THEY THOUGHT I WAS DEAD: SANDY'S STORY

THEY THOUGHT I WAS DEAD:
SANDY'S STORY

PETER JAMES

MACMILLAN

First published 2024 by Macmillan
an imprint of Pan Macmillan
The Smithson, 6 Briset Street, London EC1M 5NR
EU representative: Macmillan Publishers Ireland Ltd, 1st Floor,
The Liffey Trust Centre, 117–126 Sheriff Street Upper,
Dublin 1, D01 YC43
Associated companies throughout the world
www.panmacmillan.com

ISBN 9781-5290-3143-0 HB
ISBN 978-1-5290-3144-7 TPB

1 3 5 7 9 8 6 4 2

A CIP catalogue record for this book is available from the British Library.

Typeset by Palimpsest Book Production Ltd, Falkirk, Stirlingshire
Printed and bound by CPI Group (UK) Ltd, Croydon, CR0 4YY

Visit **www.panmacmillan.com** to read more about all our books
and to buy them. You will also find features, author interviews and
news of any author events, and you can sign up for e-newsletters
so that you're always first to hear about our new releases.

TO MARGARET DUNCTON – my hawk-eyed vigilante!

PROLOGUE

A lot of us screw up in life, some more than others, and some of us screw up pretty much most of the time. I'm there, right up among the big screw-ups. To paraphrase my favourite comedian, the late Peter Cook: 'I've made loads of mistakes in life and I could repeat them all exactly.'

That's pretty much how I feel.

I read a poem once that I think was called 'The Dash'. It talked about that mark, that hyphen you see on gravestones, linking the date of birth and date of death. It's always struck me as curious that the important thing on those headstones is the two dates. The dash in between is inconsequential. Maybe that's because human lives are generally inconsequential. Is all that matters that we were born and that we died?

But surely everyone has a story to tell? They may not have invented the wheel, or split the atom, or solved the Riemann hypothesis . . . But surely a lot of people deserve more than that tiny dash, don't they?

This is my story. I'm just fleshing out the dash a bit on my odd little life.

1

26 July 2007 – The day I leave

My name is Sandy. I'm driving from Brighton towards Gatwick Airport and I'm nervous as all hell. You would be too if you were me, right now, I promise you. I keep looking in my rear-view mirrors for someone following me. Silly, because no one can possibly know – yet – what I've done.

I've just left my husband, Roy, but he certainly won't have a clue at this moment – he's immersed in his work as ever, on a murder case. It's his thirtieth birthday today and we're supposed to be going out to dinner tonight – we have a reservation at our favourite restaurant – us and another couple – our closest friends. It's a big deal your thirtieth, a milestone. I'd even asked the restaurant to make him a cake with a marzipan goldfish just like his pet, Marlon, on top.

Bad timing, I know. If I'd had a choice, I'd have picked any day but this one. But I don't have that luxury.

I'm not just running from my husband, although that's part of this story – he's a decent guy who doesn't deserve what I'm going to be putting him through. A decent guy but not an ideal husband for me. No, I'm running from a mess I've got myself into – a real, proper mess. A death threat from someone the police have in their sights as a highly dangerous Person of Interest. My husband knows the man, he's talked about him, believes he is behind several killings, but the fact is that the Major Crime Team don't have enough evidence to arrest him. Yet.

3

Roy doesn't know I have an involvement with this man. He has no idea that I'm the next person he is intending to kill. He doesn't know how terrified I am.

He doesn't know I am taking someone with me, either, but that's another story, for later.

And I've no idea what Roy will do when he can't find me or call or text me. I've not left a note or anything corny like that. But I have left pretty much all my personal stuff, other than just a couple of small photographs he won't miss. He's a smart detective, so I guess he'll start by using all those great skills he has at tracking down murder suspects, both current and long past.

But he is going to find it hard to track me down, for one very simple reason.

I no longer exist.

2

Roel Albazi was forty-seven years old, stocky and squat, and dressed in mismatched Versace. He was Albanian and had lived in England for many years. He had a shaven head, tattooed neck and a pencil-thin moustache that ran down either side of his mouth to his chin. Adorned with a gold necklace, big rocks on his fingers and a bling watch, he sat outside the pizza restaurant in Shoreham High Street that was one of his legitimate business fronts, sipping a macchiato and smoking his short cigar, which was nearly down to the stub.

He had the physique of the kind of non-negotiable muscle you'd find outside any nightclub door on the planet. From a distance he looked a thug and not a man with a degree in international law. A hard man, you'd think. Not someone who would be afraid of anyone.

Until you looked closer and saw his frightened eyes.

He was very afraid right now of one person. Her name was Song Wu. She was a lot richer than him, a lot more ruthless and a lot more powerful. And she owned him – pretty much – since making his company, Albazi Debt Recovery International, an offer he should have refused but could not, three years ago. The offer had been a vastly lucrative contract to work for her company exclusively.

It had been an invitation to sup at the Devil's table, he was well aware of that, but he thought he could handle it. The money on that table just too good to turn down.

5

And the deal had been too good to last.

And at this moment he was in deep trouble with Song Wu.

There was a rumour that she liked to have people who crossed her – or defaulted on her – cut up alive, and then she watched the videos. But Roel Albazi knew it wasn't just a rumour.

Before his rise from mere debt collector to Fu Shan Chu in the triad run by Song Wu – effectively, in Mafia terms, her underboss – she'd made him watch the video of his predecessor. It was an hour long and involved kitchen knives, a rotary bandsaw and a chainsaw. The man was still conscious fifty-five minutes into the procedure. His mistake had been trying to broker a deal with another employee to siphon off some money. He didn't understand about loyalty. This employee was Chinese, and Albazi's predecessor fatally did not get the way the triad connections worked, and how a Chinese person would always be loyal to another Chinese person over a westerner.

Song Wu was third-generation English, but she was still as pure Chinese as the day her family had left Hong Kong back in 1954. Her father had amassed an empire of thirty-five restaurants and takeaways across the south of England, twenty Chinese grocery stores and a wholesale business supplying Chinese restaurants around the UK.

Privately educated at one of the nation's poshest girls' schools, she had reacted to racist bullying with a ferocity that soon made other pupils steer well clear of her, and she found she enjoyed both the power and inflicting pain. Within five years of her father's death, she had added a dozen more restaurants, a string of launderettes, two fully legal casinos in England and another five around Europe, as well as seven stone of body weight to her existing twelve. She liked an excess of food, but she liked an excess of money even more. She was a glutton for cash. Profits made her eyes light up; losses made her face flame. Nothing melted the ice that was her heart.

She had two brothers who were directly beneath her in the family hierarchy but dealt with other areas of her business. Silent figures in the shadows who executed their sister's instructions with precision. Albazi wasn't aware of anyone who admitted to knowing them, or even having seen them, but everyone in the Song Wu organization feared them.

It was from the Casino d'Azur group that she hauled in the biggest gains – but only in part from the actual gaming tables. The highest margins came from her business model of loaning cash to gamblers who had run out of luck. They were given big loans, always short term, with interest rates of fifty per cent per month. Defaulters were sent a video of someone being tortured, which self-erased after one viewing. Most paid up pretty fast, finding the money somehow. And that was partly because Albazi vetted the people the Casino d'Azur lent to very carefully in advance. He made sure they had assets they could turn to, in desperation. Assets such as the unmortgaged portion of their homes.

But at this moment, Albazi was a worried man. Two people he'd approved big loans to in the past three months had, separately, done a runner, and Song Wu had not been happy. Albazi knew she suspected he was lying to her and had cut some kind of a deal with these people behind her back. Now this third person wasn't showing up either, and he was feeling physically sick at the thought of having to tell Song Wu. She was going to be even more certain he was double-crossing her.

Every five minutes Albazi methodically checked his watch and each of the three phones lined up on the metal table. Traffic streamed past. Pedestrians streamed past. But there was no sign of her. And no message.

She had given him her word. Assured him. They had an appointment. An assignation. At 12 p.m. today she was going to turn up with the £150K she owed him.

7

PETER JAMES

It was now 12.20 p.m. Then it was 12.25 p.m. Then 12.30 p.m.

Yet again he checked the middle phone, the one she had the number for, the one they always spoke or texted on. No message.

Bitch.

He stubbed out the cigar in the ashtray. She might think she was clever, but it wasn't clever not to pay him. Sure, the interest rates were high, but so they should be as he never took security for the loans. All of them were on trust and he made sure he collected what he was owed. Always. However long it took. His customers paid either with cash or with their homes or with their lives. He preferred the cash but killing a debtor – and very publicly – served as a great warning to others. Call it a marketing cost.

He picked up the phone on the left and dialled. It was answered almost instantly.

'Sandy Grace,' Albazi said. 'Find her. Now.'

3

I'm on the M23, heading north, and the slip road to Gatwick Airport is coming up a mile ahead. If I take it, I guess that will be the point of no return. How does a relationship get to the point of no return? I have often asked myself if there is a way back to our once blissful marriage. But it is like a broken glass: however brilliantly it gets repaired, there will always be cracks. Roy might call them tiny fractures, but for me they are significant.

Of course, the heat of that first passion can't last, however much we fantasize it will. We go through stages with any 'significant other'. First, we fall in lust, then we fall in love, then we hitch our wagons together and steadily rumble and bounce along Reality Road. Whether we have kids or not, some are destined to end up in some form of compromised state of contentment. Acceptance of our lot. And that is fine for many people. But I want more. I've always wanted more. I *need* more. I just feel the compromises I have to make are too many.

That may seem selfish, given my husband is not a bad person, but it's the only way out I can see. I think it will damage Roy less if I disappear than if I have to tell him what I have become and what I have done. It would ruin his career having a wife who has got into this situation and I can't help feeling that I would, forever after, be an embarrassment to him. The proverbial albatross around his neck.

All I can say is that it isn't easy for me. I dislike myself entirely. I hate what I have become. I wish, desperately, it hadn't got to this.

I like Antoine de Saint-Exupéry's description of love as not gazing into each other's eyes, but looking in the same direction together. I think he got that from Dickens, who was always mentioning people sitting in 'companionable silences'. But wasn't that because they had nothing else to do in his day? No internet, no computer games, no Amazon to browse, no Sky Sports.

So when does that oh so subtle change in your relationship start? The first night that you share a bed and don't make love? The first morning you leave home forgetting to say *I love you*? The first time you don't notice your significant other's new hairstyle? The day you forget the anniversary of when you met? The day you realize, for whatever reason, you no longer come first in your significant other's life?

Tick that last box for me.

The reality of being married to an ambitious Major Crime detective is that you will often come second – sometimes to a corpse.

The more I go over and over this in my head, the more I realize that whatever I now do, even if I somehow sort out this mess, too much has happened for our relationship to continue. I'd always carry the lies and live in fear of Roy finding out about my sordid other life. I have to leave.

Selfishly, it is easier for me if I pass on some blame to him, so I consume myself with thoughts of what he could've done to prevent me getting into this mess: maybe he did prioritize his job over me, maybe he didn't love me enough. That I'm just an appendage, the person who makes the bed, who does the shopping, who cooks, that he doesn't care for my career or any of my ambitions to use my interior design skills, so long as I turn up to functions on his arm. But deep down, if I let myself go there, I'm just trying to ease my guilt.

He's actually a bloody good guy. I should find his dedication to his job a positive thing, but I use it against him. I'm a disgrace. He's better off without me.

Just over a year ago. Our wedding anniversary. He never forgets any significant dates and he'd booked a restaurant as a surprise – our favourite seafood restaurant in the Brighton Lanes – where we had gone on one of our very first dates. He'd sorted a taxi so we could both have a drink, and he'd given me a beautiful present, a white gold eternity ring. I felt bad because I hadn't given him anything special.

This was the evening when I made a terrible decision.

4

2006 – One year earlier

We are in the back of the taxi. Roy has his arm around me and we are all loved up. All these years of marriage and still in love. I feel hugely grateful despite so long trying, fruitlessly, for a baby, which has been arduous and draining for us both.

We are heading east along Church Road, Hove, one road north of the seafront. A wide, buzzy street, lined with shops, cafes, bars and restaurants. The driver is a young, friendly guy. His plate says *Mark Tuckwell*. Roy and I are chatting to him, like we always do to taxi drivers, waiters, shop assistants, pretty much anyone, really. We both share an insatiable curiosity about people. I'm sure Roy banks it all, though, somewhere up in that ten-gazillion gigaflop processor inside his skull, whereas I just remember faces. But I know my husband too well. I can see that all the time he's chatting to this driver he's looking through the windows, taking in both sides of the street, and suddenly he yells, 'Stop! Stop! STOPPPP!'

And my heart stops.

I know what's about to happen because it's happened before. Roy, with his damned near photographic memory, has spotted a villain he's been after for a year, or maybe longer, walking along the street.

As the driver pulls hard over to the kerb, Roy already has his door open. 'Darling, order a bottle of bubbly – I'll see you at the restaurant as soon as I can.'

12

Then he's gone.

The time is 7.30 p.m.

At 8 p.m. I'm sitting in the restaurant, English's, with a bottle of Champagne, reading the menu over and over. And over. Roy calls with an update. He has chased this suspect down Western Road for over half a mile, finally rugby-tackling and pinning him to the floor at the Clock Tower.

He's now on his way to the custody centre at Hollingbury. He can't hand this charmer over to anyone else yet, because of something to do with *chain of evidence* – after finding Class A drugs on him. But it shouldn't be a problem, he assures me. It's early evening, so he will be able to process him through custody quickly, and then join me.

It's now 10 p.m. I've spent much of the past two hours reading the menu until I've learned it by heart, and texting my best friend, about my progress on this increasingly boring and increasingly non-romantic date. A combination of the booze and the boredom and I'm really pissed off. It's escalating in my head, and I can't stop it even though the evening started so well.

On the plus side I've eaten an entire basket of delicious breads with a fish paste and a very yummy butter, and I've almost finished the bottle of Veuve Clicquot. And now, Roy has just called with yet another update.

For some reason I don't fully understand, he's still stuck in the custody centre but will be with me, he promises, faithfully, in twenty minutes.

I read out the menu to him and he chooses scallops for his starter and monkfish for his main. I select a bottle of Chablis from the wine list, hang the cost. Although I'm feeling a bit smashed and know I shouldn't drink much more.

It is now 10.15 p.m. and Roy has texted to say he is still delayed. I'm so ravenous I've had my starter and half of the bottle of Chablis. Not sure if I'm feeling more pissed or just plain pissed off. Through my haze of alcohol the restaurant appears to be emptying. Actually, it is *empty*.

Am I really the only person still here? I look around and see tables all tidied and laid for lunch tomorrow. Around the corner a couple of waiters are chatting by the bar. One of them has just asked, with a slightly desperate look on his face, if I would like my main course or would I still prefer to wait. I can't remember what I said to him, but I seem to recall ordering some chips. Or French fries, as I'm in a posh place.

Then I hear footsteps clumping down the stairs, and I see a tall man I vaguely recognize, and he appears to vaguely recognize me, too. Everything is vague at this moment. I'm definitely drunk. Last time I went to the bathroom – some while ago – and peered into the mirror, even my hair looked drunk.

This guy is tall, good-looking in a kind of supercilious way, as if everything around him is beneath him, and sharply dressed in a dark jacket, crisp white shirt and tailored jeans. His loafers are so polished they are like black mirrors. I've seen him before somewhere, but I can't think who the hell he is. But he's walking over to me with a knowing look. When he speaks his voice is posh and measured. 'Sandy Grace, right?'

I give him a guarded, 'Yes.'

I'm finding him a bit intimidating. And I'm still trying to think who the hell he is. He smells nice, a cologne I don't recognize.

'Charming little restaurant this, isn't it? Are you and Roy having a pleasant evening?' He looked down, and I could see he was clocking the untouched other side of the table, the glasses and plates and cutlery.

'Well, I can't speak for Roy, but mine's been a bit rubbish, actually.'

He frowned. Or rather, looked pained. Or bewildered. 'Right,' he said, awkwardly. 'Yes, OK. Right – well . . .'

He looked around him, as if expecting Roy to materialize – perhaps from the loo – at any moment.

'He's not here,' I said to put him out of his misery.

'Not here? You've been stood up?'

I shook my head. 'Not *stood up* – not exactly.' I explained the events. When I finished I picked up the bottle of Chablis from the ice bucket and showed him there was still some left and offered him a glass. He hesitated, saying he was driving, then he said, 'Why not, I've not drunk anything all evening,' and accepted, sitting down and clinking his glass against mine. 'I've also been stood up,' he said.

'Seriously?'

'My date never showed.' He shrugged a *What-the-hell*. 'You're wondering who I am and where we've met before, aren't you?'

It threw me, because he was right. 'I'm trying to place you,' I replied diplomatically and took a stab. 'Sussex Police, right?'

'I'm a DI, we met at the Sussex Detectives' Ball, at the Grand Hotel in Brighton, last October. I was on the next table to you and your husband – we chatted briefly about how terrible the comedian was. I'm down on secondment to Sussex Police from the Met – briefing the force on counterterrorism.' He held out his hand and gave a very clammy, limp handshake for much longer than I was comfortable with, all the time staring into my eyes. 'My name is Cassian Pewe. Maybe I can give you a lift home?'

Have you ever come across someone who you found both attractive and repulsive at the same time? If not, you've never met Cassian Pewe. Snake charmers work by hypnotizing venomous reptiles. Cassian Pewe is the reverse. He's the supercilious reptile with the silver tongue and the golden looks. I knew he was dangerous, but as we talked, there was something about him – I can't explain what exactly – I found mesmerizing. Hypnotic?

When it got to 11.15 p.m., and the remaining staff in the restaurant were clearly dying to go home but too polite to say so, Roy rang, his voice full of apology. He was still at work, he said, and he would make up for this evening but best I get a taxi to go home.

I hung up on him. Then I accepted Cassian's gallant offer to give me a lift home in his white convertible Jaguar. He told me it was a classic, although I don't know much about cars, but it was rather gorgeous, with its soft leather seats and mahogany dashboard, and he was clearly proud of it. It was snug and warm inside, with the roof down and the night air blowing in our hair and on our faces. In my woozy state I imagined for a moment we were in the South of France, Cannes maybe, instead of Brighton.

When we pulled up outside our house ten minutes later, I saw Roy's car wasn't on the driveway. He was still at work, still playing with his prisoner. Cassian Pewe suddenly switched off the engine, and before I knew it, had slipped one arm around my neck, pulled me towards him and kissed me passionately on the lips.

Shocked, I was again both attracted and repulsed. Then he stared into my eyes, in the faint glow of a streetlight above us, and said, 'I really like Roy. I like him a lot.'

'Well, I hope you don't kiss him like that,' I replied.

5

I'm faced with a choice as I approach Gatwick Airport. The North or South Terminal? If I had a coin, I'd toss it. I decide South. So many decisions I'm completely free to make.

It's 1.45 p.m. Horrible Roel Albazi can only just about now be figuring I'm a no-show. My mirrors are still clear. But just for belt and braces, to be certain no one is following, I do a full 360-degree loop around the South Terminal before driving up the ramp of the short-term car park. Roy is not going to be happy if he gets stuck with the bill, the size of which will depend on how long it takes them to find my car. But the car is in my name, so it really shouldn't be a problem for him.

I take my ticket and the barrier rises in front of me. Symbolic in a way, as I drive through and into my new life, which begins with an empty space between a white Porsche Cayman and a purple Nissan Micra on the fourth floor of the short-term car park. I lock my little Golf – I've no idea why, habit I guess – toss the keys into a convenient bin, then walk across the bridge into the terminal building.

One bonus, in the situation I find myself in, of being married to a detective is the stuff I've learned from Roy that most people would never, ever, even think about. Like how to disappear in our online, digital world.

How to vanish without trace.

17

Like I'm about to. I am so nervous. Then I remind myself I have no choice.

It's weird when I look at my left hand and don't see my wedding ring or my engagement ring, which have been part of my fourth finger for so long. There's just a faint white band of skin that isn't suntanned. I may have to pawn them, hopefully not, but not too close to home, in case pawnbrokers become a line of enquiry. I dig my hand into the pocket of my lightweight denim jacket as I stroll around the Departures concourse because I'm oddly self-conscious about that white band, my naked finger.

After stopping at WHSmith to buy a newspaper, I head over to the British Airways check-in area, join a short queue and then check in to flight BA 2771 to Malaga. No luggage, I tell the polite young man behind the desk who is looking at my passport.

After a few moments of tapping on his terminal, he hands my passport back to me. 'Have a nice flight, Mrs Gordon.'

Instead of heading for security, I head for the loos. Once securely locked inside the ladies', I open the small holdall slung over my shoulder, pull out a dark brown wig and tug it on. Along with a large pair of dark glasses. Then I reverse my denim jacket, so it is now white. Tug off my jeans and replace them with a sensible skirt. Next, I make my way across to the EasyJet check-in area.

Fifteen minutes later, thanks to my second false passport, Sandra Smith is allocated seat 14C on EZY 243 to Amsterdam. When she arrives, with just hand baggage, she will check in to a London City Airport flight under the name of Sandra Jones. On entering the arrivals lounge there, she will see a limousine driver holding up the name Alison Shipley.

Alison Shipley will be whisked away from the airport in the back of a black Mercedes S Class driven by a courteous man called Meehat El Hadidy, following directions on his satnav to East Grinstead.

Taking her towards her new beginning.

6

They called him Tall Joe, although he was actually very short. Two inches shy of five feet, with a shaved head, snooker-ball shiny, and the body of a Sumo wrestler, he looked even shorter than his height. He had a problem with walking, due to knackered hips from too many fights, so that he strode along in a kind of pendulum motion that had something of the drunken sailor about it, swinging each leg past him and then sort of throwing his body forward. It looked pretty clumsy, but that was deceptive. Nothing about Tall Joe was clumsy. Joe Karter was a man of precision.

He was also a man of light and dark. On the light side, he was scrupulously polite, funny and charming – charming so long as you paid what you owed, when you owed it. On the dark, he was an aikido eighth dan black belt who had killed two men with his bare hands – and five in more painful ways – permanently disabled another eight, and had become a legend in prison, when serving lengthy time for GBH, by throwing a fridge down two flights of stairs, during a tantrum.

Not many people ever messed with Tall Joe Karter, which was why Roel Albazi employed him. If you owed money to Albazi's boss, Song Wu, when Joe Karter, always dressed in a suit and tie, looking like an overgrown schoolboy, knocked on your door, you paid it, or you made arrangements, fast. Albazi, and his associate, Skender Sharka, always ensured that any of their debtors who had fallen behind were made aware of Tall Joe Karter's CV.

Albazi was stressed before he picked up the phone to call Joe, and the fact that his bagman was sounding so calm was making him even more stressed. Not just one but *two* people he'd given substantial loans to, to cover their gambling debts, had gone missing – done runners. And Joe was in the middle of sodding nowhere, in his car, cheerfully telling him that he didn't know where they were.

The wife of one, Alan Mitten, who owed £30,000, plus £15,000 of interest, had just told Joe that she hadn't seen her husband in three weeks and even if she never saw him again it would be too soon. She'd been served a foreclosure notice from the mortgage company, her car had been repossessed and the bailiffs were coming this afternoon to take their furniture. So far, Skender Sharka was making some headway but not quickly enough. Although he was confident of finding him within the next twenty-four hours.

Tall Joe was even more hopeful about the other, Robert Rhys, a lawyer who owed £25,000 plus £15,000 interest. He was close to getting an address. And as soon as Rhys was located, Karter said he would meet him to arrange a payment plan.

'What payment plan do you have in mind?' Albazi quizzed.

'I'll ask him which bone of his body he would least like me to break, boss,' Tall Joe replied in his deep, cheeky-chappie voice. 'So I'll break another one – a toe or a finger – and tell him I'll break another one every twenty-four hours, saving the one he really doesn't want me to break to last, until he's paid. He'll pay tomorrow, boss, I'm confident.'

'He's a card player, isn't he, Joe?'

'Poker.'

'So he won't want you to break his fingers, will he?'

'He won't, boss.'

Albazi thanked him and hung up, fretting about Alan Mitten. He was a double-glazing salesman and his employers hadn't heard from him for over two weeks. At least Robert Rhys had decent employment, a partner in a small firm of solicitors. He would have equity in the firm, although the fact that he was in his late forties and living in a flat gave a clue to his gambling habit, that maybe he'd never amassed enough to afford a house. Gambled it all away. Hopefully Tall Joe would work his magic. Poker with your fingers in splints would not be a good prospect.

He leaned back in his swivel chair in his sixth-floor, white-carpeted penthouse office above his restaurant. It had a magnificent picture window view to the south across the river Adur to the houseboats on the far side and the English Channel beyond, and another across Shoreham High Street to the north. He pulled up a map on his screen. His loyal right hand, Skender Sharka, towered over him, looking down at it, too.

Sharka, a freak of nature, was six foot six tall and totally hairless. He'd been nicknamed 'Deve' at school, which translated into English as 'Camel', because he had two lumps on his skull. He was a gentle person, gentle in all he did, gentle even when he killed.

They'd worked as a team for the past decade, he, Sharka and Tall Joe, collecting debts that weren't legally enforceable – mostly drug debts – and then Albazi had been approached by a representative of Song Wu with the proverbial offer he could not refuse. Although subsequently he had realized the offer was too good to be true.

The tracking system of locating his debtors, devised by Sharka, was highly effective. People in hiding generally did not travel far. Those who needed to hide in a hurry rarely went out of their comfort zone. Albazi had had enough debtors go bad over the years to warrant his investment in the latest technology, with algorithms created by Sharka, whose principal method of tracking people was through payments to a source on the internet who had access to all the different phone companies' records. By cross-referencing numbers, he'd been able to see the burner phones each had bought in the mistaken belief these would make them invisible and impossible to track. It worked so brilliantly Albazi had only ever lost one completely. But he had dealt with that swiftly, by having the man's parents and then grandparents, back in Albania, tortured and murdered.

Now, Song Wu was not happy with him, and he cursed himself for getting reckless. In truth, he hadn't done the full due diligence he would normally do on a customer before lending them the money, he had come to rely too much on his debt-collecting abilities. On top of Mitten and Rhys, and with Sandy Grace playing games, the situation was a whole lot worse.

He sometimes felt his relationship with the Song Wu organization was like being a man trapped in a watery cul-de-sac with a crocodile. So long as he kept throwing it chickens, the crocodile would keep smiling. And all the time growing bigger and needing more chickens . . .

'So where is she right now, Skender?' he asked.

From the moment, a month ago, when Sandy Grace had first defaulted on a repayment instalment to his boss, Tall Joe had placed a tracking device on her car. It was a magnetic transponder, attached beneath the boot, so small she would only have found it if she had been searching for it specifically. Its current location showed as a small blue dot on a map on the computer.

'Brighton, boss. Looks like she's in Churchill Square car park.'

Albazi studied the screen carefully as he drilled a hole in the tip of a Cohiba Robusto, then put the stubby cigar in his mouth without lighting it. 'So she might be trying to get the cash together, as she promised. One hundred and fifty thousand pounds in cash – in fifty-pound notes. Her time is running out. Let's hope she's taking the threats seriously.'

Albazi lit his cigar carefully with his gold Dunhill, turning the end over and over in the flame until it was burning evenly.

His face disappeared in a cloud of blue smoke. His disembodied voice said, 'So wait. Watch the blue dot. Tell me when it moves again.'

Skender assured him he would.

'Know what's going to happen to you and me if she fails to deliver?'

'No, boss.'

'You don't want to know.'

'OK.'

'Which is why I'm going to tell you.'

7

Where does anything really start, in life? For me, Sandy Grace, or for any of us? The lightbulb moment some people talk about, that sudden flash of inspiration that pops seemingly from nowhere. Or maybe nothing so dramatic, just a simple spark of excitement when we suddenly find ourselves more alive than we ever did before – because we've found our mojo – or whatever.

Or the polar opposite. The feeling one morning, when you wake up, that today is the first day of the rest of your life and you don't want the rest of your life to be this same old, same old, any longer. That was how it was for me. A very short while after I first met Tamzin.

I've heard that a bad back is one of the symptoms of un-happiness – when life is not panning out how you want it to be. Maybe that's true – or maybe people with bad backs say that because misery likes company. Whatever, I'd ricked my back trying to move a sofa into a different place in the living room. I wanted good feng shui in our new home – all that ancient Chinese stuff about bringing balance and good vibes into our living spaces.

So I got great feng shui and a messed-up back. Or, in medical terminology, prolapsed discs L4 and L5. I had sciatica for a year – if you've never had it, you are lucky. You have no idea how painful it is. Think of sliding a red-hot wire all the way down inside the skin of your leg, from your bum to your foot, and then

24

twisting it a few times before plugging it into a live socket for several seconds. I'm not exaggerating.

My best friend, Becky Jackson, had joined a Pilates class. Like Roy and me, she and her husband had been struggling to conceive, and she'd read in a magazine about two women with infertility problems who had been helped by Pilates. Becky gets most of her information from magazines. She was raving about how Pilates made her feel, and her instructor had told her it could help my back. So I gave it a go. And one of the girls in the group was Tamzin Heywood.

And within a few weeks, two things happened. The first was that my back improved dramatically. The second, that I wanted to be Tamzin Heywood.

Badly.

So badly I lay awake at night thinking about her with pure, undiluted envy. It was her lifestyle. I thought about everything she had that I didn't. Someone once told me that the secret of life is to know when it's good. And she was making me feel the exact opposite of that about my life.

My rather grey little life. In our grey house. Just a couple of years ago it was my dream home. Detached, four-bedroom – well, three and a half really – with a good-sized rear garden, and so close to the sea you can hear it. I put my imprint on it, the inside is light and airy, all minimalist, and I created a Zen garden in the rear. I really thought it was fine, lovely, far grander than the bungalow in Seaford where I grew up. Our *forever* home.

I'd planned the children's rooms; the eventual loft conversion, when we could afford it, where we could wake in the morning with a sea view – well, a partial sea view anyway. Then I went to Tamzin's house.

Shit.

She and I are the same age. I'd always liked nice clothes but I'd never been fussed about brands – before now. She wears the coolest – and of course most expensive – gym kit brands, as well as insanely bling and covetable Prada trainers (£550), she has gorgeous hair and, naturally, perfectly manicured nails. Perfect everything.

Her husband, Ferris, owns a string of estate agents, but Tamzin's no idle kept woman, no vacuous airhead *Housewife of Brighton*. Of course she isn't. She's a passionate animal lover who spent two years recently studying to qualify in canine myotherapy – that's dog massage to you and me. It's her passion – as well as her own source of income – helping dogs with their mobility and muscle health. Being a fellow dog lover, I immediately admired that about her – and respected her for it. Roy and I agreed a long time ago we could never like anyone who doesn't like animals.

Tamzin and Ferris live in a house styled like an Italian palazzo in Roedean, an exclusive enclave at the eastern extremity of Brighton – where an expensive girls' school is located. Their house has a sea view to die for, out across the English Channel, and all the toys. Indoor and outdoor pools, tennis court, gym, sauna, steam room, the whole enchilada. She drives a convertible Porsche with a personal plate. I drive a ten-year-old Golf that had 90,000 miles on the clock when we bought it.

But it's not just their house, it's their whole lifestyle. They have a debenture at Wimbledon, which means they go to all the best matches throughout Wimbledon fortnight. They are members of Glyndebourne so they go to the opera regularly throughout the summer season, all dressed up fancy. My envy of Tamzin and her life really came out when they invited Roy and me to see *Carmen*, but at the last minute he had to cancel because a dead body had been found in a park.

So I went alone and was determined to have the best time. We all had way too much to drink, and they invited me back to their house after. Their three kids were sleeping over at the grand-parents'. Tamzin convinced me to stay as it was so late, and we were all so drunk. Ferris went up to bed leaving Tamzin and me drinking a magnum of white.

I texted Roy a drunk message: **Don't wait up, back at Tamzin and Ferris's. Magnum open. Party time! Love you. X**

It was all so hedonistic. We were laughing, spinning each other around and dirty dancing to the music. Then she surprised me by kissing me as we danced, her soft tongue on mine. Everything slowed down. My God, it felt like the best kiss ever. I'm ashamed to say it but I was smitten, I just didn't think of anything or anyone else at that moment. Not Roy. Not Ferris. I was selfishly in lust and out for myself. We ended up making love together on the sofa in the living room then crashing out in each other's arms.

I woke up at 6.30 a.m., with the hangover from hell, my head was thumping, and I was alone with just a blanket over me. As soon as my thoughts allowed, I felt embarrassed. My face reddened as I imagined my parents' reactions. Then more embarrassment at why I cared about my parents' bloody reactions at my age. But this was not my house. What if the kids came back at any moment? I'd outstayed my welcome; I should leave and get back to Roy. I painfully pieced back together the night and snuck out before they got up, closing the front door with almost no sound behind me.

Then came the long walk of shame home, high heels in my hand, clearly last night's clothes. I texted Tamzin to say thanks for a great evening, wink, kiss. Then I vowed to get my drinking under control. Seriously. Sort my life out. My grey boring life. Find happiness in my life with Roy. I loved him and desperately wanted our marriage to work, and still hoped beyond hope that we would have a baby.

But when I think back on it, no surprise, that's when the dissatisfaction with my life really started. I couldn't get that fling out of my head, I'd enjoyed it. I craved it.

The worst thing of all was that Tamzin was so damned friendly towards me afterwards. As well as being genuinely warm, kind, funny, generous and interested in everyone, she never, for one moment, seemed to take her privileged life for granted. She never mentioned our brief encounter, not once. It was as if it had not happened. Not that it could have continued, of course, but, looking back, it was another rejection. And it hit me hard because I had enjoyed it. It took up way too much of my thoughts. What if this, what if that. One thing I knew for certain: Roy must never know about it – it would ruin him. Well, it must never happen again, and I must work harder at my marriage. What sort of a wife was I? I ended up feeling disgusted with myself.

That summer, when I had quit my full-time job with a firm of accountants to work part-time as receptionist at a doctors' surgery – our infertility specialist had advised me I shouldn't do any stressful job – we were invited over to her house a lot. Such happy, fun afternoons around the pool, with some very nice wines from their cellar. Sometimes in the company of their three beautiful and polite kids – with their equally beautiful, and dutiful, nanny. And always with their two adorably daft and soppy golden retrievers, nuzzling us for cuddles and ever-hopeful of treats.

I so wanted her life and that night together had just intensified those feelings. Not that I could tell anyone. And the problem was that I wasn't just envious – Tamzin had made me start to question my entire life. And to be fair on Roy, that wasn't his fault, it was mine. When I met him, all those years previously, my life – and my aspirations – were very different.

Roy is two years older than me, but in some ways it often feels much more. He's so stable, so calm, so wise. I was nineteen when we met, and my life up until that point had pretty much been a train crash. I am an only child, as is my mother who was born to German parents. But, unlike modern Germans I've met, she totally lacks any sense of humour. She's just a cold fish, and bitter at the hand life has dealt her, in the shape of my seriously weird loser of a father.

He worked all his career as a car mechanic in a small garage in Eastbourne, and spends his retirement building scale model Second World War aircraft, like Spitfires, Hurricanes, Wellingtons and Halifaxes, as well as all their German counterparts. He likes to tell the few visitors who come to their home in Seaford these were aircraft his father had flown in the war, first as a fighter ace with seven kills, then a bomber pilot.

He has always maintained – and still does – that his father was one of the Dambuster heroes, whereas in reality he had been an aircraft fitter and had never been posted anywhere near 633 Squadron. Partly on account of the fact he would have been just fourteen years old at the end of the war.

And to make it worse, my mother has always gone along with it. Maybe, when I look back at her in a charitable frame of mind, I wonder if it's because she was traumatized by what her country did in the war, and this was some weird way, in her weird mind, of her assuaging her guilt.

She had been brought up in England and eventually, to her regret (my supposition), met my father and lived unhappily ever after.

I haven't read much poetry, but I did come across a few lines I really liked from someone called Philip Larkin about how your parents fuck you up.

Oh yes. That resonates. I was fourteen when I first decided I didn't want to live a life like theirs.

8

Early July 2007 – Looking back

My mother is an observant Lutheran who believes we are saved from sin by God's grace. My father and I had to pray twice a day. For the first thirteen years of my childhood I lived in fear of losing that grace. Then at school I met Simone Oster, who was totally rebellious.

Tall, with a shock of curly hair, she was wonderfully wicked. First, she got me into smoking cigarettes, then a week before my fifteenth birthday, she got me drunk and . . . we kissed on the floor of the summerhouse in my parents' garden.

It felt really weird, my first proper kiss. I had expected it to be with a boy because all my friends were doing that, but at the same time, it made me feel so alive. My biggest, best-kept secret.

It made me feel, *Screw you, parents! I'm now a grown-up. I don't need you. Catch me if you can!*

They caught me. Right in the act. No getting out of it. Their shocked faces as I was mid-snog with Simone, my hands cupping her bottom, in their chintzy conservatory at the age of fifteen. *Schnerkly*, I'd call the decor. Maybe I made that word up? I don't know, but it fits. If you'd seen their reaction, I may as well have committed some heinous crime. I was grounded in my bedroom, delivered the blandest of food, forbidden to ever touch a girl in that way ever again, and told to read the Bible. I didn't know what I felt back then about my sexual preference, I was exploring. I know now that I had feelings for both sexes, but my parents, who were stuck in the Dark Ages, blocked out any possibility of me having any sort of sexual relationship again with a girl. And that was that. When I was old enough, I was to find a man who would be the 'provider', get married, and my sole purpose in life would be to eventually give them grandchildren. That was the only path acceptable to them. I guess that added to my rebellion then and now. Maybe.

God, it was all just so damned boring and not how I saw my life. I had ambition, determination, resilience, and knew I would not settle for that.

In truth, the next four years were something of a blur. I had a few boyfriends along the way – none very serious – smoked a bit of weed, doing the minimum work at school to scrape through exams, and impervious to the shitty reports of *could do better* that landed with my parents.

When I was eighteen I met Vince in a nightclub just off Brighton seafront. At the time, he was supercool, tall, long dark hair, totally confident. I liked him at first. Probably because he gave me coke for the first time – we snorted it together in a cubicle in the women's toilet. I used to see him around and about on various nights out and we flirted but never did anything – well, except coke in the loos. He was thirty, over eleven years older than me.

One night I was out with Becky and a bunch of other friends – we were planning to large it as one of them had just got engaged. It was going to be a BIG NIGHT OUT.

We'd arranged to meet in the Brighton and Hove greyhound stadium on the outskirts of Hove. I'm never naturally punctual but for some reason I arrived early, just before 7.30 p.m., and it was quiet. A few people were hanging out around the bar and just one of several tables was occupied by a bunch of smartly dressed people. Three guys and two women. I didn't give them a second glance; actually not entirely true, there was one of the guys who looked fit – he could have been Daniel Craig's kid brother – but he didn't even see me – or so I thought.

Being alone gave me the chance to get in the mood. I swigged down a large glass of Sauvignon Blanc and was on my second when in swaggered Vince with a couple of mates. For some moments he didn't spot me, and I held my breath hoping he wouldn't see me at all – I wanted to move away from that life before it got me hooked. I knew, even then with occasional recreational drug use, how easily influenced I was.

He looked like a combination of Elvis and Al Pacino but without either of their handsome features.

And of course, as luck would have it, he spotted me almost instantly.

And came over. 'Hey, babe!' he said, looking around at the empty chairs of the table I had bagged. 'All alone? Get you a drink? I've got some good shit, want to score?'

'I'm fine, thanks.'

He looked at my glass, which was now almost empty. Then he stared hard, too hard, at me. 'Let me guess, Savvy B? A large one?'

'I'm fine, thank you, Vince.'

He leaned in towards me. I could smell the stink of cigarette smoke on his clothes, hair, breath. 'You're not fine at all, are you, babe? You're missing me, aren't you?'

His pupils were enlarged and his eyes pinballed around. He was high on something, as ever.

'I'm fine,' I said, calmly – and thanks to the two glasses of wine, courageously. 'I don't need anything, thank you, Vince.'

He nodded. 'Oh yes, you do. You want me, don't you? You just don't want to admit it.'

'Actually, Vince, I do not.'

He sat down next to me, nudged up close and put his arm around me. 'You want to know what it's like to fuck me, don't you, babe?'

I told him to leave me alone.

He nuzzled my ear.

'Leave – me – alone – Vince,' I said and pulled away.

He followed.

I must have raised my voice louder than I had intended when I said, 'LEAVE ME ALONE!'

Because suddenly the fit-looking guy in the smart suit – Daniel Craig's kid brother, who'd been at the table – was standing next to Vince and looking down at me. He had a nice, commanding voice. 'Is this man bothering you?'

Vince rounded on him. 'Who the fuck are you, nancy boy?' His stance was aggressive, his arms pulled back, as if he was about to either punch or headbutt him.

'Let's just say I'm someone who knows who the fuck you are. Probably carrying drugs, right?' He jerked a finger at the table where his companions sat. 'See them? They're all cops, like me.' He pressed his face so close to Vince's that their noses almost touched and said, 'You've got white stuff around your lips. Been sniffing babies' bums? Talcum powder, is it?'

Vince suddenly looked uneasy, his stance turning passive. He appeared momentarily lost for words.

'Tell you what,' Daniel Craig's kid brother continued. 'Because I'm in a charitable mood tonight, I'm giving you a choice. You either disappear out of this bar right now or I'm searching you and nicking you for possession and you'll be spending the rest of your Friday night in the custody suite at Hollingbury. You have exactly three seconds to decide.'

Vince required just two of those seconds to process this information. Then he legged it.

I looked up at my knight in shining armour. Into gorgeous, intense blue eyes full of warmth and smiles. 'Thank you,' I said.

'You OK?' he asked.

'I am now. Thank you, again.'

He continued to smile. 'Want to join us for a drink?'

'I'm afraid I'm on a friends' night out,' I said, hesitantly. 'But they haven't arrived yet, so I could join until they do.' I didn't want to sound too keen but at the same time fancied him like hell.

He gave me the biggest smile.

Once seated, I started chatting to the man next to me, thinking how to break the conversation and chat to my rescuer. I leaned across the table and our eyes locked. 'I've been given a tip! Always bet on any dog that does its business before it races!'

'You mean watch and see if it has a crap?' he joked.

'Very sharp, you must be a detective!'

'No,' he replied, 'not yet. But I'd like to be one day.'

I felt such a connection to him. But then, out of the corner of my eye, I saw Becky and a bunch of the others walk in and the moment was gone. I so wanted to stay with him longer.

He asked if I could stick around for one more drink but, reluctantly, I told him I had to go as my friends had arrived.

He handed me a card. 'Well, if you ever fancy meeting up, give me a bell.'

I glanced at the card before pocketing it. The printed words read: *Constable Roy Grace, Brighton Police.* Beneath was a contact number.

I put the card into a zippered compartment in my handbag, very carefully.

An hour later, slipping away from the group on the pretext of going to the loo, I called him. We made a date.

9

Roy excited me so much, in those early years. On our first date, those clear blue eyes felt as if they were drilling deep into my soul, and I loved his curiosity – he seemed to genuinely want to know everything about me. None of my previous relationships had ever questioned me the way he did. And I liked it. I felt he really cared. And he made me laugh.

He made me feel wanted and secure, but more than anything, he excited me. It was as if a light that I never knew I had inside me had suddenly been switched on. I felt I was finally clear about my sexuality, and about who I wanted to be with for ever – I didn't have eyes for anyone else.

His life seemed so glamorous and adventurous, compared to my dull job at the time working as a receptionist – well, at least until I asked him what his first case had been. He blushed and, grinning, told me he'd been called to help on the investigation into the theft of a donkey.

The ridiculous thing was that, even though I really wasn't fond of my parents, at the age of nineteen I still craved their approval, a life-long habit I have been unable to shake off. My mother, who had banned me from having any sort of sexual relationship with a female after that traumatic incident with Simone, had also been dismissive of all previous boyfriends I'd risked bringing home (most I didn't). Surprisingly, however, she thought a policeman was respectable and took – almost – a shine

35

to him. It was the nearest I'd ever seen her to showing any warmth to any of my friends.

Poor Roy made the mistake of feigning interest in my father's model aircraft. He bored Roy for hours on end with stories about his own father's exploits in the war. Re-enacting dogfights he'd had, shooting down Messerschmitt Bf 109s and Dorniers and Heinkels, notching up his kills. He acted these out like pageants, swirling his little aircraft through the air, reeling off the ammunition and bomb loads each plane was armed with – and had left.

Because it was early days in our romance, it was a while before Roy, who had worked it all out the first time he had met my father, told me he had actually done the maths and realized that my father was making it all up. Fortunately, it amused Roy. I'd been scared he might run a mile after meeting my parents, but he didn't, he recognized just how very different from them I was. I later learned that one of the attributes of a good detective is to be able to read and understand people. Emotional intelligence. And curiosity.

He never truly warmed to my parents, but he was always scrupulously polite to them, and always curious about them. I admired that about him, and that he was non-judgemental.

Which was just as well as they are complete cheapskates. Like, for example, my mother would buy all her Christmas cards for the following Christmas in the January sales. Not that they had many people to send them to – a few cousins and Joan and Ted. So far as I knew, the only friends they had. But hey, she must have saved at least £2 doing this. Then, oh boy, the night Roy came round and did the traditional thing, of asking my father if he could marry me. My father cracked a bottle of sweet sherry, then after two glasses, which clearly went to his head, effusively declared we must all go out to dinner the following weekend to celebrate – and it would be their treat.

So the next Saturday we went to their local, which my father said had something of a reputation as a good food pub. My father, Roy and I ordered our starters, which was fine, although my mother, frugal to the bitter end, said she couldn't manage one and would just have one course. But then it came to ordering the mains. Roy went for a T-bone steak, which was the most expensive thing on the menu – not by a huge margin – maybe £7 more expensive than the other mains. My mother, quite appallingly, holding the menu up, turned to him and said, 'Do you really need that steak, Roy?'

'Actually,' he replied calmly, 'yes, I do.'

If I had to pinpoint the moment when the first fissure in Roy's relationship with my parents appeared, it was then. A T-bone steak.

And my pathetic father, as if to appease my mother by economizing on the wine, ordered just a half-bottle of house red, to last the four of us all evening.

I loved Roy for his stance over the steak. Loved him so much for that.

10

When did it start to really go south? My dissatisfaction with my life began soon after I met Tamzin and envied her so much. When I realized I wanted so much more than I had – and unless I made some changes, so much more than I would *ever* have. I know now that I matured through my twenties, my hopes and dreams became more cemented, and I could see that my life dragging out as it was would bore me. I needed more.

Looking back, there were a few things building up that on their own might not have led to me leaving Roy but together they created a monster that eventually whacked me in the face and left me with no obvious alternative. One sad little building block happened on a wet Tuesday in May. I'd gone out in my lunch hour, at the medical practice where I was then working in reception, to buy a copy of the *Argus* newspaper. Roy had texted me that there was a big piece in it about a murder he was working on.

He was newly promoted to DI and this was the first case on which he was the Senior Investigating Officer, and I was proud as hell of him. And there on page five was a very handsome photograph of him, with a quote beneath it. Something about being on the verge of a breakthrough with the case. We kept all his cuttings in a scrapbook.

While I was in the newsagent, not a gambler by nature, I bought a lottery scratch card on a whim. I'd never bought one before, and I hadn't realized there was such a range of choices. The lady behind the counter was really helpful, actually – scratch that, no pun intended – she was just a brilliant saleswoman. I'd gone in to buy a newspaper and came out having spent £40 on scratch cards and a bunch of lottery tickets – at a time when money was tight for us. We'd just bought the house we loved, close to the seafront, for more than we could really afford.

We had overstretched ourselves with the cost of furnishing and decorating it but the house really was in a dilapidated and sad state. It needed more money spending on it than we had. I just suddenly thought, you know, if I could get lucky with a scratch card or a lottery ticket, then all our financial problems would be over. And, on the third scratch card, I couldn't believe my eyes.

Five hundred pounds!

Seriously.

I went back to the newsagent to make sure I hadn't got it wrong. She gave me ten fifty-pound notes, with a big smile. I was walking on air! I bought a bottle of Champagne on the way home, planning to crack it open when Roy had finished with his case and was no longer on call. But I couldn't help telling him the moment I saw him, excitedly. He wasn't excited, not really, not in the jump-up-and-down way I'd hoped. Sure, he was pleased about the £500 we suddenly had, but he told me it was beginner's luck, to be happy with that and to forget doing it again.

But I couldn't. The lightbulb was burning brightly inside me. This could be my path to a lifestyle like Tamzin's. I bought a bunch more scratch cards and lottery tickets the following week. And I won again, incredibly, first £25, then £100 and then another £500! I bought a pond for the house from a garden centre, but this time I didn't let on to Roy it was out of my gambling winnings – I told him my parents had given it to me. I'm not sure he believed me, because he knew what tightwads they are. As another example of that, for last Christmas my father's present to Roy was a rather horrible golf club tie, which, I found out, he'd won in a tombola at his golf club. And, worse still, it had a tiny bit of egg inside the tip – which meant someone had worn it – OMG.

So anyway, I figured I was on a winning streak. By sheer chance, that Saturday I was going with Roy to an evening of greyhound racing. It was in support of a charity we really cared about as dog lovers, the Brighton Retired Greyhound Trust. And it felt special to go back to the place where we had first met.

It's a three-course sit-down dinner, during which you get to bet on six races – all very civilized and easy, smiling servers bringing betting slips to the table. I knew nothing about greyhounds at all, other than that I think they look beautiful. Somehow, I picked five of the six winners, and at the end of the evening, with my £270 profit in my purse, was kicking myself for not placing bolder bets.

But what I did know was that I was really beginning to like this gambling malarkey. I felt signs – whatever – something telling me I had what it took to be a winner.

Not that Roy was impressed. A few weeks later he was rummaging through our kitchen bin, looking for a receipt he'd thrown away by mistake, and found a whole bunch of scratch cards I'd bought, where I'd won nothing – just a temporary losing run. A few hundred pounds, no big deal. But he was furious, partly because I'd hidden it away but mostly because he added up the amounts and was shocked with what he saw as my frivolity, when we were in a financially tough time. He just looked so exasperated, and it made me feel guilty. I can still see his face now. An expression not of anger, but disappointment. The worst kind.

I tried to make myself feel better by reminding him that he played a regular game of boys' poker with his chums, every Thursday evening that he was free. He pointed out that they set a limit, so no one could lose more than £100 in any poker evening, and repeated to me that the scratch cards he'd found totalled over £500.

Paraphrasing Shania Twain, that didn't impress him much.

To tell you the truth, that wasn't impressing me much either. But I knew it was just a passing glitch. From now on I would keep my gaming to myself, then one day soon I would surprise Roy with our solution out of this financial crisis. We didn't need millions and millions, but a big enough win to lift the stress from ourselves and live in our lovely home and be happy together. Be a little bit more *Tamzin*. That's how I liked to describe it.

I'd got the bug. The BIG WIN was out there, waiting for me. I just had to find it. And I would. I was convinced of that. Me and – well, let's just say a lot of other hopefuls.

I was smarter than all of the other hopefuls. I really did think so.

Although I'd had a dismal school record, the one subject I was good at was maths. And I reckoned I'd worked out a winning formula.

I was going to be the one. The modern version of Charles Wells – the Man Who Broke the Bank of Monte Carlo.

Bring it on!

11

Early July 2007 – Looking back

I realized there was a whole world of gambling beyond just scratch cards. So I opened an account with a firm of bookmakers and had a go at the horses. I began secretly reading *Sporting Life* as well as the racing pages in the daily newspapers, and looked up a number of websites that told you how to win – or at least to have the best chance of winning.

Factoring in my skills at maths, I had three wins, seven places and forty-two losers in the following month. Not great, I had just £800 left in my dwindling savings. Then I came across a piece online about a guy, calling himself the Cincinnati Kid, who reckoned he made £100K a year at online poker. He played the time zones. He figured out, for example, that at 3 a.m. in Los Angeles it was 11 a.m. in London. People playing a poker game, especially an amateur one, say in LA at that time, were likely to be tired and a little drunk, whereas he was fresh and alert. Smart.

Roy had taught me how to play some of the varieties of poker when we'd been on holiday in Mykonos one summer. I boned up on it online, then put it into practice, in the hours between the end of my shift at the medical centre and Roy getting home. But winning wasn't as easy as the Cincinnati Kid made it sound.

I favoured Texas hold 'em, but after another month working the time zones – Australia was perfect for me, with games going well into the small hours in just about every major city – my £800 had increased to just £1,152. Although they might be tired and drunk, one thing I learned about Aussie gamblers – they were still pretty sharp. Five weeks later, and although I'd had a few good wins, I was down to £731. Wherever that BIG WIN was lurking, it wasn't in the dens of lone Aussie gamblers.

I was beginning to think that initial run of luck had been just what Roy had said it was all along, and nothing more. Beginner's luck. That I was chasing a dream. But then something happened that was to change my thinking. And, ultimately, change the direction of my life.

12

Spring 2007 – Looking back

A charming guy of about thirty came into the medical practice. He had grey eyes, shiny hair and a really calm aura. He walked up to me with a confident smile.

'Hi, I've an appointment with Dr Mair.' He locked eyes with mine.

I couldn't help smiling back. Not that I was looking to get his approval. But. You know, he had a presence about him, and I liked it.

His name was Jay Strong. He asked me if I lived locally and did I have a few spare minutes to tell him about Brighton; he was looking to buy a flat with his husband, and he wanted to know where the good areas were and where to avoid – from a local, not an estate agent. He told me he worked as a croupier at a posh gaming club in London, in Mayfair, where the clientele were mostly rich Middle Eastern visitors to the city. He didn't know anyone here and, to be honest, he seemed a little lost. Well, that got my interest! I knew I could help him with some local knowledge, and I love nosing around streets looking at houses. I hesitated just for a moment, checking in with myself. 'Sorry, no. I can't tell you about Brighton,' I said. 'But I can *show* you!'

We arranged a time to meet, obviously outside of my work hours and, although I knew he was gay, I still felt a little guilty. I'd definitely tell Roy about him later so nothing to stress about, though he'd probably be a bit jealous if he saw him and wonder why I'd said yes. But this random, some might say fateful, connection was too good to be true and I was excited to learn more about this world where I was destined to be successful. For now, though, it was my exciting secret. My new career.

And for the next two months, Jay made up for the something that was missing. This friendship – and the attention – that I realized I craved. He was like a 'brother from another mother', I'd say, the sibling I never had. To outsiders we may have looked like a couple, but I was careful where we met and always had an alibi lined up. Learned that from the best! I wholly believed that Jay and his husband, who I'd not met, would be people I could eventually introduce Roy to once I'd won big. How could Roy not like them after Jay showed me how to make us thousands of pounds?

What Jay didn't know about gambling wasn't worth knowing and I lapped it up, learning about this new world and finding a way to bring in some well-earned money. A tip he gave me, on the promise I would keep it to myself, was how to win in a casino.

'Look for a bored croupier at a roulette wheel,' he said. Simple as that.

He explained that most casinos require the croupier to spin the wheel every few minutes, regardless of whether they have punters at the table or not. The ones that don't have anyone at the table, or just a solitary punter, relieve their boredom by aiming for a target – and the easiest target is zero because it stands out from the alternate red and black by being green. And it has the added bonus of being the casino's advantage. Anyone can bet on zero, but most punters don't. The croupiers practise their spin of the wheel and toss of the ball, seeing how close they can get that little ball to that green slot.

Jay told me to find a quiet table and a bored croupier, and lay my bets around the numbers either side of zero. He said that's what he does when he goes gambling himself – and he almost always wins.

I discovered there's a casino in Hove, close to where we live, called the Casino d'Azur and I tried out his advice the very next day. I was made to feel instantly welcomed there. The atmosphere was exciting, with chandeliers hung from high ceilings, all the different gaming tables, the cashier behind a barred window, the smart serving staff. It felt a privilege to be there, although in reality just about anyone could walk in off the streets, buy some chips and start gambling.

I imagined myself in a Bond movie, but as I walked into the main gaming room, instead of glamorous people in tuxedos and elegant dresses sipping Martinis, I saw a couple of little old ladies perched at slot machines, a solitary Chinese man in a rather tired-looking suit placing chips at one of the three roulette wheels, and two men in jeans and T-shirts at a blackjack table.

Only one of the two other roulette wheels had a croupier, and just like Jay had said, he was spinning the wheel at his empty table. I wandered over, with £50 in chips. And guess what?

Jay's advice won me a shitload of money!

That first afternoon, anyway.

Beginner's luck?

13

There was something I found deeply seductive about the roulette table and had done since I first started. About the whole casino experience. The way the staff pamper you, bringing you drinks, charming you, making you feel you're a somebody, that you are important. That you are part of an exclusive family, the fraternity of real players.

This was some difference from the rather bland experience of buying scratch cards in a newsagent's. Every time I had done that, even when I had that first sizeable win, I felt a little like some kind of closet gambling addict. But here in the casino it was so different. There was a sense of magic in the air.

I loved the rituals and the sounds. The calm of the room; the focus all around us at the poker and blackjack tables; the quiet punctuated by the occasional shout of joy from another group at a roulette table.

I started small, tentatively, gently, testing my maths. And I kept winning, I couldn't help it. It was like I had the Midas touch, as if I wasn't following that little ball but it was following me. I walked away just before Easter with over £2,000, and another day with nearly £3,000. And I felt liberated. So powerful!

And said nothing to Roy, not yet. But truly they were happy days.

And even better, the casino was almost exactly halfway between work and home. My commute on foot – which I did when it wasn't raining – took me almost past the casino's entrance, luring me inside. And especially since I won a bucket load that very first time: £740 – to me that was big – and I was winning even bigger every day.

I left work at 1 p.m. and Roy was rarely home before 7 p.m. That gave me the whole afternoon at the roulette wheel. And the brilliant thing, I realized, was that this was a pretty dead time for the casino.

Playing the bored croupier strategy served me brilliantly in those weeks. But after my early surge I hit a losing streak and, a few months on, my careful records showed I was now up by a princely £132. Not exactly the jackpot I knew was waiting for me.

There was a Chinese guy of about fifty, whose name I learned from overhearing the croupier addressing him respectfully as Mr Yuchi. He wore a neat suit and smelled of stale cigarette smoke and had taken to joining me at my table, which annoyed me because it meant the croupier was no longer so bored. But Mr Yuchi played the roulette table like no one I'd ever seen.

He literally covered vast areas with stacks of chips – and these were high-value ones; some I could see were £50, others £100, and on some numbers they were six, eight, ten deep.

I watched him discreetly. Then I realized his method. It was simple and crude. He was basically playing the odds. If you tossed a coin and it came up heads, you'd expect it to be tails next time. If it was heads again, you'd expect it even more so to be tails next. Heads for the third time and for sure it had to be tails next. But if it wasn't, then the fourth time, surely.

It wasn't any different at the roulette wheel, apart from the risk of that green zero. Every time that little ball landed in a slot it was either red or black. I began counting. Over the next two weeks I never saw either colour come up more than four times consecutively. Yes!

I had a new strategy.

Bet on a colour – red. If black came up, bet on red again, doubling the amount. Then again. Then again.

The first time I tried it, it worked a treat: £5 on red, black came up; £10 on red, black again; £20 on red, black again; £40 on red – red came up! £80 back for a £75 investment. Beats the hell out of the stock market!

The second day I went bolder: £50 on red, black came up; I doubled, £100 on red, black again; £200 on red, black again; £400 on red, black yet again.

And I was out of chips.

In between the next spin of the wheel I ran to the cashier, drew £500 off my credit card – my own one, not our joint account – and returned to the table. Black came up four times in a row, while I waited, then I put the lot on red. Four conspicuous piles of twenty-five-pound chips.

Black again.

Shit, shit, shit.

Mr Yuchi must have seen my disappointed face because he gave me a smile and a *don't worry about it* shrug.

So I didn't worry about it. Just a momentary glitch. I had another hour before I had to leave and head home. I went back to the cashier, who sat in her little booth behind the counter, and asked for another £500 in twenty-five-pound chips.

But moments after I put the card into the reader I saw her frown. She was a rather prim-looking lady in her sixties, with the kind of dyed hair that goes a little orange, in a bun on top of her head. Although she must have recognized me, as I'd been drawing money out or cashing chips in now daily for months, she looked at me like I was a total stranger. 'Declined,' she said.

'Declined?' I echoed. 'What do you mean?'

I had to work hard to suppress my anger – I blame my parents, they kindly allowed me to develop a bit of an issue with how I dealt with situations that made my anger spiral out of control. I could feel it really rising now. I had to have a word with myself, it wasn't her fault that some bank robot with a screwed-up algorithm was denying me credit.

'Your card's declined, sweetheart.'

'How can it be? I've got—'

Then I was quiet for some moments. What actually did I have in it? A week ago, when I had last checked my balance, I had nearly £9,000. OK, I'd had a few bad days, but there was no way I'd lost that much.

Was there?

I tried to calm myself down. To think clearly. I was aware there was someone standing behind me. 'OK,' I said, 'let's try a smaller amount – two hundred?'

Orange Hair asked me to re-enter the card. 'I'm sorry, it's still declined.' This time she looked almost smug about it. There was no way I was letting her win anything over on me. Recklessly – I know – I pulled out the joint HSBC card Roy and I had and handed it to her. With the kind of nonchalant bravado I know Tamzin would have shown, I said, 'I'll draw a thousand from this.'

As I turned around, with twenty crisp fifty-pound notes in my hand, I saw it was Mr Yuchi standing behind me, holding an armful of chips to be cashed. He gave me a polite nod.

I exchanged my cash for chips at the table. Determined to make up my loss quickly, I asked the croupier at my table for fifty-pound chips.

And lost the lot in twenty minutes.

It was 6.30 p.m. Roy had messaged me to say he wouldn't be home until 8 p.m. tonight. I sat at the table debating what to do and cursing my stupidity. It was the middle of the month, and our HSBC credit card statement came through on the twenty-sixth – just over ten days to go. It was still a printed statement, back then. I knew that Roy never checked it too thoroughly, he would just glance through it, looking for anomalies.

If I could just replace that £1,000 before then, he probably wouldn't notice; even if he did, I could tell him the bank had made an error, which it had corrected.

But the question was: where was that £1,000 going to come from? At that moment, all I could think was that it would come from drawing out more cash and winning it back.

But it turned out there was another solution.

Mr Yuchi.

He came back to the roulette table and sat beside me. Although we'd exchanged glances numerous times over the past weeks, we had never actually spoken. 'You have cash flow problem?' he asked, his voice short, clipped, but kind. 'Need buy more chips?'

'Just having a bad run, I guess,' I replied and gave him a smile.

He slid his hand inside the breast of his jacket and pulled out his wallet. For an instant I honestly thought, totally irrationally, he was going to give me some cash. Instead, he pulled out a business card and laid it down on the baize in front of me. 'You call him, he always help. Not ask too many questions. Very nice man. I have to go to work now, see you tomorrow!'

He slipped off his chair before I could even thank him.

Ha, that seems such a joke now. Such a sick joke. But back then it felt this friendly man with the stained teeth, who reeked of smoke, had thrown me a lifeline. Rather than a death sentence.

I picked up the card. It didn't have much on it. Just a phone number and a name.

Roel Albazi.

14

Roel Albazi was a total slimeball, but I had one thing in my favour – from the moment I first met him, in his fancy clothes, in his ritzy office with its white carpet, hung with erotic art, and smelling of a no-doubt expensive cologne, I could tell he was trying it on with me. Yuck. His was the kind of flirting that's both overt and subtle at the same time, the kind you get from men who consider themselves God's gift to women.

But I figured if I played along, he might cut me some slack. And he did. He cut me slack all the way to £100,000 of debt. On my unspoken promise.

Well, not exactly a promise. I played the flirty card so well each time we met, while more and more cash advances kept coming. He knew my husband was a cop and that, by association, I was trustworthy, good for the money. What he did not know, and I did, was that he was on my husband's radar. But that didn't bother me, I needed his money, and I was certain that with his continued extended credit I would eventually hit a winning streak. It was a mathematical certainty. I just had to keep going, continue raising my stakes after each loss until it all came good again. The classic gambler's folly, I've since realized – chasing your losses.

Out of the first tranche of cash he advanced me, I covered off the missing £1K from our joint account, so no awkward questions from Roy. But that was small beer compared to the catastrophic losses at the table that followed.

52

Without my fully realizing it, my life was turning, day by day, into a perfect storm. I had started to take Valium to help with the anxiety I was feeling constantly and, if I was honest with myself, it was becoming as habitual as the gambling. I had made the mistake of having an on-off affair with Cassian Pewe, the man who Roy despised more than anyone on the planet – and I was starting to intensely dislike Cassian, too. I had missed my period and I was getting panicky. I now owed almost £150,000 to a man who both repulsed and frightened me. Roel Albazi repeatedly told me over the phone his boss was concerned that I wasn't paying anything back, and hinted none too subtly that sleeping with him might buy me some time. Yuck.

I was thinking more and more often that the way out of this extremely serious situation was to run away from it all. Run away from the shame I'd cause myself and Roy and start over somewhere. I had no idea what I wanted to do, I just knew I wanted a different life and to escape this never-ending anxiety.

I couldn't turn to my parents.

I'd started drinking a bit more than usual. On top of the Valium this was not a good mix. I knew I needed to come off the tranquillizer but it felt like a quick way to relieve some of my problems, so I just took it secretly instead. Taking the easy option.

My dream of a lifestyle like Tamzin's had crashed and was now burning. Tamzin was expecting another child and I'd heard nothing from her. It was impossible for me to envy her life any more than I did. She would now have the perfect new baby to go with the perfect everything else. And she clearly didn't give me a second thought. I wasn't anyone of significance to her, just someone she met passing through. Who she just happened to have had a drunken fling with. End of. But I couldn't get her out of my mind. And, just to add to everything, my best friend, Becky, told me she and her husband, Elliot, had made the decision to emigrate to Australia – he'd had a job offer and they would be leaving at the end of the month. The only person I felt I could rely on, about to leave my life.

I felt totally adrift. I was a boat that had broken its mooring and was in a storm-tossed sea heading onto rocks. And there wasn't anyone I could turn to. How could I tell my husband I'd run up a gambling debt of nearly £150,000 to a murderous loan shark?

I did try to talk to Becky, but suddenly I felt I didn't know her any more. Her head was now in Australia. All she was interested in was showing me the website of the house, eight minutes' walk from Bondi beach, that Elliot and she had rented for a year with an option to buy. And showing me magazine pictures of their dreamy ideas for the kitchen, the lounge and the master bedroom – and of course the deck and the barbecue area. And the baby room, too – she was three months pregnant. She offered me the chance to help her with the interior design, saying how much she valued my creative input, but I just couldn't muster up the energy to do it. I felt like I had already become one of the ghosts of her past life.

Of course you and Roy will come and stay, won't you? You must!!!

Our Pilates instructor had gone off to Thailand at the start of that summer for a two-month-long wellness convention, or something or other, so the girls' group didn't meet twice a week as it had before.

I felt so lonely, suddenly. And scared. And utterly lost. I had to find a huge amount of money. Sure, we had some equity in the house, but no way near enough. Besides, I could hardly say to Roy that I owed all this to a gangster he was gathering evidence on. My only hope was that he busted Albazi. But when – quietly fishing for information – I mentioned his name at home, it didn't sound like the police were anywhere close, yet.

There was a time in my life when I slept like the proverbial log. Now I lay awake, dozing intermittently throughout each long night, and in the mornings opened my eyes, exhausted, with the sense that the whole world was out to get me.

The calls and texts from Albazi were getting more frequent and less and less friendly. Then, one morning, I saw a car parked in our street, just across the road from our house. We lived in a quiet residential area of neat semi-detached and small detached houses. We lived among decent people in a nice neighbourhood.

This was not the street for a black car with blacked-out windows to be parked.

I'd never thought about suicide before. Amongst his skill sets, Roy was, back then, a suicide negotiator for the police. He could be called out at any time of the day or night. It might be to talk someone down from a high-rise window ledge or a cliff-top, or on one occasion a teenage girl who had doused herself in petrol and was threatening to set fire to herself with a cigarette lighter. That one hadn't ended well.

I knew how much the attempts upset him, even the ones he foiled. He maintained that however desperate someone might be, there was always a way through, always some light at the end of the tunnel if only they could be shown it.

In the same way, he believed there was decency in almost everyone, however rotten they might seem at first. He used to say that everyone's journey to a custody cell began in the family home in the first years of their life.

But that June afternoon, as the little ball nestled between the frets of the only green slot on the wheel, the croupier, using what looked like a posh version of a windscreen scraper, swept up the last of my chips and my last hope.

I was done.

Feeling utterly desperate. My credit card was all but maxed out and I was trapped. If there was any light at the end of the tunnel, it was the train coming towards me. I really seriously began considering killing myself. Perhaps I should end it all?

Could anything be worse than where I actually was right now? Frightened. Possibly pregnant with a baby I longed for but couldn't fully explain; a husband who loved me so much but was never good enough for me. A twisted web of acquaintances who knew me a bit but didn't really. Doubted by my never proud parents. All my savings blown. Abandoned by my friends. No idea where my life was going. Alcoholic . . . maybe? Probably not. Addicted to Valium? Probably. And gambling. Maybe? Who knows. Am I there yet? Does anyone know? When do you know?

And a debt that was going to turn very ugly very soon, and that was frightening me the most. I was getting increasingly frequent phone calls from Roel Albazi, which I started to ignore. Then he sent his flunkey. A bald-headed guy of around forty, who was taller than the front-door frame of the doctors' surgery. He was scrupulously polite, had a big smile and spoke calmly, as he accosted me on my way out of the office. He asked me if it was all right to have a word with me.

As we were on a busy street in the centre of Hove, which made me feel pretty safe, I told him that was fine. He then leaned down and, face to face with me, very gently and very kindly, said, 'My boss, Mr Albazi, doesn't want you to come to any harm. But he needs a repayment plan. He's worried for your safety, he likes you, he doesn't want to see you end up dead. But it is not in his gift to protect you.' Then he winked at me, and before turning and walking off, he added, 'I think it would be nice if you called him. Mr Albazi would appreciate that. Make an appointment, perhaps? But make it soon. While you can. While you are still alive. You are much too young to die.'

15

It was 8.20 a.m. and I was worried the chemist might not be open yet, as I headed to work. After several gloomy days of rain, summer was back and as I walked through glorious early morning sunshine, I was feeling more positive than I had in a long while. I'd barely slept all night, having made my decision that I would do a pregnancy test today. When I'd looked it up online, it said it was best to do it in the morning.

I'd also made another, firm, decision about what I would do if it was positive.

There were normally two of us on reception in the mornings, but my colleague, Julie, was away on holiday, and once I got behind the desk it would be non-stop all morning, with no chance to slip out to the shops until I finished my shift at 1 p.m.

To my relief the chemist was open. After a quick chat with a helpful assistant, who explained how to use the testing kit and even excitedly wished me 'good luck', I was on my way with a small box in my handbag. The box had a cover pic showing an elegantly shaped blue-and-white plastic tube, with a tiny window in it. On the top of the box in bold yellow it proclaimed: *OVER 99% ACCURATE.*

I went into the surgery via the rear of the building, but as I approached reception I could see there was already a queue of people, the young, the old, the very nearly dead and one old boy slumped in a chair, white hair sticking up as if he had just been electrocuted and who looked like he could actually be dead.

I took their names in turn, ticking them off the list, then told them to take a seat and the doctors (there were six) would call them.

I just wanted to go to the loo. To open my pregnancy testing kit. To find out!

I couldn't wait.

Anyhow, most of the people waiting in line didn't need me. Their doctors would come out and summon them in. I took the opportunity to stick a BACK IN 2 MINS! sign on the counter, grabbed a urine sample pot, which the girl at the chemist told me was easier to use, scarpered through the door behind me and into a cubicle in the ladies', closing and locking the door behind me.

I took the box, branded Clearblue, out of my handbag and ripped it open with clumsy, nervous fingers, breaking a bit off a nail in the process. They were all chipped anyway, long overdue for a visit to the nail studio. I always avoided going for as long as possible, because the sweet young girl there was a chatterbox who drove me mad, talking non-stop. Anyhow, now I needed to spruce up for my new life. I made a mental note to book an appointment. Then I unfolded the instructions and read them carefully.

Two minutes after dipping the test stick into the sample pot, not even thinking what carnage might be going on in the waiting room, there was just a single red line. Not pregnant.

Seriously?

I wasn't sure how I felt about this. On the one hand, I was elated considering the mess my life was in, but at the same time, deeply disappointed. I wanted to be pregnant and I didn't want to be.

'Shit,' I said. 'Shit, shit, shit, sh—'

I stopped. Stared wide-eyed at the tiny window. Was it my imagination?

A second line was starting to appear, very faintly at first.

It got steadily brighter and darker. Until it was as strong and thick as the first line.

Twin red lines now. Parallel.

I stared at them, numbly, then sat down on the loo seat and stared at them even harder. For reassurance I took the package out of the bin where I had shoved it and read the wording in yellow at the top. *OVER 99% ACCURATE.*

My skin seemed to have taken on a life of its own, as if it was crawling around my body independent of the rest of me. It was a weird sensation. It stopped then started again. Like I was covered head to foot in a colony of millions of ants or something. I shook, hard, and yelled, 'Stoppit! Stoppit! Stoppit!'

Then I heard my name being called. It was Rosie, who ran the accounts. 'Sandy? You OK?'

Yeah, I'm fine, apart from my skin taking a walk around the block. 'Yes, thanks, great! Just – a friend – teasing me!'

'You sounded really distressed.'

I owe a man who is threatening to have me skinned alive £150,000 that I don't have, I'm about to leave my husband and I've just found out I'm pregnant. Should I be sounding distressed?

'I'm fine, Rosie, thanks! Never better!'

16

The post in our road used to get delivered around 9.30 a.m. on weekdays, long after Roy and I had gone to work. So now, as I was only working part-time – on our fertility consultant's orders – I was the one who got to it first.

It used to be after I got back from the casino and before Roy was home, but now, since I'd been cleaned out – having gone all-in, as they call it in gambling speak, a week previously – I was home by 1.30 p.m. most days. The first thing I would do after scooping up the post and checking it for any nasty surprises was to take a Valium. I would be feeling better in minutes. Better, but full of shame, now it dawned on me that this was an addiction that was probably getting out of hand and couldn't be good for my baby. It did, however, enable me to face the shit.

The shit called Roel Albazi.

And the problem of finding £150,000 to pay him. Without telling Roy. And without the benefit of a fairy godmother. It was time for action.

It wasn't going to come from remortgaging our house, for sure. So where on God's earth was I going to find that kind of money? Of course, I should never have lost it, but then, Albazi should never have fed me all the loans he did. Probably, if I hadn't been in some kind of altered reality, thanks to my messed-up mind at the time, I would never have let this happen. I did not have a clue what to do, I was terrified of Roy finding out and I was more scared than I'd ever been in my life. Albazi – and his goon – were making my life a waking hell.

Two days ago, Albazi sent me a text. I wish I'd never opened it, because it shocked me in a way that nothing ever in my life had, before. His message read: **Hey Sandy, just thought you'd like to see this video of a person me and my boss loaned money to, who failed to repay it. I'd hate this to happen to you, because you are such a nice person.**

I clicked on the website link. What I saw made me sick, and I mean physically sick – throw-up-in-the-bathroom sick. A man in his thirties, Hispanic-looking, lying on a bench, like one you'd find in a physiotherapist's or chiropractor's clinic. Except his hands and feet were bound. And he was naked. Someone, off-camera, began to slash him with a carving knife. I turned away, but – I don't know how or why – I kept turning back, although I muted the sound to stop the screaming.

I was terrified that, even if they didn't come after me, what if they came after Roy? I wanted to tell Roy, but I was stupidly scared both of how he would react, but also of what might happen to him if he went after Albazi. I still loved Roy. I cared for him. None of this crap was his fault. He was the same Roy Grace I had married. He'd stayed the same, consistent, decent human being who genuinely cared about making the world a better place. But I was no longer the same Sandy Balkwill he had married. I wanted more than being the wife of a parochial Sussex homicide detective.

And thanks to that, I was in deep trouble.

I'd even googled to see if gambling debts were legal and learned that, if incurred through legal gambling, they are enforceable. I'd found several gambling debt support groups all offering advice, but none of it helped. I went as far as asking Becky for the phone number of a friend of hers who was a paralegal in a big law firm to see if she could help me, but I chickened out of calling her – I don't know why, but all I can think, looking back, was that I was more scared of Roy finding out than I was of any retribution by Albazi.

Sure, Mr Albazi, go ahead, torture me, kill me and solve all my problems in one go. Because, Mr Albazi, the money I owe you isn't my only problem. There's another big problem that makes me want to run away even more.

This baby I am carrying. The baby I have wanted for so long – and yet I don't know who the father is.

17

So, even though the money from my latest pay cheque was now in my bank account, and despite my growing anxiety over what I was going to do about my debt and the baby, I avoided the temptation to nip into the Casino d'Azur and try to improve on it. Instead, listening to the sensible voice in my head for once, I headed straight home from the surgery, stopping only to buy a tuna mayo wrap for my lunch at my favourite deli. Not that in those dark days I had any appetite at all. Food had become nothing more than fuel. I ate mechanically, to live.

Arriving home around 1.30 p.m., I scooped up the mail from the floor, and sifted through it, standing up at the kitchen table. It was mostly bills and the usual rubbish – but among all the takeaway fliers, along with a renewal notice for our fridge warranty, was a plain envelope, classy paper, with my name typed. It caught my attention as it included a reference to my maiden name on the envelope.

I opened it, quite carefully, but the first thing I saw as I opened the double-folded letter, on equally classy paper inside, was the name and address of a Brighton law firm. Hobart-Widders, Solicitors and Commissioners for Oaths.

I instantly had a sinking feeling. Was I being sued? For the money I owed?

Then I read on:

Dear Mrs Grace (née Balkwill),

I am writing to you on behalf of a law firm in Reutlingen, in the state of Baden-Württemberg, Germany, who have asked us to help trace you.

They wish to inform you that you are a beneficiary in the estate of Frau Antje Frieburg, late of Gegesten 2, Mehen Strasse, Reutlingen.

I would need you to please provide identification documentation to ensure we are corresponding with the right person before we can release further information or a copy of the will. I am sure you will understand this information is of a sensitive nature.

We would require photo ID, such as a passport or photo-card driving licence, and proof of your residential address, such as a recent utility bill or bank statement, ideally dated within the past three months. If it is inconvenient for you to attend our office in person in order for us to copy your ID and verify your identity, please let the undersigned know and we can make alternative arrangements.

Yours faithfully

Carolyn Smith, BA, LLB.

I sat down and read the letter again. Then a third time. Several thoughts and questions were flying through my mind. The first was who the hell was Frau Antje Frieburg? Had the solicitors made an error and located the wrong beneficiary? And how much money might I have been left?

I googled the name, but nothing came up that remotely matched. But as my mother's parents were German, I figured if we did have a relative of this name, she would know. After some hesitation I called her.

It wasn't something I did that regularly, because, to be honest, calling my mother was never a great experience. I would always have to endure a litany of moans about something. Last time, a few weeks ago, it had been a list of all her ailments, followed by moans about her long wait for appointments with all the specialists she was certain she needed. It was followed by complaints about the Seaford bus service, about the rise in costs of just about everything, the weather, the paint flaking off their house a year after it had been repainted – by my father, to save money – and their car, falling to bits and my father too mean to replace it.

It took a long time for her to answer and I expected it to go to the answer machine. Although it turned out it had long since ceased to work ever since my father, a serial bodger, had tried to fix something on the volume control. She was a little breathless and as joyless as usual at hearing me. She greeted me with, 'I was in the garden, weeding. You cannot believe how the weeds come up this time of year.'

'I have the same problem here,' I said.

'No, we have really bad weeds. We have particularly tough weeds in Seaford – they have to be resilient to cope with the corrosive sea air.'

We actually lived closer to the sea than my mother and just a few miles along the coast, but I wasn't interested in arguing about weeds. I was too excited by the letter, although I was trying not to get over-excited. 'Does the name Antje Frieburg mean anything to you, Mum? If I'm pronouncing it correctly?'

There was a long silence. I thought for a moment we'd been cut off or, as she was prone to do when annoyed about something, she'd just hung up. 'What did you say?' she asked, finally, her voice sounding a little shocked.

'I asked if you knew the name Antje Frieburg – like, who she is?'

'Antje Frieburg, did you say?' She repeated the name slowly and disdainfully.

'Yes.'

There was another long silence. I finally broke it by asking, 'Do you – did you – know her, Mum?'

'Why in God's name are you asking me about that bloody bitch?'

18

July 2007 – Looking back

Two hours later, I entered the rather sterile first-floor reception area of the West Street offices of solicitors Hobart-Widders. The solicitor had a brief gap in her afternoon appointments, due to a cancellation. In my handbag I had my birth certificate, marriage certificate, passport, driving licence, a week-old electricity bill and our quarterly council tax demand, for belt and braces.

Carolyn Smith was on the phone, I was told by the receptionist. Her assistant would be along in a minute – meanwhile I was directed to take a seat. I perched on a small, semi-circular sofa, with a coffee table with several magazines laid out, as well as today's *Argus*. But my head was buzzing too much to look at any of them, too much to focus on anything at this moment but the name, Antje Frieburg.

Who had named me as a beneficiary in her will.

And who made my mother spit blood.

Turns out Antje Frieburg was her paternal aunt – one of her father's three sisters. It took me a while to get it all out of my mother, because there was clearly a lot of anger and bad blood. She was the one member of her family who had done well – not just well, she was massively wealthy. She had married a German industrialist, a cousin of the Krupps family, and his family had amassed a vast fortune during the Second World War supplying steel to Hitler's war effort.

It wasn't this my mother was angry about. It was that after she and my father had married, she had asked her aunt if she could lend them some money to buy a house in England, and her aunt had loftily replied that if she'd wanted to live in style, she should not have married a working-class aircraft fitter.

But I barely heard the reason for my mother's hatred of her aunt. What I had heard was the word industrialist.

Industrialist!

It was spinning in my mind! Like the wheels on a one-armed bandit.

Kerchingggg!

I did some more googling after ending my call with my mother. I linked the words Frieburg and industrialist, and now I got a hit!

Claus Kauffman-Frieburg, married to Antje. He had died fifteen years ago. His company had factories in Kassell, Frankfurt am Main, Dusseldorf and Cologne, and their head office in Tübingen – close to Reutlingen.

For the first time in a long while I was suddenly feeling optimistic and happy again. As I looked up Claus Kauffman-Frieburg on Wikipedia, he showed as, at the time of his death, the 231st richest man in Germany. I had been joking about a fairy godmother, but now it seemed maybe it wasn't such a joke after all . . .

Just how much had this aunt I had never heard of and never met left me? Enough to pay off odious Albazi and to set myself up in a new life somewhere abroad? Hastily, I start to think through all the options in my head. One of which is being able to pay off Albazi and stay with Roy, but I know it has gone too far for that. God, I have been so stupid. If only I'd realized I'd be getting some inheritance, I'd never have needed to get sucked into gambling. But then again, even if I'd not gambled and got into such a financial mess, there was still the mess I'd got into with Cassian. And this pregnancy. I know in my heart that, whatever money this inheritance is, I can't go back to 'normal' with Roy. My life is now somewhere else far away. The prospect of this half terrifies me and half excites me. I try to focus.

How much money did the 231st richest man in Germany leave his wife, Antje? Hundreds of millions? Why had she chosen to leave some of her wealth to me, having rejected my mother's request for help all those years back? Perhaps she had no children and had simply decided to leave it all to more distant relatives.

How much was coming to me? That was the burning question. Would there need to be protracted correspondence with her lawyers in Germany? Roel Albazi had given me two weeks to repay £150,000 before the interest kicked in again and the debt went up. Could I get Antje Frieburg's inheritance within that time frame?

And how fast could I find out just how much it was? I didn't dare to try to guess, although I did wonder, with a tingle of excitement like a caffeine high, if it might be in the millions. I was going to find out soon enough.

I looked up, suddenly, to see a young, smartly if conservatively dressed woman in her mid-twenties, standing in front of me. 'Mrs Grace?' she asked. 'I'm Carolyn Smith's assistant, Sonia Golding. Carolyn Smith can see you now.'

19

July 2007 – Looking back

Carolyn Smith's office was small, and made even smaller by several piles of documents tied with pink ribbons on the floor, a row of filing cabinets against one wall, and bookshelves laden with legal tomes on the other. The window looked out and down onto the constant flow of traffic up and down West Street, and I caught the smallest glimpse of the sea, a quarter of a mile to the south.

The solicitor was a good-looking and friendly lady, with long brown hair. She was smartly dressed in a pale blue linen two-piece over a white blouse, and sat behind a glass-topped desk stacked with more documents, a computer and an elaborate phone-intercom. Facing the desk were two Perspex ghost chairs.

A Law Society practising certificate hung on one otherwise bare wall, and arranged along a bookshelf I could see a photograph of a fit-looking man in his forties, with short, dark hair and dressed in tennis kit, brandishing a racquet, and another showing two blond, curly-haired teenage boys. A third was of a spaniel, face almost squished against the camera lens, that looked like it was laughing. Strange what one remembers.

I read somewhere that years after you meet someone you might not remember their name, or even what they looked like, but you will always remember how they made you feel.

'Gorgeous dog!' I said.

'That's Jim,' she replied. 'The love of my life – well, next to my husband and my boys.' She smiled warmly and held out her hand, shaking mine. 'Very nice to meet you, Mrs Grace. So,' she continued, seating herself behind her desk and moving into formal lawyer mode, 'you've brought me some proof of ID?'

Sitting opposite her, I opened my blue handbag – which looked a little like the expensive Mulberry bag I secretly craved – that Roy had bought me last Christmas, and produced the envelope containing the documents I'd brought along and passed them across the desk.

She put on a pair of glasses and studied each one of them in turn, taking her time – taking so much time I began to wonder if I hadn't brought what was needed. Then she called in her assistant and asked her to photocopy them, before looking back at me with a smile. 'Good,' she said, 'that's all perfect. I'll return the originals to you in a minute. So now I can release this letter to you.'

Opening a pink file folder on her desk, she took out a sealed envelope with a row of German stamps on the plain white envelope, and handed it to me.

Typed on it was: *Sandra Christina Grace, née Balkwill, Brighton, England.*

I looked at her. 'Do you know what it says?'

'I don't,' she replied. 'My job was to ensure it went to the correct addressee – we had to carry out a number of checks to establish there is no other person with the same name and background as yourself. You don't need to open it now – it's your private letter, take it home with you and open it later if you'd prefer.'

I was in turmoil. I desperately wanted to open it and yet, at the same time, I was scared. What if . . . ?

It was a question I hardly dared ask myself.

What if it was a massive disappointment?

Equally, what if it was a vast sum of money? I would need to hide that from Roy and I was sitting in front of someone who might be able to help me to do that – legally.

The paper felt a little flimsy, like the airmail envelopes my mother used to correspond with her relatives in Germany, back in my childhood. But it also felt like there was more than just a single sheet inside. 'I'd like to open it now,' I said. 'Just in case I need your assistance.'

'Of course!'

I began to tear at one corner of the envelope. But, as I did so, Carolyn Smith reached across her desk towards me, holding a slim, elegant silver paperknife.

I took it from her and slit the envelope open with a shaking hand.

20

I was right, there wasn't just one letter inside, there were two, stapled together.

The first, written entirely in German, was on old-fashioned, embossed corporate letterhead, the law firm's moniker, *Fischer Volks*, at the top, and two columns of names, all with letters after them, in much smaller print beneath. Evidently a substantial company, if these were all partners.

I was about to hand it to Carolyn Smith when I realized the stapled attachment was a translation. Somewhat in pidgin English, I saw, as I began to read.

Dear Fräulein Sandra Balkwill,

I act, on behalf of my firm who are co-executor of the estate for the lately deceased Frau Antje Frieburg of Reutlingen, in the state of Baden-Württemberg, Germany.

Beneath the terms of the will within this late deceased lady's wishes, you are nominated as a beneficiary. If you can be so troubled as to be making connection with our office, it will be of assistance to us to please guide you as to your satisfaction of your inheritance.

Hoping we hear from us soon.

With sincerely your regards

Julia Lutz

Junior Partner

I handed the letter across the desk to the solicitor, who read it in silence for some moments. Then she looked at me. 'Not a great translation, is it?'

'Done by a budgerigar?'

She smiled. 'Let's hope it's laid a golden egg.'

I nodded, very hard, thinking how good that would be. It could change everything. 'So what happens next?' I asked, trying not to sound over-excited or anxious, but very conscious of Roel Albazi breathing down my neck.

'Well,' she said, 'I can email her, informing her I've verified it is you, then it's over to you to communicate directly with her.'

I shook my head. 'No, I – I'd like you to do that.'

I explained to her that I did not want my husband to find out about this inheritance, which – although I did not tell her – I had every expectation was going to be massive. Life-changing, for sure. I asked if she could represent me in handling the money, when it came in. I mentioned that I was potentially planning to leave him, and that I wanted the money to be paid into an account I still legally held in my maiden name.

She replied that she could not see there was any issue with that. And as my solicitor, she would carry out any instructions regarding my inheritance that I gave her.

She then had a call on her intercom that her next client was in reception. She glanced at her watch and told me to make an appointment with her assistant for the following day. Also, to fill in all the forms she needed to take me on as a client, and by tomorrow she expected to have heard back from the German law firm, with further details – and hopefully the amount of my inheritance.

I was so excited I barely slept all night. My tossing and turning repeatedly woke Roy, and I was riddled with guilt. He'd been working around the clock for the past week on a nasty case – a charred body found in a burnt-out car – and was shattered.

But I couldn't help it, I was dreaming of the fortune I was certain I was going to inherit from the estate of Antje Frieburg, widow of Claus Kauffman-Frieburg.

I did wonder why she had dropped the Kauffman, but I didn't wonder that much. More on my mind was the fact that Antje Frieburg was the widow of the 231st richest man in Germany. I felt so confident that I texted Roel Albazi, telling him I was coming into an inheritance and would have sufficient funds to repay him entirely within just a few days, a week or so at the most.

He messaged me back that he was glad to hear this. When could he expect the first payment?

I told him there would be no 'first payment'. He would be getting the whole lot in one go.

He sent me back an emoji of fingers crossed.

I ignored it. Albazi was history. The debt was history, and sadly, but inevitably, my husband was about to be history too. This had gone too far for me to go back to normality now. I had to be brave and see it through. I was heading to a new life, an heiress, with a baby growing inside me.

My only decision now was where to go?

And Germany was very much on my mind. Germany felt like my destiny!

I finally fell asleep, and despite my guilt and anxiety I had a very happy dream. It might not have been so great if I'd known what Carolyn Smith was going to tell me in the morning.

21

'You are not serious? Tell me you're not?' I blurted at the solicitor – now *my* solicitor – who had just given me the details of my inheritance.

I saw the top of a bus glide past the window behind her, the pane blurred by pelting rain, hunched figures with gloomy faces on the top deck, just visible between the slats in the horizontal Venetian blinds of her office. And I thought about another bus I'd seen go by yesterday, in the sunshine, and just how good I had been feeling sitting here in this same ghost chair.

How excited I had been for my future. How I had been thinking . . . *Goodbye, buses, it'll be taxis, limos and helicopters from now on – and no more flying cattle class! I'll be turning left on planes in future, or maybe, if the amount of my inheritance is large enough, it will only ever be private jets, living the life, living the dream! Living like Tamzin* – and I'd had a sudden memory about that amazing drunken night with her. About making love and kissing her, and falling asleep in her arms. My mind drifted and I was enjoying it.

I'd even thought that maybe I'd set up my own charitable foundation one day – to help causes I believed in, and to make people see the good in me. *Isn't that what really drives every big donor to charity? Altruism and ego make good bedfellows, don't they?*

That was yesterday. When my world was a sunny place and I was foolishly getting carried away spending vast sums of money that I didn't then know I didn't have. Now my solicitor had just rained on my parade, in keeping with the shitty day outside. And my anxiety was the worst ever.

Carolyn Smith, dressed in a crimson top, with a lace ruff neck, over black trousers, looked more formal than yesterday. And she had totally misread my reaction.

'It's a nice sum, isn't it, and out of the blue!' she replied, all breezy.

'A nice sum? Seriously?' I was staring back at her in utter disbelief – and maybe denial, too. Disbelief at the amount she had just read out to me, and disbelief she could think that was a *nice* sum.

'Thirty thousand pounds, that's a pretty nice amount of money, don't you think?' she said, like she was congratulating a small child on a sandcastle or a painting of a dog. 'And because your aunt is a foreign national, due to a magnanimous gesture by the UK government some time ago, you won't have to pay any inheritance tax on it.'

For a moment I was lost for words. I could sense my disappointment turning to anger. I tried to remain calm. I needed to keep Carolyn Smith onside, despite how much she was irritating me. I kept telling myself not to shoot the messenger. But it was hard with all my dreams crashing and burning around me. Only thirty sodding thousand pounds. Shit. Shit. Shit.

'Mrs Smith – Carolyn – what you don't know is that Antje Frieburg was married to one of the richest men in Germany,' I said, my voice rising. I was struggling to keep down my rage. 'For Chrissake! That's just shaking her bloody petty cash tin at me. It's like she's saying, *Hello, distant Englisher relative, have a few crumbs!*'

Carolyn Smith was now looking at me with an expression I couldn't read, then she shrugged a take-it-or-leave-it and that really pissed me off. And set me off.

'You don't understand, do you?' I said to her, more loudly than I intended, and jumped angrily to my feet. I took some breaths to calm myself, staring at her but not knowing really what to say.

She eyed me back silently for a few moments. 'Please sit down, Mrs Grace.'

'My mother was right when she called her a bloody bitch!' I said, sitting back down. 'It's just not as much as I'd hoped.'

'Hoped for what?' she probed.

'It's not your problem,' I replied. 'I'm sorry. I – I let my imagination run away – it does that sometimes. I ought to cut its sodding legs off, hobble it.' I shrugged. 'You see, a bigger amount would have solved all my problems.'

She looked at me sympathetically. 'Mrs Grace – can I call you Sandra or Sandy?'

'Sandy,' I said bleakly.

'OK, Sandy, let me tell you something.' Her tone was gentle, coaxing. 'As a probate lawyer, I see people every day who are disappointed with the amount of their inheritances. They were expecting so much more and only got a little. Everyone who sits where you are sitting, and is disappointed, thinks life isn't fair. And they are right, life isn't fair. Not many people are ever satisfied with what they've been left, and yet almost everyone is better off than they were before that relative died.' She smiled and shrugged, then massaged her neck for some moments. 'I'm afraid Gandhi was right in something he once said – and don't take this the wrong way: *The world has enough for everyone's need, but not enough for everyone's greed.*'

'Greed?' I echoed, my anger rising again. 'Is that what you think it is? It's not greed, I'm desperate.'

Giving me a quizzical look, she interlocked her fingers. 'Well, as I'm now your solicitor, or about to be, would you like to elaborate? You can tell me – under client confidentiality.'

I so much wanted to tell her. I badly needed to confide in

someone, just to unburden myself. But, as I stared across the desk at her, I suddenly felt so scared and inferior. There she was in her expensive clothes, her name on the company letterhead, living her dream – so I presumed. And here was I, a total mess, hooked on diazepam, deeply in debt to a very dangerous man, and about to leave my husband. I shrugged my shoulders and said, simply, 'I guess I was just hoping – like you say most of your clients are – for more.'

'It's like they say,' she responded, looking at me curiously, 'many of the things you can count, don't count. And many of the things you can't count, really count.'

I said nothing, just sat there thinking hard.

'Now let's get the paperwork sorted,' she continued, matter-of-factly.

I took a deep sigh, then tried to snap out of it, searching for any thread of positivity to hang on to. Thirty thousand pounds. If I got lucky – and my luck was long overdue for a turn for the better – I could turn it into a lot more. At least the £150,000 I desperately needed to pay slimeball Albazi.

My whole body shuddered each time I thought about him and thought about what he would do when he found out I didn't have all the money I'd promised him.

'How long will it take to receive this money?' I asked her.

'International banking transfers can be done pretty much instantly,' she replied.

'You mean you could have this in your client account before the end of today?'

'If that is your instruction, yes.'

'And once you have received the funds, could you pay them in cash to me?'

Carolyn Smith paused. 'I could, yes, but under money-laundering regulations I would have to ask you what you planned to do with the cash.'

'And if I said stick it on a horse or a roulette wheel, what would happen?'

'The answer is nothing. It's your money, you would be free to do what you want with it.' She frowned. I could see from her puzzled expression that she had no idea what I was saying or planning. Or how badly I needed to multiply that amount by five.

That I was already thinking of the various points on the roulette table where I would place my chips. And trying to ignore that irritating voice inside my head that was telling me to be sensible and to at least not risk the lot.

Carolyn Smith told me it would take her a couple of days from receipt of the funds from Germany to get me the cash. A couple of days was good, I told her. A couple of days would give me time to think clearly. But even as I left her office, an anguished plan was taking shape in my mind.

22

The Song Wu Corporation headquarters were housed in a massive seven-storey building that was part warehouse, part offices. It was one of many ugly precast concrete structures that rose, with the very barest nod to Planning, in the building frenzy that followed in the aftermath of the Second World War. If anyone wanted to be anonymous, this New England hill area of Brighton, a short distance from the station, was the place to do it.

The ground floor and basement contained the vast range of food products, mostly imported from China, which the Corporation supplied to restaurants and specialist grocery stores around the south of England. On the floors above were the administration offices.

It was one of Song Wu's affectations that visitors to her penthouse office were never permitted to arrive under their own steam, they were always *brought* here in a blacked-out Mercedes, and Roel Albazi, sitting in the dark rear of the car that had collected him from outside his office in Shoreham, had never liked this.

It was all part of her psychological play. Making visitors – and all visitors were here for business purposes – feel a little out of their comfort zones, a little beholden to her, and a little bit weakened and subservient. If a meeting went well, you were chauffeured back again afterwards. But if it did not go well, you were escorted to the receiving bay and then you were on your own. Albazi knew the game but what choice did he have?

The inscrutably silent chauffeur – just like all the Song Wu staff – did not respond to any of Albazi's attempts at conversation. Twenty minutes after collecting him from outside his Shoreham office, the Mercedes dipped down a steep ramp beneath a rising, shuttered door, into the lower level of the ground floor, passing a forklift truck stacked with pallets, and pulled up in front of the metal gate of the elevator.

Albazi's door was opened by a security guard with a rictus smile and equally dead eyes, who pressed the button for the elevator. The wide metal door opened as painfully slowly as the creaking, groaning and clanging ride up that followed. Albazi wondered every time he came here why Song Wu didn't spend just the tiniest bit of her fortune on modernizing at least the lift – surely it drove her nuts too? But then, everything about this place indicated someone who didn't care about their surroundings, just what it enabled – the money.

Except for her office itself, that was something else. As the elevator finally stopped with a jolt, the doors opened onto what could have been an anteroom in a Chinese palace. High, domed ceiling, bright red, gold, black and mother-of-pearl, with ornate lanterns, huge vases and figurines on plinths. At the far end were double bamboo doors, ornately latticed, with a clone of the guard down below standing in front.

As Albazi approached along the mosaic tiled floor towards him, the guard put out his hands, cautioning him, then patted him down. Only when he was satisfied that the Albanian was packing nothing more lethal than a mobile phone did he pull open the double doors to reveal Song Wu's opulent office. Although Albazi had been here on many occasions, it never failed to impress.

She sat behind her magnificent, uncluttered, black lacquer desk, with a view through the window behind her across the streets and terraces to the east of the city and the racecourse, staring imperiously at her visitor. She was plump, but her girth was elegantly disguised inside a red silk blouse embroidered with Chinese symbols and tied at the front with a huge red bow. Matching bright red fabric earrings, like miniature sash cords, hung either side of her face, and a large ruby pendant on a gold chain nestled among the fleshy folds of her neck. She wore gold rings on each of her fingers, the nails of which were immaculately varnished.

A solitary joss stick stood in a jade incense burner on either side of the desk, from which rose little coils of jasmine-scented smoke. The only other objects on the desk were three exquisitely carved ivory photograph frames facing away from him, a red leather-bound notebook and a red pen.

If Song Wu was anyone else, Albazi was certain she would be considered obese, but she wasn't anyone else. Somehow, she managed to carry her size with elegance, and even elan. Compared to the rest of her body, her face seemed disproportionally small, but she was strangely attractive, Albazi thought, with a perfect complexion, and black hair harshly raked back into a chic bob. She had a tiny rosebud mouth and eyes the colour of a glacier. He had once been to a Gilbert and Sullivan operetta and she reminded him a little of the caricature of the queen. But there was no humour in Song Wu's world. Or music. Or, so far as Albazi could tell, joy.

Without moving a muscle, both her arms resting on her desktop, she said, 'Sit down, please, Mr Albazi.'

He sat, knowing better than to attempt any small talk.

As he perched on the edge of one of the two chairs facing her, Song Wu said, calmly, 'You don't know where they are, Mr Albazi?' Her cut-glass English had no trace of an accent and she spoke with an almost girlish voice like a rather old-fashioned BBC newscaster. 'Two hundred and thirty-five thousand pounds of my money? How do I know these people are real?

How do I know you have not just made them up, Mr Albazi? Invented them as a way to steal my money, just like your predecessor?'

Her voice was getting louder, icier. But she remained deadly calm, too calm.

Roel Albazi sat uncomfortably, trying hard to look confident, although inside he was shaking. He was trying to focus, remembering what was important. *Mianzi – Face.* He needed to show Song Wu this and to allow her this, too. *Face.* Strength and respect. But being in her presence took all his confidence away. The whole ritual of arriving here was designed to do exactly that, he knew.

'We have located two of the defaulters,' he lied. He was trying to sound strong and hard, to keep *face*, but his voice came out small and almost reedy. 'Alan Mitten and Robert Rhys. Skender has their addresses, he is going to sort them out.'

'Sort them out?'

'Collect.'

'And this Sandra – Sandy – Grace? What is the update?'

'We are on it.'

'*We?*'

'Me, Skender and Karter.'

She gave Albazi a strange look. He couldn't figure it out but it unsettled him. 'You and Skender and your little gorilla. You are very dependent on Skender, aren't you?'

'He's a good man, as is Joe Karter.'

'I decide on who is a good person and who is not, Mr Albazi.'

'Of course. But they both worked for me for ten years before I – we – began to work for you and I completely trust them to do any job I give them.'

'You would struggle without Skender?'

Albazi shrugged. 'I take care of him, I don't think he's going to be leaving me anytime soon.'

'Really?' she said, with the trace of a smile that made her look colder, not warmer. 'He's not leaving you?'

'No.' Albazi felt his Adam's apple rise. His mouth felt dry, his stomach was churning. He felt queasy and needed a drink of water. But to ask for anything would be weakness. Loss of *face*.

'So, Mr Albazi, you had surveillance on Sandra Grace for several days, yes?'

'Yes, Skender kept watch on her. And two other people I use when I need them.'

'A watch twenty-four-seven?'

'I didn't feel that was necessary.'

Her eyebrows raised into two small, dark arcs. 'You did not? You did not feel it was necessary to put twenty-four-hour surveillance on someone who owed me one hundred and fifty thousand pounds? Was that to save you the expense of paying Mr Skender and other people more than you needed?'

'No, we were attracting too much attention from some of the Graces' neighbours. A lady who lives in the house directly opposite is the local neighbourhood busybody and she marched up to Joe Karter, banged on the window, told him she had taken down the registration and demanded to know what he was doing. He told her he was a location scout for a movie company. After that, he moved further up the street.' Albazi shrugged. The look she was giving him was really frightening him. Acidic bile rose in his throat and he swallowed it back down. His insides felt like they were in a blender. 'I have no reason to believe Sandy Grace is a flight risk.'

'You look very nervous, Mr Albazi. Is there something you are failing to tell me?'

'No – I'm aware that it is not good, but we are on it – on all three of our defaulters.'

'I think you are better off without Skender,' she said. 'It might concentrate your mind if you are not delegating to your flunkeys.'

'He's a good man – Joe too – they both are,' Albazi replied, but his voice tailed off even before he had finished the sentence. He was distracted suddenly by one of his three phones ringing. Apologetically, he pulled it from his pocket and looked at the display. It was a number he did not recognize. Looking back up at Song Wu, he said, 'This is the number Sandy Grace has. It could be her calling me.'

'You'd better answer it.'

He stood up and turned away from her, tapping the phone and putting it to his ear. 'Hello?' he said. But there was no sound from the other end. Conscious of Song Wu watching him, he said again, 'Hello? Who is this? Hello? Hello?' After several more seconds of silence, he hit the red button and turned back to her with a shrug. As he sat back down he said, 'Whoever it was must have been in a bad reception area. Hopefully they'll—'

His voice froze in his gullet as he perched back on the edge of the chair and saw the three ivory photograph frames on Song Wu's desk, which had all been facing away from him. All three now faced him.

One was a bearded, very old and contented-looking man in a floppy hat, with a fishing rod in one hand and a cigarette in the other, on a riverbank.

Another was of a couple in their sixties standing behind a higgledy-piggledy stall stacked with drab jumpers and sweat-shirts. It was in a street outside a shop that had a display of lurid phone covers and advertised, in Albanian, mobile-phone repairs – all makes. The man, tubby and sad-faced, had a mop of grey hair, wore a black top and baggy jeans. The woman, of similar build, and dressed in shapeless clothes, was holding up a garment for a customer.

The third contained a photograph of a handsome, dark-haired woman in her late thirties. She stood in front of an ornamental pond with spouting fountains, her arms around an almost impossibly cute little girl of about three, with long dark hair.

Albazi was transfixed by them. The old man was his grandfather. The couple behind the clothes stall were his mother and father. The woman with the little girl, in front of the ornamental pond, was his sister and her daughter – his niece.

'Next time you come to see me, you come with two hundred and thirty-five thousand pounds. You will come to me in exactly forty-eight hours, with the cash, a money-order, a letter of credit, whatever. My car will collect you. Are you very clear of the consequences if you don't? Which one of these three photographs will not be here on your next visit?'

For some moments, Albazi barely heard her.

Song Wu's message could not be clearer. In the Albanian community, there was a culture of retribution being carried out against innocent members of the target's family, back home in their country.

His insides in turmoil, Albazi barely made it back out through the double doors and down to the lower level. There was no Mercedes like the one that brought him here. Only the security guard, who pressed the button to raise the shuttered gate.

He just got up the steep concrete ramp before he sank to his knees and threw up on the pavement.

23

Without turning round to look back, Albazi staggered to his feet and, wiping his mouth with his handkerchief, hurried away through rain that was falling steadily. When Song Wu gave a deadline, she meant it, precisely. No leeway.

Another twenty-four hours or so and, between them, Tall Joe and Skender Sharka would have collected from two of the defaulters, Alan Mitten and Robert Rhys. Both men had told Albazi they were sure they would be paying up, either the entire debt or a large instalment, and their instincts were rarely wrong. When you threaten to break a man's bones or kill his children, he finds the money and pays up pretty quickly.

But Song Wu had wanted to see him today and when she wanted to see him, Albazi knew, there was no option to delay for twenty-four hours. She told you the time and you were there.

Sandy Grace was going to have to come up with the money. It would be nice to put additional pressure on her by threatening to go to the local paper, the *Argus*, and let them know that a detective's wife had run up gambling debts of £150,000. But there was one problem with that – Song Wu's moneylending business wasn't licensed and the publicity could be very bad for her. If the news reached the Gambling Commission, and it would, she would almost certainly lose her licences to operate her casinos.

Meantime, he had a very big problem on his hands. To safe-guard his family back in Albania, he needed to appease Song Wu and quickly. She wanted £235,000 in cash in forty-eight hours. He could come up with it, but using a dangerous strategy.

He kept a cash float in the secure safe in his office of half a million pounds of Song Wu's money, for loans to gamblers like Sandy Grace. It was audited once a month by one of the Song Wu corporation accountants, who came to his office and checked the cash against the loans. The most recent audit had taken place less than a week ago. He could hand over that £235,000 by giving her back some of her own money without her realizing. That would buy him three weeks to get all the cash. More than enough time.

He climbed into the rear of a taxi at the rank, gave the driver his address and relaxed back in his seat, feeling a lot better at that thought. Pulling out his phone, he called Sharka's number, wanting an update on progress, and also to discuss another loan applicant whom Sharka was checking out. After several rings it went to voicemail, which was unusual – normally Sharka answered instantly. 'Hey, man,' Albazi said. 'Call me.'

Fifteen minutes later, as the taxi crawled along in a long queue at temporary roadworks, heading towards Shoreham Harbour, Sharka had still not returned his call, or even, at least, texted to explain why not. He hit Sharka's number again and again got his voicemail after several rings. This time his message was less friendly. 'Hey, Skender, what the hell? Call me right away, it's urgent, man.'

24

Normally the drive from the centre of Brighton to the small five-storey building in Shoreham, where he owned his pizza restaurant as well as, five floors above, his penthouse office and apartment suite, took around twenty minutes, and a little longer in the rush hour. But it was only midday and he'd been in the taxi for over twenty-five minutes, and they'd not yet made it past Hove Lagoon, the children's playground with two boating ponds and a cafe.

'What's going on?' he said to the driver. 'We haven't moved in five minutes – what the hell?'

Two exasperated hands rose in the air in front of him. 'Roadworks!'

The wipers kept up a steady, rhythmic clunk-clunk, and droplets of water blurred the views from the side windows.

'Shall we cut inland?'

'I was there earlier. Roadworks also – we'll be moving again in a minute.'

Albazi looked at his phone. No message from Sharka. He called his number again, and once more got his voicemail. He left an even angrier message, then sat back and reflected on those photographs of his family on Song Wu's desk. With anyone else it might have been an idle threat, but not with her. In the years of taking her handsome payments, he'd seen enough to know that just as her organization was an efficient money-making machine, it was an equally efficient killing machine.

90

The traffic finally inched forward and they began picking up pace as they passed a green temporary traffic light then travelled along a single-file, coned lane. The solitary landmark chimney of Shoreham power station slid past to their left, then warehouses along the wharf, the refiner, a berthed dredger.

A few minutes later, as they approached Shoreham High Street, the traffic came to an abrupt halt again. A police car on blue lights, siren screaming, shot past then stopped a short distance in front of them, blue lights still flashing.

Albazi could see through the windscreen that vehicles ahead were starting to turn around. A police officer with a white cap approached a van that was in front of them. Moments later, the van began turning round. Then the officer reached his taxi.

The driver lowered the window and the officer said, 'I'm sorry, sir, the road is closed due to an incident and is likely to be closed for some while.'

'My passenger's got to get to Shoreham High Street, what do you suggest?' the driver asked.

'It's only a quarter of a mile,' the police officer said, shooting Albazi a glance. 'To be honest, he'd be quicker to walk. The whole of Shoreham is at a standstill.'

'What's actually happened, officer?' the driver asked.

'An incident – that's all the information I have at this moment,' he replied.

'I'll walk,' Albazi said. It would take him less than ten minutes to get to his office, although he'd be drenched by the time he got there. He paid the driver, climbed out and strode off quickly, turning his collar up and bowing his head against the hardening rain, a nagging feeling in his gut that something was wrong.

He passed the clubhouse of the Sussex Yacht Club, and a recently finished block of flats on the harbourfront. Vehicle after vehicle was turning round, and nothing was coming from the opposite direction. A few hundred yards ahead he could now see a blaze of flashing blue lights, and two marked police cars angled across the two-lane road, blocking it completely. Behind them was a line of blue-and-white tape. Maybe a car crash?

He tried Sharka again – and still got his voicemail. 'Hey, man,' Albazi said. 'What the hell's going on? Call me back!'

A young, uniformed police officer was standing in front of the tape, holding a clipboard. As Albazi approached her, he saw debris all over the pavement and road a couple of hundred yards further on – almost directly in front of his pizza restaurant. It was mostly furniture, he realized. It looked at first glance as if a removals lorry had overturned. Filing cabinets, some of their drawers open, files spewed out and getting sodden on the wet tarmac; two sofas, a swivel chair, a shattered desk – his desk, he realized with dawning horror. His bed, his clothes, his paintings, sculptures, books, computer, phones, fridge, drinks cabinet, the bottles lying all around, many broken. His prized cigar humidor, with over four hundred Cuban cigars, many spilled out and being ruined by the rain. Sparkling shards of glass everywhere.

He stood for a moment, in numb disbelief at what he was seeing. Had Sharka gone mental? Was this his doing – some kind of a protest? He looked up and could see the wide window of this side of his office was mostly gone.

Bewildered, he said to the officer, 'Those are my things. I need to go through.'

'I'm sorry, sir,' she said. 'I can't allow that.'

'You don't understand.' He pointed along the road, then up at the top floor of the building. 'That's my office, these are all my things.'

She had the decency to look shocked. 'Have you annoyed your landlord or something, sir? Or is it a domestic dispute?'

'I own the building, that's where I live and work. I don't know what's happened, I need to go through.'

'I'm sorry, sir, I'm not authorized to let anyone through.'

'You've got to let me – I—'

He was interrupted by the sound of a large vehicle behind him; at the same time, his phone pinged with a message.

'I'm afraid you'll have to wait, sir – unless there's a way you can get in at the rear of the building? I'm afraid you can't come through here.'

He turned to see a low-loader truck halt at the tape.

'How long?'

'I can't say, sir. It's likely to be some while.'

'You are joking?'

The main entrance to the building was at the side, but he needed to go through the cordon to access it. He glanced down at his phone and saw the message.

Next time you disappoint me, it won't just be furniture.

He stared at the message in rising fury, as another police officer untied one end of the tape from around a lamp post to allow the vehicle through. Albazi seized his chance and, ignoring the shouts of the officer with the clipboard, ran through the opened cordon, breaking into a sprint, dodging around the debris of his office and home, ignoring more shouts, and into the side alley, where the main entrance door to all the parts of the building above the pizza parlour was sited. It was ajar.

He went straight in, past the creakily slow old lift, and began racing up the flights of the fire escape stairs. As he neared the top he heard a loud bang, followed by another, then another. BLAM-BLAM-BLAM.

He hesitated but it didn't sound like gunshots.

BLAM-BLAM-BLAM again.

He took the final flight silently, on tiptoe. As he reached the top he saw a tall police officer and a shorter, burly one, standing outside his closed front door, trying to break it open with their yellow metal battering ram.

'Officers!' he called out. 'Stop, this is my place!'

They both turned to face him. He held up a small bunch of keys. 'I think you'll find it easier to use these,' he said.

The tall officer, who was perspiring, said, 'I dunno what your door's made of, but it would keep a tank out.'

'It would,' agreed Albazi, as he turned the key in the first of the three locks. 'It would stop a seventeen-pound tank shell.'

'Get many of those fired at you, do you, sir?' asked the burly one, her face red from the exertion in the stuffy hallway.

'I have a debt collection business,' Albazi replied, turning the second key. 'Not everyone likes me.'

'A pissed-off customer is it, do you think?' the tall one asked. 'Broken in and thrown all your stuff out?'

'No one breaks in here,' he said, as he turned the final key. Then, holding his breath, scared of what he might find, he stepped into his normally beautiful hallway. Immediately he heard the sound of running water. Then he realized the deep pile carpet was sodden. There were shadows on the walls where some of his paintings had hung, now lying on the road.

'Skender!' he shouted out. 'Skender!'

'Someone in here, sir?' the tall officer asked. 'But the door was locked, surely?'

'They all lock automatically when the door is shut,' Albazi replied tersely. Water was pouring out from under the bathroom door. He strode up to it and flung it open. The room was empty, but all the taps of the washbasin, bath and the shower were turned on to their max. Water was pouring over the top of the huge double-tub and the copper washbasin. Splashing across the floor to reach them, almost in tears, he turned off the taps.

'Got a spiteful girlfriend or something?' the burly one asked. Her colleague had stepped away and was walking into another room.

'I don't have a girlfriend,' Albazi said. 'I—'

There was a shout from the other officer. 'In here!'

Albazi, followed by the other officer, hurried along the hallway and into the scene of devastation that had, just a few hours ago, been his immaculate, beautiful office. Blood red paint had been sprayed randomly over his carpet and up the walls. For some moments he was so incensed that he completely failed to notice the motionless, naked figure of Skender Sharka, lying where his bookshelves had been just a few hours earlier.

His huge, muscular body lay sprawled out at an odd angle, as if he was trying to swim the crawl along the floor and had frozen in mid-stroke as his arms hit the wall.

25

'No!' Albazi screamed. 'No, no, NO!' He ran towards the motion-less figure. 'Skender, Skender!' He turned to the two officers, nearly hysterical. 'That's my friend! My employee!'

Then, to his joy, as he knelt, he saw movement. Sharka, the palms of both his hands flat against the wall, turned his head and made a sound that was part moan, part grunt. It came from deep in his throat. He made it again, more urgently. Then again and shook his shoulders, turning his head towards Albazi.

'You OK? You OK, Skender? What's happened?'

Sharka made the same sound again. It was as if he was trying desperately to speak but could not get any words out. Had he had a brain bleed, Albazi wondered? Had he been hit on the head and was delirious, or was he on some drug? Although he doubted that, Sharka never drank and never took drugs.

'Tell me,' Albazi asked, 'who did this? Did they hurt you? Drug you?'

'His hands look like they're stuck to the wall,' the male officer said.

Then when Sharka tried to reply again, Albazi realized he was unable to open his mouth to speak. He saw what looked at first like a line of spittle between his lips, but then as he looked closer he saw it was solid. He reached out a finger and gently touched the area. It felt hard.

96

Then he realized.

'Your lips, Skender, someone's glued them shut, right? With some kind of superglue?'

Sharka nodded.

'His hands, too,' the female officer said, examining them carefully but gently. Addressing Sharka, she asked, 'Are you able to move them at all, sir?'

He shook his head.

Albazi heard her colleague radioing for an ambulance. He turned to her and said, 'I think warm water and soap might help.'

There was a staccato voice through the radio. Then the tall officer said, 'There's an ambulance on its way, sir, they'll know best what to do.'

The female officer was checking Sharka's pulse. He looked at Albazi, bewildered and, for the first time that Albazi had ever seen, frightened.

'You'll be OK, man. I need to know what happened. Who did this to you? I need to know this.'

But in reality, he knew already. The message on his phone was from the same number the anonymous caller had used when he was in Song Wu's office less than an hour ago. A burner for sure.

In her office, Song Wu had been quizzing him earlier about Skender. Now he realized it was more than just quizzing, it was a subtle hint, which in hindsight could not have been clearer. She sent messages to people when she was angry with them. Brutal messages.

'Do you have any idea who might be responsible for this?' the tall officer asked.

'No, none,' Albazi lied. 'But Skender must have let them in. He either knew them or they tricked him.' He squeezed his arm, just a little. 'I'll get you sorted,' he said.

Sharka's face contorted into traces of a smile and he nodded.

'Did you recognize who did this?' he asked. And from the look in his eyes, Albazi knew he did.

But Sharka again shook his head.

26

Two days later, at 2 p.m., I was back at the Casino d'Azur. It gave me the greatest pleasure to walk up to the cashier who had not that long ago told me my credit card had been declined. Now, using some of my inheritance, sliding £5,000 in cash – fifty-pound notes – across the counter, I told her the denominations of the chips I wanted.

I headed with my stash over to a roulette table with no punters, and an even more bored-looking than usual croupier. He looked a little like Clive Owen in the movie *Croupier*, but without the good looks or charm. His bow tie was wonky, he had a dusting of dandruff snow on the collar and shoulders of his tuxedo and he wore a watch that looked as cheap as it did flashy. I can remember him so clearly and yet he barely even acknowledged me, I could have been air.

I perched on a stool, carefully stacked my chips on the baize at the edge of the table. Six piles of red, black and purple chips, each with a black-and-white chequered rim. The red were £5, the black £25 and the purple £100. I was so nervous. I needed this to come good today, I really needed it.

Before placing any bets, I watched him set that wheel spinning slowly, then flick the ball. Rattle, rattle, rattle, rattle. Silence. The ball nestled in black 28. He spun again. Red 19. Both numbers were within a close arc around zero. The next was way off target – if zero was his target – black 24, on the far side of the wheel. But then the next was red 3, just one number away from green zero.

And the next was black 15, just one number away from zero again, this time on the other side of the wheel. Shit, this guy was good!

I waited for another throw.

Red 32. This number was adjoining zero!

He had his eye in, for sure. But, if I placed a bet, would the sly bastard still continue on his bored strategy or change it, to beat me?

I placed a tentative, fairly low opening bet, covering several numbers either side of the wheel. One hundred pounds in total. And one came up! But I'd gone for low odds, so my winnings weren't huge – my stake back and a net gain of thirty quid. But an encouraging start.

The croupier was on autopilot as he pushed a purple, black and single red chip towards me, his mind was somewhere else altogether, and from his expression it wasn't anywhere great.

Then, as I contemplated my next bets, I was conscious of someone joining me at the table. For a moment I thought it was the Chinese man, but when I glanced up, I saw a man I wouldn't normally have bothered to look at twice – at first. He had a tattoo of a serpent rising up above the collar of his pink shirt. I've never gone for men or women with overtly visible tattoos, I can't explain why, but I've always found them a turn-off.

Tattoo man wasn't in any way pretty boy movie star or catwalk handsome. He was swarthy – Greek, I guessed – correctly, it turned out. But there was something attractive about him – he had a presence. He exuded confidence in the way he moved, the way he sat and placed his stack of chips on the table and the way he turned and nodded at me with an amiable smile. 'Nice win,' he said, with a slight accent. He looked like he owned the place. He was the kind of man who would always look like he owned whatever place he was in. And, as he fixed his hooded, brooding eyes on mine, he looked, for an instant, like he even owned me.

It occurred to me he might be one of Albazi's henchmen. But he looked too classy. An expensive, lightweight bomber jacket over chinos, and a gorgeous Hublot watch – I only knew the brand because Roy had always liked their designs, but they were way above what I could afford to buy him. His dark brown hair was short, but not quite close-cropped. He smelled faintly of a very masculine fragrance.

I shook my head, eyeing the mountain of chips he had in front of him. 'I should have put down more.'

He shrugged and spread a bunch of chips over several numbers just before the croupier intoned in a small voice, 'No more bets.'

The ball came to a halt between the frets either side of the number 4. One of his bets – a purple, one-hundred-pound chip – lay smack in the middle of the number. Netting him a gross £3,600.

'Nice one,' I said, as the croupier began stacking his winnings.

He shrugged again and held out his hand. 'I'm Nicos.'

'Sandy,' I said, shaking it.

'What are you doing here?' he asked. He again spread a bunch of chips across the roulette board, before turning back to me.

'What does it look like?' I replied.

'Is anything what it looks like?'

'You sound like my husband,' I replied. 'He has a very irritating habit of answering a question with a question.'

'Is he a cop?'

That knocked the wind out of me. 'Why do you say that?'

He shrugged again, his powerful-looking shoulders. 'Takes one to recognize one.'

That instantly made me wary. 'You're a police officer?'

'Was.'

'Here in Sussex?'

He shook his head. 'In Greece.'

'OK.' I frowned. 'So, from the few words we've exchanged, you've come to the conclusion my husband's a police officer?'

'A detective,' he said. 'Who probably doesn't know his wife has a gambling habit.' He smiled and stared even harder at me. 'What else does he not know?'

I don't know why I said it – it was completely reckless. But I felt safe with this guy. 'I guess . . .' I hesitated for a moment. 'I guess he doesn't know I'm not working on my marriage.'

He barely showed any reaction. 'It wouldn't take a rocket scientist to figure that out, Sandy.'

I saw him glance at my wedding ring. And noticed he wasn't wearing one. The roulette wheel was rattling slowly across the frets.

It stopped at black 31. Where he had two purple chips.

'You're on a roll!' I told him.

'Maybe. So far so good. But if you stand by the roulette wheel for long enough, all your chips will eventually disappear into the casino's bank.'

'So why are you doing this?' I asked as he spread even more chips over an array of numbers.

'Why? Because I'm laundering money,' he said, nonchalantly.

'What do you mean, *laundering* money?'

'Hiding it from the Inland Revenue, Sandy. I play the arc – it's a roulette strategy where I'll lose around three per cent of my money, if I play for long enough. But no one in the Revenue will have any way of finding out how much I've bet and how much I've lost.'

For some moments, I thought this hunk was crazy. 'What business are you in that you need to hide – launder – money, Nicos?'

'Zero!' the croupier announced.

Brazenly, without lowering his voice, and without a trace of disappointment as the croupier cleared away all his chips on this losing throw of the wheel, he replied, 'I'm a drug dealer.'

27

'A drug dealer?' I said, unsure for a moment whether he was joking. But he just sat staring back at me and gave me a smile. I hoped he was joking.

I should have been instantly disappointed in him, but I wasn't. My rebellious streak liked the idea of me, the wife of a detective, sitting at the roulette table with a drug dealer. Kind of reminded me of that TV series I loved – Roy had liked it too – *The Sopranos.* Watching it had been something we'd enjoyed together in recent times. Thinking about that made me feel guilty for a moment.

Nicos looked me directly in the eyes. He knew, as well as I did, that we both felt some attraction to each other. He asked, smiling, 'Does that put you off me?'

'Why are you a drug dealer?'

'Why are you a gambler?' he shot back.

'There you go again,' I said. 'Just like my husband, answering a question with a question.'

He raised his thick, dark eyebrows, smiling again. 'We've barely met and we're already bickering like an old married couple.'

He said it with such charm and such good humour that I laughed. 'Maybe if all couples got their bickering out of the way within the first five minutes of meeting, there would be a lot more marriages that lasted.'

He gave me a kind of wistful smile that seemed to contain so many secrets, then turned his attention back to the table and the wheel, which was already spinning, the ball rolling at speed around the rim. He spread chips across some of the grid of numbers, with careful precision, then looked at me. 'No bets?'

'I thought I might see what I could learn from you.'

The ball rattled around the frets.

'No more bets,' the croupier said.

This was the moment in the game that I always found the most exciting. The final seconds as the wheel slowed down, the rattling continuing as the ball, almost with a mind of its own, dropped first into one slot and then another before popping out back onto the rim, and finally coming to rest in yet another slot. But Nicos wasn't even looking at the wheel, he was looking hard into my eyes.

Then he picked up one of his chips from his stash. A purple one with the same black-and-white chequered edge as all the others. He held it up between his finger and thumb.

'Seventeen,' the croupier intoned. He followed it, as if imagining he was in Monte Carlo, by adding, 'Dix-sept, noir.'

Out of the corner of my eye I could see Nicos had laid a whole stack of purple chips on 17, but he didn't even glance away to acknowledge the croupier, as his substantial winnings were pushed towards him. He just continued to hold that purple chip in front of my face. 'You want to see what you can learn from me, Sandy? This is what you can learn. What do you see?'

'A purple chip.'

'Take it,' he urged.

'Take it?'

He held it out. 'Take it. Hold it. Tell me what this chip means to you.'

He put it in my hand. Was he gifting it to me? As I closed my fingers around it I was puzzled, unsure what he was getting at. 'The fact that it's purple means it is worth one hundred pounds?'

'You're heading in the right direction.'

The wheel was spinning again.

'I guess – I could put it on a number, or red or black, or a group of numbers on the table and maybe win a lot of money, or lose it all. Or I could take it to the cashier and walk away with one hundred pounds in cash.'

'Exactly.'

'No more bets,' the croupier announced. He might as well have been talking to himself.

'I'm not with you, Nicos.'

He looked straight back at me. 'You are, you've told me exactly what the chip means to you. You can have a flutter on the gaming table and maybe turn it into several more chips, or you can take it to the cashier and walk away with £100. What you are holding in your palm is currency. Money. Money is the only thing in life you can really trust to be what it is.'

'Unless it's a forgery?' I quizzed.

He shrugged dismissively. 'When was the last time you were denied anything because the coin or banknote in your hand was a forgery?'

'So far, never.'

'Well, the chip you're holding, you know the cashier here will give you one hundred pounds in cash for it. You know what that money will buy you – in a supermarket or a garage or nail studio or a London theatre. It's a certainty. You have a one-hundred-pound chip, the cashier isn't going to tell you it's only worth ninety pounds. You go to the checkout at Tesco and the person there is not going to tell you that your one hundred pounds in cash is only going to buy you eighty-five pounds of stuff. Money is the one thing in life you can trust. The only thing.'

'The only thing?'

'Sure. People lie – spouses, business partners, friends, siblings. Money is dumb, money never lies. It's binary – everything or nothing. You have it or you don't.'

I tried hard to think of something that would contradict him, but I was distracted by the wheel spinning again. I tried to hand him back the purple chip, but he dismissed it with a wave of his hand. 'Put it on a number. Or any combination. If you win, you can pay it back; if you lose, it's gone, it was nothing. Have you ever been on a winning streak – like a *real* winning streak, where you just could not lose?'

'When I started gambling,' I said. 'That's what got me hooked.'

He smiled, those hooded eyes opening wider and appraising me. 'There is nothing on earth that can match the feeling of a winning streak. It's better than any drug, any amount of booze, any orgasm, right?'

'Any that I've had so far,' I conceded.

He suppressed a smile.

A dangerous look. Dangerous for me. Because I fancied him. But I tried to play it cool – and to remember why the hell I was here in the first place, this afternoon. To try to convert my meagre inheritance of £30,000 into the £150,000 I owed Roel Albazi.

But I didn't want to stop talking to Nicos, because he fascinated me.

Keeping my voice low, I asked, 'What drugs do you deal in?'

'Cannabis. Nothing else. I'm not a moralist, but I believe it should be legal – so I'm just doing my bit to help the process along.'

'That's your justification?'

He shook his head. 'You have power over your mind, not over outside events. Realize this and you will find strength.'

'Meaning?' I asked.

As he replied, he placed a bunch of chips over more numbers and sections of the board. Not wanting to be left out, I put down a few randomly, including the purple one he had given me, barely looking at what I was doing. The wheel began to spin.

'Do what you believe in, what you *really* believe in. Live your life doing that. If you do anything else, anything you don't really believe in, then you are a failure. You want to know the best description of success I know?'

'I've a feeling you are going to tell me.'

His eyes stayed deadpan. He shrugged and said, 'Success is the person who wakes up in the morning, and goes to bed at night, and in between gets to do what they want to do.'

'So you're a success because you are a drug dealer and that's what you want to be?'

He spoke flatly, without emotion. 'A dealer in a drug that *should be legal*. A drug that helps people through illness, a drug that helps people realize their potential and their dreams.'

The ball rattled over the frets. I wasn't even sure which colour and which combination of numbers on the board I had covered.

'Twenty-two,' the croupier announced, sounding even more bored, probably because he didn't have our attention. '*Vingt-deux, noir.*'

All my chips were cleared away. It took only a quick glance at my stash to see that my original £5,000 was already halved.

'Can I buy you a drink at the bar?' Nicos asked suddenly.

I'd found before, on occasions when I was losing steadily, that stepping away from the table and returning later could change my luck. It was 2.30 p.m., a strange time to be having a drink, but what the hell, one drink might help.

'Sure,' I said, secretly justifying it to my baby bump. 'A vodka Martini, Grey Goose – and an olive.'

He gave me an approving look, and five minutes later we were seated on bar stools, having given our orders. Nicos asked, in a very caring tone, 'OK, so what's really going on?'

'What do you mean?'

'You are a very troubled lady, aren't you?'

I stared hard back into his eyes. Those alert, nut-brown, all-seeing eyes. 'What kind of detective were you, in the Greek police?'

'I was in the army first, doing my military service. When I got my – discharge, I think you call it – I joined the police in Athens. After four years I got offered a promotion to detective, which I took. Then someone saw I was good at interviewing suspects and I was made an interrogator. I did it for six years, interviewing everyone from political asylum seekers to drug dealers – and I just got disillusioned. I thought to myself, here I am, Nicos Christoforou, on a shit salary, interrogating these arrogant drug dealer bastards with vast sums stashed away we'll never find. Sure, they'll get hefty jail sentences, but when they come out in ten years' time – less for good behaviour – they'll be multi-millionaires, and in ten years' time I will still be Nicos Christoforou, still on a shit salary.'

'And?' I asked.

'And now I'm here. Just as bad as all the shitbags I locked up, but a lot smarter and a lot richer than most. And while some are still in jail, I'm here, talking to a most beautiful woman, and I mean this, a truly beautiful woman.'

'Really?' I said, with a smile. 'I thought you were talking to me?'

He gave me a strange look. He was humouring me, but there was a flash of something dark behind his smile, and in his eyes. As if he was someone who did not like being interrupted or wasn't very good at taking a joke.

He went on. 'A beautiful but a very troubled woman. You need help, don't you – and I'm not talking about counselling. You are in a lot of trouble, I think. I'm only telling you all my background because I can see you are really facing some trauma now.'

I stared back at him for a long while, my mind whirring, my emotions in shreds. 'What exactly do you know about me?' I asked.

He gave a shrug. 'I didn't do any research, Sandy, if that's what you are thinking. I can see it in your eyes.'

'See what?'

'Fear.'

Of course, he didn't know it then, nor did I. But one day the fear would be in his eyes.

28

'Fear?' I replied.

'If you spend six years as an interrogator in my country, where perhaps the police aren't quite so concerned with being as gentle with suspects as they are here, you learn to read fear in someone's face. Not nerves, not worry, *fear*. Real, raw *fear*. Understand me? It's what I see in your face.'

Somewhere near where I was sitting, but it might have been a hundred miles away, I heard the rat-a-tat-tat-tat-tat of the roulette ball, then silence. My throat felt tight, my mouth dry. At that moment our cocktails arrived, in proper Martini glasses I was pleased to note. Both contained a large green olive on a stick. And as all proper Martinis should be, the glasses were filled right to the very brim, the drink almost slopping over the top.

Nicos raised his and we touched glasses with a distinct, classy crystal *chingggg*. I took a sip. It was dry, cold as ice, and almost instantly it made me feel happier and more confident, as this drink always did. And it made me like Nicos even more. But at the same time, I was a little wary. He seemed almost too good to be true and one lesson I'd learned in my life so far was to trust your instincts – if something seems too good to be true, it probably isn't true.

'That fear you see is a monster called Albazi who is after me over a hundred-and-fifty-thousand-pound gambling debt that I've managed to rack up. There. I've said it. I've not told a soul this, you understand. And I'm not really sure why I've just told you.'

Could he be working for Albazi? Or was I just completely paranoid, given the shit I was in?

'I think you're a hard lady, right?'

No one had ever called me that before, and I wasn't immediately sure how to take it. Compliment or criticism? But the way he was looking at me made me smile. 'Maybe.' Then, what the hell, I don't know where it came from, but something popped in my head. I took another sip, a bigger one this time, then held my glass out towards him, like I was challenging him to a duel, and said, 'You are right, I'm hard. I drink cocktails made from the tears of my past lovers.'

He studied me in silence for some moments, as if absorbing this very seriously. Then he studied his glass, slowly twirling it around by the stem. 'I never realized before, the reason Martinis are so potent. Now I'm educated, thank you.'

He smiled. We touched glasses again, then he looked at me carefully, as if I was a page of a newspaper he was reading and, finally, said, 'So, Sandy, what are we going to do with you?'

It's strange how you get feelings about people, but in that simple line, I knew, for sure, he was on my side and had nothing to do with Albazi – he wouldn't even know the Albanian existed. It felt so good to say my problem out loud to someone who didn't know me, someone who wouldn't judge me, someone who had been through some deep trauma themselves. A weight was lifting from my shoulders, and I was feeling a little safer.

I looked at my glass and there was barely enough of the clear liquid nectar left to cover the olive. Had I drunk the whole thing already?

It had gone to my head. And in a very nice way. I drained my glass. Emboldened, the alcohol doing most of the talking, I replied, 'The first thing we are going to do with me is teach me how to be hard to find. Unless you have a problem with that?'

'You want to be hard to find?'

I nodded.

'You want to disappear?'

'Perhaps. How would I start?'

'You start with your digital footprint. May I see your phone?'

'Well, there's two actually, the second one I only got this week.'

I pulled them from my handbag and handed them to him. The second phone was my secret phone, the one I'd bought to see me through my leaving Roy. I called it phone B. I hadn't wanted Roy seeing any messages from Albazi and phone B was just for my eyes.

Nicos asked me to enter my PINs for him. I did so. For some moments he concentrated on the first phone in silence, bringing up what looked like a variety of menus. Then he pulled out his own phone, laid them side by side, and concentrated fiercely. I heard the occasional beeps. He repeated this process with the second phone. Finally, he handed the phones back.

'What were you looking for? A bug?'

'I'll explain.'

29

Nicos did explain. If someone wanted to follow you or just find you, there were several ways they could download tracking software onto your phone. The most sophisticated ones would send back to your stalker your exact location to within a few feet.

As I wondered whether Albazi had downloaded something like this onto my personal phone, Nicos told me the Greek police, in their endless war on drug traffickers, had developed some effective blocking software, and that's what he had installed on my phone. He couldn't guarantee it would be one hundred per cent effective, but he did think it would at least make me harder to find.

I told him I had a bit of a problem with that, in case it made it harder for him to find me. I instantly regretted it, because it came out all wrong. But he seemed fine with it. He just grinned and said, 'The day I cannot find you, Sandy, is the day you'll know you are truly safe.'

That was the first time I kissed him. It wasn't exactly the most romantic kiss of all time. I just leaned across – almost falling off the stool in the process – and gave him a quick peck of gratitude on the cheek. 'Thank you,' I said.

He barely reacted. After I'd sat back down he fixed a stare on me. 'So let's talk about this Albazi. When most people want to be hard to find, it is because they are having an affair, but this is not your reason.'

'You really are – were – a detective, weren't you? Just like my husband,' I said.

His face unreadable, his eyes still fixed on mine, he retorted, 'I hope not. If I was your husband, I wouldn't want to ever let you out of my sight. There isn't anything I would want to look at more than you.'

It was about the cheesiest chat-up line I'd ever heard. But he said it with such charm it felt like a warm tornado was swirling through my insides. This was getting dangerous. I desperately tried to think of something clever to say in reply, something meaningful, something polite but distancing, but my brain didn't want to deliver. Instead I said a rather vacuous, 'Thank you, that's nice.'

'Nice,' he said, in blank echo. The way he said it was like he had tossed a coin into the air and would only decide after it had landed whether it was heads or tails – and what either would mean.

'And you?' I asked. 'Are you married?' And I found myself nervous as I awaited the answer.

'I was.'

'You're divorced?' I tried not to let the relief show in my voice.

'Eleni died,' he said flatly.

It was strange but something bothered me that he'd used her name. It implied the wounds were still raw, that he was still hurting. But it did make me realize, for the first time, that he was vulnerable. He took another sip of his drink then stared down at his glass.

I sat in silence for a brief while, thinking how to respond. Finally I ventured, 'I'm sorry. Was it recent?'

'Eight years ago.'

'Do you have kids?'

'I did,' he said and stared back into his wide-rimmed glass. He looked mournful now.

'You did? What happened to them?'

'Twin boys. They were two years old. They died with their mother in a car crash.'

'God, I'm sorry – I didn't – didn't mean – to—'

He waved a dismissive hand. 'It was a long time ago, life moves on, because it has to. I erased it. I swept it away, into a compartment of my mind, locked it and threw away the key.' He shrugged.

'I'm sorry,' I said again, aware it sounded lame. 'What happened – the crash – how did that happen?'

'I'll tell you some day, maybe, but not now. I want you to tell me more about you. And I will of course know if you are telling the truth or not.' He smiled but it suddenly had more the coldness of a professional rather than the warmth of a friend.

'Of course you will, you're an interrogator.'

'You know the reason people lie? It's when they are afraid. Did your husband tell you that?' He smiled again. This time there was a tad more warmth.

'No, but it makes sense.'

'Sure it does. We are programmed by our genes to do whatever it takes to survive. That's why truth is the first casualty of every war. And we are all guilty of something.' He raised his eyebrows.

'So we are all liars?' I replied.

'That would depend how you define truth.'

'Answering a question with a question again,' I chided.

'If that's your only problem with me, I'll take it,' he said and then grinned.

I suddenly looked at my watch and it was almost 5 p.m. But I didn't want to get off that bar stool. I didn't want the afternoon to end. I had been steadily munching on the endless bowls of nuts, olives and spicy crackers the barman put down, trying to curb my hunger, and now I was trying to figure out how three totally amazing hours had passed.

Safe. He made me feel safe, the way that Roy had made me feel safe, too. At this moment Nicos made me feel more wanted and more alive than I could ever remember. Had it been like that in the early days with Roy? Maybe a little, but we had both been so young then. Barely more than kids. Nicos was a man who seemed both physically and mentally strong. He was so not my type, yet the moment I stepped out of the casino, and into the heat of the late afternoon sunshine, all I could think was that I wanted to see him again soon. Desperately soon.

We'd arranged to meet here tomorrow at the same time. But it was not soon enough.

As I walked towards home, my phone pinged with an incoming message. I pulled it out of my handbag with a smile, expecting it to be from Nicos. But my smile evaporated. It was from Roel Albazi.

30

Hi Sandy, told my boss about your inheritance. She's pleased to hear that, but she really needs a firm date for the loan repayment. She wants it within four days. You OK with that? She wouldn't be happy with a late payment, if you understand. Can you confirm and I'll let her know.

If you do have a problem getting the money through in that period, then a letter from the lawyer for the executors confirming the funds are coming, and stating when, might buy you some time – but not much.

I deleted the message.

Mistake.

Moments later another text came through from him, and this one really chilled me.

Don't play games, Sandy. I might be Mr Nice Guy and on your side but my boss isn't, trust me. When I send you a message, I don't expect you to delete it, I expect the courtesy of a reply. My boss doesn't play games with people who don't pay what they owe. You've already seen evidence of that. I'm doing my best to protect you, but default and it will be out of my hands, and you don't want that, believe me.

Shit. Albazi could see what I was doing on my phone? A bug? How else could he know I'd deleted the message, unless he was close by, watching me?

I was walking along New Church Road, a wide street, one

block north of the sea, a mostly residential area of large Edwardian houses, many converted into medical practices, a few high-rent low-rise blocks of flats, a church, and light traffic even though it was now rush hour.

I stopped and looked around but there was no one nearby. A youth struggling with a skateboard on the other side, and an old, blue-rinsed lady, dressed for the Arctic, seemingly oblivious to the temperature being over 30 degrees, walking a trio of Pekineses on leashes, a good hundred yards behind me, making me cross that she would walk her dogs in this heat.

So Albazi had installed something on my phone. If I'd not met my new friend Nicos, I'd not have known someone could even do this.

And despite the heat of the day, I felt a sudden, wintry chill of fear.

I decided it would be smarter to reply than not. To perhaps buy some time.

Message received and understood. All good.

As soon as I had sent it, despite Albazi's instructions, I deleted the message thread. Not that Roy would have seen it, even on my usual phone. I can't remember the last time he looked at it. He had no reason to because he trusted me. But, being paranoid, I'd changed my PIN on that one also, without telling him. Something else I'm not proud of . . .

31

Maybe the guilt should have stopped me lying, sitting opposite my husband, when he asked me how my day was. I told him I'd gone for a glorious walk along the seafront this afternoon. Probably over-egged it a bit by waxing lyrical about how beautiful the shore looked with the tide out.

All the time I couldn't stop thinking about Albazi. About how he knew I had deleted his text. Hopefully Nicos could look at my phones again tomorrow and see if he could find something else, something he had missed.

Except, now, I'm starting to doubt Nicos, big time. Have I been a total fool? Is Nicos working for Albazi – and instead of removing a bug or something that Albazi's put on my phone, has he installed something else? Just schmoozing me to fool me?

And succeeding?

I barely heard Roy talking about his day, about how he'd been in court, in the witness box for most of the day being cross-examined by – in his words – a complete bastard of a barrister called Richard Pedley.

All I could think was that another Valium pill would help with my troubles. I am worried sick.

As Roy stops eating, to check an incoming text – he's the on-call SIO tonight – I sneak a look at my phone B, which I always keep on silent in the house, hoping that maybe there is a text from Nicos that might reassure me. But there isn't.

119

How do I tell Roy that I owe £150,000 to a Brighton hoodlum he's planning to arrest? It's just not an option.

What I don't yet have is a robust plan. My mind feels like one of those IKEA flatpacks you open up, and the contents lie in all kinds of different pieces that you have to somehow assemble to get your finished kitchen cabinet, or whatever it is. The cabinet is my plan, but I don't know what my plan really is, any more than I know what the cabinet should look like.

Here are the absolutes of what I do know at this stage, and in no particular order:

One: I am pregnant.

Two: I cannot let Roy know what I've got myself into.

Three: I have a very short window of time to pay Mr Albazi.

Four: I have almost £30K left, in a rucksack, in the spare room.

Should I take it all to the casino and go shit or bust? It's big stake money. If I got lucky, it would solve one of my problems. Well, two actually. I could pay back Albazi and I'd have enough to start a new life.

I look at Roy, sitting opposite me at the table in our modern and minimalist kitchen, which I designed and am proud of. And I love the view of our garden behind him – all my ideas, which Roy also liked – but, to be honest, I don't think furniture and interior – or exterior – decor are his thing. He'd have been happy if I'd told him I wanted a rustic farmhouse kitchen, or an industrial look, or one that was bright purple. I'm not even sure he would have noticed if he'd come home tonight and the kitchen was completely different.

He'd probably do the same as he always did, which was to walk through the door, kiss me and ask me how my day had been, then tap the goldfish bowl, say hello to Marlon and drop in a couple of pinches of food. He'd remove his jacket and tie, pour each of us a drink – no alcohol for him if he was on duty – sit at the table, scan through the *Argus* newspaper, followed by the website for updates, and maybe ask if I could turn the volume of the television down. And then he'd realize, finally, the kitchen was different but only by going to find something that's not in the place he was expecting.

To be fair, he does pull his weight about the house and he does his equal share of the meals, something microwavable from the freezer or a salad that he would be unable to overcook or grill or fry to a cinder. And he's very good with eggs. The best egg scrambler in the world and he has mastered the perfect poached egg. That I shall miss along with everything else.

I watch him now, in the blue-and-white-striped shirt from Gresham Blake I bought him last Christmas, which is creased and crumpled after this long, sticky summer's day, sleeves rolled up, digging his fork into the macaroni dish (from the freezer), along with a passable Greek salad that I've managed to rustle up.

He is still reading something on his phone, and a wild thought crosses my mind. What if he is only pretending this is a work message and really it's a text from a mistress?

Wishful thinking, I know, to appease my own guilt. He's too decent to have an affair. Roy's the virtuous one, and I'm the shallow imposter of a wife. Sometimes in these past months, when I'm lying awake in the middle of the night, while Roy sleeps the sleep of the innocent, I think *fair play to him.* He doesn't deserve me, he deserves someone better than me, someone who will love him for who and what he is.

Often, during those long, lonely hours of the night, I question myself. Do I really want a lifestyle like Tamzin's? Would that actually make me happy? Is my life actually OK as it is? Am I, like so many others, unable to simply be grateful for what I have?

Maybe. There are a lot of shallow people. But there are also a lot of talented people with something to offer the world, whose lives are unfulfilled because they never got the chance they deserved. Maybe because they married the wrong partner.

Like me?

On occasions, when we've met a real pair of oddballs, Roy and I have agreed, a bit jokily, that there's someone out there for everyone. But there is someone out there for Roy, it's just not me. It's someone who would be content to play the role of honest, supportive wife – and that is really not me. I've failed as a wife and I'm ashamed of what I've let myself become. I've been unfaithful, I am living a lie, I'm scared – and I can't deal with his dedication to his job.

Being the other half of a Major Crime detective, I've realized, is not something I am good at. The detective gets the glory, the headlines, the press conferences and the promotions. The *significant other* gets the cancelled birthday and anniversary dinners, the solo Christmas, and short shrift if you put your foot down.

A twenty-year-old university student has just been raped and murdered. Hello, is our dinner date at our favourite Italian really more important than my husband talking to the victim's parents, trying to comfort them, to reassure them, to help them find some meaning in their lives that have now been destroyed for ever? God, and I had so much been looking forward to the fritto misto!

It's always going to be an argument you cannot win. So you go with the flow. But, if you want the truth, in my view only dead fish go with the flow.

I may come across as a total flake, but I don't think I am. I realize my husband does a very important job. But I'm important too. I'm *me*.

And I'm pregnant. If I do nothing, I am trapped. I've desperately wanted a child for so long. There is no way I would get rid of this gift. But the moment I tell Roy, that's it, I would be stuck. And I'd be stuck with a secret I cannot bear to hold. So that's not an option. I'm going to have to leave before he finds out. I have a way out but it's not going to be easy. I will take my gambling problems with me and leave Roy to his career without tarnishing it. Now Nicos has arrived in my life I have another option. Maybe he could stake me to win the money I need, or if he's really loaded, he could pay off my gambling debt entirely. All things I'm considering. Along with when I can take my next Valium, but I really need to stop taking that.

And actually, the timing of my departure from this life could hardly be better. Albazi expects the money within four days, or a letter from the lawyer confirming my inheritance. As neither are going to happen, I'm going to have to do a runner and go into hiding. Could Nicos really help me?

Ironically, the person who *could* help me is Roy – by arresting Albazi. Problem solved – or at least delayed.

Trying to sound nonchalant, as if I was merely making small talk, but desperate for some information as I carry this weight on my shoulders, I interrupted his reading of the long message on his phone by asking, 'How's that case going with that nasty Albanian guy, the one with the funny name – Abbassy or something? Are you close to an arrest?'

'I can't talk about it, Sandy,' he replied without looking up.

'Can't talk about it?' I said, a little more petulantly than I'd intended.

'You know I can't,' he said.

'*You know I can't,*' I replied, mimicking his voice. But he ignored me and that annoyed me even more. 'It's ridiculous, I'm your wife, we shouldn't have secrets.' I nearly bit my tongue, well aware of my hypocrisy. I badly wanted to share this stress with him, with anyone.

Roy looked up. 'You know there are work things I can't tell you.'

'Leslie Pope said Dick tells her everything.'

Dick Pope was a colleague of Roy and the four of us were good friends.

'Well, he shouldn't, it's not professional and it could get him into a lot of trouble.'

'I'm not asking you to share every detail. You mentioned this guy a while ago, so I was just curious – you said something about torture and murder.'

'We're making progress, OK?' he said abruptly. 'He and his two henchmen are particularly dangerous people. They've even threatened police officers making routine enquiries and they don't do idle threats.'

'So is this the headless torsos case you're working on – Operation Mullet?'

'Sandy, I can't say, OK? I've said too much already.'

'I *can* keep a secret, Roy.'

'Have you never heard the saying, "If you tell a secret to one person, you've told the world"?'

'Well, that's bloody charming!'

He excavated another forkful of macaroni.

As I watch him eat, I'm thinking about another problem – it is Roy's thirtieth birthday in four days' time and I've not yet bought him a present. He has hinted for some while that he'd like a new watch – I'd like him to have one too, the tatty one he wears is an embarrassment. He's made a big hint about a Swiss Army watch and, at £60, that's a lot more in my budget range than the six-grand Hublot I saw him admiring in a shop window a while ago.

Although here I'm hesitating and it saddens me. This might be the last gift I'm ever going to buy him; should I go cheap or at least give him a parting gift from my inheritance? Something to remember me by for ever?

My heart tells me to go for the Hublot.

Common sense tells me the Swiss Army watch.

I've always prided myself on being sensible.

32

Alan Mitten and Robert Rhys had been sensible. To Roel Albazi's relief, after Tall Joe had finally tracked them down and popped along to see them, the money they owed magically appeared in less than a day.

But Sandy Grace was not being sensible. He wasn't trying to help her because he was being altruistic, he was simply looking after his own skin. If Song Wu was reckless enough to come down hard on the wife of a cop, the police would be all over it - and very quickly all over him.

But whatever the police might do was nothing compared to what Song Wu might do to him or his family back in Albania if Sandy defaulted, after she discovered, through the monthly audit, that Albazi had paid her back with her own money.

He knew full well how much of an interest Sussex Police took in the local Albanian community, and steps they had been taking to engage with it, which only made all Albanians here even more suspicious of their motives. During the hours of questioning by the police he'd had to face since the devastation of his office and the humiliation of Skender, it was clear they believed it was the work of fellow Albanians, and they were going through all his links to them. A little too thoroughly for his liking. He had the distinct impression they were using the incident as an excuse to delve deeper into his own private business world and that was making him very uncomfortable.

He was also angry, very angry indeed at Song Wu, for what she had done to his office and home, and the humiliation of Skender. And angry at his impotence. Angry because he knew there was nothing he could do to get back at Song Wu, to get even with her, without putting his family back in Albania at even bigger risk.

She had sent a clear message to him. A warning. Letting him know how vulnerable he and his team were if they upset her.

Skender was fine after his ordeal, and quietly determined to get revenge on the two henchmen from Song Wu who had done this to him. He told Albazi they'd tricked him into opening the door, then floored him with a taser and, he presumed, then drugged him before stripping him and applying the glue, as the next thing he knew he was naked on the floor, unable to open his mouth or remove his hands from the wall.

Albazi's office and apartment were uninhabitable, and until the repair work was done, he had checked into the Grand Hotel in Brighton. His computer equipment and physical records had been trashed, but he had a backup of everything and was able to function again quickly. And, to Albazi's relief, the safe, which he had not told the police about and was concealed behind fake kitchen tiles, had not been touched.

All his attention was now focused on Sandy Grace. Thanks to two bugs, loaded onto her phone, and the third, a magnetic one placed under the rear of her little VW Golf, he could keep track of all her movements. Even more importantly, he could hear all phone conversations she had, in real time. Or recorded, for those he missed.

This guy Nicos, whoever he was, who thought he was a hotshot with phones, presented a threat. What rock had he crawled out from underneath?

He needed to be eliminated and fast.

33

23 July 2007 – Looking back

Nicos was late. We'd arranged to meet at 1.30 in the Casino d'Azur and it was now 2 p.m. I was starting to get concerned, all my random fears that he might be in cahoots with Albazi growing stronger with every minute that he did not appear.

My head was in a very strange place. My anxiety was through the roof and my self-medication by way of another Valium was not helping. Nicos had a snake tattoo running down his neck. Could I trust someone with a tattoo like that? Why was I even so bothered about his tattoo? As goes the last line of one of my favourite films, *Some Like It Hot*, 'Nobody's perfect.' The universe seemed to have gone weird on me, as if it was against me, and having a big joke at my expense.

I was dangerously in debt. I couldn't stay with my husband, as I would bring no end of humiliation on him, and I very definitely did not want to tell him I was pregnant. Because then I would be stuck. Stuck in a relationship I could not be in any more, even if I somehow managed to sort the Albazi shit out, and trapped by a lie.

The lie that Roy was the father.

He could be, but, shamefully, so could Cassian, who I had slept with a year ago, but also more recently just before I told him I didn't want to continue seeing him. I was faithful to Roy for most of our marriage. Not that I'm trying to justify anything.

Right now the only option I can see is to leave Roy before my bump starts to show. And before Roel Albazi's boss sets the knifeman on me. Thanks to my small inheritance, I've got enough cash to tide me over for a bit. So long as I don't lose it all this afternoon on more spins of the wheel.

But where do I disappear and how?

There were two of us in this now. Unless the test was wrong. But that was unlikely.

OVER 99% ACCURATE!

I was actually gambling sensibly for maybe the first time since I'd got the bug. Just small stakes this afternoon – one-pound and five-pound chips. Just as well I was keeping my stakes low, because I was on yet another losing streak. The roulette wheel wasn't speaking to me, the ball wasn't speaking to me, nor were the numbers and colours. Only the nice young croupier was speaking to me, but even she wasn't saying much, other than she liked my hair colour, and she asked me where I'd bought my cream blouse and seemed excited when I said Zara in Brighton. She had a day off tomorrow and would go there, she said.

I started to raise my stakes a little because I was increasingly annoyed about Nicos. He was definitely a no-show. Great. How had I misjudged him so badly? I was now certain he was an Albazi plant and I was just a dumb sucker. Over the next half-hour, gambling recklessly, I lost the equivalent of about thirty Zara blouses.

And my patience.

3.25 p.m.

Sod you, Nicos. Go to hell. My anger was making me reckless. I dropped another £5,000 on the wheel. Great stuff. I'd managed to turn £30,000 into £20,000. And dwindling.

Suddenly, my phone, which was on silent, started vibrating. I looked down: it was a call from Roy. I ignored it.

I wanted so badly to take another Valium to calm down even

though I knew it was becoming more and more of an addiction. A way to cope with the crisis I had got myself into.

I was about to reach for one when, over two and a half hours late, I saw Nicos across the far side of the room, heading towards me with an urgency and a look of apology that instantly melted all my anger towards him.

I felt a thrill at seeing him that I found hard to put into words. Like I'd taken a drug that instantly filled me with warmth and confidence. I didn't need the tranquillizer, I had the sense, at that moment, that my future had walked into this grand room that was filled with gaming tables and hung with chandeliers. My white knight. Not in shining armour, but in a lightweight leather bomber jacket, black T-shirt, blue chinos and brown loafers.

On Nicos they looked incredibly sexy.

I raised an arm, signalling him to stop in his tracks, held up my phone and pointed to it, then with the index finger and thumb of my free hand made a zip-it sign across my lips.

He stopped and nodded. He got it.

Of course he did, he was smart.

I turned my phone off, waited until the display had died completely, then gave it a few more seconds before I gave him the thumbs up, and he continued over to me, hooded eyes locking onto mine.

'Forgive me,' he said.

Just the way he said those words in his charming accent, while smiling at the same time, made me feel ready to forgive him instantly, before even hearing his apology.

'To be this late is inexcusable,' he continued. 'It was a flight that was badly delayed. I had important business. I'm so glad you are still here.'

I gave him a reproachful look. 'What business was more important than me?'

Instantly I regretted saying those words. They sounded pathetically shallow. So not me.

To my relief he grinned. 'The business of protecting you, Sandy Grace, OK?'

'Maybe.' I said it with a teasing grin.

He produced a small phone from his jacket pocket. 'We will communicate via this from now. Switch your old phone back on only when you absolutely have to. And be very careful what you say when it is switched on.' He looked at me sternly. 'If I'm going to keep you safe, you must always do exactly what I say to you. I'm making good plans for you.'

I looked back into his eyes, searching them for any hint of deceit. But if it was there, I couldn't find it. 'You're making plans for me, Nicos? Is this like a *job* phone? Like the one my husband is attached to?' I laughed. 'I barely know you.'

'Do you *really* know anyone, Sandy? How much does someone let anyone else into their life – even their husband or wife? Isn't trust a gut feeling?'

I shrugged. 'I guess it is,' I said.

With his stare fixed on me, he said, 'There is no mathematical equation for trust. No matter how long you and I spend in each other's company, you will never really know me any more than I will know you, beyond what I choose to let you know, and beyond the superficial.'

'Fine,' I replied. 'So let's be superficial. I know nothing about you. Tell me about where you grew up, tell me about your parents. Your family?'

He shrugged. 'I was raised on a small island in the Aegean Sea, Mykonos. It's a cool place, but I didn't appreciate that when I was a kid.'

'I know it,' I said. 'I absolutely love it there. I've always wondered what it is like out of season, as I've only been as a tourist and it's so busy. But so beautiful, those white buildings against the blue skies, stunning!'

'It is very quiet in the winter months, that's when I like it the most. My father was a tobacconist, with a little shop in the town selling cigarettes, cigars, soft drinks, ice creams, cold cappuccinos. My mother worked with him until she got cancer, when I was twelve, and died a year later. My sister and I helped my father out in the shop during our teens.' He hesitated. 'You want more?'

'I do,' I said. And I genuinely did.

'I guess my horizon was bigger than the tiny island of Mykonos. When I joined the army I wanted adventure, but I never saw any action. So when I was discharged, as you call it – I think – I figured maybe the police would be more my thing. I moved to Athens and after being promoted to detective was asked to be an interrogator. Since then, bigger opportunities beckoned, and now a new one beckons.'

'Which is?'

'Helping you to hide.'

I remember looking at him, still unsure quite where he was coming from, and asking him, 'Why do you want to help me?'

He stared at me levelly. 'Because I like you.' His eyes sparkled with charm.

I tried to read his expression. To find a subtext. But beyond his eyes there was nothing but steely resolve.

'I know you need to hide. And you have three days to do it. I can help you. Trust me, I've had previous experience. But you will really have to trust me. If I tell you, *jump*, will you do that?'

'I guess that will depend on how high,' I replied, smiling.

He gave me a deadly serious, almost mesmerizing look then said, 'In the situation you are in, Sandy, that is really not funny. If you want me to help you, I need you to take me seriously. Are you able to do that?'

We stared at each other for several seconds. 'I am,' I said finally.

'Good,' he replied. 'I've found out a little about the people you owe money to. These are not nice people. When you tell them you cannot pay they are not going to pat you on the head and say, *Never mind, dear, let us know when you can.*'

'I'm aware of that.'

He shook his head. 'You've led a protected life, married to a cop. Taking that loan from those people, you've stepped into a jungle where the normal rules of society don't apply. Even if you stayed with your husband, he wouldn't be able to protect you. Believe me, Albazi is a nasty man, but the people he works for make him look like your favourite childhood uncle. You understand what I'm saying?'

'I do,' I replied.

'So get real.'

34

23 July 2007 – Looking back

I got real.

Albazi wanted full payback in three days, and that wasn't going to happen. Which meant, as Nicos so eloquently put it, I had three days to get my shit together and then vanish.

I was putting my trust in a complete stranger, by his own admission a drug dealer, and yet strangely I did now completely trust him. Or maybe I just really, desperately *wanted* to trust him?

Nicos was taking care of everything. I was going to have to change my name, but he was dealing with that. I was going to have to change my appearance. And, just as importantly, he drummed into me repeatedly that, if I went ahead with this, I would have to leave everyone and everything I loved in Brighton behind. There would be no tearful reunion. No, 'Hi, darling, I'm home. I'll explain . . .'

The more I tried to think straight about the enormity of it all, the harder it got. I was schoolgirl-excited one moment, then scared witless the next. There really were only two options, or so it seemed. Either I fessed-up to Roy and we figured out something together. Or I just disappeared. But either way our house was already mortgaged to the hilt and I really didn't know how much Roy could do, other than arresting Albazi. That would be a short-term solution, for sure. But a long-time nightmare for me, because the longer I left it, the more likely it was that Roy would find out I was pregnant.

I lay awake for much of that night, my scalp feeling tight, like it was a bathing cap. I was leaving my husband, my friends, my parents and every other part of my life. Three days in which I had to seem totally normal to everyone, while all the time planning not a weekend break, or a fortnight's holiday in the sun, but my complete disappearance. For ever.

I would be gone. Properly gone. With a man I barely knew, who had made all the arrangements, which included coming up with some new identities. All I had to go on was just my gut instinct that he was some kind of a guardian angel. I guess I've always believed that somehow people like Nicos find us at times in our lives when we need them.

It was that way handsome Roy Grace, with his Paul Newman eyes, had found me all those years back. And now Nicos just appeared. He told me it was the first time in his life he had been in the Casino d'Azur. He told me he wasn't sure why he had gone in, but the moment he saw me, he knew the reason.

Sounds corny, but in my muddled state I guess I was ready to believe anything.

I was up against two ticking clocks. It felt like those ones you see on top of briefcase bombs in movies, with big red digital countdowns, so you can see time is running out for the hero to defuse them. But I was pregnant and that bomb was not going to be defused – not after all those years of trying for a baby.

Finally, I had what I wanted most of all in the world.

I should stop taking the Valium, I knew. I would, I promised myself and my baby, I would stop as soon as the stress was off. I think my baby knew, I felt we already had a bond, an understanding between us. My baby was cool, we were already a team. A very cool team.

But as those days and hours ticked away my confidence was ebbing, too. I didn't see Nicos, we just spoke on the 'job' phone he'd given me, and that wasn't helping calm me much either.

None of it was feeling real. I walked around and around the house – it wasn't a big or grand house in any way, it was pretty ordinary. The estate agents had it in their brochure as *four-bedroom*, but in reality it was three bedrooms plus a large cupboard with a window, but I'd always loved it. Well, until I compared it with Tamzin's. Built in the 1930s with a few pieces of timber on the front facade to give a mock-Tudor effect, it had a tiled carport out front and a small, fenced garden at the rear, which I'd turned into something very exotic, with stones and flowing water and pathways and greenery. A proper sanctuary. We'd spent so many back-breaking hours creating this I would of course be sad to leave it, and felt sentimental at times during those days.

There was much about the interior I'd be sad to leave, too. The Little Greene-branded paint in the shade of 'flint' throughout the rooms, and mostly black furniture – all part of my minimalist interior plan. But was there anything I wanted to take with me for my new life, wherever that would be? Nicos had talked about Valencia in Spain and Jersey in the Channel Islands. I had no idea what, if anything, might work out with him, but he was my portal into my new life at this moment. Once I was out and with a new identity, I could decide whether there was any future with him, or perhaps with someone, somewhere in the world, who I had not yet met.

I desperately wanted to talk to Becky. But she was in Australia with a big time difference. Not that that was an issue. I guess the issue was that if I told her what I was planning, for sure at some point soon after I'd gone Roy would call her and then she would have to lie to him – or worse – not lie.

Nicos had drummed into me repeatedly: *Tell no one.*

I told no one.

35

26 July 2007

D-Day.

I get out of bed this morning feeling like I've a stomach full of frogs on crack cocaine. My eyes are raw from lying awake most of the night, churning my decision over and over. This morning I am Sandy Grace. But when I get into bed tonight, I will be Sandra Jones. I should be excited about my new life; I'm not, I'm shit scared.

I'm still trying to convince myself I'm not nuts, entrusting myself to a man I barely know – and a criminal by his own confession. On the other hand, it is exactly what I need right now, a good criminal mind. And I keep reminding myself that I would have still been in this situation even if I'd not met Nicos. He's actually making it far simpler for me, and I am grateful I can tell someone and talk about it.

But still, every few minutes I'm minded just to call it off.

Then I think of the good reasons I can't.

On top of all this, it's Roy's thirtieth birthday and I have to go through the charade of normality. Since we first got together, birthdays have always been special. Breakfast in bed for the birthday boy or girl. Then dinner with friends later. And when possible on our birthdays, we'd take the day off and have an outing. But – luckily – he cannot take today off.

I've been watching the green dial of the digital clock all night long, ticking away the minutes agonizingly slowly. I'm watching it now: 5.31 a.m.; 5.47 a.m.; 6.11 a.m. Roy is normally an early riser but today he's still deep asleep. Good, let's get this over with. I slip out of bed, pull my dressing gown on, slide my feet into slippers and then creep into the bathroom to brush my teeth.

I go downstairs and take the tiny cake with the single candle out of the cupboard where I've hidden it, and open the miniature bottle of Champagne I'd bought online – I know he's not supposed to drink on duty but one mouthful won't matter – and pour him a glass. I'll drink the rest of it.

I've bought him a very rude birthday card – which I always do – it has HORNY BEAST! printed on the front; I've got to keep today as normal as possible, so he doesn't suspect a thing.

I carry the Champagne, cake with the candle lit, card and his presents on a tray up to the bedroom and as I enter I start singing, 'Happy birthday to you . . . Happy birthday to you . . .'

Believe me, my singing voice is truly terrible, it's enough to wake the dead. And it does the trick, it wakes Roy.

'Oh my God!' he says with a big, loving smile.

The smile that once would melt my heart, but now I can't find the love. It's a protection against what I am about to do. If I let myself slip into the guilt, I will not do it. He takes the tiniest sip possible of the Champagne, and I, his wife, bride of many summers, step out of my dressing gown, slip into bed, naked, beside him, and down half the glass – to lighten the mood – while he opens the card, laughs and then kisses me. A big, loving kiss. I try not to think. It's all getting too much. I am aching. Then I hand him his presents one at a time, looking away when I think my facade will crack. I am barely able to mask my pain.

I start with the least exciting, the running shorts and then the top that he had been hinting he wanted. Next the aftershave, which delights him – he sprays some on my neck and then on his. Finally he opens the BIG PRESENT full of expectation. And I haven't disappointed him.

As he rips open the package containing the Swiss Army watch, Roy simply says, 'Wow!'

He grabs me and holds me, planting many kisses all round my neck and on my lips. I am breaking, this is the hardest thing I have ever had to do. I know I need to stay strong, but this is torture. I don't hate Roy, he's not a bad person. But there's no way I can change my mind now. We hug tight, my head over his neck, facing away, so he can't see the tears streaming down my face. The enormity of it all just whacked me so hard at this moment. Roy tenderly caresses me and does everything he knows I enjoy. Usually. When I'm not about to walk out the house and never return. We make love and I plant my face into the pillow to mute my sobbing, hoping he won't notice. As we climax, my emotions and the guilt overwhelm me and I feel like telling him everything, putting the duvet over my head and crashing out here in this bed for ever. But I know I can't hide here. The bad things will find me. We lie there together for a moment in silence and I wipe a tear from my face, which he sees. Roy asks me, 'Hey, you OK?' And I turn my face away and say of course I'm OK, convincingly. I wonder if he will remember this moment when I am gone. We are silent for a while.

His job phone goes and it snaps us out of this reverie and gives me the strength to even be slightly annoyed, because this always happens. I quickly regain my composure and my mind is straight again. I am doing this. I am leaving.

The first thing I did after getting up and showering was to phone in to the doctor's surgery saying I felt a bit unwell but that I would see if I improved. I barely had to act, my voice sounded terrible. This would avoid raising any suspicion if I left later due to sickness.

Next I took a final walk around the garden trying to not let myself get distracted by the pangs of conscience. I couldn't help but feel sad. Then around the house, to see if there was anything

THEY THOUGHT I WAS DEAD

I should take with me, something sentimental or something I just might need – that would fit in a single holdall along with the essentials I had already packed. I knew I couldn't take much with me and I couldn't take things from the house that would be missed, so I had to leave the photographs of Roy and myself. I didn't want to leave him any clues, not beyond abandoning my car at Gatwick Airport. I had a good amount of Valium that I could take with me until I'd weaned myself off it. That was always the plan, just the right time had not yet occurred for the big weaning-off event. It would. I again promised myself and my baby.

Nicos was very specific. Anything that could give a tell-tale footprint I had to leave behind. Which meant my credit cards and my personal phone. The plan was to leave a trail at Gatwick for anyone looking for me. But before I set off, I needed two things – we were out of paracetamol, because I'd been taking so much in recent days to try to sleep, and I wasn't confident I had enough fuel in my Golf to get to Gatwick Airport. I'd been meaning to fill up for days but, whatever, I hadn't. I'm sure Freud would have had something to say about it – I was being anal or retentive or something because my inner *me* didn't really want to leave. But one of the things I had learned from Roy was how often it was the simplest things that got criminals caught – such as a tail-light out or driving erratically. Or maybe running out of petrol on the way to Gatwick Airport . . .

The first flight I was booked on was the 16.12 BA 2771 to Malaga. To make that in good time I needed to leave here by 1 p.m.

When I'd plucked up the courage I got in my car to head to Boots in Hove to pick up some bits. But, ridiculously, because I hadn't said goodbye to Marlon – the dumb goldfish Roy had won at a funfair shortly after we were married – I got out of the car and went back into the house. I can't explain it, but I would have felt bad leaving without saying goodbye to him. Going back in,

139

even just minutes after I'd left, felt like being a visitor to someone else's house. Mentally, I'd left. I pressed my face up against the round bowl, blew him a kiss and dropped in a pinch of food. He opened and closed his mouth, looking mournful as ever. Guess that's about as good as it gets in human bonding with a goldfish.

I had just one more problem to overcome and that was our incredibly nosy neighbour, Noreen Grinstead, who lived directly opposite us. She was a jumpy woman in her fifties, the local hawk-eye, who knew everyone's business in the street. Almost every time I went outside, there she was in her rubber gloves, either cleaning their cars or hosing the tiles of their carport, day or night, winter or summer. I think it was her cover for snooping.

To my relief, as I came back out of the house, she wasn't there. Sometimes there is a god.

Driving away from my home for the very last time, just after 1 p.m. on 26 July 2007, I had three different passports in my handbag – thanks to Nicos calling in a favour from a Brighton forger, who had once specialized in them. Nicos had paid for them himself and would not hear of my offering to reimburse him. In my desperation to get away from Albazi I never stopped to think through in any detail what motives Nicos might have. I was just grateful for his strength and his help.

I also had three different-coloured baseball caps, three wigs and three changes of clothes all stuffed into my fake Louis Vuitton holdall – a bag I'd bought on a short holiday we'd had in Dubai a couple of years before.

The bag also contained the very bare essentials I needed, in terms of toiletries and clothes, as well as a bottle of water and a small photograph of Roy and me. We'd had it taken in one of those booths on the Palace Pier, years ago, when we were first dating. The way Roy looked then, so handsome, so happy, I guess that's the way I want to remember him, always.

At the bottom of the bag, wrapped in newspaper and carefully sewn into a false compartment I'd created, with a concealed zip, were two books on pregnancy and bundles of fifty-pound notes left from my inheritance. Enough to tide me over for some while if I decided to move on from Nicos.

It's a strange thing, planning to disappear for ever. It kind of freezes your mind – or at least it did mine. I'd had very little time to think of what to put in that one holdall; very little time to think about everything from my life up until then that I wanted to keep.

I really struggled to think of anything.

Roy's the one for that, with all the stuff he likes to collect – old records, old inkwells, everything meticulously organized to the point of being borderline OCD, of course, in his office and at our home.

I stopped at Boots in Hove, where I bought some toothpaste and the maximum number of paracetamols I was permitted. Then I left and filled up with petrol, right to the brim. When they eventually found my car, with a full tank, they would be confused.

I checked my phones. There were several messages on phone B. They were all from Roel Albazi, the only number he had for me. To my disappointment, there were no messages from Nicos on this or my 'job' phone either and he, of course, had both numbers.

The first from Albazi was at 1 p.m.

Hey Sandy, you're running late!

The second, still friendly, was just after 1.30 p.m.

Hey Sandy, what's going on, I'm waiting for you. Did you get the time wrong? Or the date wrong?

The third, at 2 p.m., was the turning point, where the texts began to be less and less friendly.

Sandy, what are you playing at? I warned you not to mess with these people.

There were more, getting progressively angrier.

I ignored them all.

36

Roel Albazi sat at the marble oval table in his apartment above the pizzeria in Shoreham. He had long ago learned never to be knocked down by any adversary and within a week of his home being trashed, while it wasn't perfect yet, it was habitable again, filled with rental furniture. But despite that, and the whisky inside him, he was feeling nervous as hell. And knocked again. By a new adversary.

Sandy Grace.

It was 8 p.m., Friday evening. Skender Sharka, patched up with a few bandages on his face and arms, and Tall Joe sat at the table either side of their boss. All of them had a glass of Chivas Regal, filled by Albazi from the rapidly emptying bottle on the table.

'OK, so this is the update on this woman,' Albazi said. 'I don't know what interest this Greek guy, Nicos Christoforou, has in her. Maybe he wants to fuck her.'

'Or has already?' Tall Joe suggested.

Albazi did not react. 'Nicos Christoforou is a piece of work. He makes out he's all Mr Nice Guy, telling the world he only deals in cannabis because in his heart and soul . . .' He paused to place his hand on his chest, in mock solemnity and, mimicking Howard Marks's Welsh accent, said, 'I do not believe in hard drugs.'

Both his colleagues grinned.

'That asshole Nicos tells everyone that he wants cannabis to be legalized because of all its health benefits, so he announces

142

that's what he's doing, that he's on a mission to convert the world to the magical healing wonders of cannabis, of hemp oil, grass, weed, ganga, whatever the hell you want to call it. That may be true – but what he's saying about himself is complete crap!'

He refilled everyone's glass then went on.

'I've found out all about Nicos Christoforou, thanks to the Song Wu research team. He's got links with drug corridors from Thailand, the Philippines and two cartels in Colombia. He's supplying Class A drugs into Spain, via Valencia, and to Jersey in the Channel Islands, and he has supply networks around the world. Most of his stuff comes into England through Liverpool. In 1996 he was imprisoned on a twenty-five-to-life jail sentence in Zanzibar on a drugs importation charge, before escaping on a yacht in 2001– after some bribery. Zanzibar still have an international warrant out for his arrest – but of course not in the name of Nicos Christoforou, that is some alias way down the line. The warrant is out in his real name, Constantine Angelos.'

'Where does he live, boss?' Sharka asked.

'Good question,' Albazi replied. 'He seems to live out of a suitcase. The last permanent address anyone can find for him was a villa in a fancy suburb of Athens, twelve years ago. He had a wife and two children who were blown up by a car bomb intended for him. That's when he changed his name and vanished – until he ended up in prison in Zanzibar.'

Tall Joe said, 'So this *Nicos*' – he waggled his hands in the air – 'might be the clue to finding Sandy Grace?'

'Or whatever she's called now, yes,' Albazi said. 'She was due here yesterday at 12 p.m. with all the money and she was a no-show. She's not responded to any of my messages. She had agreed, absolutely no question, to turn up to see me with the £150K she owes. She never showed, so where is she?'

'You need to hear this, boss,' Tall Joe said. 'I have traced her to Gatwick Airport and a Sandra Smith, who I'm sure is her, took a flight to Amsterdam and disappeared, but good news was told to me in a boozer at lunchtime today by a mate who's a private pilot. One of his regular clients happens to be Nicos Christoforou.'

Suddenly he had Albazi's full attention. 'Seriously, Joe?'

'Seriously. He regularly flies him in and out of the country, mostly from Shoreham or Goodwood, or if it's a jet then from Biggin Hill.'

'Flies him where?'

'Jersey, mostly. Spain sometimes – Valencia is a regular round trip.'

'I guess Nicos flies privately because he's got stuff he doesn't want to put through an airport scanner, right?' Sharka said.

'That would be a pretty good guess,' Tall Joe replied.

'Your pilot friend,' Albazi said, thoughtfully. 'He's bent, right?'

'Bent as the proverbial nine-bob note.'

'How much of a bung would he need to tell us when and where he's flying Nicos next?'

Tall Joe gave an impish smile and made a circle with his forefinger and thumb. 'He's already told me that, boss. Tomorrow morning. He's got two passengers – Nicos Christoforou and a lady.'

'Called?' Albazi asked.

'Sandra Jones.'

Albazi smiled and nodded slowly. 'When people change their names, they often keep their first name because it's easiest and it feels familiar. I think there's a pretty good chance this Sandra Jones is Sandy Grace, yes?'

'No question,' Tall Joe said. Skender Sharka agreed.

'I've seen the copies of their passports filed for the flight plan.' Tall Joe put his laptop on the table and pulled up the photo page of a passport. He turned it so Albazi could see it clearly.

Albazi studied it for a moment. It was Sandy Grace's face, but she looked quite different with long, wavy red hair. He nodded. 'It's her, for sure. Nice work.'

'Always!' Joe said.

'Do you know which airport and at what time they are flying?' Albazi asked.

'I do, boss. Tomorrow. Biggin Hill on a chartered Citation jet, which my pilot friend flies, to Valencia. Scheduled departure time 10 a.m. They overnight in Valencia and then the jet drops them off in Jersey the next day.'

'That's very interesting, Joe,' Sharka said.

37

There's a stranger looking at me, giving me a curious, almost mocking eye. She's saying, *Ha, imposter!* She looks like something out of a fashion magazine from the 1920s, with her bright lipstick and the way those long red curls slant down her face. You could picture her dancing the Charleston in one of those slinky outfits.

I can't believe I'm looking in a mirror.

It's me.

Was me.

Hello, Sandra Jones!

Gratitude is a strange thing.

I was so grateful to Nicos but I was also now feeling angry with him. Angry, I guess, because he'd been so persuasive, so confident. He's convinced me to believe in him. Now, thanks to that, I'm totally out of my comfort zone. At least, in my addled mind, 'comfort zone' had been my life this morning, before I left – before everything changed, while I was still *old* me. Now I was *new* me and not yet liking it much. In truth, I was not liking it at all.

I'd go so far as to say that I was actually hating it, and wondering if I'd made a very big mistake. Wondering if it was too late to do anything about it.

New Me was sat in a small, pleasant, but sparsely furnished bedroom on the first floor of Saint Hill Manor, the British HQ of the Scientologists. It was kind of like how I imagine it might feel to be on your first night in boarding school. Different sounds, different smells, different terrain, different vibes, unfamiliar voices. Very strange and disorienting.

There was a tall bookshelf, stacked mostly with hardbacks and paperbacks by L. Ron Hubbard, and a modern television screen. A table with a bottle of mineral water and a glass. I had a view out over several modern extensions and what looked like a mock Norman castle, surrounded by almost fanatically well-tended lawns, and a lake.

But despite feeling lonely, nervous and lost, I did at least have one positive. Roel Albazi sure wasn't going to find me here too easily.

So far, on this first crazy day of my new life, Nicos had delivered everything he'd said he would. My passports, my Gatwick flight reservations, and his friend, Hans-Jürgen Waldinger, here at the HQ of Scientology. Hans-Jürgen had made me feel welcome, showed me my room and given me the timetable for meals. Not that I had any appetite for food, I felt on the verge of throwing up, from nerves, at any moment.

Hans-Jürgen, a good decade older than me, was from Munich, and spoke cultured English with the hint of a German accent that I found very charming and quite flirtatious, and he seemed to belong here, as if he was part of the management. He was tall and good-looking in a kind of arty-academic way – long centre-parted hair and retro spectacles, and dressed fresh and cool for the summer heat in trainers, thin chinos and a short-sleeved white shirt. He was confident and quite tactile with me and, when he looked at me, it was with an intense, penetrating gaze as if he was reading something deep inside me that made him smile, that I didn't even know was printed there.

Whether Nicos had briefed him or it was just his natural way, to my surprise, Hans-Jürgen made no attempt to start introducing me to Scientology – in fact, it was almost the reverse. I told him I had relatives near Munich and he said how much he missed the city and was planning to move back soon. I asked him if he was going to remain involved with Scientology there and he said he was not, very pointedly. He then whispered a strange thing to me, which perhaps I should have taken more seriously. 'Be careful of Nicos, he's a dangerous man. Any time you are in trouble you can come to me.'

38

After Hans-Jürgen had left, I felt even more unsettled and on edge. I sat in the armchair and buried my face in my hands, thinking, *Shit, what have I done? Shit, shit, shit.*

Was it too late to reverse it? I had my 'job' phone or even phone B; I could call Roy right now, tell him everything and he would forgive me and we would sort it out.

And get Roy killed in the process by Albazi?

I started thinking about what clues I'd inadvertently left that Roy would find.

My laptop, which Nicos had insisted I leave behind, would be the first thing he would start checking. Well, once he had cracked my password. We didn't have any secrets and in the past he always knew my password. But that was before I started online gambling. I'd changed it then to stop him from finding it out. I imagine some of the boffins in the Police High Tech Crime Unit would be able to crack the password easily enough. But I'd cleared the history caches on the search engines, so maybe my laptop wasn't going to be of much help to him. But, God, I wished I had it with me now. Just to have something to do to occupy myself.

They'd find my car at the airport, of course, but I didn't know how long that would take. What else would Roy find? He'd be able to get my phone records, but my personal phone records would show nothing untoward. He'd speak to my friends, but

I'd not told them anything. Nor my work colleagues. Weighing it up, I felt so far, with Nicos's help, I'd covered my tracks pretty thoroughly.

My window was open and it was a fine summer evening. I heard the drone and clatter of a lawn mower a short distance away and I could smell the scent of freshly cut grass. It made me think of my beautiful garden – that I would never see again. And suddenly, for the first time in this hectic day, the full seriousness of what I had done began to overwhelm me and I started sobbing, uncontrollably.

When I calmed a little and dabbed my eyes, I put my hand on my stomach, apologized to my unborn baby and popped another Valium – then started trying to think it all through.

What was Roy doing now? Was he wondering where I was? What would he have done when he saw my car wasn't there?

Dick and Leslie Pope would have got all dressed up to go to Roy's birthday dinner, at the Gingerman, one of our favourite Brighton restaurants. What happened when I didn't turn up?

I was never going to speak to them or see them again and that made me really sad.

One of the things I've learned from my years with Roy is that you need to be anal to be a good detective. Painstaking, methodical, highly organized. How did he ever fall in love with slapdash me? The attraction of opposites?

Don't get me wrong, I'm not saying that was a fault with him. The fault was with me. Always me. Because I always wanted more than I had. *Ah, but a man's reach should exceed his grasp, or what's a heaven for*, right? Robert Browning said that. I think he meant that if we wanted to achieve anything, we always had to strive beyond our limits, beyond our comfort zone.

39

I was very definitely out of my comfort zone by now. I reached for an L. Ron Hubbard book, called *Dianetics*, just for something to do, and as I grasped it my phone pinged with an incoming message.

From Nicos. Finally.

You made it to first base 😊 **X**

That 'X' had a strange effect on me. Was it the first indication of any affection towards me in a text? Or was it my mind hoping?

Hans-Jürgen had given me a number to call him on if I needed anything. When he answered I told him I couldn't find the minibar in my room. 'I am the minibar,' he replied, which made me smile for the first time today.

Twenty minutes after telling him what I would like, he appeared at my door with a miniature vodka, a small can of Fever Tree tonic, a slice of lemon, an ice bucket and a glass.

I thanked him, and as soon as he left, I took a moment to prepare the drink, then downed it. Then dialled Nicos. When he answered, asking me how I was, I replied, 'Am I doing the right thing?'

'Get real, Sandy,' Nicos replied, almost coldly. His voice sounded different from yesterday, the last time we had spoken. Yesterday he was my friend, saviour and future lover. Today he sounded like a transactional businessman.

'Get real?' I shot back. 'Is that how you answer any problem I have, *get real*? How much more real is this supposed to be?

I've left my husband and my home and I'm never going to see either of them again. I have my entire life crammed into one holdall and you're telling me to get real? The holdall's not even sodding real.'

'If you don't like it, ask Hans-Jürgen to call you a cab and go home. No one's holding you hostage. Call your husband, tell him you're on your way home.'

There was a long silence then he hung up. I did actually consider it yesterday, initially for one nanosecond, then for longer. Then I thought about the conversation we'd all have at the restaurant, starting with Dick Pope or Leslie asking me how my day had been. *'Pretty uneventful,'* I'd reply. *'You know, same old, same old.'*

I've always been interested in ancient history. I remember reading about life when all humans were nomads, and the concept of owning property did not exist. There were no wars then. Wars only began when our ancestors stopped wandering, created farms, put boundaries around and grew crops and whatever. The day we humans started owning property was the day we started wanting more. And then more. And began killing for what wasn't ours.

So it was actually incredibly liberating to know I had the contents of my entire fake life in that one fake bag. On the one hand I didn't care about property any more. I didn't care that I theoretically owned fifty per cent of our house. If I was disappearing for ever, that was part of the cost. But on the other hand, I missed it already, knowing I would never go back there. I tried to shrug it off.

Lobsters and crabs shrug off their shells as they grow. They're not sentimental creatures, they'll just grow new, bigger ones. And they'll keep on doing that every time they become too big for the next one. When a lobster or a crab discards its shell does it feel sentimental about it? Or does it simply move on and grow a new carapace to protect it from all the predators out there? Living in the moment?

Does our past actually mean anything? Shouldn't we just live in the moment, in the *now*? I remember that was how I had been feeling yesterday, finally driving away from my home to Gatwick.

The most nervous I had ever felt in my life. Now, by definition, a nomad. But with a small feeling of a sense of adventure. Of liberation. Along with the doom. But I focused on the future as much as I could. With my mantra of 'mind over matter'. With three different passports and three different identities in my bag.

I did wonder whether that was overkill. And had told Nicos so. His response was that I either trusted him or did not. He explained there were over four hundred CCTV cameras at Gatwick Airport, but they were monitored by just three operators. It wasn't easy to track someone's movements across the airport's two terminals – North and South – and it would be harder still if the target kept changing ID.

It was for the same reason he'd given me three passports. When Roy realized I had gone missing – properly missing rather than just not coming home – the airports would be checked – along with all the ferry ports and much else. The more I obfuscated, the less chance he would have of figuring anything out.

It was the reason Nicos had insisted I left my car in the short-term car park, to confuse Roy further. I guess, from knowing his methods, he'd start by applying the ABC rule. Assume nothing, Believe no one, Check everything.

So he would not assume it was necessarily me who had driven my car there. He would check the CCTV, but there was no guarantee he would see me leaving the car park and entering the airport. After that point, with all my rapid costume changes, it would make it even harder. And if he got as far as checking my name on any flights out, he wouldn't find it.

Nicos was smart. He really was.

Right now, I'm aware of how much he helped me escape from a marriage that was probably doomed. But more, much more, he helped me escape a killer who I owed money to.

And almost seamlessly.

Another text pings in. It's from Nicos.

Car picking up 8am tomorrow. Private jet flying us from Biggin Hill. Be ready for some sea and sunshine! XXX

40

I read and re-read that text. *XXX*

Previously there had just been an X. Now it was *XXX*.

But actually, sitting in my lonely room that evening, after being upset by our brief and cold conversation, I felt good about that sign-off. *XXX*.

Good, because despite his periods of coldness, it felt, seeing this, that there was affection in that sign-off.

Was that how he viewed me? Was that why he had done all this for me, because he fancied me? I could live with that, right now, I really could. I'd liked him the moment I first saw him and much though I was now angry with him – in part – I knew I was beholden to him and I had the sense that our immediate futures were at least linked, if not entwined. And tomorrow we were out of here. That felt good.

It probably sounds crazy, but despite Hans-Jürgen's strange warning I really did want to trust implicitly this person I barely knew. There was something about him that gave me confidence. Perhaps a combination of his background, his moral stance over drugs, which I totally got, and the way he was with me. If he had once put his arms around me and pulled me to him and kissed me, I would have kissed him back. But he hadn't.

He told me the best way to disappear would be to hide in plain sight, playing the long game, while over the next few days my Roy and other police officers did their thing of looking for me.

Alerts at all ports. That kind of stuff, and all the time I was just twenty miles from home. Hiding out in a room overlooking fields and a beautiful lake, having long but infrequent chats with Hans-Jürgen Waldinger about pretty much every topic except Scientology.

I had a lot of time to think during this past twenty-four hours of my incarceration in that room. On Hans-Jürgen's advice, to avoid my getting caught up in any awkward conversations with other people there, or being recognized, because my face was now on television, I only left it to go down to meals with him. I could have read more, but the only books on my shelves were about Scientology and I wasn't into religion of any kind.

Growing up with parents who were devout Lutherans – more my mother, but my dad went along with it – had made me stay away from religion as much as possible. And I cringed watching my father comply; he was so bloody weak he would bend if a fly farted on him.

Maybe my hosts, the Scientologists, had answers but I wasn't in any mental state to study anything or to concentrate on anything. Most of my time I just sat, nervous whenever I heard footsteps come along the corridor. Scared it would somehow be Albazi.

This morning, Hans-Jürgen brought me a copy of today's *Argus* newspaper. I couldn't believe it, but there was a photograph of Old Me on the front page. Beneath a bold headline: FEARS GROW FOR DETECTIVE'S MISSING WIFE.

I read the story beneath. It really was about me, about Old Me, about someone who used to be called Sandy Grace. About when I was last seen, my last purchases of paracetamol, toothpaste and petrol. My car found abandoned in the short-term car park at Gatwick South.

'*Sandy had not boarded any flight,*' Roy was quoted as saying at a press conference. My plan had worked.

He then went on to say, '*When I last saw my wife, at 7.30 a.m. yesterday, she was in a happy mood and looking forward to going out to celebrate my birthday that evening. I'm not able to speculate what might have happened to her, but I have grave concerns she may have been abducted and is in great danger.*' He looked so visibly upset and that was hard for me to see.

A text pinged in. It was from Nicos.

U awake? Hope they're looking after you. You should be safe now. The Biggin Hill diversion is in place. XXX

Three XXXs again. That didn't escape me.

But I was confused by what he meant. What Biggin Hill diversion?

41

At 6.30 a.m., Roel Albazi drove his ageing black Range Rover, which was on cloned plates, out of the small parking area beneath the apartment building. He drove carefully, although he had a false driving licence corresponding to the registered keeper of this car, well aware that he had been on the local police radar for some while. He had recently been interviewed under caution in connection with loan sharking, during which he had been asked about his association with Joe Karter and Skender Sharka. He had successfully – at least so he thought – convinced the police that he did not do business with either and had no idea of their whereabouts.

Tall Joe sat behind him and Skender Sharka's huge bulk filled the front passenger seat, his knees pressing against the glove locker. Inside the locker was Albazi's Glock 17, its magazine filled with seventeen 9mm soft-nose bullets.

He hoped he wasn't going to have to use it, but he was so angry this morning that he was fully prepared to. Against Nicos, against Tall Joe's pilot friend, and against that bitch Sandy Grace, if it came to it.

All three of them in the car were in a bad mood, not helped by an Albanian folk song blasting at them in all directions from the massive speakers, a woman's voice wailing a lament accompanied by hard twangs from guitar strings.

As they drove up the ramp, Sharka leaned forward, reaching for the sound system's volume control.

'Don't fucking touch it!' Albazi said.

'It's hurting my ears, boss.'

Waiting for the garage doors to rise, Albazi held two clenched fists in the air. 'This is my music, OK? This gives me strength! This gives me what I need to think, understand?'

'OK, boss, OK!'

'I don't think you two understand shit,' Albazi said, accelerating up the ramp and out into the early morning light, turning right, following the arrow of the satnav, which had Biggin Hill Airport as its destination. 'This is my music, OK? This is my soul!'

He drove in silence for several minutes, all three of them in the vehicle nursing god-awful hangovers, which Tall Joe's fried breakfast for the three of them, half an hour ago, accompanied by some very strong coffee, had done just a little to alleviate.

'What I'm not understanding, boss,' Sharka said, 'is your plan.'

'The plan is to get my client's money back. Any part of that you don't understand?' Albazi fired.

'Quite a lot.'

'You're not understanding my plan?' Albazi challenged.

'That's right, boss.'

'Maybe that's because I don't have a fucking plan, all right? I just know the bitch and the Greek are going to be at Biggin Hill for a 10 a.m. flight and we are going to be two miles from it, on the only road they can take there, by 8 a.m. At some point, Sandy Grace and I are going to be having a quiet little chat, during which I'm going to tell her that the Border Force officers here and in Valencia will be very interested in knowing that she travels under two different names, and the best way to stop that happening will be to pony up the money she owes Song Wu.'

Opposite Shoreham Harbour, Albazi turned left into Boundary Road, which was residential for a quarter of a mile and then was lined on both sides with shops. Heading up a gradient, towards a level crossing, the light turned from green to amber.

PETER JAMES

'Shit!' He floored the accelerator and the Range Rover powered forwards, bumping over the rail tracks just at the light turned red. Albazi, feeling in a reckless mood, kept the accelerator floored, the speedometer crossing 70mph. It was a 30mph limit but at this hour he was sure there wouldn't be any police around.

They were approaching the junction with the Old Shoreham Road, the traffic lights there green also.

80mph.

He was a good two hundred yards from the lights, when they turned amber. He kept going.

'Boss!' yelled Sharka, alarmed.

Ignoring him, Albazi crossed the line to enter the junction on red, and shot safely over to the other side.

'We got plenty of time to make it to the airport, boss,' Sharka said. 'Our ETA right now is 7.25.'

But Albazi barely heard him. He was focused on his rear-view mirror. On the blue flashing lights that had suddenly appeared in it.

42

Another thirty minutes and Tom Miller would have ended his long night shift, with four rest days ahead to look forward to. He planned to spend as much of them as possible with his fiancée, Steph, watching *Grand Designs* episodes that they'd recorded on television and traipsing around DIY stores, getting ideas for their new home together – a bargain, if something of a doer-upper, close to the station in Worthing.

Single-crewed, due to his regular partner calling in sick, the twenty-eight-year-old traffic officer had just finished booking a lorry for speeding along New Church Road, and was about to make a right turn up towards the Old Shoreham Road and the fast route back to base, when he saw the kind of driving he hated. An old model Range Rover with blacked-out windows barrelling past, way, way over the speed limit – recklessly over it – towards the junction with the Old Shoreham Road.

He pulled out after it, and saw, to his horror, that it was approaching traffic lights that were on amber, and then red, far too fast to stop, and held his breath as it ran them, straight across four lanes of traffic that was mercifully light at this still early hour.

Moron! he thought. He could have just let it go and headed back to base at Arundel, logged his car mileage, signed off and headed home to Steph. Just one more asshole and one more accident waiting to happen, but he wasn't that kind of police officer. He couldn't let anything go, ever, when it came to idiotic driving. He switched on his blues and twos, slowed as he approached the red lights, saw a clear gap in the traffic and floored the accelerator of the marked BMW estate, immediately switching off his siren as he entered the wide residential road on the far side, conscious that many people would still be sleeping.

As he closed the gap to the Range Rover, he flashed his head-lights once, then again. The vehicle in front seemed to hesitate for a moment and Miller felt himself hoping this would turn into a pursuit. *Go on, punk, make my day!*

He gave the driver another flash of his headlights, then a clear *whup whup* of his siren. The vehicle showed no sign of stopping and the man in the rear kept looking back at him, then seemingly saying something to the two men in the front.

The vehicle's left indicator began blinking, then a brake light came on. Just one brake light. *Great*, Miller thought. *Got you on that, too!*

The Range Rover stopped in front of a row of semi-detached houses on the wide road. He pulled up directly behind it and, leaving his blue lights flashing, climbed out, tugging on his white hat. The men in the vehicle seemed to be acting suspiciously but he couldn't see exactly what they were doing.

As he reached the driver's door, the illegal, heavily tinted window slid down. He saw a man behind the wheel who looked Eastern European, stocky and squat, with a shaven head, a pencil-thin Fu Manchu moustache, and adorned in bling. The kind of thuggish look Tom had come to associate, unfairly he was sure, with old model Range Rovers. But particularly with ones that had lowered suspension and their windows blacked out heavily. The driver might as well have had VILLAIN tattooed across his forehead.

'Good morning, officer!' he said with a slight accent, all charm, flashing a smile full of expensive dentistry.

'Are you in a hurry, sir?' The police officer took a closer look at the enormous guy next to him and the Sumo wrestler clone on the back seat and none of this looked good to him. One of the things you learned in the Roads Policing Unit was profiling vehicles. Did the occupants match the vehicle they were in? And the faces of all three characters were ringing a faint bell. He was sure he had seen them in a recent briefing, when Persons of Interest were flagged.

'The light was amber, officer,' the driver said.

'It was, sir, yes, at least fifteen seconds before you reached the junction and went over on red. Are you the owner of this vehicle?'

'I am.'

'Can you tell me the registration number?'

Albazi reeled it off, a touch too smugly for Miller's liking. As the man spoke, he clocked the alcohol on his breath, but for a moment said nothing. Instead he took a couple of paces back, radioed in the number and asked for a PNC check. Then he asked the driver, 'Have you been drinking, sir?'

'Oh sure, like it's 6.45 in the morning. Doesn't everyone wake up and have a stiff drink?' Albazi grinned broadly.

'I would hope not, sir,' Tom replied. 'Especially if they're getting behind the wheel of a car.'

'Yeah, well, me and the boys had a couple of beers last night. But that was all. May I ask why you've stopped us?'

'You failed to stop at a red light and you also have a defective brake light, sir. In case you are not aware, some of the worst road traffic injuries occur when a vehicle is T-boned, which is the kind of accident running a traffic light causes.'

As he spoke, he was looking at the satnav screen on the Range Rover's dash. It showed Biggin Hill as the destination, which further increased his suspicion about these characters. Had he stumbled across drug smugglers? 'In a hurry to leave the country, are you? Or are you just plane spotters?'

Moments later, Tom received a radio call. He walked away from the vehicle until he was out of earshot.

The control room operator said, 'Tom, the index you've given me for this vehicle shows it was written off following an accident three months ago.'

'What's the name of the registered keeper?' Miller asked, his suspicions now confirmed.

'It's registered to a Guy Rolliston, with an address in Sheffield.' Thinking fast, the PC thanked her. He could see all three occupants of the car looking at him and it made him feel increasingly uncomfortable – and wary. Something was wrong. Instead of asking her to call for backup, and risk being lip-read, he put on a broad smile while secretly pressing the emergency button on his radio phone. Then, as he walked back to the driver's door of the Range Rover, he discreetly requested backup.

'Can you tell me your name, please, sir?' Tom asked calmly, trying not to show any real concern.

'Guy – Guy Rolliston.'

'May I see your licence, Mr Rolliston?'

'Of course.'

Tom Miller struggled to think that anyone could have sounded – or looked – less like a Guy Rolliston than this shady-looking character behind the wheel. Guy Rolliston sounded like the name of an accountant. He took the slim, pink card, looked at the photograph and carefully examined it, studying the name and date of birth. He was playing for time and trying not to let it show. Backup could be anywhere from a couple of minutes to half an hour away, depending on where any vehicles were located. But, despite being nervous, he decided to press on with his gambit. An intermittent stream of vehicles passed. He thought it unlikely he would be assaulted here in broad daylight on a main road.

'Mr Rolliston, I have reason to believe you may be driving under the influence of alcohol and I require you to take a breath test. Would you please step out of your vehicle.'

Miller produced a breathalyser from the tailgate of his BMW, assembled a fresh tube in front of Albazi and stood next to him while he blew into it. Moments later the indicator turned red. He showed it to Albazi, then said, 'I'm sorry to tell you, sir, you have failed the test. I'm arresting you on suspicion of driving while under the influence of alcohol and I will be taking you to the Brighton custody centre where you will be given the opportunity of a second test.'

'What the fuck?' Albazi shouted at him. 'I've not drunk since last night!'

There was a moment of stand-off while they eyeballed each other. The police officer braced himself to deal with a headbutt from the driver, which he sensed might be imminent. Then to his surprise the man's body language turned less aggressive, almost compliant. Miller cuffed him and led him to the BMW. Just as he was pushing his head down, his prisoner shouted to the big guy in the front seat of the Range Rover, 'You know what you have to do?'

'Yes, boss.'

Miller turned to him. 'I hope your pal isn't thinking of driving your Range Rover, even if he is insured. This vehicle has a malfunctioning brake light and the front windows are darker than the legal limit. This vehicle cannot be driven until both defects are rectified.'

'We have important business!' Albazi shouted in frustration from the rear of the police car. 'You need to understand!'

'Need to understand what, exactly?'

'I thought you were a police officer,' Albazi said. 'Not a comedian.'

'So how exactly are we supposed to get home?' the short, very fat guy in the back asked.

PETER JAMES

'You are on a bus route, sir. If you choose to get in a vehicle with clearly illegal blackout windows – and with a driver who has been drinking – then I'm afraid that's your problem. What's your name?'

'Freddie Mercury.'

'And your mate is Brian May, right?'

'Yeah!' Tall Joe said. 'How did you guess?'

'I'm psychic – I have the *gift*.'

Miller returned to his vehicle and slammed the rear door shut on Albazi, trapping him as the child locks were always on, then turned to see both men standing by the Range Rover, one even taller than he had looked, the other short, a tiny head on top of a swollen body, like something out of one of those old Michelin Man adverts, he thought.

They were both looking around in near panic, as the wail of sirens howled above the din of the passing traffic.

'So Biggin Hill, eh?' the traffic officer said. 'Quite an historic airport – Second World War aviation is one of my passions. Four hundred and fifty-three pilots and ground crew died at Biggin Hill during the war – did you know that?'

Skender Sharka and Tall Joe stared at him as if he was insane.

'But between them all they shot down one thousand, four hundred German aircraft. Not bad, eh?'

There were headlights and blue lights coming towards them, from two directions now.

'Think about it,' Tom Miller went on. 'If it hadn't been for those brave pilots at Biggin Hill, we might all be speaking German right now. Maybe it wouldn't be so bad, eh? German is a nice language. *Mein Fahrer wurde festgenommen.* Sounds a lot nicer than *my driver has just been arrested*, don't you think?'

166

43

Just when I'd been getting really excited about leaving this place and jetting off, Nicos had called. All bets were off, I needed to stay where I was. He would explain when he was back in the country later in the week.

And this morning, the headlines of the online *Argus* shouted at me.

'EVIL' FINANCIAL EXTORTION GANG BUSTED

Below was a reassuring quote from Detective Inspector Roy Grace. '*I can confirm that, after months of intelligence work in partnership with the National Crime Agency, we have now arrested the suspected ringleaders, Roel Albazi, Skender Sharka and Joseph Karter, of what I can only call an evil gang of predatory lenders.*'

It was such a good feeling, after the weirdness of my confinement, where every sound of footsteps along the corridor outside my room filled me with dread that there would be a rap on the door from Roy, or Roel Albazi, to be feeling a little safer.

When Nicos finally came to visit, later in the week, he explained the whole plan – for us to fly out from Biggin Hill – had been a bluff to flush out his regular private pilot, who he suspected – correctly it seemed – of being a complete slimeball, and taking a bung from Albazi.

I showed the piece to Nicos and he just smiled like *I told you so*.

He then made it clear that there wasn't going to be any private jet trip to the sun anytime soon. Albazi was in police custody and likely to be charged, but unless he was considered a serious flight risk, he would almost certainly be released on bail, with his trial many months away. Many months in which he would be free to come after me.

Nicos told me he had business overseas and that I should stay here, in this safe haven, until after my baby was born, and then I could move on, somewhere abroad with him, to my – our – new life.

It was strange. I felt trapped by my circumstances, yet free at the same time. I had nothing to worry about other than the nagging fear of Albazi appearing. But at least I was surrounded by caring people who I knew would protect me, and I busied myself doing everything a dutiful mother-to-be should. And I promised my unborn child I would be the best mother it could possibly have. The best mother in the world.

44

March 2008

I spent the next eight months of my confinement, as the Victorians would have called it, at the Scientologists' HQ, during which time I gave birth to my baby son. I didn't gamble once in all this time, not even with scratch cards, nothing. I really felt I was over it. Over my addiction and off the Valium, finally. Maybe it was my hormones, all changed now I was in mother mode. Whatever, it felt great, as if I'd managed to prise a monkey off my back.

That day my son was born was truly one of the very best days of my life. I cried with happiness, holding my beautiful baby in my arms. Less than a week later was another of the best days of my life, when I read that Roel Albazi had been sentenced to fifteen years in prison.

I was well cared for, and for perhaps the only time in my life, I actually felt almost carefree, apart from just one nagging worry.

Strapped into the plush, mushroom-coloured leather seat of the jet, I was feeling oh so safe! I was aware of the wheels bumping along the tarmac beneath us as we taxied. My baby, fast asleep in his carrycot on the seat beside me, did not stir. So far, he was an amazing baby, defying all the stuff I'd read online about what a nightmare these little people could be.

But I knew it was still early doors . . .

And that nagging worry persisted. Would Roy find me? And what would happen when he did?

Nicos had collected me from the Scientology HQ at 8 a.m., in a chauffeur-driven black Bentley. Hans-Jürgen had escorted me down to the front entrance and it was strange, because there was a lot I'd wanted to say to him during the past months – so much, in fact – about what he had meant about Nicos, about why he himself was really here, why he was leaving the Scientologists and what he planned to do when he returned to Munich, but I was feeling fragile, and scared, and Hans-Jürgen, all in clinical white, walking in silence, hair flopping around his face, looking every inch a man on a mission, hadn't been doing anything to improve my mood.

But then, as he held the rear door of the car open for me, just before I climbed in, he said, 'If you are ever in Munich – *München*, *ja*? – give me a call, remember what I said.' He pressed a card into my hand.

Nicos was sitting up front, next to the driver, shouting into his phone in Greek at someone, and acknowledged me with a single waggle of his free hand. For the entire journey through the rush-hour traffic, which took about ninety minutes, Nicos made call after call, never once turning to look at me or my baby. On one call he spoke Spanish, then on another a language I did not recognize, but could have been Russian, then Greek again, then French, I was pretty sure. The common denominator between them all was his angry voice. He was sounding mightily pissed off with everyone he spoke to.

But that was his style, his negotiating voice, his language, in whatever actual language he was speaking. The only language the low-life shitbags he did business with understood.

But now, finally, in the plush interior of the Cessna Citation jet, seated across the aisle from him, I saw a whole new Nicos. Kind, sweet Nicos. The concerned, caring man I had met just months ago in the casino, who had facilitated my escape from my old life, but who I barely knew. I'd only seen him a handful of times since.

He reached out and took my free hand and squeezed it gently, as the aircraft began to accelerate. My baby gurgled.

My stomach felt as if it was being pressed into my seat back. The bumping intensified for a few moments then stopped completely. Through my window I saw the ground dropping away. Roads, fields, houses, turning to miniature versions of themselves, turning to Toytown. It felt like we were climbing almost vertically. I saw wisps of cloud, then more cloud, then it all went grey outside the window.

Nicos kept his grip on my hand as we continued climbing. Then as we broke out through the cloud cover into glorious sunshine, he leaned towards me, put an arm gently around my neck and pulled me towards him. Closer, then closer.

Then our lips touched.

He kissed me. Then he kissed me again, with more intensity.

We were still kissing five minutes later.

Finally he broke gently away. 'How you feeling?' he asked.

'Oh, you know, pretty average.'

'Me too,' he said.

'Where are we actually going?' I asked. Not that I really cared. Right now anywhere, absolutely anywhere at all, was good with me.

'Jersey,' Nicos said. 'In the Channel Islands. You'll like it there. It's cool.'

My son gurgled again. It sounded like he approved.

45

Jersey, Channel Islands, 2011

My beautiful golden-haired boy, who is three and is going to be so handsome, is my best friend on this little, beautiful rock, just nine miles by five in size. He's the one constant and reliable thing in my messed-up life. Sometimes I wonder who is looking after who because without him I would be nothing. He's what I live for now and the reason I am not already dead from the drugs I'm now dependent on.

It's ironic. I was once a gambling addict and managed to get that out of my system, and now I'm a drug addict. How did it get to be like this? I used to manage my anxiety with tranquillizers like Valium. But that was under control to some extent, or maybe it wasn't. So much has changed. So much can't be retracted. So much I wish I'd done differently – or never done at all.

He has a German name, my son. Bruno. My insistence. I had wanted to put down roots after leaving England, and those roots, I felt, from my maternal side, were German. Nicos was fine with that. He was fine with pretty much everything, because he had me trapped. Coercive control I think they call it.

The person who helped me escape from my perceived hell was now the person who had me trapped in a worse hell. He did it oh so subtly and over time. He knew my weaknesses and he played on them. First the Valium, which to be fair I'd wanted and needed, he had obtained for me to my delight and relief. But then some-where along the line it changed. Heroin. Me, Sandy Grace, hooked on heroin. How did that happen? Here I was, shaking and begging for the next hit. And there he was, the man in control of it all – in control of when my next hit came. I am under the spell of the man I thought was my saviour, the man I was in love with, and there is no way out that I can see.

I try to think back to how it happened and when I do, my memory gets all hazy. Nicos had friends here who threw wild parties in their massive houses, with weed and lines of coke galore, and in those early days on this island I went along to them happily, loving meeting all these characters who seemed genuinely to like him – and me. Nicos knew all the best and fun places to go, restaurants that were hidden treasures, like Green Island, and bars, like the speakeasy the Blind Pig. And I loved the coke. One day – I can't remember exactly when, but I must have already been off my face on something – Nicos convinced me to start trying heroin. He said it was only addictive if you let it be. And stupid me, who trusted him then, who loved him crazily then, believed him.

This is my life now. I can't remember when I last did any real exercise, and I can't give Bruno the love and attention he needs even though I so desperately want to. I let him get away with everything because I just don't have the energy to fight it, or I'm too out of it. My screwed-up brain tells me it's wrong. I know I'm creating difficulties down the line – spoiling him, I guess. I never knew it could be this hard to be a mother. Even a rubbish mother like me.

And, if things could be any worse, I still do not know who his father is.

I had thought back then, in those final weeks before I left Roy, that I would find everything I wanted in my new life – not that I knew what exactly I did want. And four years on, I still don't. All I know at this moment is that I don't want the life I'm now living. It feels at times that I'm a parasite inhabiting someone else's life, not mine. Or is it a cuckoo that does that? I often feel I'm being mocked or punished for turning my back on what I had, for failing to realize when it was good.

Sure, on the surface, my life appears pretty glam now.

We live in a cool penthouse apartment, with curved windows overlooking a beautiful bay, St Aubin, to the west of Jersey's only town, St Helier. Nicos has a very flash powerboat that we had some fun times on, in those early days, visiting all the neighbouring islands like Sark, Alderney, Herm and of course Guernsey – where he did a lot of business – as well as pounding the waves over to Saint-Malo and Carteret in France. And sometimes on a fine summer's day we would take a picnic and a bottle of rosé and just cruise around a section of Jersey's stunning, craggy coastline, dropping anchor in an empty bay and swimming in the sea, which was often crystal clear but always a little bracing.

I learned that Nicos had chosen Jersey as his base long before I met him. Demand is constant and the profit margins are huge, mainly because the street value of drugs here in the Channel Islands is four times higher than on the British mainland. And there are no organized drug gangs vying for their share of the market. He owns a string of nail salons here and in Guernsey, as well as on the mainland – all cash businesses that are, so he had told me repeatedly, perfect for money laundering.

I went along with all his shit because I had no choice in the spiral I'd got into. But I'm not so far gone that I can't scheme and plan.

And dream.

God, how many times have I thought back to my life with Roy? Never in all the years I was with him had I been afraid of what mood he would be in when he walked in through the front door, regardless of whether he had been drinking – which was rare – or after something at work hadn't gone his way – which was a lot of the time. He was always calm and gentle and caring.

I'm scared every time Nicos comes home.

He constantly uses the power he has over me. He never lets me forget that all he needs to do is make just one phone call to blow everything for me. To taunt me, during our worst rows, he holds his phone up to my face and shows me Roy's private mobile number programmed into his speed-dial. And he taps it with an immaculately manicured nail.

One perk of being here, I have to admit, is that I do genuinely love this island that I now call home. I made some really nice friends soon after we'd first arrived, but my drug addiction has taken its toll on my reliability. To the point where I've lost all interest in everything but my new best friend. Heroin.

Horse, Nicos calls it.

And the worst thing of all is that much of the time I really don't care about anything else.

There isn't any feeling in the world like those immediate minutes after a hit. I feel so powerful, so profoundly happy, so on top of the world. Everything seems possible and everything looks so rich, so intense, so vibrant.

When I piss him off, which is often, because he tries to mess with my head all the time and I'm not so far gone I can't fight back, he simply withholds my next fix.

Those magical first few months after we'd arrived in Jersey were like an extended honeymoon. We were deeply in love, so I thought. Nicos was travelling constantly and he'd take me everywhere, telling me a day without me wasn't worth living. We went back and forth to Valencia, which I fell in love with, to Colombia, Manila, Bangkok and Taiwan. It was an amazing life of private jets or first-class flights, limousines, huge suites in five-star hotels. Bruno stayed behind in Jersey with a nanny, because Nicos did not want him around. He didn't want to have to share me with anyone, and I was so besotted with him I went along with it.

Part of his negative attitude to Bruno was, he claimed, I'd never told him at the start that I was pregnant – and OK, I guess he was right, I had kept it quiet. All part of the strained mental state I was in. I wasn't even sure, back then, that I'd be able to bring a child into this world. I was hugely stressed by everything and doubted that I would go full term.

When I finally did tell him that I was pregnant, on his first visit to the Scientologists' HQ, he told me he was happy, and it would be *our* baby, *our* child, and he would always love and take care of it. That was just bullshit. *Love* Bruno? More than three years on and he doesn't even like him.

To be fair, he paid the fees at an expensive private nursery school for him, and spoiled him rotten, buying him – in my opinion – far too much pointless designer clothing and ridiculously expensive toys. And Bruno, sensing he was onto a winner here with Nicos, was good as gold with him, a charmer from birth.

I think back often to that first year or so in Jersey, which really was so great. In addition to Nicos's colourful friends, I'd met several mothers at the nursery school, and we all got on brilliantly. I did think at first I might become good friends with two of the mums I met there, one called Alex who had a son Bruno's age, and another, Beth, who had a daughter a few months younger. I had coffee mornings at the Royal Yacht, and the occasional lunch with them at a very elegant restaurant called Quayside and we always had a good laugh. But Alex's husband was a prosecutor – not someone I figured Nicos would be too happy to meet, and Beth's was a teacher – who I met briefly and decided Nicos would have zero in common with.

But I spiralled more and more into a chaotic state as the heroin took increasing hold of me. And my new friends – part of the new life I had been building, began to move away, dropping me one by one – so subtly I barely noticed it was happening. My calls stopped being returned, my Facebook messages were getting fewer and fewer *likes*. Also, and I wasn't aware of this at the time, but I realize it now, looking back, Nicos must have been systematically deleting text and voicemail messages from my phone when I was out of it.

So we live a pretty insular life now. One thing that amuses Nicos is that a senior police officer lives directly beneath us. On some evenings, Nicos could have flicked cigar ash onto his head. 'He'd die, wouldn't he?' Nicos would say, with a big grin. 'He'd just fucking die if he knew who this guy living above him really was!'

Sometimes I'm tempted to go down one floor and knock on the police officer's door and tell him and end this hell.

One day soon I think I will.

46

Love and hate. Extreme emotions so far apart, yet so much closer than we are aware. They evoke such strong feelings that they can blur your vision – not what you can see just with your eyes, but with your mind too – until you can no longer distinguish the boundary between them. That's how living with Nicos was making me feel.

Love and hate come from the same place deep in our hearts. And in my relationship with Nicos the darkness and the light lived side by side in a kind of increasingly uneasy and volatile alliance.

It was about 11 p.m., I was on the sofa with a glass of white wine, watching a documentary on television – well, watching through my right eye, my left one was almost closed and I could barely see anything through it. I was praying that eye wasn't permanently damaged. Yesterday Nicos had got mad at me. Why? Because I wouldn't let him punish Bruno for throwing a tantrum and breaking a bottle of wine. Bruno hadn't wanted to go to bed – a frequent occurrence – and in his fury accidentally knocked a bottle of red wine off the breakfast bar – admittedly an expensive one – which smashed on the floor, spraying its contents all over part of Nicos's precious white carpet.

This changes things for me. Nicos crossed a threshold, hitting me for the first time. And I am more and more concerned with his anger towards Bruno. I know he could hurt him. He's been punishing him almost daily for just about anything that annoys him – like leaving his socks in the living room, or not putting away his toy cars, or not taking his shoes off after coming in from outside. Bruno is too young, how would he know to do that, for goodness' sake?

Nicos often yells at him now, and raises his hand as if to slap him. I see Bruno cowering. I scream at Nicos, and tell him to stop. But calm as a summer breeze, he just grabs hold of me, asserting his power. The look he gives me is intense, terrifying. And always he knows he holds the ultimate trump card. My drugs. My anonymity. He has me just where he wants me. Dependent, in so many ways. Much to my disgust – or is it self-loathing?

I can feel it all escalating, I think he will hit Bruno soon.

And when he does I will—

Oh God.

I'm crying again. Crying myself to sleep. *To sleep perchance to dream.* I'm thinking about that quote from *Hamlet. In this sleep of death what dreams may come?*

For me, it's so often the same dream. I'm with Roy. He is smiling, holding me, so glad that I am back. I feel so intensely happy.

Then I wake and Nicos, stinking of cigars, is lying beside me, drunk and snoring.

47

Jersey, Channel Islands, 2011

There is so much I miss about Roy in these increasingly hellish days with Nicos. I'm missing him more and starting to regret increasingly what I've done. One thing I miss especially is Roy's kind nature. He would never treat a child or anyone in this way.

He would have made a good father, a truly fine one. He'd have instilled good values into Bruno, such as plain decency. What was Bruno learning from Nicos, other than fear and violence? And from pathetic me? Nothing. Last night I'd had enough, and snapped. I'd yelled at Nicos not to touch my son, and I now had a painful shiner of a black eye to show for it.

I'll dodge the question if anyone asks about it – I'll say I'm fine, that it was a genuine accident, I walked into a cupboard door. I guess because I am still terrified that Nicos will carry out his threat and tell Roy about me. Tell him the truth.

I would love to find a job just to get out of the flat, but Nicos won't hear of it. Sometimes I try to argue but I am scared – scared about what he is capable of. The increasing violence. Especially when he drinks, he is very angry and doesn't know his own strength. But there is the other reason I'm scared of him, too. Thanks to my blindness in seeing it coming and Nicos's clever manipulation, I'm so heavily addicted to heroin and sometimes cocaine – as well as alcohol – that I'm totally dependent on him.

I realize now that the wild social life he threw me into when I first arrived on this island was all for a reason. To help him worm his way more into Jersey society through his charitable donations – and in doing so increase his contacts for his core business of drugs. When he met me in the casino he was looking for someone just like me and I fell for it.

It makes me so sad to look in a mirror now at the clothes I'm wearing, which Nicos bought me and insists I wear. Baggy tops and trousers to hide my weight loss and my bruises, the track marks, the damage to my veins. My face shows how drawn the drugs have made me, my sallow skin, which was once so rosy. I think how good I have got at using make-up as a disguise, but underneath it all I am crumbling. I hide myself away and barely see anyone.

And yet, despite all the attempts Nicos has made to break me, he has still not yet broken my spirit. There is still a little bit left inside, a corner of me that he hasn't yet got to, that tells me I have to get out of this dangerous cycle of addiction.

I owe it to myself and to my son.

This week I read a piece on drug addiction in the *Jersey Evening Post* that could've been written just for me. It was about a doctor called Deryn Doyle who runs a clinic helping addicts. It got me thinking more clearly than I had done in a while. If I could speak to her and get some help, secretly without Nicos knowing, maybe I could get off this drug dependency – and with that, out of this relationship.

In my more lucid moments, I think, *What relationship?*

Our relationship has gone from lovers to adversarial strangers, held together by a bond.

He supplies my drugs – holding back if I annoy him until I am desperate and pleading with him – and in return I play the role of the loving, always-smiling, presentable partner he could take on his arm to a cocktail party at Government House or to a fundraising ball for the hospice, or the Shelter Trust, or any of the numerous other high-profile charities he has managed to attach himself to.

He certainly won't imagine I could get myself off the drugs – and that gives me all the more determination to do it. It's not about proving him wrong, it's about self-preservation. I am *almost* ready to do it. I will book to see Dr Doyle, and then after a few more hits, maybe I will be free of this. Please God.

I know in all honesty I have tried and failed coming off the drugs recently, but it seems through Dr Doyle's clinic I may have access to some help. Addicts can be cured, can't they? 'Clean', they call it. I want just two things right now. The first is to be clean. The second is for Nicos to have no idea that I am.

He was out at a meeting tonight and I was glad about that. Four years ago I'd been crazy about him and now I hated him so much I could hardly bear to be in the same room. I can't stand him touching me. Recently sex with him had pretty much stopped – coinciding with the day, three months ago, I started noticing the smell of a perfume on him that definitely was not his own.

He had 'meetings' three nights a week and would never say anything about with whom or what it was about. I had long stopped bothering to ask, it just made him angry when I did. *It's a meeting, right?* he would snap. *A business meeting, some-one has to earn the money to keep your little bastard at school.*

The programme I was watching, when the front door crashed open, was a documentary on the Colombian drug cartels, focusing in particular on a monster called Pablo Escobar. Nicos had dropped his name casually on a few occasions, like they'd been good mates. In his dreams. And yet I could see them being two fish in the same seas, except that Nicos was, rela-tively, a wannabe minnow and Escobar had been a Great White shark.

There was a time when, at the sound of Nicos coming home, no matter how late, I would have jumped up and thrown my arms around him. Now I looked up anxiously.

That was the time when he would have run over to me and thrown his arms around me.

A time long past.

'Where the fuck did you get that wine?' was his opening gambit.

'From the fridge.'

'So why didn't you put it back in to keep it cold?'

It was a fair point. The half-full bottle was sitting on top of the breakfast bar. Nicos was right, I should have put it back into the wine fridge that was built into the bar. But the truth was I was drinking it so quickly, I didn't have to worry about it getting warm. I was celebrating my future, when the drugs became just a part of my past, part of life's rich tapestry. Granted, I hadn't got there yet but at least I was thinking about it and that was worth a celebration.

He was drunk and furious. A dangerous combination, and a regular one.

He peered at the bottle. 'Can't you read, woman? Are you illiterate or something? This was on the bottom shelf of the fridge, which I told you never to touch.' He held the label in front of my face.

Chassagne Montrachet 1997, I noted. I knew I shouldn't have said it, but I couldn't help it, I was drunk myself and angry – more angry than scared at this moment. 'It's old, so I thought I'd better drink it before it was past its best before date,' I replied.

'You stupid bitch.'

That was the last thing I remember hearing before my hair felt like it was being wrenched out of the top of my head.

My next memory was waking up, feeling dizzy, with a blinder of a headache, and looking at my watch. The back of my head felt sticky.

Sticky with blood.

It was 3 a.m. I was lying on my back on the kitchen floor,

bleeding from the back of my head. When I see Nicos come over to me the first thing I think is that he's there to comfort me, to take away the pain. Instead, he injects me with a hit of heroin.

And weirdly, I'm grateful.

48

Jersey, Channel Islands, 2011

I can't even remember when it was that my pity had turned to hate but I truly hated Nicos. He'd lost his wife and kids. That's got to have a massive impact on anyone's psyche, so for a while I tried really hard to feel something for him. He had shown me kindness when I needed it, and without him I know I would not have been able to leave my previous life behind without a trace. So I always felt I owed him for turning up at the right time. Sadly, any hope of him loving me in the way I first loved him never came, he played on my weaknesses like the bully he was. The heroin. The threat always hanging over me that he could reveal who I was at any moment. I was putty in his hands. I needed some of the balance of power to swing my way. And it took me a long time to find the strength and the right time to do something about that.

When he started hitting me, I knew there was no going back. I had to get off the heroin and get out. But that is no easy task. Heroin gives that euphoric high that takes me away from all my shit, but the addiction is overbearing. I hate myself for it.

He was raging at Bruno last night, another major incident. Bruno had done nothing wrong. My poor boy was so desperate to get away he fell over, cracking his head on the corner of a glass table so badly I had to get him to A&E at the hospital, where they put in eleven stitches. I couldn't even drive him there as I was drunk and drugged, which makes me so ashamed and I'm sure the taxi driver was judging me.

185

This morning I had woken up more desperate and determined than ever to get off the drugs, to be free from this. I just took a little hit, promising myself it would be one of my last. I'd got good at negotiating with my inner voice about why it was justified this time, and that it would be my last or one of my last, in order to give myself a little way out in case I slipped back or needed another hit. It was 11.32 and I thought Bruno was playing in the room next door. I came round in my drug daze to see him sat opposite me, my needle in one hand, pressing it tentatively against the skin of his opposite arm. My heart literally stopped.

At 11.37 this morning, I vowed to change.

The tipping point. No more drugs. Ever.

Seeing my vulnerable, curious son sitting there with my dirty drugs in his hand. The dirty drugs that Nicos got me hooked on. It couldn't get any lower.

49

Drugs came into Jersey via planes, boats and the mail – fake Amazon parcels being favoured by some dealers. Nicos had a local Customs officer in his pocket, keeping him very sweet indeed with regular payments into a Panamanian bank account.

Panama was one of a decreasing number of countries in the world where you could open a bank account with no questions asked and, equally important, no replies given to questions from prying law enforcement agencies.

Sticking to his strict business maxim of keeping his friends close and his enemies closer, Alan Medcraft was as close as an enemy could be. Having obliged the Customs and Immigration officer by depositing, over the past few years, half a million pounds – and counting – into his Panamanian bank account, Nicos had enough on the guy to have him banged away in La Moye – the island's prison – for much of the rest of the fifty-year-old's active life.

'Symbiotic!' Nicos liked to announce whenever the man was in the apartment. 'Alan and I have a *symbiotic* relationship.'

I think Nicos liked the sound of that word more than he actually understood what it meant. It was typical of the way he behaved generally, using brute reason instead of brute force – except with me, where it was usually the reverse.

He liked to invite Medcraft up to our apartment, and ply him with vintage whiskies and cognacs and fat Cuban cigars – which stank the apartment out for days. Although, to be honest, I didn't mind that. It masked the smell, that seemed to be increasingly common, of the alien female perfume on Nicos. Although the fact that he had a lover – or maybe more than one – was fine by me if it meant he left me alone.

Medcraft was no dormouse. He was a good six foot tall, looked like he worked out, and could have given Nicos a beating if he chose to. He had a shaven head and a sly, slimy smile that said, in my interpretation, *I'm corrupt as fuck. But try proving it!*

He was an invaluable asset to Nicos, giving him intel on any particular operations the Customs and Immigration officers were carrying out, or what area they would be focusing on in the coming weeks. And even more importantly, diverting attention away from Nicos's chosen supply route for his next big consignment. Sometimes that would be a drop from a light aircraft flown over from the south coast of England or the west coast of France, other times it would be a yacht out at sea with which Nicos would rendezvous in his own boat.

He once told me how that worked. He would take a briefcase full of cash, concealed inside a sailing bag, and meet the drugs yacht several miles offshore. Sometimes, Alan Medcraft would have prearranged a major operation on the other side of the island as a distraction.

Nicos had also let slip, whether from bravado, to impress me, or because he was genuinely nervous of them, that the people he met out at sea were not to be messed with. Anyone who crossed them never got a second chance. They were members of a violent Liverpool gang, controlled from his prison cell by its founder, Saul Brignell, who had direct links with one of the Colombian cartels. His gang distributed drugs in major quantities throughout the British Isles, via lorries, boats and helicopters. They boasted that no one who had ever crossed them was still alive.

Then Nicos told me he'd been offered the deal of a lifetime. A consignment of crystal meth, cocaine and heroin, available in a week's time via a rendezvous at sea, with a street value in Jersey, when cut, of around £20 million. The deal was on offer to the first Jersey dealer who could come up with £1.2 million in cash.

Nicos told me he had that money. It was stashed in a secure storage unit near Brighton. But he'd been warned by Alan Medcraft that Jersey Customs and Immigration were mounting a major operation on both the private and commercial airports and the ferry port over the next month, and that he was very much on their radar.

Suddenly, behaving all sweetness and light to me for the first time in many months, Nicos asked me how I would feel about driving to Brighton and fetching the money.

Seriously, £1.2 million?

You have a new name, a new look, no one in the Brighton area is going to recognize you. I give you the security code and the two keys for my locker at the storage depot. You drive over on the ferry in your car – and they won't be interested in you. Alan told me they are not targeting anyone with a Jersey licence plate. Anyone asks you why you're going or why you've been to England – and they won't – you just tell them it was for a funeral.

He hadn't needed to try hard to convince me at all, I would have bitten his hand off for any chance to be away from him for a few days. And what he didn't realize, because he was so wrapped up in his own greedy plans, was that this was perhaps a deal of a lifetime for me. This was my way out. Although I tried my best to look like I really needed to think about it, full of nerves and not in any way enthusiastic.

I had a bright red MX5 which I loved, and the idea of a few days blasting up English roads faster than the 40mph limit here in Jersey filled me with joy. And I was glad to be able to take Bruno with me, and get him away from Nicos.

My potential plan, which still needed some serious thought, was making me feel happy for the first time in a very long while.

One thing worried me: even though I knew I now looked totally different from Old Me, and I had a convincing passport as Sandra Jones, I was still pretty nervous about going anywhere near Brighton, just four years after leaving.

But the opportunity was too good to miss.

And I had that plan – rough, unformed, just a tiny germ at this stage, but a plan nonetheless. The opportunity to escape from Nicos, with Bruno, and start a new life. The gift he had inadvertently given us. People talk about all their Christmases coming at once. It was all my Christmases, all my birthdays and more, so much more.

A new life was something I had been craving even more than my next heroin fix. But as long as I was on heroin I was dependent on Nicos and knew I couldn't leave him. I only had the chance to escape once, so I had to do it well.

And now there was good news on that front – or at least reasonable news. Since meeting with Dr Deryn Doyle, I'd been trying to wean myself off heroin, but the side effects were horrifying. I felt nauseous and vomited a lot, as well as having diarrhoea and agonizing stomach cramps. I constantly felt paranoid and was unable to sleep. I took to drinking more alcohol, but all that did was make my cravings for heroin stronger.

I thought I could come off the drugs through willpower alone, but I couldn't, and now I really needed this to work and to do it without Nicos knowing. I went back to see Dr Doyle and she prescribed methadone, which would take away the craving without giving the amazing high of heroin. And it would also alleviate the withdrawal symptoms.

The journey of a thousand miles begins with the one step, I kept reminding myself. It would be a long, hard fight to freedom, but I had started it. I was on my way.

Through an anxious and uncertain facade, I told Nicos I would do it.

50

It was a very strange feeling, sitting up near the front of the Condor car ferry as we approached Poole harbour on this Sunday afternoon, with the seriously swanky homes of Sandbanks lining the entire waterfront to the right. Some of the most expensive properties in the UK, and anyone with a ferry ticket and a pair of binoculars could peep right into their living rooms – or bedrooms if that was your thing.

They'd have a great view today, on this glorious afternoon, with barely a cloud in the sky.

Suddenly I had a thought. What if I had a pair of binoculars and could stare into Roy's living room right now? What would I see? Four years on?

Would I see him with a new woman?

And if I did, how would I feel about that?

Something twisted deep inside me. I suddenly felt like when I was in need of my next drugs fix. As if all the lights in the universe had been extinguished.

I didn't want to think of it, of Roy with someone else.

But could I blame him?

Did I actually want to wish some kind of curse on him, banishing him to life on his own, a life of celibacy, a life of – what exactly? A life of darkness, of never-ending missing me?

Maybe he'd already forgotten about me?

Maybe if I looked through the window of our house – home

- with those binoculars, I would see him with a beautiful new lady, a couple of kids, playing one of his beloved collection of 45rpm vinyls.

And how would I feel about that, about seeing him happy?

The hollow feeling of dread in the pit of my stomach told me exactly how I would feel.

Bruno, on the seat beside me, was absorbed in a comic. It was a big deal returning to England after all this time. It may not seem a long while to have been away, but it was over three years that I had lived abroad, in Jersey. My car, down on Deck B, was on Jersey plates and Sandra Jones had a Jersey licence.

She had a whole different past to Sandy Grace, too. I'd figured that, even before Nicos had told me to think about it. I was Sandra Jones, from Battersea, London, where I had been working as a receptionist in a large doctors' practice before moving to Jersey to be with my boyfriend, Nicos Christoforou, who worked in the finance industry for a trust company. That was his cover. Half the people on the island seemed to work for trust companies. Just saying the words 'trust company' was a great way to cauterize the trailing ends of any awkward conversation about what he actually did.

The shore was getting closer and larger, the reverse of it shrinking beneath my window when I had left this island on a private jet three years back. And I felt increasingly nervous. What if I got pulled over by a passport officer because they'd spotted an anomaly?

Don't be daft, I told myself. I'd already used the passport on countless trips with Nicos and it had never been questioned. But there was one thing I did need to do. Bruno unintentionally prompted me, 'Mama, I need a peepee.'

I climbed out of my seat, a little unsteady on my legs as the boat rolled in the swell, and gripped the handrail with one hand and Bruno's arm with the other. Then I made my way to the ladies' and locked us in a cubicle.

After Bruno had relieved himself, I took the powder compact out of my handbag, opened the clasp and stared at the contents. The powder. The *horse*. Nicos had given me this, thinking it would be sufficient to get me through the trip.

And, oh God, it was so tempting to keep it, to risk going through Customs with it, just to have a fix when I got to our hotel.

I stared at it.

Hesitating.

But I'd already made my decision. I had to stick to it. Had to. For Bruno. He looks at me so trustingly sometimes, as he did just then. He thinks I'm so much a better person than I really am.

I took a deep breath and tipped the contents down the loo and flushed it while Bruno was distracted. Then we headed back outside and while he washed his hands at one basin I debated whether to wash the powder compact clean, but I decided not to take the risk of leaving any residue, and simply dumped it into a bin.

And it was like a huge weight suddenly floated away.

A couple of minutes later as I sat back down beside Bruno I felt so happy I hugged him. And even the grumpy look he gave me couldn't dent my elation.

51

September 2011

As I drive my little red Mazda down the ramp, into a sunny afternoon, a young woman in a yellow fluorescent jacket signals for me to slow right down to avoid the sports car bottoming out, and I obey. Bruno doesn't notice anything apart from the weird pink monster on his screen, that I can see out of the corner of my eye.

Moments later we are on English soil – well, English *concrete*, technically – in a queue of cars heading for the exit of the ferry port. It feels seriously strange being back in England. Like, I shouldn't be here, that I am a fugitive. Hell, this is my country, I have every right to be here.

Yes, girl, you do. But just don't ignore the shitstorm that awaits you if you're recognized.

Just as I thought that, I realize we are nearing the Customs shed. Two people, also in hi-vis jackets, are seemingly selecting cars at random to make a right turn, past a row of bollards and into the shed. I can feel myself perspiring, although everything is kosher; I wasn't carrying anything to worry about now – well, apart from the methadone I had acquired to get myself clean. But that would be OK, surely. And at least my passport had been well tested over the past three years travelling as Sandra Jones.

To my relief, Bruno and I are ignored and we carry straight on. Two minutes later I am following my satnav screen as it takes me alongside the harbour for a short distance before turning me inland and into the labyrinth of residential streets of Poole, or Bournemouth – I'm not exactly sure where I am. But one thing I am excited about, on this whole weird trip, is being able to hold the three-spoked wheel and put my foot down on the faster roads.

It is such joy when I finally clear the conjoined towns and hit the M27 motorway and just bloody go for it! Third gear up to seventy – then fourth and up to ninety . . .

As I stare ahead, past the bulge in the bonnet, at the horizon hurtling towards me, I'm feeling such an empowering sense of liberation – and elation – and—

Stupidity.

I hit the brakes hard, dropping down to what now seemed a ridiculously slow 70mph. I really do not need to be stopped by the traffic police. But at this moment I am honestly feeling like I'm in a foreign land where the rules don't apply to me. Because, like before, I don't actually exist!

Then suddenly I am scared witless. Blue lights in my mirrors. Instantly, a freezing fog swirling in my stomach and spreading through my veins.

Shit, shit, shit.

Bright headlights now, bright even against this daylight, and strobing blue lights, too. It looks like I've a full-on mobile disco coming up behind me.

I'm gripping the wheel so hard my knuckles are white. My speed is now a rock-steady 67mph. I'm already trying to think of a plausible excuse when they pull me over. So far, I haven't come up with it.

'Faster, Mama!' Bruno commands.

The disco is getting closer by the nanosecond. I hear the siren flailing the air. Those lights and sirens do not give them a right of way – they are merely asking permission to come through, I remind myself.

Not that that is going to help me at this moment unless I pull over and block them. And how stupid would that be?

Then, to my amazement, in a whoosh, accompanied by a howling crescendo, the car has gone past and is already in the distance. It is followed seconds later by a dark, unmarked BMW, blue lights also flashing. Then another.

It takes me some moments to realize I'm fine. The bandits have gone. But all the same I keep my speed to a sensible 75mph – no point *painting the devil on the wall*, as my grandmother used to say. It was an old German expression that I can still remember.

Suddenly, as we pass a large construction site to our left, Bruno yells out excitedly, 'JCB!' Then an instant later, 'Komatsu!' Then after barely pausing for breath, 'Doosan!' He was currently obsessed with diggers and excavators, and his favourite toy was a remote-controlled bulldozer I had got him for his birthday. Bruno switched obsessions every few months. Previously it had been dinosaurs and other prehistoric monsters. Before that, worms. He had jars of the wriggly things in his bedroom.

I was beginning to wonder, privately, if he was on the autism spectrum. Whatever his obsession, it pretty much takes over his life. His entire bedroom had been prehistoric-themed after his worm phase. Now it was digger-themed. Earthworks. Cranes, all kinds of construction site stuff. A tiny bit advanced for such a young boy? Or just the sign of an enquiring mind? Whatever, I couldn't love him any more at this moment. We were a team and away from Nicos. We would be OK with anything life threw at us. I looked at him and felt a huge sense of pride and love.

An hour later, the satnav tells me we are thirty-two minutes from my destination in Shoreham, a few miles west of Brighton.

And Bruno looks up from his screen to tell me he is hungry and that he needs to pee again. Then he shouts out, 'Takeuchi, Mama, Mama!' pointing at a massive digger at the roadside.

I glance at the car's clock, and then my watch, to check it – don't know why I do that, but I always do. It's 5.30 p.m. and I'm very jittery, seeing all this familiar scenery on the A27, on the approach to Chichester, at being this close to Brighton, to Roy, to Albazi even if he is banged up. I realize I need to pee very badly too. But more than that, I've got cramps in my stomach, I'm starting to perspire but I'm feeling cold, like having a chill, but it's not that, I know exactly what's happening. I can feel my heart racing.

There's a sign to a service station. It's coming up now. I'm so frazzled I almost miss the slip road and have to brake hard, cutting in front of another car that flashes me angrily. Then as I approach the pumps and the cluster of buildings beyond, I tug my black baseball cap further down over my forehead. Silly, I'm seriously not recognizable any more, not with my long, wavy red hair and – I guess – with a young boy.

You'd have to be a pretty good detective to link me to the missing Sandy Grace.

52

Seventy miles away from the service station that Sandra Jones had just pulled into, Prisoner Number FF276493 was on a call on his contraband phone in his cell in HMP Belmarsh.

The maximum security prison, in south-east London, a ball-and-chain's lob away from the Thames, had housed in its time some of the UK's most notorious villains, including Great Train Robber Ronnie Biggs, child murderer Ian Huntley, Islamic terrorists and an assortment of other charmers. The author Jeffrey Archer had also once enjoyed its hospitality and so had disgraced former MP Jonathan Aitken.

At 5.50 p.m., Prisoner Number FF276493, in his former life always attired in Armani or Versace, now wore a washed-out pea-green T-shirt, baggy grey tracksuit bottoms and plimsolls, and on his wrist in place of the Breitling was a crappy eighteen-quid watch he bought before coming in. Ending the call, he put the phone back under his pillow, then shuffled from his cell to join a queue of fellow prisoners on his floor of B Wing, to collect his evening meal off the steel trolley.

Anger burning inside him was a constant of Roel Albazi's life now. He peered at the contents of his cardboard tray suspiciously, to make sure it was what he had ordered the previous day and they hadn't given him a bloody vegan pile of crap again, in error. Satisfied, he carried it back to his cell. Two foil containers sat on

198

it, one marked *Shep pie*, the other *Sponge pud/custard*, along with a plastic knife, fork and spoon and a paper cup.

As he had done at this same time for pretty much the last four years, he began the solitary ritual of his evening meal by slouching on the edge of his bunk and placing the tray down on his lap. He peeled the lid off the shepherd's pie, then dug his plastic fork into the potato crust, releasing a whirl of steam.

Although ravenous after a hard workout in the gym, he hungered for something else more important to him than food. Revenge. The desire for it burned away 24/7 in his heart. He was feeling utterly frustrated, helpless and isolated. And uncharacteristically despondent. Everything was crap, constantly crap, and it just seemed to be getting more crap. One of his key contacts on the outside, an Albanian cousin, had stupidly just been busted for drugs.

Normally his hot meals were tepid by the time the trolley had been wheeled over to his wing from the kitchens on the far side of the prison, so when he took his first mouthful, he was startled by the scalding heat of the meat and potato, his tongue instantly frizzing. 'Fuck!' he shouted in anger and hurled the foil container at his cell wall, just a few feet away.

Most of the contents splattered from the container into a mess on the floor, the rest sliding down the sludge-green wall.

'Oh for fuck's sake!' he yelled again, even louder.

'Fuck you!' a voice yelled from a few cells along the wing, then another.

The chorus continued to grow to a crescendo, but he ignored it. He was thinking, as he did endlessly when he wasn't thinking about Sandy Grace, about Song Wu.

Song Wu showed him no leniency. Instead he had messages delivered from her, sometimes by a Chinese fellow-inmate, other times by a prison officer who seemed to revel in it – and was probably in Song Wu's pay, he reckoned. Messages that taunted him. Messages about his family back in Albania.

Messages about those three ivory photograph frames on Song Wu's desk, that had all been facing away from him at the start of that fateful meeting with her over four years ago, and then were suddenly turned towards him.

The very old, bearded man with a fishing rod on the side of a river. His grandfather. He'd been found drowned in that river two weeks after Albazi had been arrested.

The second photo, of his mother and father, in their sixties, standing behind a market stall stacked with clothing. Both of them were burned to death in a fire in their tenement block, four weeks after his arrest.

The third photograph was of a dark-haired woman in her late thirties, standing in the city of Tirana hugging a little girl of about three. His sister, Emina, and her daughter – his niece, Aisha – both of whom he adored. Both dead, their little Fiat crushed by a truck. Six weeks after his arrest.

There was a chart on the wall above his pillow that he had made himself. His countdown-to-release calendar. If he kept his nose clean, he would be out of here in six years' time.

At least he had a very substantial amount of money stashed away in Albania that the British police hadn't been able to find. They'd seized all his other assets under the Proceeds of Crime Act. But he would be able to live fine after his release and he would still have some good years left. Not that he was concerned about that now.

His focus at the moment was on the prison officers here, and privileges. It wasn't luxuries he wanted but information, and he knew the game. An army could only march as fast as its slowest soldier. Just as a chain was only as strong as its weakest link. And however secure a prison might be, it was only as secure as its most corrupt officer.

It hadn't taken Albazi long to find him. Not once his cousin had gone to Albania, on his dollar, returning with cash to flash.

Serious cash. Thanks to that, Albazi had his mobile phone and, pretty much whenever he needed it, crucial access to the internet.

Tall Joe Karter, the idiot, would have been out in two years' time if he hadn't been so goddamn stupid. Albazi had had the full download: a bully of an officer had been picking on Tall Joe, who was in the Category B prison HMP Gartree. Joe had been training in the gym throughout his time there, and finally lost it with the officer after one taunt too many. One morning, he threw him down an entire flight of stairs, fracturing his skull and breaking his back in two places, confining him to a wheelchair for life. Tall Joe wouldn't now be released until less than a year before himself.

But the good news was that Tall Joe would be badly in need of money when he did come out. And the even better news was that Skender Sharka, who'd received the most lenient sentence of the three of them, was now out and in contact with Tall Joe's pilot friend. And tasked with finding Sandy Grace and killing her when he did.

Albazi hated Sandy Grace more than he had ever hated any human. He held her responsible for the deaths of his grandfather, his mother, father, sister and niece. And what he hated most of all, not that he would ever admit it, was that she was a woman and had outsmarted him.

Only when she was dead would he be able to move on. And turn his attention to Song Wu. This bitch might think she was safe, invincible, protected by her triad ring of guards.

One day, he promised himself, she would suffer more than his family had suffered.

But for now his focus was Sandy Grace. He went to sleep on his hard bunk and even harder pillow, every night, thinking of her face.

Every day I wake in my cell and know you are still alive, Sandy, something else inside me dies.

It was exactly the same every morning. All that changed was the depth of Roel Albazi's anger towards her. It just kept on growing deeper. The fuse burning down. Getting shorter.

He knew, thanks to Sharka's work, that Sandy Grace had changed her name to Sandra Jones. He also knew her address in Jersey, thanks to the information Sharka fed back to him. He liked knowing that. Liked knowing something that her husband did not, and nor did the press.

He'd followed the press and media stories of the mystery of missing Sandy Grace, in the immediate aftermath of her failing to turn up to meet him that July day back in 2007. Her disappearance had become a major story, even making the national press for a short while.

According to the papers, the detective's wife had seemingly vanished into thin air. For a long time the speculation had been rife that Detective Inspector Roy Grace had murdered his wife himself. Plenty of people were reported in the media saying if anyone knew how to do it, it would be him.

The fact that there were barely any clues, and possibly a string of red herrings, only served to reinforce the suspicion on Roy Grace.

Sandy had left work early the day she vanished. From analysis of her credit card, she had bought some paracetamol and a tube of toothpaste at a branch of Boots in Hove then filled her VW Golf with petrol. Shortly after – at the time she should have turned up in Shoreham with the £150K she owed him – she had seemingly abandoned her car in the short-term car park at Gatwick South, and apparently vanished off the face of the earth. He knew different.

Albazi might not be able to reach her now, from the confines of his prison cell, but the day would come. The day when he would fly straight over to Jersey and knock on her door. And then rip the smug bitch's throat out with his bare hands.

THEY THOUGHT I WAS DEAD

That thought was the reason he marked off every single day on his calendar with a large black cross.

It was his reason to live.

53

September 2011

On the occasions when Roy and I had friends around for dinner we liked to play party games after the meal, when everyone was well lubricated. The games were all pretty harmless, except for one, the Truth Game. That was dangerous and Roy hated it when anyone suggested it.

It was dangerous because when loaded with drink, the booze took away people's inhibitions, making them want, all of a sudden, to unload their confessions: tell everyone the worst things they had done; their secret desires; the thing they were most embarrassed about. Often it was too much information! My old dear friend Tamzin said she and Ferris played it at a dinner party they gave and it resulted in one couple getting divorced. Wasn't it T. S. Eliot who said that humankind cannot bear very much reality?

One question invariably would be: what is the worst thing you have ever done?

What I am about to do is truly one of the worst things I have ever done. I have £1.2 million tucked up in a suitcase in my car. I know it is dishonest money and it does not belong to me. But this is not a time to be virtuous. I am not about to tell the world where it has come from. And I don't need all of it anyhow, so no dramas.

54

September 2011

In the service station loo, behind a locked door, I shot up methadone, and it started to calm me, rapidly. I then peed, refuelled
and got us something to eat, and Bruno and I had a mother-and-
son date night in the car park before driving on to the Malmaison
at Brighton Marina for an early night.

Nicos had helpfully instructed me that we must spend a
minimum three nights in England, so as not to create any suspicion
with the Jersey Customs and Immigration team when we return.
He said the Border Force officers scrutinize the manifests of the
airlines and ferries, and people making round trips in a short space
of time, such as twenty-four hours, will often trigger suspicion.

It is such a relief to spend three nights away from Nicos, and
some time instead with just Bruno. I'm planning to take him to
see the lions at Longleat safari park tomorrow.

Our twin-bedded, tastefully styled room is feeling like a sanctuary after the long stressful day and I'm finding it calming,
particularly as Bruno is now fast asleep, and I can finally open
the heavier and bigger-than-I-had-expected suitcase that's sitting
on the floor. It doesn't look anything special, just a big, cheap,
soft-sided suitcase – I guess that's the point, ordinary and bland
to avoid suspicion.

I'd collected it on the way here, from the storage depot in
Shoreham, using the keys and the code Nicos gave me to access
his locker. Now I heave it up onto my bed.

Pop-pop go the twin metal catches.

I lift the lid. And . . .

Oh my God!

It's the smell that hits me first before anything else! It's never really occurred to me before that money has a smell, but it really does. It's not the glorious smell of musty paper you get in old libraries, it's tangy, intoxicating, a seductive perfume full of promise. It smells of the French Riviera, of fast cars, of slinky black leather gloves, of expensive lingerie, of jet planes – and above all . . .

It smells of freedom.

I'm high on the smell and mesmerized by the sight. I've seen plenty of movies in which villains have suitcases full of cash, but . . .

Shit . . .

I've never actually seen a real suitcase full of real cash, until now. Bundles of fifty-pound notes. Bundles and bundles. And bundles.

And more bundles. All neatly stacked.

And more bundles still. All held together with red elastic bands.

I count one bundle. There are a hundred fifty-pound notes; £5,000 a bundle.

An hour later, after I've finished counting, I'm looking at £1.2 million. I whisper it out aloud to convince myself I'm not dreaming. 'One million, two hundred thousand pounds!'

As they call it in criminal slang, one point two million quid in *folding*.

Nicos told me it would be a doddle. Collect the suitcase, spend three days in England, and then return to Jersey.

Great.

But I'm not comfortable leaving a suitcase containing over a million quid in our hotel room. Or our car parked with that amount inside.

And here's another problem that smart Nicos hasn't antici-pated. The suitcase is almost too big for the boot of my little MX5. And that gives me another problem. Where is the rest of our luggage going to fit?

Then I'm struck with a thought. And it's a thought that I really like. And the more I think about it, the more I like it.

How about I take some of this money to the Rendezvous casino a two-minute walk away? That would help sort out the oversized bag issue!

And £1.2 million would be so cool to gamble with.

If I could figure a way to get that debt paid back to Roel Albazi, I never need to think of him ever again. I'd feel a lot better. I want to be a decent person, really. I guess that's something my Lutheran mother instilled in me.

Do the right thing.

But that would mean taking up gambling again and that's not really doing the right thing. Maybe it would lead me back down the dangerous path of gambling addiction, and it wasn't lost on me that was why I was in this situation to begin with. Nicos never allowed me the opportunity to gamble once we moved to Jersey and luckily there are no casinos there. Instead, he got me hooked on heroin. One addiction to another. At least it did stop my out-of-control gambling habit. But just this little flutter would be OK. It was all I could think of and the obvious way into my new better life. Just a little of the money, win it back and more, raising no suspicion when I take it back as promised to Nicos, pocketing the profit. I felt confident and in control.

I could ask the reception to help me find a local approved babysitter to watch over Bruno while he slept, disappear next door to the casino, just an hour or so, all anonymous.

The more I think about it, the more I like the idea.

Just one big bet – two at worst. £150K on red or black? Double the money and, bingo, out of trouble! Not that I'm worrying that

I'm in any trouble – four years on, Roel Albazi in prison probably has bigger things on his mind. And anyhow, I've no idea how I would get the money to him.

God, my mind is so messed up.

But this money is burning a hole. I could turn it into so much more and Nicos would never know. I hand him the suitcase in three days' time, with £1.2 million in it. And I'd have another million or more, stashed secretly. And I'll use it to get away from him.

It's a good plan.

Game on.

I'm feeling lucky tonight!

55

The ferry back to Jersey from Poole takes four hours. And four hours is a long time when you've got a kid sitting next to you who keeps wanting to play throaty lion roars at full volume on his games console.

I made the mistake of downloading the sounds for him. Angry lion roars, hungry lion roars, attacking lion roars. He thinks they are really funny and keeps giggling, but no one else sitting around us on this packed seating area at the front of the *Condor Liberation* is particularly amused. Each time he pulls his headphones plug out of the side of the player pretty much the whole ferry gets treated to the sounds.

But that's the least of my problems at this moment. I have a much bigger one. Which is that it didn't go too well at the casino three nights ago. Nor did it go too well two nights ago. Nor last night.

Not well at all.

In fact, that's really a bit of an understatement.

It would have quite suited me not to return to Jersey at all – today, at least. Instead I would have preferred to stay on and try to recoup my losses, but Nicos needs me – and the money – back urgently. Today. Not tomorrow, today. Late tonight he has a rendezvous several miles out to sea with another boat for this big deal – his biggest deal ever – and the calm weather is about to change. Tonight is the window, the tide is right and the forecast is calm seas. Tomorrow night a force seven, gusting nine, is fore-cast. A heavy sea for two boats to meet alongside mid-ocean without real danger. It would have to be tonight.

Of course I don't tell Nicos over the phone of the major problem I have. And I'm relying on the fact that I will delay our return by enough time that if Nicos starts checking the money, he's going to be in a very big rush, too concerned with heading out to sea for his rendezvous to count every single banknote.

I'm really relying on that quite a lot. But I have some distraction ideas in case I need to use them.

I'm well aware of the calibre of people he is having his offshore rendezvous with. The reputation of the gang headed by Saul Brignell, which controls, if the press is to be relied on, up to a quarter of all heroin to the south-west region of the British Isles.

And Nicos is relying on me to have collected the £1.2 million they will be waiting for, forty-four nautical miles north-west of Jersey, at midnight. He has a cunning plan that he told me about before I left for England. The drugs will be wrapped in waterproof packaging. After he loads them onto his boat, he will only travel a couple of miles back towards Jersey, then he will drop them into the ocean, at five different points, each marked with a small red buoy – the same ones the local lobster fishermen use.

Then over the next week, he will accompany a bent local fisherman, called Adam le Seelleur, to haul up each package in turn and bring them back to shore along with the rest of his catch.

So smart, so cunning.

But my plan is even more cunning.

56

'Where the hell have you been, you stupid bitch?'

That was the greeting Nicos gave myself and Bruno as we arrived back at the flat after three days in England, just before 7.30 p.m.

He was shaking with rage. Scarily so. I was convinced he was going to hit me again and, still holding the suitcase of cash, I stepped in front of Bruno, protectively. The bastard could hit me all he wanted but never my son.

Nicos looked like a demon was inside him. He paced up and down the apartment, seemingly fixated on his watch. 'Do you have any idea what the fucking time is? What the fuck have you been up to? You should have been here four hours ago. I've got a deadline – you know I've got a deadline. It actually crossed my mind you might have run away with all the cash or gambled it! But I know you'd not be that stupid.'

'I texted you,' I replied. 'The ferry from Poole was late,' I lied. 'I texted you that.'

'Why didn't you get a fucking plane?'

'You told me to take the ferry.'

He looked at his watch again. 'If I'm late for the rendezvous, you know what's going to happen? The whole deal could be off. Do you understand?'

'Maybe you could ask the ferry company for compensation,' I replied, mockingly.

'That's not even funny,' he snarled, snatching the suitcase out of my hand, dumping it on the floor, then kneeling and popping it open.

And suddenly I felt a catch in my throat. Shit. Shit. Shit. Please no.

As he raised the lid he said, 'Let's just check all is in order, shall we?'

His words filled me with terror. I stood, frozen. I knew he was on a deadline, which was why I'd deliberately arrived back so late. I honestly thought he would have just grabbed the suitcase and rushed off. I turned to Bruno and told him to go to his room. Obediently he towed his little Trunki off.

I watched Nicos stare at the tightly packed bundles of fifty-pound notes, each held together with a red band. I was bricking it. Taking more of his time than I'd hoped he had, he lifted out one bundle at a time along the top layer, flicking through each of the banknotes in turn like a bank teller, then putting them down on the floor. His eyes darted up at me constantly, suspiciously. He looked at his watch again and I thought he was about to close the lid. Instead he began to remove the second layer.

I tried to appear carefree, but my hammering heart felt like it was going to break loose inside my chest. He removed one, checked it, then another, then another. Out of the corner of my eye I saw Bruno come back into the room.

'I'm hungry, Mama!'

'I'll get you something in a minute, darling.'

I was watching Nicos checking through the second bundle, when I heard a crash and a sound like pebbles rattling across the floor.

Bruno, standing on a chair, had pulled down a box of Cheerios. They had spewed out of the packet and were everywhere.

'Jesus, you asshole kid!' Nicos yelled. 'You—' Then he looked at his watch again. 'Shit, I have to go.'

'I'll clear it up,' I said.

'Fucking right you'll clear it up.' He hastily crammed the bundles back inside the suitcase, closed the lid, then lugged it into the hall.

The door slammed shut.

He was gone.

57

The *Bolt-Hole* was Nicos's private in-joke. Well, not completely private, because it was Sandy who had suggested the name for his boat to him. *When the time comes to flee Jersey in a hurry, that'll be our bolt-hole, right, Nicos?*

One of the keys to living on this island and trying to stay under the radar of the police and all other authorities was to not look flash. For that reason he drove a bland, six-year-old Honda SUV, which was fine for the island's narrow roads, and he flew in and out on British Airways or EasyJet, or sometimes, to vary things, on the little twin-prop Blue Islands flight to Southampton. He mostly only used private jets when he was out of sight of Jersey.

So far as the Jersey Revenue knew he was a Greek guy who owned a number of small-time nail studio businesses, lived in rented accommodation and paid his taxes. Even his sleek thirty-eight-foot powerboat was dressed down to look like many of the other sport-fishing boats in the marinas of St Helier, St Aubin, St Catherine's and Rozel, with a pair of rod-racks sticking out of the stern.

At 8 p.m. on this fine evening, the sun travelling down the clear blue sky before soon bouncing off the horizon, he parked his SUV opposite the yellow-painted edifice of the Normans hardware building. Dressed in a windcheater, jeans, a peaked cap and boat shoes, he then hefted the large, heavy, red and

214

black Musto waterproof holdall out of the tailgate, along with – just for effect if anyone was watching him – a fishing rod.

Then he walked as jauntily as he could, trying to mask the heavy weight of the bag, trying to appear to all the world like a guy off for an evening's fishing, hopefully to bag a bluefin tuna or some bass at the very least. He ducked through a gap in the railings and looked down for a moment at the vast array of boats moored to the network of pontoons. RIBs, dinghies, sailing yachts, speedboats, cigarette-shaped racing powerboats, cabin cruisers, fishing smacks and a handful of serious, ocean-going multi-million-pound superyachts.

Seagulls swerved around above him and rigging clattered in the light breeze as he carefully made his way down the stone steps and onto the pontoon where *Bolt-Hole* was moored, at the far end. The salty tang of the sea and smell of boat paint and varnish and rope, as well as the cawing of the birds above, took him momentarily back to his childhood, to all the times he'd accompanied his uncle, who was a fisherman, out to sea.

Jersey had one of the biggest tides in the world, its land mass increased by over one third at low water. And at low water this harbour basin was mudflats, with everything on it stranded. But he had three full hours before that happened. After his rendezvous, where he would make the switch of cash for the drugs, it wouldn't be until 4 a.m. tomorrow before there'd be a high enough tide for him to get back into the harbour. But he wasn't worried about that for now. All part of his cover that he was out night fishing, and he fully intended to try to catch some fish after the rendezvous, to bring back and maybe cook for supper tomorrow.

Sandy wasn't crazy about the way he cooked fish in their flat, on an open skillet with lashings of olive oil and garlic. She said it stank the place out for days.

Well, she wasn't going to have to worry about that for too

much longer. After this deal was complete and he'd got the full value for the drugs in Jersey, he was planning to do exactly what Sandy had done, and disappear.

And Sandy wasn't going to be part of that plan.

58

Less than thirty minutes after Nicos fired up the four Mercedes diesel engines, *Bolt-Hole* was making great headway, the twin propellors throwing up an arcing mare's tail wake, the tall white pinnacle of La Corbière lighthouse already a tiny speck astern in the rapidly fading daylight. And Sandy and Bruno were even tinier specks.

He double-checked that the transponder, which would reveal his position and course to the coastguard's radar, and also to anyone with a marine tracking app on their phone, was switched off. On a private vessel of this size, there was no legal requirement to have it on – it was purely for safety, so that other vessels could see him.

Exactly what he did not want.

He'd also made sure the port, starboard and masthead lights were off. In this falling darkness, he should now be pretty much invisible. And he would maintain complete radio silence. Not that it was likely the coastguards would be listening, he had learned. Their role was mostly around marine safety. Drugs they left to the Customs.

They would have been clocked on the Noirmont Point radar – during the war a German underground command bunker – and again on the Corbière radar at the western extremity of Jersey, but no one would have taken any notice of him. Just one of hundreds of small boats sailing around the Channel Island waters,

and just another dickhead who'd forgotten to switch on his transponder – and nav lights. Or maybe a bolshy Jersey or French
fisherman – of which there were dozens – ignoring the regulations.

The boat's expensive speaker system was pumping out music.
Feel-good songs that Nicos shouted along with. He loved driving
this beast of a machine, which could top 50 knots in a calm sea
and outrun anything the coastguard could throw at him – if it
ever came to it. He loved all the electronic displays, especially
the ones that showed him, on the instrument panel, an X-ray
view of the engines working, the pistons and cams rising and
falling. But best of all was the digital navigation system.

The waters around the Channel Islands were notoriously
tricky. They were booby-trapped with submerged rocks and
treacherous currents, such as the Alderney Race, where the
current could run as fast as 12 knots, propelling some hapless
yachts backwards. Even with all his years of experience with
boats, he treated these waters with respect.

But tonight, now well clear of land and heading out into deep
water, following the satellite navigation set to the agreed rendezvous point in Hurd's Deep, just shy of fifty nautical miles from
Jersey, he had no worries. Secure in his padded seat, he made
constant small adjustments to the wheel, maintaining his course,
leaving the island of Guernsey just twinkling lights now, well to
his stern, on the north-west course he had set. The increasing
Atlantic swell was throwing the boat around and he reduced the
speed to 20 knots below her maximum.

He was in more of a hurry than he had wanted to be after the
Cheerios incident, but he was still happy he'd left plenty of time
for the rendezvous. The echo sounder was showing the depth of
ocean beneath him, steadily increasing over the next two hours
from 20 metres to 50 then 60. Suddenly, as if they had gone over
an under-sea cliff, the depth increased to 175 metres. They had
hit the channel known as Hurd's Deep.

'Woah,' he said aloud and to no one. 'That is deep, man!'

Deep meant safe, but uncharacteristically he began to feel nervous. Saul Brignell's minions were never the friendliest people to do business with. Although they always delivered quality. But . . . the thought occurred to him that he was heading out into the Atlantic Ocean to rendezvous with a bunch of England's most ruthless gangsters, with £1.2 million in cash in his Musto bag. That was a lot of money, even in the world of high-end drug dealing. And that meant a lot of temptation. What was to stop them from double-crossing him, simply taking the cash and dumping him overboard into the pitch-black sea? With 180 metres of water beneath them. There was just him. No witnesses.

There was nothing, he knew. Nothing but the strange honour that existed between villains – most of the time. Reputation, that was all. Screw a major player in the criminal fraternity and word would get around fast.

Hurd's Deep was on the main shipping lane north from Cherbourg, on the French coast, to the English Channel. It also connected with the lane from Liverpool – from where Saul Brignell's boat was likely to have started its journey, probably around this time yesterday, Nicos estimated.

The choice of rendezvous location, by the Brignell team, was a smart one. The chosen point in the Hurd's Deep channel was well away from all likely detection. Out of radar range from both the Channel Islands and the French coasts, too far south for the British navy to be patrolling, and too far out for the Channel Islands Customs cutters. Because of its distance from the nearest land and also because it was a known dumping ground for toxic and nuclear waste, there weren't likely to be many fishing boats around.

He took a long swig of Liberation IPA beer, followed by another; comforted both by the thought and by the alcohol, he took a third swig and stuck the bottle back in the holder on the dash. Then he lit a cigarette and inhaled deeply. As he blew the sweet smoke out through his mouth and nostrils he was looking steadfastly ahead, keeping a watchful eye for small fishing boats that might be out at this hour and for any fisherman's marker buoys that could foul his propellors. But it was unlikely there would be any fishing buoys out in this channel.

The prow of the boat rose and fell and pitched and yawed in the increasingly big sea and he felt the first wave of nausea.

Shit, don't let me be seasick! Come on! He was rarely seasick, but just sometimes it came on. He felt a stab of panic. Last time it happened, he was flat out on a bunk down below for four hours, wanting to die.

To distract himself, he once more checked the compass coordinates for the RV on the satnav screen: 49°39'00.0"N 3°05'00.0"W.

The RV point was twenty nautical miles away – safely outside the twelve-mile radius that constituted the Channel Islands territorial waters. It was now 10.15 p.m. and he wasn't due to rendezvous with the Brignell boat until 11.30. He slowed right down, but the boat began rolling and pitching even more. He increased the speed, faster, faster still, pushing the throttle handles forward, opening up the four engines to their max, feeling the thrill of acceleration as the boat surged forward, the front rising up onto the plane. It thumped, crashed, rocked, but flew. It was a wild ride. 'Yee-ha!' he yelled out aloud. It was curing his nausea!

The fuel gauge readout showed he was burning a gallon of diesel every two minutes. But he didn't care, the adrenaline coursing through him had kicked his hint of seasickness into touch. He was feeling great now, really great!

Some moments later, after another swig of beer and a drag on his cigarette, his thoughts returned to Sandy as the boat leaped on like a wild, bucking animal, into the darkness. He surfed a wave, then corrected harshly with the wheel as it yawed left, then right. How was he going to rid himself of her?

When he'd first met Sandy in that casino, four years ago, she'd reminded him so much of Eleni. But Eleni had been so easy to manipulate and never put up a fight. Sandy had turned out very different. He reflected that it had been partly his doing, with getting her into recreational drugs then this spiralling into addiction of a much more serious nature with the heroin. But he felt she deserved it. She was too much of a live wire if left to her own devices. That woman needed to be controlled. And as for that kid, he needed a bloody good slap.

Nicos sensed there was a vulnerable person beneath that carapace, but in the time they'd been together, he'd not been able to reach it. She talked repeatedly about the husband, the big detective guy she had abandoned, and he got the sense, constantly, that she regretted what she had done. But when he'd told her if that was how she felt, she should go back to him, it always turned into a row.

What he could not figure out was that she wouldn't contact the husband she had loved, yet had recently talked about making contact with her parents, who, she had told him, she didn't even like. She just craved their attention like some pathetic child.

But at least from a business perspective, his relationship with Sandy had worked out fine. He'd succeeded in getting her completely drug-dependent, so that she would do anything he asked of her.

Getting back to the task, he took a final drag before stubbing out the cigarette, and a final swig of the bottle, then set the navigation onto autopilot and jumped down from his seat.

And immediately, after just a few paces across the deck, downhill one instant, uphill the next, he started getting the roundabouts. Staggering back towards the wheel, the boat rolled sharply over to port and he fell, just grabbing the backrest in time.

Then it heeled to starboard.

He made it back into his seat and reduced speed. The nausea began to overwhelm him again. One cure for seasickness that worked in daylight, usually, was to stare at the horizon. But there was no horizon. Just darkness through the windscreen now, as black as a coal cellar. The weather front that had been forecast was arriving early, heralded by clouds that were shrouding light from the half-moon and stars. He pushed the throttle levers forward again to flat out, and as the boat surged, his seasickness receded once more.

Maybe it would be smart to stop trying to check the cash in the suitcase inside the Musto waterproof bag. Sandy had collected it from the storage unit and he had no reason to suspect it wasn't as he had deposited it there, over a year ago. She wouldn't have dared touch it. He'd long instilled in her head that if she ever tried to double-cross him, he would make both her and the kid pay.

Bob Marley – and the Wailers – belted out, '*Don't worry about a thing . . . 'cause every little thing gonna be alright . . .*'

He liked this song. And Bob Marley was right. It was, it was all going to be all right!

Hell yes!

Hell it was dark out here.

The only sign of life was the increasingly faint flashes of the Les Hanois Lighthouse at St Peter Port, a long way to his stern. Ahead was the vast blackness of the Atlantic Ocean. And way, way, beyond the fuel range of his boat, the Azores, and then the east coast of America.

But long before then, in approximately one hour and seven minutes, according to the satnav, he would rendezvous with a boat sent by Liverpool drugs magnate, Saul Brignell, with £1.2 million worth of drugs, that he would be able to sell to his contacts in Jersey for around £15–20 million. He'd move it in bulk, quickly, and leave the bigger risks to the dealers, cutting it down to fifty-pound bags and selling it on the street. It would be reckless to do it himself, even if the rewards would be so much greater, double the value or even higher. Not worth the risk, he felt. After all, he wasn't a greedy man.

So sweet. The best deal of his life.

Then bail out of this area. Quit while he was ahead.

Leaving flaky Sandy behind. He would vanish. He knew where he was headed. But she would never find him because, just like Sandy Jones, Nicos Christoforou was not his real name. Of course, Sandy still did not know this.

59

The satnav was showing a distance of just four nautical miles to the RV position: 49°39'00.0"N 3°05'00.0"W.

Less than a minute later, far ahead in the darkness, Nicos, still fighting off seasickness, saw to his relief a faint white dot. It disappeared in the heavy swell then reappeared moments later, a tiny bit brighter, a tiny bit larger.

It vanished again, then appeared again, brighter still.

He flashed the prearranged Morse code signal. Two long flashes; one quick flash; one long flash again. It was the letter Q. A question. *Is this you?*

Two long flashes followed by three short ones came back. Morse code for the number 7. It was their prearranged signal for *Yes!*

Then, for belt and braces, he flashed back the code for 1-4. Then received back the code for 2-2, in case any clever dick on a boat out there thought it would be fun to join in the numerical sequence.

Smiling with relief, he switched on the navigation lights and the powerful forward-facing searchlight, thinking, how did they say it in English? *Happy days!*

Then another Morse-coded message was flashed at him: 'Port or starboard?'

'Starboard,' he messaged back. Then activated the switch for the starboard side fenders to lower.

Two minutes later, the superstructure of a substantially larger boat than the *Bolt-Hole* – a good hundred-foot long, he guessed – materialized out of the darkness. A powerful beam shone into his eyes, then raked the foredeck. Within moments the boat was alongside and two burly men in black sweaters, jeans and plimsolls had jumped down from it onto *Bolt-Hole*'s deck, instantly securing ropes around front and rear stanchions.

Moments later, a short rope ladder dropped down over the deck rail. Nicos switched off the engines and, holding the red sail-bag, stepped, unsteadily, out of the wheelhouse, his nausea gone but replaced now by a nervous flutter inside him. He was utterly defenceless, in the middle of the sea, with over a million pounds in cash and, doubtless, some of the nastiest people he had ever dealt with waiting at the top of that ladder.

He looked up at two shadowy figures ten feet above him. Not wanting to risk climbing the ladder with the bag, he shouted at them to lower a line. When they had done so, he looped it through the handle of the Musto bag, securing it with a knot. Then he reached up and grabbed the coarse rope sides of the ladder and began hauling himself up, only too aware of the sea beneath him and the weight of the two boats that would crush him to death instantly if he fell.

The ladder swayed precariously as the boat rolled in the swell, tossing him away and out, like an unwilling acrobat, then a second later slamming him into the side of the hull.

Finally, after a good minute of hard exertion, he drew level with the deck of the Brignell boat and two strong pairs of hands gripped his arms reassuringly and landed him on the deck.

It was an impressive craft, from what he could see of it from here, the bobbing searchlight from *Bolt-Hole* fleetingly illuminating parts of the deck area. It was all of a hundred feet and probably more, and it had a helipad, on which sat, crab-like, a small dark helicopter.

'Yer all right?' a Liverpudlian accent, friendlier than he had anticipated, asked.

'I'm fine.'

Two men stood in front of him, big guys, bigger than him, wearing sweaters against the chill. One was holding his Musto bag.

'The boss is waiting for yer.'

'Saul Brignell?' Nicos questioned.

'No, Mr Brignell is still in his suite at HMP Wakefield. His associate, Mr Davis, is looking forward to meeting yer.'

Nicos had only met Saul Brignell once before, at his office in Liverpool, two years before he had been arrested, when he'd first decided to target Jersey as a potential market. Brignell had agreed to supply him with crystal meth, but it had for some while been only a relatively small amount. In the blunt way Brignell had, he'd told Nicos, 'I'll be sniffing your bottom for a while. When I'm confident that you're not a cunt, we'll start doing proper business. Do we understand each other?'

Tonight was the first time they were doing 'proper business'. Even though Brignell was in a prison cell. He'd heard rumours about his associate, Crazy Nigel Davis. When you first met him, he would appear all charm, even a little nervous with a twitch. But upset him and you would unleash an out-of-control fury.

The Liverpudlian who had spoken to Nicos, and was now carrying his bag, led the way, with the other right behind him, his boat shoes squeaking on the teak deck. Glancing uneasily at the two men who were still on his own boat, Nicos followed him through double doors, down wide, steep steps into a lounge that was fitted out as a facsimile of an English pub. There was a bar with a row of beer pumps and a row of optics behind. Shelves lined with whiskies, brandies, gins, vodka, rums, Baileys, advocaat and a vast variety of other liqueurs lining the rear wall – all in lipped shelving that would prevent them from falling off in a rough sea.

In front of the bar were several wooden tables, which Nicos could see were fixed to the floor, as were the chairs, and there was cushioned banquette seating to both the right and left, as well as a couple of pinball machines and a jukebox. There was even an authentically fake Persian carpet covering most of the floor.

All that was different to any of a thousand other indifferent pubs was the smell. The smell that used to be a staple of every pub and bar in the land. A smell that Nicos still missed and which brought a smile to his face now, despite his returning nausea from the motion of the boat's floor beneath his feet.

Standing behind the bar, with a pint of Guinness in one hand, a lit cigarette in the other, and looking every inch mine friendly host, stood a tall, elegant figure, thin as a reed, his right eye winking away like a lighthouse beam.

Nigel Davis wore a slim-fitting open-neck white shirt, with cufflinks sporting large emeralds, a Richard Mille watch of the kind favoured by Formula One drivers, and blue jeans. Spikes of silver hair had been meticulously brushed forward into a short fringe. As he spoke, the whole left-hand side of his face twitched, his eye half closing. 'Nice to meet you, Nicos,' he said, speaking slowly, drawing out each word as if he had to give it great thought. 'Welcome to the Black Lion. Ever been to a pub in the middle of the ocean before?' His smile turned into another twitch.

'No,' Nicos said. 'I haven't.' The man's phoney friendliness made him uncomfortable.

Davis drew on his cigarette, then tapped the ash into a retro, red Craven-A ashtray on the bar top. 'You're very welcome. All those fucking rules back on shore, like the smoking ban, don't apply. So what can I get you to drink, Nicos? On the house!' He roared with laughter as if this was the best joke in the world.

Nicos smiled politely. 'Well, I guess because we're at sea, maybe a tot of rum?'

Another twitch. 'You know how much a tot is, Nicos?' Davis ducked under the bar, produced a half-pint tumbler and pointed to halfway up it. 'That's a lot of rum. If you drank a tot, you'd be totally pissed. Great if you were going into battle in a wooden warship where you were likely to have your legs blown off by a cannon ball. Not so great if you were trying to handle the electronics of a modern warship. That's why the Royal Navy stopped it. July the thirty-first, 1970. That was a shit day for the navy – I was a young rating then, and I remember it.' He scowled. 'I often thought I'd like to meet one of them members of the Admiralty Board who made that decision – that I'd like to meet him on a dark night, know what I mean? But I'll give you a tot, and you can drink it while I count your money – how's that?'

'Sounds good,' Nicos said.

'Yeah. I'm under strict instructions from Mr Brignell to take very good care of you.' He crushed out the remains of his cigarette, ducked under the counter and produced a large brandy snifter. Then he reached behind him for one of the bottles of dark rum at the right-hand end of the shelf.

This boat might have been a lot bigger than his, Nicos thought, but it was pitching and rolling every bit as much and his nausea was returning. Maybe the rum would help. He made his way unsteadily to the nearest chair and sat down heavily.

Moments later, Nigel Davis strolled over almost jauntily, like a seasoned sailor, holding the snifter filled near to the brim with dark liquid, which he set down on the table in front of Nicos. 'Here we go. So no slight on your integrity intended, Mr Christoforou, but I need to be able to tell the boss that you are as honest as he thinks. Are you good with that?'

'Mr Brignell knows he has no need to question my integrity,' Nicos replied. 'But fine, go ahead.'

Davis nodded at the Liverpudlian who had carried down Nicos's bag. 'Open it, Jerry.'

Nicos took a closer look at him, as he unzipped the red bag, pulled out the pale blue suitcase inside it and laid it on the floor. Jerry was a classic man-mountain, with a face like beaten metal and lopsided hair, shaven on one side and lank, shiny with gel and jagged on the other.

He popped open the catches of the suitcase and lifted the lid.

All of them looked down at the rows of fifty-pound bank notes, each bunch secured by a red elastic band. The Liverpudlian took the top layer out, counting as he did. 'Ten thousand . . . twenty thousand . . . thirty thousand . . . forty thousand . . . fifty thousand . . . boss.'

Nigel Davis watched approvingly.

The Liverpudlian began on the second layer. 'Sixty thousand . . . seventy . . . eighty . . . ninety . . . one hundred . . . one hundred and ten thousand.'

Then he stopped. For a moment he froze. Then he said, 'Boss, you'd better take a look at this.'

60

I'd only met Adam le Seelleur twice before: once when he'd come to the apartment to do business with Nicos and once at his boat in St Helier harbour. On both occasions, even though it was summer, he wore a white bobble hat, oilskin jacket, gum boots and a face that displayed not an iota of humour or friendliness. Taciturn was the most favourable description I could apply to him.

I could understand his reasons for doing business outside of his trade, which was lobster fishing. He told me the first time I met him that a decade earlier he'd pull up sixty lobsters on a normal night, now it was down to ten, and his cut from the middlemen averaged £5 each.

With his grizzled seadog face and heavy beard he could have been anywhere between fifty and seventy. And he could have featured in one of those television commercials for frozen fish fingers, except the old seadogs in those kinds of commercials were always smiling and jolly, whereas Adam le Seelleur had not smiled on either occasion. He'd looked at Nicos and at me with a kind of disdain.

Whether it was simply because he was a true-born Jersey bean and we were newbies, parvenues, or whether there was an element of judgement of us, a sort of disgust at what Nicos did – although he was happy to take the money, far more than he could earn in months of hard work at sea – I didn't know.

And I didn't care. In a strange way, by making it plain he didn't really like either of us, I saw a certain honesty there. I felt I could trust him.

Which was why when he had said 11.30 p.m., very firmly, I was confident he would be there. He'd told me earlier this evening, after Nicos had left, that the shipping forecast was for it to have clouded over by then and there would be no moonlight to show us up.

Twenty thousand pounds had bought his loyalty, a deal I'd arranged before going to England to collect that suitcase, and now I had the money to pay him. And it did make me smile to think Nicos was paying for the trip! Paying out of the £1.2 million he now thought he had with him on the *Bolt-Hole*.

Maybe I had just one regret – that I wasn't on the *Bolt-Hole* to see the bastard's face when he opened the case. But I suspected it wouldn't be pretty.

I checked my watch. It was just gone 11.10 p.m. and I was in the back of the taxi, an old and bumpy people-carrier thing, with Bruno, fast asleep, leaning against me. All of our possessions were in the back, in two suitcases, and my trusty fake Louis Vuitton holdall, still with the £20,000 in cash sewn into the bottom, that had been there for the past four years, on the floor between my legs. Plus I'd added a further thirty thousand pilfered – although I prefer to say *borrowed* – from the suitcase. A decent enough nest egg. Four days' supply of my methadone was also sewn into there. For now, it was working and although it wasn't easy being off the heroin, I was determined to make it work. No way I was going back to my drug-addicted life.

Hasta la vista, baby. To the dirty drugs and to evil, manipulative Nicos.

As we wound down the steep, twisty and beautiful hill of Bouley Bay, I felt the faintest twinge of nostalgia. I'd walked down here and up again, and cycled it a few times, and it's a tough bastard, I can tell you. But in daylight the view of the bay at the bottom is worth it. So many great views here in this beautiful island. I'm going to miss a lot of things. Pretty much everything except Nicos.

A few hundred yards before we reached the bottom of the hill, the taxi driver, whose name I saw on his badge was Toby McMichael, turned into the entranceway of the low-rise apartment block, which was the address I'd given him. I paid the meter fare of £15 with a twenty and told him to keep the tip.

He offered to carry the bags in and up to my apartment, but I thanked him, told him we were fine, then stood with Bruno in the warm night air laced with salt from the sea below and exhaust fumes from the departing cab, watching the tail lights, waiting for them to disappear on up the hill.

'I'm hungry, Mama,' Bruno said.

He was always hungry. Or tired. So I always kept a stash of whatever his current favourite snack was in my handbag and pockets. At the moment it was Crunchies. I gave him a mini one. The moon was breaking through and there was just enough light to see. I picked up all the bags, and with Bruno absorbed in unwrapping his treat, we walked on down the hill, past the creepy edifice of the long closed-down Bouley Bay Hotel – which felt like something from a horror movie – and on towards the jetty.

I checked my watch again. It was 11.20 p.m. The bay was quiet, the only sound the steady wash of the sea against the pebble beach. Ten minutes to go. Ten minutes to either Adam le Seelleur arriving or finding out he had double-crossed me. And if he had?

I hadn't paid him a bean yet. He'd wanted the whole twenty thousand upfront. I told him he would get ten thousand when he arrived at the jetty and a further ten thousand when we arrived in France. So I had a pretty good feeling he would turn up.

But the closer it got to 11.30 p.m., the less good that feeling became.

We passed the wooden shack and outdoor tables of Mad Mary's cafe and suddenly, almost on cue – just a little behind schedule – the sky clouded over.

I put down the bags, pulled out my phone and switched on the torch. Then, struggling with the bags and the torch, as Bruno was nearing the end of his chocolate bar, we walked along the stone pier, as instructed, and stopped several feet short of the end, with steps going down into the water. I stared out to sea. There was nothing, I thought, absolutely nothing so dark as the sea at night.

There was a bench at the end of the pier and we both sat down, and I fished another Crunchie out for Bruno.

It was starting to get chilly now, being right over the water. Bruno complained that he was cold and tired. I barely heard him, I just kept staring out into the blackness of the bay for any sight of a shadow moving. Listening for the sound of an engine. The thrust of a prow through waves.

But I couldn't see anything. Or hear anything.

Don't burn your bridges, the saying went.

But that was exactly what I had done.

Adam le Seelleur had suggested this bay as the safest place because there was zero radar coverage here. A few miles to the south there was a radar station that could detect up to six miles eastwards, just beyond the Minquiers group of islands. But by steering well to the north-east, we would avoid detection, he'd said.

The risk was when we approached the west coast of France, close to the port of Saint-Malo, we would probably be picked up on French radar. But it was unlikely anyone would show interest in a small fishing boat arriving in the port in the early hours of the morning. Just like a dozen others returning from a night's commercial fishing that had forgotten to switch their transponders on – or had deliberately turned them off in order to poach undetected in the Channel Islands' waters.

11.35.

11.40.

He wasn't coming, was he? The bastard.

Then I felt my phone, in the back pocket of my jeans, vibrate, and at the same time heard the double pips signalling a text. Was it Nicos? I felt sudden panic. Bruno and I should be safely on our way to France now, not stuck here. Especially considering the frame of mind Nicos was going to be in after discovering what was in his suitcase.

I tugged it out and looked at the display, which was lit up. Relief surged through me. And joy! It was from Adam le Seelleur.

5 mins. You there?

I replied instantly with a chequered flag emoji. Then I whispered to Bruno, 'The boat's here in a few minutes, darling.'

I don't know why I was whispering. There was no one around; I could have shouted if I'd wanted. Bruno didn't hear me, he was asleep.

Suddenly, I heard a rustling sound, like paper. And what sounded faintly, so faintly, like an engine. Then – or was it my imagination? – a shadow that seemed darker than the darkness it was moving through. Moving towards us.

Moments later, a torch beam shone in my face.

61

Nicos looked in disbelief at the suitcase on the floor.

Tight bunches of fifty-pound notes, secured by red elastic bands, were stacked up beside – £110,000 so far in this bundle.

He carried on counting. But was shocked to see an increasing number of the bundles had been altered and contained newspaper to bulk them out along with the fifty-pound notes.

After a couple more layers he realized the rest of the suitcase was packed tightly with nothing but newspapers, which Jerry methodically pulled out and laid down. All of them, from the headlines and front-page photographs Nicos could see, were no more than a couple of days old.

'What the fuck?' Nicos said, almost silently, to himself. He took a large sip of his rum.

The Liverpudlian carried on, as if expecting to start finding more cash underneath the papers. He kept on removing more and more newspapers, all from the same day, until he reached the bottom.

Nigel Davis's face changed from benign to furious. He lit another cigarette. 'What's going on, Nicos, you want to tell us?' His nervous twitch looked like it was going critical.

'I – I . . .' Nicos uttered, then fell silent. 'There's been a mistake.'

'Crap at maths, are you?' Davis asked, his voice tight with pent-up rage.

'There's been a mistake, I'm telling you!'

'Perhaps the mistake was trusting you?' Nigel Davis said. 'The boss was right, wasn't he, when he said to count your fingers after shaking hands with you?'

'I'm telling you, there's been a mistake,' Nicos said, his confidence eroded, realizing he was sounding more like he was pleading.

He was thinking fast. He'd checked every damned bundle of fifty-pound notes himself and there had been £1.2 million worth of them when he'd put that suitcase into that storage locker last year, not wanting to risk the sniffer dogs at any of the London airports, or bringing it in through Jersey airport. Much safer to let Sandy and her kid, returning home on the car ferry, on Jersey plates, bring it, with a layer of the kid's clothes on top, like he'd told her.

So where had the money disappeared? From the locker or in transit? It was Sandy, he knew. The bitch – she—

His train of thought was interrupted by Nigel Davis standing over him, his face twitching more crazily than before. 'Do you have any idea how much this operation has cost Mr Brignell? The fuel for this boat, all the risks of loading the cargo – and you try to stiff us with the decades-old newspaper trick?'

Nicos raised his hands. 'You need to understand – it's not me – I'm not the one who's done this. Look.' He tried to mask the desperation in his voice and demeanour. 'Look, guys – so there's just over a million – so just give me that amount's worth of gear.'

'Seriously?' Nigel Davis said. 'You really think we've come six hundred fucking miles for this? It is not what we agreed.'

'Like I told you,' Nicos said, 'there's been a mistake – I'll correct it – I'll sort it.'

Davis stared at him and he twitched again. 'A mistake? So you didn't check it before you came? Or did you think we're a bunch of suckers, a bunch of honky-tonk boat people without a maths O level between us?'

Nicos shook his head, desperately trying to think his way out of this. 'Look,' he pleaded, 'Saul knows this is not how I do business.'

'Saul knows, does he?' Davis retorted. He dug one hand into the right-hand pocket of his jeans and took another drag of his cigarette with the other. 'So the rest disappeared by magic, did it, Nicos?'

'Not magic but—'

'Sleight of hand, perhaps?' Davis gave him a warm, disarming smile. And yet another twitch. His expression changed but Nicos barely noticed.

'Yeah, sleight of hand.' He nodded vigorously. 'Yeah, sleight of hand. That's it!'

'You know the stock-in-trade of magicians, don't you, Nicos? Distraction?'

He frowned. 'Distraction?'

'They get you to focus your attention in a different direction, so you don't notice when they remove the rabbit from the hat, or drop the coins up their sleeve, or do this!' As Davis said the words he pointed his cigarette up towards the ceiling.

While Nicos craned, looking upwards, presenting his neck as the perfect target, Nigel Davis pulled a switchblade, razor sharp, from his pocket, and with one swipe sliced cleanly through the Greek's throat.

Blood instantly began to spurt from the cut as Nicos raised his hands to his throat. He tried to speak but just a gasp came out. He stared in disbelief at the man in front of him holding the blade. He kept on trying to speak as he sank to his knees, shaking and gurgling as he dropped forward, before finally falling silent.

'You're really making a mess,' Davis said. 'Mr Brignell won't be happy about this. He likes everything immaculate. He really doesn't like a mess. He's going to be very pissed off with you.

And you don't want to be around when he gets pissed off. So it's just as well you won't be.'

He stubbed his cigarette out in Nicos's right ear. There was no reaction.

Ten minutes later, a spare anchor chained securely around his midriff, under the glare of a powerful spotlight, Nicos was lobbed over the deck rail. His body belly-flopped onto the black water, with a splash and a moment of turbulent white foam, then there was just the blackness of the surface of the sea again.

The depth here was 135 metres. Far too deep for most scuba divers to operate. It would take a submersible to find him. And that's if they even knew where to begin to start looking. Not that there was likely to be much left of him within a few days.

62

'Baked beans!' Bruno had suddenly woken up, and to my concern was running excitedly in and out of the wheelhouse onto the rear deck of the boat. He appeared to be pointing up at the sky. 'Baked beans!' he said again. 'Baked beans, Mama!'

I had no idea what he was talking about. 'You're full of beans, suddenly, aren't you, darling?'

'Noooo, Mama!' he said, stamping his foot and still pointing upwards. 'There!'

The sky might have clouded over, giving us cover from the moonlight, but the payback was the sea getting progressively rougher in the rising wind. I was starting to feel a little queasy and was more than happy to go out of the shelter of the cabin into the fresh air of the heaving deck, despite the strong stench of rotten fish and disinfectant.

Adam le Seelleur had become marginally less frosty after we'd left Bouley Bay and headed out into the open sea, telling me we were taking a long route to avoid the slim chance of being picked up on the St Catherine's radar, and he'd pointed out our position on the satellite screen. We were currently one nautical mile west of the Les Minquiers, a group of islands and rocks nine miles south of Jersey. Nicos, Bruno and I had picnicked there in happier days.

I was looking up, trying to see what Bruno was pointing at so excitedly. And then suddenly I saw it. There were twin aerials on

239

the roof of the cabin. And on top of one was something that did look like a can. I switched on my phone torch and hauled myself up onto the roof, hanging on a little precariously, but the distraction was keeping my seasickness at bay.

I pointed the beam up and saw a tin of Heinz baked beans stuck to the top of the right-hand aerial. 'You are right!' I shouted back to him.

Then I jumped down and went back into the cabin, followed by Bruno. 'Are you aware someone's stuck a tin of baked beans on the top of one of your aerials, Mr le Seelleur?'

He was sat at the wheel, a swinging, gimballed compass in front of him, staring ahead into the darkness through the windscreen. 'What of it?'

'I thought you might want to know,' I replied, a little taken aback by his curt reply.

'I do know,' he said, his voice surly again, then continued staring ahead. He reached up and made an adjustment to the navigation screen. 'Why would I not know?'

'I – I thought maybe it had been put there by some kids as a prank, or blown there.'

'I never put to sea without checking my boat carefully, lady. There's nothing on board that shouldn't be here. Except you and the kid,' he said, rummaging in his oilskin jacket pocket. After a moment he produced a packet of cigarette papers and a pouch.

'What's that?' Bruno asked him, pointing at a green screen with elliptical dots moving across it.

'The radar, kid,' he said. 'I use it to hunt for fish. Except we're not hunting fish tonight, are we?'

'Why not? Why aren't we fishing?' Bruno asked.

Le Seelleur began rolling a cigarette single-handedly. As he did so he shook his head, turning to me. 'That's the transponder aerial. The can muffles the signal. I put it there to stop us being tracked. A beer can would work fine too.' He sparked his cigarette with a plastic lighter and moments later, as he exhaled, I smelled that delicious sweet, pungent aroma.

It was tantalizing.

I'd quit smoking soon after Roy and I had married, but he had carried on, admittedly only having the occasional cigarette. But there were times when I honestly believed he only did it to piss me off. I was tempted to ask le Seelleur now if he could roll me one. But I hesitated because Bruno – in his awake mode – would see me.

Instead I went down for'ard, and into the boat's primitive loo. Here I took a small amount of methadone.

Emerging a couple of minutes later, the world without Nicos already seemed a better place. It was amazing to be out here, in the middle of the sea, on the way to my totally new life!

The colour of the darkness seemed so intense. So black. Our wake sparkled like a trillion Swarovski crystals scattered behind us.

Then I remembered something very, very important.

My phone. Well, what was now my old phone. My old 'job' phone.

I looked at my watch. 2 a.m. Then at the phone.

And something struck me as odd. No text or WhatsApp from Nicos. No missed call. Odd but good. Great, in fact.

The display glowed a deep blue. I checked quickly through my messages just to be sure there wasn't anything I had missed or needed to respond to.

Like what, doofus? Duh!

Then I threw it over the side and never even heard the splash.

'Bye bye, old life!' I murmured. Aware this wasn't for the first time. But, hell, who was it who said that life is a series of chapters in a book?

Time to turn the page.

And I had another phone. The one I had bought in England

two days ago, with a great package allowing me to make calls in Europe at no more cost than those in England. Nicos didn't know this number, of course, and I had no intention of ever giving it to him. In my mind, Nicos was already part of my history.

It seemed only minutes later that our captain was pointing ahead, through the wheelhouse window. There was a faint yellow glow in the distance, but as I looked I could see a clear bright red light to our left and an equally clear green one to our right.

'See them?' he asked. 'The red and green?'

'I can.'

'Marking the channel taking us to Saint-Malo harbour entrance.'

He hit a couple of switches on the panel in front of him, turning on the port and starboard navigation lights as well at the masthead light, and looked back at me, still taciturn but at least not frosty. 'Now we're legal.'

It seemed he had warmed to me – to us. Not that I thought he was ever going to be my best mate, but at least – maybe I'm flattering myself – he did seem to be a little more friendly as we approached the harbour moles, still in the pitch darkness of the cloudless night.

Bruno was now fast asleep on a bunk down below, seemingly oblivious in his tiredness to the musty smells of damp and the noxious reek of diesel fumes. It was just a relief he'd not been seasick on the entire voyage.

Dawn would be starting to break soon. Dawn of a new day and the start of my – our – new life.

I'd booked a rental car from Sixt, who were located at the Saint-Malo ferry terminal. The only problem was they didn't open until 8.30 a.m. Our skipper had already made it clear he wasn't going to hang around and risk getting questioned by any port officials. As soon as we were off his boat, he was back out to sea and looking to do some proper fishing, so that he would return to Jersey with a catch and not arouse any suspicion by berthing empty-handed.

The sea was calm and the air was much warmer now we were in the shelter of the harbour. If we couldn't find a cafe, we'd hunker down on a bench or in a doorway. My sleepless night was starting to take a toll on me.

I woke a grumpy Bruno and, perfunctorily assisted by Adam le Seelleur, who had reverted to his default setting of surly, we managed to safely get the luggage and Bruno up a steep, slippery stone staircase and onto the quay.

'Good luck,' le Seelleur said, with a level of enthusiasm that reminded me of one of the miserable croupiers at the Casino d'Azur every time I placed a bet.

I watched the fisherman descend those steps, agile as a mountain goat, unwind the rope from around a bollard, then jump aboard his boat, which was already drifting away from the quay.

I sat on a bench, holding Bruno's hand, our bags on the ground in front of us, watching the lights of the boat as they headed towards the harbour mouth, both the lights and the beat of his engine getting weaker and quieter with every second that passed.

'Mama, why can't we go fishing with him?' Bruno asked, suddenly.

'Because,' I said, and paused, searching for an answer. 'We have a long journey ahead of us.'

'Why?'

I looked at my son, almost too tired to answer. 'Because we have a long way to go.'

'Is Nicos coming with us?' he asked.

'He's busy, darling. I don't think he is.'

Bruno gave me a strange look. Then, out of the blue, he said, 'I'm glad!'

Astonished and delighted by how perceptive he was, I said, 'You're glad, my darling? Why?'

'He's not nice. You're sad when you are with him, Mama.'

Those words, those few words, coming from my little son, almost brought tears to my eyes. How could he be so wise?

God, I just wanted to scoop him up into my arms and hug and hug him. And hug him again.

I put my arm around him, staring down at the fishing boats and the yachts, their rigging clattering in the wind. I sat there like that for a long time, and although I had no idea what really lay ahead, other than a twelve-hour drive, I felt a sudden burst of optimism.

Everything was going to be all right. It was going to be just fine. And this child of mine was my biggest ally.

I looked down at him and mussed his hair with my right hand. He swept my hand away, irritated. 'Don't do that, Mama.'

I grinned. There were so many times when he seemed far too advanced for his age. 'Why not, my darling?'

He did not reply for some moments. When I looked at him, I saw the reason – he was asleep.

God, how I envied him that, at this moment. We had a twelve-hour drive ahead of us and I'd not so far had one wink of sleep. I closed my eyes and tried, sitting upright, with Bruno leaning against me. And managed at least five minutes.

Then I was wide awake again, fretting about the journey ahead, and about what we would find on arrival.

Meantime, there was something much more pressing. My methadone was running dangerously low. I really needed more. I had enough to get me through the next three days, but beyond that I was on my own.

And *on my own* was not a good place.

63

'MAMA!'

I don't know which it was that woke me up. Bruno's scream, his frantic shaking of my arm or the blare of the oncoming truck.

A bloody great idiot coming at me on the wrong side of the road. Headlights blazing, horn blasting. I could see the driver's face, he was so close. He looked horrified.

Tall trees to the right and to the left.

Oh Jesus.

'MAMA!' Bruno screamed again, in utter terror.

And then I realized.

I was completely on the wrong side of the road. Heading straight at the truck, a massive green beast of a thing, horn blaring like the lungs of some prehistoric monster.

I swung the wheel and somehow – it felt like inches – managed to steer our rented Golf over to the right.

Shit.

I was drenched in perspiration.

And shaking at the horrific realization.

I had fallen asleep at the wheel and had drifted right across the road, into the path of an oncoming petrol tanker. I'd nearly killed my son and myself.

I blinked away tears of tiredness, slowing right down and checking the time. It was midday. I'd been driving for three hours, after a night of almost no sleep at all, in the heat of the sun, which

I felt inside the car despite the aircon. Some while back I'd turned off the autoroute to avoid getting jammed on the Périphérique around Paris.

We were approaching a town or a village now, to my relief. I slowed even further to comply with the 50kph speed limit, still shaking and drenched in perspiration, and looked for a cafe, badly in need of a strong coffee. A very strong one. And I hadn't eaten anything on the boat, nor had Bruno other than chocolate bars. I saw a cafe, with a small car park, and tables outside in the morning sun.

Five minutes later, Bruno was drinking an Orangina and I was sipping a double espresso, followed by Red Bull, while we waited for Bruno's croque monsieur and my cheese omelette to arrive.

Bruno was absorbed in his electronic game. I studied the Google maps on my new phone. Avoiding the Périphérique had added two hours – in theory only, I knew – to our journey. We'd been driving for three hours, which meant, if all went well, we would arrive in Munich sometime around 11 p.m. Too late, I decided. I began to search on my phone for a cheap hotel towards Strasbourg, an Ibis or a Mercure, and saw one that would then give us just a four-hour drive to Munich the next morning. While I did, I was thinking about Nicos. About how he had got on last night with his rendezvous.

These were people not to be messed with, he had told me. They'd come a long way for this deal and, if it worked out, it could develop into a major slice of the lucrative Channel Islands drugs market for the gang. They weren't going to be happy when he opened that suitcase, that was for sure. While the thought of that made me smile, it also made me concerned. I'd learned over the past four years that Nicos in a good mood was a powder keg that could explode at any moment. In a bad mood he was dangerous to the point of out-of-control.

I was thinking hard, racking my brains about whether I had left any clue behind of where I was going. Because that was all it would take him. Just one clue, and he would find us. I could not think of any, not now anyway, to my relief.

As we sat, with a *blip-blop-blip-blop* soundtrack from the game Bruno was playing, I was increasingly aware I was due more methadone. The caffeine from my coffee and Red Bull just weren't enough, I was getting restless and very anxious. I tried to calm myself by remembering inspirational quotes from a life coach I'd found online some months back.

Don't try to know who we are. Know who we aren't. Eliminate that first.

Was that what Michelangelo meant when he talked about how he carved his astonishing figures?

The sculpture is already complete within the marble block, before I start my work. It is already there, I just have to chisel away the superfluous material.

Wasn't that what I needed to do to find – happiness? Fulfilment? My purpose on earth? My reason for existing? My mojo?

Chisel away the superfluous material in my life? And then see the true me deep inside?

Wasn't that what I had been doing in leaving Roy and now Nicos?

'How's your toasted sarnie?' I asked Bruno, who was busy shaking tomato ketchup onto it.

He didn't reply, concentrating furiously on getting more sauce from the container, and then more still.

'Don't you think that's enough, darling?' I suggested.

He gave me one of the strange, unsettling looks he so often did. One of those looks that made me think I was talking to a mature adult, and not a small boy. 'Ketchup is life,' he said.

'You think?'

He nodded. 'I know.'

'Really?'

'Mama, if we had crashed, we might both be ketchup now.'

He looked so serious as he said it, I wasn't sure whether to smile or cry. Then he focused back on his game. Within moments he was so absorbed he had forgotten all about his ketchup-spattered toasted cheese and ham sandwich.

Blip-blop-blip-blop.

'Your croque monsieur is going cold,' I said. But he didn't hear me.

I ate my omelette in silence, breaking off chunks of the baguette that came with it and wasn't fresh; it was a good day-old and plaster-of-Paris hard. I felt nauseous but needed to eat. Maybe the proprietor, a middle-aged woman with a bun, had me pegged as yet another dumb Brit who never complained.

Maybe today she was right. I wasn't in any mood to get into an argument over bread rolls. Suddenly I shivered, as if someone had walked over my grave.

Thinking about the near miss with that tanker.

Thinking about death. Oblivion.

Trying to think about what I actually wanted.

I had bolted from my life with Roy. I had now bolted from my life with Nicos.

I was heading towards a possible new life with a man I barely knew, other than having the sense that he was kind.

Hans-Jürgen Waldinger.

Heading to the address he had given me, twelve miles south of Munich, when we'd spoken on the phone three days ago. When he'd greeted me like not just an old friend, but like the person he'd been waiting for all his life.

After all my shitty time with Nicos, it was incredible to hear – and feel – the warmth and welcome in Hans-Jürgen's voice.

Sailors talk about any port in a storm.

But as we drove back out of the car park and onto the road, Bruno tapping away on his machine, it wasn't thoughts of ports in a storm that filled my head during the miles ahead. It was a sense of destiny.

I was such a mess it never occurred to me at that moment that I might need a Plan B.

64

Schloss Leichtigkeit was just about the weirdest damned place
– in a kind of good way – I'd ever seen in my life. The approach
road was a steep lane, not much wider than our rental car,
hemmed in on either side by tall leafy trees that blocked out
almost all the daylight. We drove literally through the bottom of
a medieval tower and carried on uphill. Finally, rounding a bend,
a truly extraordinary building came into sight.

I guess if Bruno had been a bit older he would have thought
we were arriving at Hogwarts and he was going to train to be a
wizard. And if he had been older still, he might have thought he
was Van Helsing arriving at Dracula's castle.

'Wow!' Bruno exclaimed. 'Is this where we're going, Mama?'

We drove between two ornate pillars, on each of which was a
large white sign with black lettering proclaiming, one in German
and the other in English, *THE INTERNATIONAL ASSOCIATION
OF FREE SPIRITS.*

Then a long, cobbled drive led us to the imposing front
entrance of the building. In a similar style to the tower and just
as old, a vast Bavarian castle rose above us. Tall, with grey stones
and red pantiles, many of the windows were just narrow slits,
and there were turrets randomly protruding along the battle-
ments. And there was an utterly breathtaking view for miles, of
mostly forestry, with some farmland, and in the far distance the
soft contours of hills fading into the heat haze.

Several vehicles were parked on the forecourt of the schloss – a line of six dark grey people carriers all in a neat row, and a handful of small, indistinct cars. It had the institutional feel of an expensive hotel or a conference centre.

As I got out of the car and unclipped Bruno from the child seat in the rear, a tall, slim woman of around forty emerged from the front door. She was dressed elegantly but clinically, all in white, including spotless trainers, in what looked to me like lab technician overalls reimagined by a cool fashion designer – someone like Gaultier. Her fair hair was pinned back, and she was holding a clipboard. There was something about her that I would have called *posh* back in England. She wasn't beautiful but she looked quite aristocratic, imposing.

'Sandra Jones?' she asked.

I saw, pinned above the breast pocket of her top, a small badge that read, *Dr Schmitt, Mentor*.

'Yes,' I said.

'We are very happy to welcome you here. My name is Julia Schmitt. I will be your Spiritual Mentor throughout your duration with us.' She spoke such perfect English I could only detect the very faintest hint of a German accent.

'Nice to meet you, doctor – er, Julia,' I said.

In truth, I was feeling a little intimidated by her. And I seriously did not like the pretentiousness of her moniker, *Spiritual Mentor*. Also, she smelled of something intense. A scent I recalled but momentarily could not place. For some reason it reminded me of the smell of a health food store. Then I remembered, patchouli oil.

'And this is your son, Bruno?'

Bruno was staring up at the building. 'Do you have ghosts?' he asked her.

She indulged him with a smile. She gave the impression there was absolutely nothing you could say to her to which she would not reply with a smile. 'Would you like to see a ghost, Bruno? *Ja*?'

He shrugged. 'They don't frighten me. I would actually quite like to meet one.'

'Well, I've never seen one here in five years. But would you like me to try to arrange it?'

He looked at her for some moments. 'I wouldn't want to be too scared,' he replied.

She looked at me and smiled, then said, 'Can I give help to you with your bags?'

'We're fine,' I said. 'Thank you, we can manage.'

'OK,' she said. '*Gut, alles ist klar!*' Then she stopped, and I knew something was coming, but I totally was not expecting what did come.

'Sandra, I'd like it for you, Bruno and I to join hands in our welcome to you here. Let us bow our heads and close our eyes to say the welcome prayer before we enter the sanctum. *Ja*?'

I frowned when she said the word sanctum, but she didn't see, fortunately. *Sanctum*, I thought. *Really?*

I looked at Bruno, his fair hair neat across his forehead and his wide blue eyes, and I could swear I saw something that matched exactly my own feeling at that moment.

I'm sure he was also thinking, *really?*

The prayer was interminable. It wasn't religious in any mono-theistic sense. It was a prayer to the world, to allow everyone who entered the portals of the International Association of Free Spirits to embrace the love, the community, the mission. To be refreshed, healed, reborn, realigned. To be set free of all our pasts.

Afterwards, as we followed her through automatic glass doors into a vast, high-ceilinged atrium, the contrast with the trad-itional, historic facade of the castle could not have been greater. It was as if we had walked onto the set of a sci-fi movie in a studio sound stage.

It felt like some kind of futuristic vision of Heaven. Everything was white. *Everything.* The floor, walls, ceiling, furniture. Even the vast numbers of real flowers, in giant white vases, were white. And there was a distinct, very pleasant and strangely calming scent from diffusers on just about every surface. The effect, for me anyway, in my strung-out state, was ethereal and slightly disorienting. As if Bruno and I had entered some kind of alternative universe.

The walls were hung with abstract paintings, all white on white, and framed ditzy new-age quotes in the spaces in between. I glanced at a few, while Bruno just stared around in awe, momentarily lost for words, which was pleasantly unusual for him.

I will form good habits and become their slave.

If you feel like you are losing everything, remember that trees lose their leaves every year, and they still stand tall and wait for better days to come.

The ship is safest in the harbour, but that's not where it's meant to be.

He who fears he shall suffer, already suffers what he fears.

There were several clusters of armchairs and sofas, as you'd see in the foyer of a large hotel, most of them occupied by people all dressed in similar white outfits to Julia, some talking, some sitting in apparent silent reflection.

I was starting to feel very uneasy – I'm not sure how much of that was down to this place, how much was tiredness from two days of driving, and how much was because my latest fix of methadone was wearing off and I was now incredibly anxious. I had only one day's supply left. What had I imagined would be here? Drug Dealers Central?

None of the people we walked past – and the majority of them looked young and beautiful, some almost intimidatingly beautiful – looked as if they had ever touched either alcohol or any forbidden substance in their lives. But everyone with whom I

253

made any eye contact smiled and mouthed something at me I could not hear. It might have been my imagination but they all seemed to be mouthing *I love you.*

Almost before I realized it, we had entered a small, equally white office. Julia Schmitt sat across a glass desk from us and passed me an iPad on which there was a medical form. I spent the next few minutes filling first my medical background – hesitating when *drugs* came up and deciding *what the hell*, to be truthful. Then I filled in Bruno's form, which was a relative breeze, while he sat beside me, his tiny hand on my knee.

I saw the frown on Dr Schmitt's face as she evidently read my opiate addiction and my weekly consumption of alcohol. But it was fleeting and then she smiled, yet again, seemingly unjudgemental, as if half the guests who registered here put down on their forms that they were substance abusers. Maybe they were.

'OK, Sandra, Dr Waldinger will be able to speak to you about any issues and requirements you have.'

That made me feel a lot easier.

She passed me a registration form to fill in for Bruno and myself, which I dutifully did. When I reached the bit about car licence plate, I told her it was a rental and I needed to take it to one of the returns depots in Munich. She said not to worry and that someone would take care of it if I gave her the keys.

But then came her double-whammy.

She produced a machine from behind the desk. 'May I take a credit card imprint, please, Sandra?'

I looked at her, astonished. 'Credit card?'

'It is normal – for all extras.' Then she gave a rather odd, knowing look. 'I think you will have some quite expensive extras?'

'Yes, of course,' I said, replying quickly before Bruno asked anything awkward.

'And for your suite.'

I suddenly felt clammy. 'For my suite?'

'Yes, the Höchster Meister has put you in our very finest suite. The Georg Wilhelm Friedrich Hegel suite. You will find such peace there, it is the perfect place to begin your regeneration.'

I stared back at her, momentarily at a loss of what to say. When I'd spoken on the phone, last week, to Hans-Jürgen Waldinger, calling him on the number he'd given me if I ever needed to contact him, telling him I needed to get away from his friend, Nicos – as he had once warned me I might – he had been utterly charming and so kind. He immediately told me to come and stay, as his guest, for as long as I needed. And I had felt again that strong connection with him I had felt four years ago, when I first met him at the Scientologists' HQ.

Now I was being asked for a credit card. Had he omitted to tell me I would be a *paying* guest?

There was no way I could give a credit card. I only had one, that Nicos had given me, for the Santander Bank in Jersey, but the moment I used that I would be traceable.

'Höchster Meister?' I queried.

'Dr Waldinger,' she replied and smiled again.

'I don't have a credit card,' I told her and she looked at me very strangely and suddenly broke into German. '*Keine kreditcarte?*' Then she smiled again.

'How much is the room?'

'One thousand euros a day, full-board, for you and your son, which will cover his daily nursery school attendances,' she replied, frowning before once again smiling. I was starting to find her smile disconcerting.

'I – I understood we are here as guests of Dr Waldinger. Is it possible to speak to him?' I asked.

She glanced at her watch. I checked on my own and saw it was coming up to 2 p.m. She shook her head. 'The Höchster Meister meditates every day between 1 and 3 p.m. It is not possible to speak to him.' It wasn't my imagination, there was a definite frostiness in her tone now. Despite yet another smile.

'You see,' I said, aware how lame I was sounding, 'I thought my son and I were here as guests of Dr Waldinger – your – your *Höchster Meister.'*

'It is correct, you are both here as guests of the Höchster Meister,' she replied. 'But I do not understand your issue, exactly.'

'I – I thought – being a guest – that meant we didn't need to pay.'

Her eyes narrowed, and I noticed she had stencilled eyebrows, which now almost met on the bridge of her nose. As she spoke she opened her arms expansively. 'Sandra, everyone here is a guest of the Höchster Meister. This institute only exists because of his immense generosity, but if no one ever paid that would not be good, that would mean everyone who came here was taking advantage of his kindness and his vision. But,' she raised a finger, 'there is something else even more important. And this is a point Dr Waldinger makes repeatedly.' She smiled again. Her expression read, *simples.* 'If something is free, then it is mean-ingless. Worthless. You do not perceive value. Do you understand?'

I didn't, but I was starting to get jittery as the effects of the methadone were wearing off faster and faster with every minute. So I dug my hand into my bag and produced one bundle of fifty-pound notes held together by a red elastic band, peeled off £5,000 and handed them to her. 'Payment in advance for five days,' I said.

She scribbled a receipt and handed it to me. 'We go to your suite?' she asked. 'Later I give you the familiarization tour.' Then she smiled again.

65

It's strange how quickly you can go on and then off someone. My first impression of Julia Schmitt, in the car park of Schloss Leichtigkeit, was of a nice lady, if a little indoctrinated. And smelling a little too wholesome.

But now, as our Spiritual Mentor led us up two steep flights of a narrow, stone spiral staircase, I was already going off her, big time. Was she being fiercely protective of Hans-Jürgen because everyone here wanted and expected a piece of him, or did she have another reason?

My addled mind was already speculating wildly. Were they lovers? Or was she hoping they would become lovers and she was jealous of my arrival here?

My problem in these recent past years was being able to think with proper clarity. Some days I struggled just to function properly, a hostage of the drugs to treat my opioid addiction, while trying to be a caring and protective mother and give out a semblance of being a normal human being, a thirty-two-year-old woman.

Had I completely misinterpreted Hans-Jürgen when I'd met him previously in England? When he had seemed so interested in my life and well-being?

Julia Schmitt was speaking and I realized I wasn't listening and had missed the first part of whatever she'd said. 'Complete mental regeneration,' she went on. 'That really is what everyone who comes here seeks and finds, if they are to look hard enough.'

Once, I would have bounded up these steps, but I hadn't done much aerobic exercise in months. As I struggled to keep up with her, lugging my two suitcases and my handbag, regretting not letting her take one of them, and getting increasingly out of breath, I grunted a reply. 'I think my body needs regeneration first!'

But my attempt at humour was lost on her. Or maybe she didn't hear it. 'Our Höchster Meister is very happy you are here,' she continued, stopping finally on a small landing, with a narrow window slit. 'He will see us soon.'

Julia put Bruno's Trunki down and he peered excitedly through the slit at the view beyond. 'Wow!'

'Please tell Dr Waldinger we are happy to be here and look forward to seeing him soon, too.'

Julia opened a door with what looked like a pass-key and frowned. '*Bitte* – sorry – please, he does not use this name any more. You must not. Here he is always Höchster Meister.'

I was tired and feeling more than a little fractious after the very long two-day drive to get here, as well having had a lousy night's sleep in a hotel last night with a rock-hard mattress and even harder pillow, sharing the room with Bruno, who took hours to settle down. 'So how does that translate?' I asked. 'Hans-Jürgen Waldinger is now *Mr Big*?'

She looked at me without a trace of humour in her expression. 'He is Höchster Meister. That is how we all address him. It is respectful.'

I looked directly back at her. 'Of course it is.'

She ushered us through into a suite, the likes of which I had never seen before. Bruno ran around excitedly, from his little bedroom into the lounge, into my vast room and then into the bathroom with its twin basins, bath, shower and bidet.

But I could barely take it in. I was starting to feel even more anxious. Next to no methadone left. Unless someone has been dependent on opiates, like me, they have no idea how it feels to be in need of a fix. Back in our early days together, when I'd really thought he loved me, Nicos had asked me to describe the feeling of needing a heroin fix. I'd told him the truth. That it felt like being in a very dark place, where all the lights had gone out. A place where you were all alone in darkness that was populated entirely with your demons.

I'd been there before and didn't ever want to go back there again.

'And this is the temperature control,' our Spiritual Mentor said.

I realized she was showing us around the suite and I had again missed something she had said. I heard a *beep-beep-beep* as she jabbed the little device on the wall. 'This is to make it cooler and this to make it warmer.' *Beep-beep-beep.*

'Where's the minibar?' I asked.

And immediately wished I'd been holding a camera to capture her shocked expression.

'Minibar?' she said.

I nodded. 'Yes, minibar.'

'There is a minibar in the kitchen area.'

I was in there almost before she had finished speaking. It was next to the fridge and I pulled it open. All it contained, to my dismay, were chocolate bars and bottles of mineral water, all labelled *Schloss Leichtigkeit Wasser.*

I checked out the fridge. It was empty.

Shit.

'How do I order wine or vodka or anything?' I asked.

'Schloss Leichtigkeit has a zero-alcohol policy,' she replied. And smiled.

'Seriously?'

'This is one thing you will learn here, Sandra,' she said. Her voice was zealous rather than judgemental. 'To become a Free Spirit is to be like a flame in the wind. But not one that is attached to the wick of a candle or the head of a matchstick. Because if you need a crutch to survive, when that crutch is gone so are you. Extinguished. Yes?'

I frowned, unsure exactly what she meant.

'Here at Schloss Leichtigkeit you will learn to become a flame that burns brightly alone, without fuel, without any external attachment or dependence. You alone will be that flame and when you graduate, you will for all your life burn brightly from just what is inside you. You will find yourself in a place of happiness and fulfilment that you never before found. You will know yourself for the first time, and what you will know will empower you in a way you would have thought impossible before you came.'

'OK,' I said, and was distracted by the sight of a thick, white brochure neatly placed on the desk in the living room. On the front cover was a photograph of Hans-Jürgen Waldinger, looking very much as I had remembered him, if a little younger in this picture. Some clever backlighting created a glow that gave him the appearance of a messianic guru.

It wasn't the first time in four years that I'd seen his face, of course. I'd googled him often, at times feeling like some kind of a fangirl stalker. And each time, such as I felt now, just as every infatuated stalker feels, those penetrating eyes were looking at me. Only me.

So close now. So many emotions whirling around inside me. Would we pick up straight where we had left off, that closeness and connection I'd felt with him back at the Scientologists? Or—

Bruno, seated on a sofa and focused on his game, brought me back to reality by suddenly calling out, 'Mama, what's the Wi-Fi code?'

I looked at our Spiritual Mentor. She smiled again. 'We have a zero Wi-Fi policy at Schloss Leichtigkeit,' she said. Another smile. These were getting smug.

They were starting to infuriate me.

The association of Free Spirits seemed less and less free.

'Today you must be tired and hungry after your journey.' She pointed at an iPad on a desk in the living room. 'All the menus are there, you may have your meals brought to your room or eat in the Refectory. Perhaps you will care to order some lunch?'

I momentarily distracted Bruno from his screen. 'Are you hungry, darling?'

'Can I have a cheeseburger? And chips with ketchup, Mama?'

'It is on the children's menu,' Julia Schmitt said. 'You will find it on page six. Oh, and I have just had a message from the Hochmeister. He will see you here to welcome you himself at five o'clock. Before then I will be back to give you your familiarization tour.'

I thanked her.

She handed me a card with a number on it. 'If you need me, whatever the time, you call on the room phone and this will reach me.'

As I took it she said, deadpan, 'There is one more thing before I leave you alone to unpack. When we meet people here, we tell them that we love them. This is very important. Our foundation is love, and this is our greeting. We do this in the common language, which is English.'

'OK,' I replied solemnly, 'thank you.'

She smiled. 'I love you,' she said.

'I love you,' I replied, feeling absurdly self-conscious.

'I love you, Bruno,' she said. But he was staring at his screen again and just frowned.

As soon as she was gone, I sat at the desk and waded through the menu on the iPad. I ordered what Bruno wanted, and a Buddha Bowl for myself. I didn't have much appetite.

Then, and I had been desperate to do this ever since arriving here, I looked at my phone. I was relieved to see there was a 3G signal, and immediately opened my search engine and typed in *Jersey Evening Post*, anxious for any possible news about Nicos. Although I had no idea what news I was expecting to find.

I scrolled down through the headlines. The main story was the plan for a new hospital for the island, which was being fiercely debated. The police were having a crackdown on speeding. There was a big piece on house prices, and alarm from the hospitality industry on the number of hotel rooms being lost to property developers building apartments aimed at the booming financial sector.

I almost missed what I had been looking for. Just a couple of column inches, the very last item before the sports news.

A major air-sea search, led by the Guernsey Coastguard, is underway following the discovery of an apparently unmanned St Helier registered motor yacht adrift ten nautical miles west of St Peter Port.

That was all it said.

Shaking, I then checked out the *Bailiwick Express*, the online newspaper of the Channel Islands. It had the same story, and no more.

Unmanned. Adrift.

I read the few words over and over.

Could it be the *Bolt-Hole*?

Unmanned.

Adrift.

I wasn't sure how I felt. What did it mean?

I sure as hell knew what it might mean.

I hadn't heard from Nicos. Then I realized of course I wouldn't, I'd tossed the phone with the only number he had overboard. But I'd checked my emails on my laptop at our hotel last night and there had been no email from him. I was half expecting there would have been one, after he'd opened the suitcase and found some of the cash gone.

But I guess I was also half expecting this silence.

The sea around the Channel Islands was a mecca for yachts in the summer months. This boat adrift could have been any boat. There was no reason to speculate about this particular one.

And yet I had every reason.

My insides were in such turmoil that when our food arrived all I could manage of our meal was one mouthful of chickpeas from my Buddha Bowl, and a couple of Bruno's French fries dunked in ketchup.

A few minutes later, I threw them both up in the loo.

66

Other than not serving alcohol, Schloss Leichtigkeit offered pretty much all the facilities I guess you might expect to find in an upmarket hotel. Indoor and outdoor swimming pools, gym, spa, treatment rooms, meditation rooms, games room, library, tennis court, bicycles available to borrow, children's play area, and a whole ton of other stuff I barely took in, as I walked alongside Julia Schmitt on our guided tour.

My mind was elsewhere. Thinking about a drifting boat. And thinking about my meeting with Hans-Jürgen Waldinger in less than an hour.

Bruno and I were conspicuous as newbies, by still being in our own clothes rather than the white uniform tunics of everyone else. I was getting a little tired of endlessly and self-consciously saying *I love you* or, whenever I chose, *ich liebe dich*, and having it equally endlessly said back to me.

Bruno, despite his hand locked with mine, was in his own little world, occasionally glancing up to me but not commenting.

I kept looking at my watch, wanting plenty of time to look my best before Hans-Jürgen Waldinger came to our suite. The man I had been thinking about often for the past four years, the man I really thought in my strung-out, stripped-out, messed-up mind might be the man I would connect with like a doting uncle and be there to support me emotionally and spiritually for life, and who had sounded so happy to hear from me just a few days ago.

THEY THOUGHT I WAS DEAD

What should I wear? How much make-up should I put on? How should I smell? I didn't have a huge choice of outfits – I'd packed a few dresses, a couple of pairs of jeans, some blouses, a skirt, my favourite shoes and trainers, and that was just about it in the style department. Of course, when we got back to the room, our tunics might have arrived, as Julia had said they were on their way. But I guess I wanted to look stand-out special for our first meeting in four years.

It was already 4.15 p.m. but, instead of heading back towards the schloss, Julia was leading us further away, insisting on showing us the acres of organic kitchen garden that enabled the head chef, formerly from a two-starred Michelin restaurant, to be self-sufficient in vegetables and herbs for our cuisine.

We finally arrived back at our suite with just twenty minutes to go before the great man was due. The mean-minded part of me wondered if Julia had deliberately left me so little time to get ready. I looked down at his face on the brochure again. It was framed by his flowing, centre-parted wavy brown hair, the similar length, covering his ears, as before, that seemed to be so much a part of his persona. And those intense – but kind – eyes, tiny smile creases on each side visible through his arty glasses.

With Teutonic punctuality, there was a ding of the bell on the dot of 5 p.m.

It was like a starting pistol had fired inside my heart, sending all my blood cells racing to see which could complete a full circuit of my body first. I was shaking and feeling clammy, and suddenly sick with nerves. I took a few tentative steps towards the door, then stopped to check my appearance in a tall mirror. I really did care about how I looked when he saw me, I wanted him to really like and care about me, to share some of his wisdom with me, to be something of a best friend.

I'd opted for a white blouse, tight jeans, my favourite platform-heeled sandals to bring me up a little towards his height, and a couple of sprays of Jo Malone on my neck and behind my ears. I dabbed some beads of perspiration from my brow, and as I reached the door, walking softly, I stood for some moments. Then I took in two deep breaths before opening it with a big, welcoming smile.

Hans-Jürgen, dressed in his white tunic, had more lines on his forehead than when I'd last seen him, deeper creases in the corners of his eyes, and his beautiful chestnut-brown hair had been infiltrated by a lot more grey than I remembered. But his blue eyes looked at me just as intensely as they had before. That penetrating gaze, as if he was reading my soul, was just as intense now. Even more so. And he smelled, very faintly, of a very attractive cologne.

He was beaming. Looking so genuinely happy. He took each of my hands in his own and squeezed them lightly. 'Sandra! So good to see you. So very good!'

His voice was so much part of his charm, too. That almost mellifluous broken English. Warm, so cultured.

He simply released my hands and stood, looking down at me. 'So good!' he repeated. Then he totally broke the spell by shooting a glance at his watch, before looking back at me again. 'All is good? Julia is taking care of you?' He glanced at his watch again and rocked on his white trainers.

I could sense he was on the verge of moving off and this was not in my script. 'Well, yes, but—'

'Something is wrong?'

'Won't you come in – have a coffee or something?' I had a terrible plunging sensation deep inside me. This was just not what I had expected. But then, what had I expected?

He looked at his watch yet again, then at me. 'So Nicos? This has not worked out with my friend?'

'Not exactly,' I said. 'No. Long story. You were right, the warning you gave me about him – if you remember?'

'*Ja.*' He shook his head. 'He gave a very big donation if we would look after you in East Grinstead those years ago. I was not sure we should take it, but then I saw you and I was glad we did.'

He gave me an intense look and smiled again. 'So glad to see you here!' Then he looked at his sodding watch again. A big fancy thing, all cogs and innards, with no conventional dial. I don't know how he figured out anything from it, let alone the time.

'I have an important telephone call in a few minutes, but I wanted to welcome you in person. I'm afraid I must go to a meeting in München tonight. Perhaps you might dine with me tomorrow tonight?'

'Well, I do have a date with Tom Cruise, but I could cancel him.'

He held his hands in the air. 'No, please do not – we can see us on another time, perhaps?' he replied, totally missing the joke.

'Tomorrow will be fine,' I said.

'You are sure?'

I nodded.

'If there is anything you need, please ask Julia, OK?'

I hesitated. But he was in a hurry. I had waited four years, another twenty-four hours was not, as a friend of mine used to say, going to change the price of fish.

'All's good.'

He gave me a look that told me he could see all wasn't good. Then he was gone. Without even saying the clinic greeting that he loved me.

I closed the door, feeling very alone. Hans-Jürgen had been pleasant. Charming as he had been previously. But distant. Distracted by something. It sure hadn't been the big reconnection I'd thought it might be. And he hadn't given me the impression he'd spent the past four years thinking or caring about me, either.

Something inside my head was shouting at me to get real. The words Nicos liked to use.

I sat back down and stared at his face on the brochure again. Then I thought about Roy. It was just gone 5 p.m. here, which meant just after 4 p.m. England time. What was he up to on this September afternoon? Was it sunny in Sussex, too?

He was at work, no doubt. But although I kept a frequent check on the *Argus* online I'd not seen any mention of him for some while.

In those last days before I'd left him, Roy was very excited about work – he'd been told by his line manager, the Head of Major Crime, that he should apply for the position of Detective Chief Inspector and had a good chance of getting the promotion. But the last time I'd seen him named in the paper he was still just Detective Inspector and that's how he was also titled on the Sussex Police website. So something hadn't worked out. And I suddenly felt a little guilty that I might be part of the cause of that.

How the hell are you? I wondered, my heart suddenly heavy.

I was missing him, dammit, despite everything. I kept denying it to myself, but I was missing him more all the time. Thinking back to the life we had and realizing that it actually had been, most of the time, pretty good.

Apart from that little issue of my gambling debt.

Apart from that, Mrs Kennedy, how did you enjoy your trip to Dallas?

I should have come clean with Roy. He would have sorted it out, he'd have found a way, he was one of life's copers, he would always find a way to deal with anything. That was one of the things I'd loved about him, how safe he made me feel.

Shit, I missed him. I missed our beautiful home.

Are you looking after the garden, Roy? Or have you let it go to rack and ruin? You were never very green-fingered, were you? You were fine with mowing, you always said that relaxed you.

But beyond that you were happy to leave the garden to me. Oh, and you did care for Marlon, the goldfish. You were diligent with him, changing his water, giving him fresh weed and always remembering his food.

Are you on your own, or do you have a new person in your life?

Do you still wonder what happened to me, after all these years? Over four years now. Gosh. Do you still think about me or have you moved on?

What would you say if I rocked up on your doorstep with my son – who might or might not be yours?

Would you greet me with a huge hug, or would you just stand there coldly and tell me to sod off?

How would you react if I told you I missed you? That I've missed you every damned day since I left you?

That the only reason I've not contacted you is out of fear? Fear that you might be so angry and disgusted with me. Fear that you might have found a new person and that you would reject me. Fear that it would be so pointless, that we would get back together and then the whole damned spiral would start over again. Fear that whatever we had together would never have been enough.

I was in no mood to go to the restaurant – or Refectory as it was called – so a little while later I ordered a meal for Bruno and myself from room service. God, how much I could have done with some wine, or something stronger, to accompany it.

Half an hour later two young men, each holding a massive tray, one looking broken by the climb up the steep stairs, delivered Bruno's second cheeseburger of the day, and a Dover sole for me. Discreetly on the tray beside my fish, potatoes and beans was an envelope.

I opened it after our two servers had departed, telling me they loved me. It contained a note from Julia Schmitt, along with four white tablets. Oh, thank God. Yes. Yes. YES!

Dear Sandra, please take one twice a day. This will take care for your heroin cravings. Tomorrow morning I will give you your programme for the path to freedom of your spirit. My colleague Fabian Katz will collect Bruno for his first class at 9 a.m. Don't forget to complete the breakfast form with your requirements and place it outside your door. Should you require turn-down service please inform the Housekeeper by dialling 7. The Management of Schloss Leichtigkeit wishes you a good evening and loves you.

I sat there for a long while after reading this, while Bruno ate his burger, messily and happily, and I let my fish go cold. I had never, ever, in these past four years, missed Roy so much and wished I was back with him. Wished so much.

I looked at my phone. It would be so easy to pick it up and dial his number.

Except, I panicked briefly, I had forgotten it.

Then it came back to me.

But I left my phone on the table. And, instead, stabbed my fork into my stone-cold fish.

67

Autumn 2011

It was probably the most comfortable bed in which I'd barely slept a wink, in my life. I both sank into it and it held me firm at the same time. The pillows were the kind I'd wanted for years and had never found. Feather clouds.

Back in Jersey, although Nicos's apartment had a magnificent sea view across St Aubin's bay and the jagged promontory of historic Elizabeth Castle, it was close to one of the island's busiest roads, Victoria Avenue. Despite our bedroom being at the back, I would go to sleep to an endless looped soundtrack of cars, trucks and motorbikes – punctuated by the occasional siren.

Last night had been complete and utter silence. And eternally long.

The new tablets had kept my cravings under control, without delivering any of the joy of those first hours after a fresh heroin fix.

My mind was alive, whirring, an engine inside my skull that wasn't responding to the off switch.

I kept thinking of that drifting boat. I tried to tell myself that it probably had nothing to do with Nicos, or me. But I couldn't shake off the thought of what might have happened to him, that he might be dead.

I wouldn't wish that on anyone and really didn't want to have to live with that guilt. I just needed him out of my life – banged up in prison would be good.

I'd left Roy. Then I'd dodged Albazi. And now run away from Nicos too. So far I'd got away with it but for how long?

I was in a country I didn't know, where I had some distant family who I had never met, one of whom had been decent enough to leave me some money in her will, although peanuts, relative to her net worth. I was staying in a place I couldn't afford, and I had a responsibility to my son.

It seemed just like my gambling. The final throw of the desperate gambler, down on their chips, is to put everything they have left on one last throw of the dice, or one last turn of the cards or spin of the wheel. It was known as *going all in.*

I'd gone all in for Hans-Jürgen Waldinger. Had he really changed, less flirty and womanizing?

At some point, I slipped out of bed and walked through into Bruno's room. He was sound asleep and I just stood and looked down at his dark form, listening to his breathing, tears coming into my eyes. My son. My only real achievement after over thirty years on this planet. I whispered how much I loved him, that I would always take care of him. I told him he deserved that. And I told him I was sorry he had such a shitty mother.

I told him he was going to make the world a better place, and then I would have achieved something.

At some point, well after 4 a.m., I must have fallen asleep because I had a weird dream involving my parents. My father, who had never flown a plane in his life, told me he'd been in charge of air-sea rescue for the Channel Islands and he knew my secret. Then my mother, who had never organized a party in her life and had no interest in doing so, told me she had put up a marquee in her back garden and invited Roy, Roel Albazi and Nicos to come and celebrate my birthday – which was, actually, not until spring.

I woke in a panic, wondering for some moments how the hell I was going to get out of the party. Then, as reality dawned, I felt so incredibly relieved it had just been a dream.

'I'm hungry, Mama!'

Bruno was standing at my bedside in his dinosaur pyjamas.

I looked up at him. Despite the thick curtains, my room was light. The clock on my beside table said 7.22.

'I think we ordered breakfast for 8 a.m., darling. Have you brushed your teeth?'

'Not zactly,' he said.

'Go and do that,' I encouraged him.

With rare obedience, he padded back out of the room.

Routinely, I picked up my phone and checked first Sky News, then I went to the *Jersey Evening Post* website. Because of the absence of Wi-Fi and having to download everything on my phone it took a while. But finally it arrived.

And I stared at the front-page splash in shock.

68

MARY CELESTE MYSTERY OF MULTIMILLION-POUND YACHT

Below the headline it read:

A full-scale search and rescue operation is underway between the Guernsey and Jersey coastguard agencies as well as Channel Island Air Search, UK and French helicopters after a St Helier-based motor yacht, Bolt-Hole, *was discovered adrift and unmanned ten nautical miles off Guernsey on Tuesday night.*

The yacht's registered owner, Nicos Christoforou, has not been seen in over twenty-four hours. The last sighting of the yacht was at 20.30 on Monday evening, as it passed the Corbière lighthouse radar.

According to an associate of Mr Christoforou, Neil Wakeling, a fellow member of the St Helier Yacht Club, he was a keen fisherman who would often go night fishing in search of bluefin tuna.

Inspector Callum O'Connor of States of Jersey Police told the JEP that the police are also concerned about Mr Christoforou's partner, Sandra Jones, and her son, neither of whom have been seen in the past forty-eight hours.

Our breakfast arrived, and, with both of us dressed in our white tunics, I ate the mushroom omelette and bowl of fresh berries

I'd ordered in almost complete silence, deep in thought, while Bruno munched happily on his cereal, intermittently humming a tune I could not recognize.

Within minutes of finishing his breakfast, he was whisked off to a kindergarten class with ten other kids his age or thereabouts. Soon after, I was collected by Julia Schmitt and delivered to a room where, she told me, I would be given the overview of the aims of the Association of Free Spirits.

Dutifully clutching the notebook I had been told to use for all I took away from the lectures I would be attending during the coming days, I joined around thirty others, right across the age spectrum, seated at desks in tiered rows in a small lecture theatre. Many of them were wearing headphones for the simultaneous translation into English, French and Spanish on offer. Not one of whom, in my brief glance around the room, I felt I had anything in common with.

On the stage stood a plump woman, probably a little younger than myself, with a tangle of frizzy hair and bright red glasses, who greeted us like the full-on, brainwashed eagle-eyed zealot for the International Association of Free Spirits she turned out to be.

I donned the headphones on the clip in front of me and selected English. And after a short while, wished I hadn't.

She talked for just over two hours without drawing breath, followed by Q&A, spouting an interminable diatribe of, in my view, totally vacuous New Age claptrap, accompanied by a PowerPoint display that alternated between happy-looking residents of the schloss, meditating, running and doing all kinds of other happy stuff, and diagrams of algebraic formulas, purportedly showing how the paths to the levels of spiritual enlightenment could be accessed through the shedding of all our erroneous preconceptions about human value systems.

These diagrams totally lost me. And the stupid-looking woman annoyed me with an intensity that increased, in a direct algebraic formula that I invented while I sat there, with every minute she spoke.

The session began at 10 a.m. and finished at 12.30. Judging from the rapt applause all around me, everyone else had taken something of serious value away from this. I stood up, feeling only that I wanted two and a half hours of my life back.

The printed programme Julia Schmitt had handed me indicated I should return at 2 p.m. for the afternoon session, following lunch, which I could either eat at a table in the Refectory, or take from the cafeteria to eat in the grounds.

I chose the latter. A *thunfischsalat* in a polystyrene tub and a mineral water, which I carried on a tray out into the gardens, and ate, seated alone on a bench beside a large lake. At one point, as I sat there in the glorious sunshine, a heavily bearded man who could have made a great department store Santa Claus, also carrying a tray, asked me something in German, in a very polite voice. I'd no idea what he wanted.

'*Sprechen Sie Englisch*?' I asked him.

'*Ja!*' he replied with a big smile. 'Would you mind if I sit here with you?'

'You can sit where you like, but I'm leaving!'

69

My afternoon session – at the start of which I noticed Santa Claus had seated himself as far from me as possible – began tediously and got rapidly duller. I wondered how Bruno was getting along, if his day was any better. If this morning we had had the induction, this afternoon looked like we were getting the indoctrination.

It was presented by a tall, thin, sanctimonious man in his forties, with a shaven head, a goatee beard and a reedy voice that I could barely hear and I couldn't understand as he was speaking in German. Then I realized – duh – I needed to put my headphones on. But again I wished I hadn't bothered. He appeared to have had both a personality and a humour bypass, and like the lady this morning, he used a PowerPoint display to ram home points, in both German and English, in large CAPITAL LETTERS.

The International Association of Free Spirits, he informed us, adopted some of the principles of Scientology, which our Hochmeister admired, but with many differences. The Scientologists espoused the *Clear*, under their banner, *THE BRIDGE TO TOTAL FREEDOM*. The International Association of Free Spirits offered similar mental regeneration, through a different process. Which he proceeded to explain over the next two hours.

All around me people in their white tunics, some wearing headphones, some not, were busily – eagerly – taking notes, just as they had all been doing this morning.

I'd not yet heard anything I thought worth writing down. I noticed someone I'd not seen this morning, who looked as bored as me. A nice-looking guy of around my age, with shambolic fair hair, seated in the row below me, along to the right, past a couple of empty chairs. His notebook appeared blank from here, and I saw he was surreptitiously texting on his phone. Then, I don't know what made him do it, he suddenly glanced over to his left and caught my eye.

He must have seen something in my face because he grinned and I grinned back. Like we were two co-conspirators. The first two members of the Escape Committee?

Then finally the speaker said something that made me smile and I did write this down, as best as I could remember it.

So many of us spend so much of our lives doing jobs we hate, in order to earn money we do not need, so that we can buy things we do not want, in order to impress people we don't like.

And suddenly he had my full attention. I liked what he had just said, even though it was a bit strange watching his mouth then hearing his words, out of sync, spoken by a female – but her English was impeccable. Then I liked even more what came next.

'The Dalai Lama said: *The more you want, the unhappier you will be.*'

He stood in silence, as if to let this sink in. 'Here at the International Association of Free Spirits, one of our key messages is to learn to be happy with what we have. Wanting what we do not have is a dark path, one that leads to discontent, jealousy and ultimately to unhappiness. Think about this for a moment: why do any of us here in this room want anything? Yes? What is it we want and why do we want it? Will a new car change our life? A new fridge? So my neighbour has a bigger house than I do. Is he or she happier than I am? Or does this person simply have bigger bills and has to work harder than I do to pay them?'

He paused then went on. 'You are all intelligent, cultured people, wanting to change your lives, otherwise you would not be here. I'm sure you will all be familiar with the name Oscar Wilde, the genius Irish playwright, poet and wit. Not noted for his punctuality, he once arrived extremely late to a dinner in London. His hostess pointed at the clock on the wall and said, angrily, "Mr Wilde, do you realize quite how late you are? Do you have any idea of the time?" Oscar Wilde glanced at the clock and replied, "And how, my good lady, can that nasty little machine possibly know what the great golden sun is up to?"'

This produced a ripple of laughter – the first time all day I'd heard such a reaction. Even my new friend smiled.

The presenter looked pleased with himself and moved a few steps to his left then to his right, putting me in mind of a ballerina elf. He opened his arms expansively and continued. 'One thing you will all take away at the end of this session is the awareness of the tyranny of one simple word. And that word is *how*? "How?" is where dreams go to die. "How?" is the question asked by people you should never waste your time with. Think about this carefully for a moment. How many of you in this room have had a brilliant idea that you've told someone you respect and they've used the *how* word in their reply? *How on earth can you achieve that? How can you ever finance this? How can a heavier-than-air machine ever fly*? How many of you ever got beyond that question: "How?" Do you think Bill Gates baulked at that question, which he must have been asked a thousand times. Or Richard Branson?'

He paused for some moments and performed another elfin balletic movement. 'If every visionary of the past five thousand years had been cowed by that word, then today we might still be living in caves and throwing rocks at each other, instead of intercontinental ballistic missiles with nuclear warheads. I'm going

to leave you with that thought. Have a good evening, everyone
- and sweet dreams!'

On the PowerPoint display behind him were the words:
SCHLAF GUT!

SLEEP TIGHT!

70

I left the lecture theatre, to my surprise reflecting on some of what I'd heard this afternoon that really resonated with me. I was looking forward to discussing some of the things I'd heard with Hans-Jürgen over dinner tonight. I hoped he'd be less distracted than he seemed before.

When I arrived back at the suite, Bruno came over and hugged my legs. He was hunched almost furtively, as if hiding behind me, and looking unusually self-conscious. I was about to ask him why he was being so clingy when I heard the doorbell and he ran off to his room.

Julia Schmitt stood there and she was not looking a happy bunny. 'May I come in, please?' she asked. 'I need to speak to you.'

We sat down opposite each other on the two facing sofas in the living room, the glass coffee table between us. 'Is there some problem?' I asked, expecting her to say something about Hans-Jürgen and me having dinner tonight.

Instead she said, 'I'm afraid the behaviour of your son is not acceptable.'

'Bruno?' I replied and instantly realized I must have sounded like an idiot. How many sons did I have here?

'He has been very disruptive in kindergarten today. He has behaved, I am informed, very contrary to the philosophy of the International Association of Free Spirits.'

'In what way?' I asked lamely.

'For a start, he took a chocolate bar from another child – a girl. These are free from the canteen, but this was the last one and she was very upset. But worse than this is he has taken the watch of another boy.'

'What?'

'Another boy in his class was showing his friends the new digital watch he got for his birthday. Your son asked to see it and this boy gave it to him. Bruno then put it on his own wrist and refused to return it.'

'Refused?'

'Yes.'

I was shocked, but . . . I had a horrible feeling she was telling me the truth. 'What happened then?'

'The teacher asked him to hand it back. Bruno had a tantrum, standing there screaming and crying and saying it was his watch now.'

God. I felt a cold, hollow feeling deep inside me. 'Where – where is it now?'

'Still on your son's wrist,' she said calmly, but with the demeanour more of a schoolteacher than the mentor she had been to me – us – yesterday.

'I will get it right away,' I said. Jumping up, I stormed through into Bruno's room. And sure enough I saw a purple, plastic strap on his wrist and a shouty watch. That was what he had been trying to hide from me.

I grabbed his left wrist. 'Where did you get this watch from?' I asked.

'Hey, Mama, let go,' he protested. 'A boy in my class gave it to me.'

'That's not what I heard.'

He burst – or rather exploded – into tears and began stamping his foot on the floor. 'He did, Mama! He did, he gave it to me!'

'He gave it to you to look at, Bruno, not to keep.'

'He gave it to me, he gave it to me, he gave it to me,' he repeated over and over, his face red, tears streaming down. 'He gave it to me, he did, I promise!'

I suddenly found myself wondering how Roy would have coped with him in this situation.

I looked up and saw Julia Schmitt, with her stern face and stern hair, looking at me and I could see in her expression she was saying, silently, *What are you going to do about this? About your little monster?*

I did, after several more embarrassing minutes of tantrum in front of a stranger, finally get the watch back off him and I handed it to Julia Schmitt.

She didn't thank me. Instead she said, 'I think your son needs to see a specialist doctor. He is not right to be here. You should not have brought him here, he is too disruptive.'

Then she was gone.

I thought we'd hit rock bottom with Nicos. Clearly we hadn't.

71

Hans-Jürgen seemed a completely different person from the cool charmer I felt I'd grown close to, back at the Scientologists' HQ, and from the person I'd spoken to for comfort in these final months with Nicos. Four years ago, after running away from my life, he had been a great mentor. But what I hadn't seen before, in those months I stayed with the Scientologists, was just how messianic he was. Back then I was just grateful to be away from Roel Albazi and to feel safe. It was as if all the time that we had been a thousand miles away from each other he had tried to close that gap by being so warm and caring over the phone. But now I was here, he seemed, at least in his body language, to be trying to push back to a distance between us again.

In this bizarre castle, running his own show, his own *cult* – because that's what we were, albeit a benign one – he was pretty much revered as a god. But he seemed to be doing his very best to appear accessible to everyone, to give the impression that if he was a god, then he was just a regular one, not special. A kind of Ordinary Joe god.

Our dinner date was something of a disappointment on several levels. I'd expected, at the very least, to be somewhere on our own, where we could talk in private. Instead, keeping up his 'just a regular Joe' god status, we queued with our trays along with everyone else at the Refectory buffet. There was hot and cold food, something-for-everyone options, each labelled for some reason with an exclamation mark at the end. Meat! Pescatarian! Vegetarian! Vegan! Nut-free! Gluten-free! Lactose intolerance!

We then sat opposite each other in the middle of one of the rows of communal tables, with other residents on either side of us, who all told us they loved us, and we told them we loved them, too. At the far end was the guy with the crazy hair I'd exchanged a smile with this afternoon. We caught each other's eye again and exchanged another WTF? smile, before I turned my one hundred per cent focus back on Hans-Jürgen, trying to break down that strange barrier that seemed to have appeared between us.

To my surprise he'd not yet said anything much about Nicos. I guess I'd told him pretty much all there was in our long phone calls. He didn't seem even remotely interested in his friend's welfare.

I started by asking him how the Association of Free Spirits had come about, flattering him with how wonderful I thought the atmosphere here was. Although . . . Privately, looking around at everyone in their clinical white tunics, I could for a moment have been at a convention of cruise ship cabin stewards.

He launched into PR mode, as if he was responding to an interview question from a reporter. As he spoke, his eyes gleamed with the cold zeal of the fanatic, although his wonderful, mellifluous voice retained all its calm and its seductive charm.

He told me the Association of Free Spirits was his brainchild and entirely funded by him. Lowering his voice, and checking no one either side of us was listening, he confided that he'd inherited a family fortune, substantially founded during the Second World War from supplying aviation components to the Luftwaffe.

What troubled me, despite his concern not to be overheard, was that he seemed to think that was OK. And of course, all these years later, maybe it was. Perhaps I was too judgemental.

Particularly as Hans-Jürgen seemed such a genuinely caring person, on a mission to use his vast inheritance to try to change the world. One of his visions, he explained – and he seemed to have many – was to reprogramme the violence in so many people's DNA and channel it into a force for good.

There was something about this that made me think of a history documentary I'd once watched with Roy, about a rock festival in San Francisco, back in 1969. It was the so-called Summer of Love, when hippies went around wearing bells and necklaces of flowers and Scott McKenzie stole the hearts of every person in the world who truly cared, with his song 'San Francisco (Be Sure to Wear Flowers in Your Hair)'.

Back then, it seemed there had been a real feeling of optimism. That yes, everyone could make the world the awesome place it should have been. *They really could! All they needed was love.*

But the Vietnam War was still raging, along with many other wars, and then the big one – 9/11, and the collapse of the Twin Towers – and the world was back to the dark place it always seemed to have been.

Except that Hans-Jürgen genuinely believed we could change it. That we *had* to change it if we were to survive as a species. I was fine with that; as the mother of a young child, I was all for doing everything I needed to change the world.

But as we continued to sit in the packed Refectory, while Hans-Jürgen concentrated on cutting into a thick piece of pork, for a moment his mask slipped and I was no longer looking at a visionary, just a rich, sanctimonious, smug guy.

I can't pinpoint when exactly or why I felt it. It was just the way he glanced around, so proprietorially. As if revelling in the fact that every single person in this grand old schloss was here because of him.

Then he looked across at me again and I suddenly saw the old warmth and the deep penetrating gaze from four years ago. 'So there is a problem with your son, Bruno, yes?'

I shrugged.

'We have some very upset parents, Sandra. If you are happy, I will tomorrow have Bruno assessed by our resident doctor, Herr Borg.' He looked at me deeply again. 'Because it is not possible to have a repeat of today.'

'Of course, I understand. Is Dr Borg a psychologist or psychiatrist?'

'Neither, but he is a very smart physician; he will assess your son and decide if he should see perhaps a child psychologist. Of course, with your permission. Would you agree to this?'

'And if I don't agree?'

His mask slipped even more and suddenly I wasn't looking at the friendly, caring Hans-Jürgen Waldinger I thought I knew, but a total stranger. A hard, cold businessman.

'If you do not agree, Sandra, then it will not be possible for you and Bruno to remain here – and this would make me sad.'

72

Autumn 2011

I stared at Hans-Jürgen for some moments, anger rising inside me, even though I knew I was in the wrong here.

'Would it?' I challenged. 'Would it really make you sad if Bruno and I left? Really? You're not giving me that impression.'

I realized, although I didn't really care, that I'd raised my voice and people on either side of us were looking at me.

He waited for some moments, then looked wistful. 'Sandra, this would make me very sad.'

'Well, I don't think I'm going to be able to remain here, anyway.'

He looked surprised. 'No? What is the reason?'

'It's a bit embarrassing – I never realized that I would have to pay to stay here. If I'd known, I wouldn't have come. I can't afford to pay around one thousand pounds a day.' I looked down at the table, at my pasta and beetroot salad. 'Not for more than a very short while.'

Then something touched my hand.

I looked up and he was holding it and squeezing, gently. And looking at me closely. Like a paternal look. 'Sandra, I have learned that if something is for free then people do not value this. But, if you have not the money, then perhaps we should look for some other way for you to pay.' He squeezed my hand again and suddenly I felt awkward. What was he insinuating?

He must have seen that thought in my eyes and he laughed

and shook his head. 'No, no, no! You are misunderstanding! Please, you must know that I am now celibate and have been for a while. I do not have sex or seek sex. I channel all these energies into here, this place and my mission.' He opened his arms expansively.

'Mission?' I asked.

Unhurriedly, he cut off another small piece of pork and chewed, then placed his knife and fork down neatly. 'There is a question I ask myself, Sandra. I've been asking it from a very young age; the older I get, the more it concerns me.' He drank some water.

'The question is?'

'It is a very simple one: would the world be any different if I had not existed?'

I reflected on this for some moments before responding. 'And are you any closer to an answer than when you first asked that question?'

He raised his arms in the air and gestured around at the fifty or so people in the room. 'I wish so. I hope that at least some of these people will make a difference because of what they learn and practise here, and at the other branches of my Association that I am going to be opening across the world.'

I felt so divided at this moment. Part of me wanted to tell him he had an ego that was out of control. But the other part of me saw such very deep sincerity. A rich man's vanity or a true visionary who had the ability to live his dream with open eyes?

After our meal he escorted me back up to our suite, but politely declined my invitation to come in for a nightcap. Not that I had anything to offer beyond tea or coffee.

'Us will see you tomorrow,' he said, in the charming way I had noticed that some Germans, no matter how well they spoke English, got 'we' and 'us' slightly wrong. 'We will make alterna- tive arrangements for your accommodation in my private suite, where I have very nice guest rooms, and there will not be any more charges. I will have everything you have paid so far refunded.'

'Seriously?'

'Of course.'

It was 9.15 p.m. and my dinner date was over.

And yet.

Hans-Jürgen was endearing.

At least he did bloody care, unlike Nicos, who was just a vulture, out for whatever pickings he could take from the carcass of human decency.

I checked on Bruno, opening his door quietly, and to my relief he was asleep. I closed it and returned to my thoughts.

God, I could have done with a drink. I reflected on his words. *Would the world be any different if I had not existed?*

Suddenly, again, I found myself turning to Roy for the answer. I knew exactly what he would have told Hans-Jürgen. It had become almost a mantra to him. A principle. It was something I had always admired about him and always remembered. Perhaps, I thought with sudden realization, it was Roy's defining quality. He would have said, '*No man ever made a greater mistake than the man who did nothing because he could only do a little.'*

Tomorrow, I decided, I would find the Hochmeister and tell him that. But perhaps he knew it already?

Then I reined myself in with a reality check. *Hey, you left Roy. Now you're quoting him. Really?*

I walked across the lounge to the open window and stared out across the parkland and the lake and the dense trees beyond, and breathed in the sweet scent of dewy, freshly mown grass.

I felt lonely, suddenly. Lonelier than I could remember. Other than Bruno and Hans-Jürgen I didn't know anyone here – and I realized I didn't really know Hans-Jürgen at all. There were a couple of dozen books on the shelves in the room, mostly in German, but I'd seen a large English section in the library downstairs and I decided I would have a browse tomorrow.

I missed having a television.

I missed so much else, too.

My thoughts returned to Nicos and his boat and what was happening. I tried, with the signal that seemed particularly feeble, to log back onto the websites of the Jersey papers, but to my frustration that timed out also.

Probably just as well.

73

The signal was better in the morning. Nicos was the lead story in the *Bailiwick Express*, and the *Jersey Evening Post*'s front-page splash for the second day running.

ABANDONED YACHT MYSTERY DEEPENS

Beneath the headline were photographs of Nicos and myself.

Was it just an unfortunate printing glitch that made my face look dark and sinister, or had someone in the photographic department of the newspaper done this to deliberately make me look like a criminal? I stared at it in horror. I looked a bit like the Moors murderer Myra Hindley. Where the hell did they get it from? Great. I read on.

States of Jersey Police have taken command as the lead investigators in the mystery of the abandoned thirty-eight-foot motor yacht Bolt-Hole, *found drifting ten nautical miles off St Peter Port, Guernsey, on Tuesday morning. Chief Inspector Callum O'Connor told this paper that they are working closely with the Jersey Coastguard and Customs and Immigration and that the boat, which has now been towed into St Helier harbour, has been declared a crime scene.*

'We are currently conducting a forensic search of the vessel,' CI O'Connor told the JEP. 'At the present time we do not know who was on board or how it came to be abandoned. The boat is modern, in good mechanical order, and the sea-state

was moderate at the time it was found adrift and abandoned. No freak waves, which might have caused a capsize, had been reported by any local fishermen or sailors.

'We are working on a number of theories, which include the owner, Nicos Christoforou, who had business interests in Jersey, and who was believed to have been on board earlier Monday evening, falling overboard. But, having done some investigation into Mr Christoforou's background, we are not at this stage ruling out foul play. We are anxious to speak to his partner, Sandra Jones, with whom, along with her young child, he shared an unqualified apartment close to Victoria Avenue. Neither have been seen since the beginning of the week.'

Not ruling out foul play? No shit, Sherlock!

I was deeply curious what they had found out about Nicos's background. And I did not like that they were anxious to speak to me. How anxious, and how far would they push to do that? I was far enough away, I thought, unaware I was about to find that Jersey might be a small island but it had a long reach. But for now I wasn't worried about myself, I desperately needed to find out what had happened to Nicos. What did the police know and were holding back? What investigations had they done into Nicos's background?

'States of Jersey Police held a press conference yesterday in which we put out an appeal to any members of the public who might have seen either Mr Christoforou or his partner, Sandra Jones, and her son, between the hours of 11 a.m. and 8 p.m. on Monday, to call States of Jersey Police, on +44 (0) 1534 612616 and ask for the Operation Sandbar incident room, or call Crimestoppers, anonymously, on +44 (0) 800 555111.'

I read the piece again, then a third time, checking for any little nugget, any hidden clue about Nicos in the Chief Inspector's guarded comments that I might have missed.

The boat had been declared a crime scene, which surely indicated they did suspect foul play. Investigations into his background led them to the possibility of foul play, they said.

'Mama, I'm hungry,' Bruno whined, walking sleepily into my room in his pyjamas and rubbing his eyes.

I put my phone down, gave him a good-morning kiss on the forehead, then suggested he get dressed quickly, so we could hurry downstairs before all the food was gone.

'Do I have to go to that class again today? They are too babyish for me,' he asked, his face squidging into a grump mask.

'Actually, my darling,' I said as an idea flashed into my head, thinking about Hans-Jürgen's request last night for Bruno to see the resident doctor – Borg or whatever his name was. 'There's someone who is going to talk to you this morning and see if there is a better class for you.'

Bruno suddenly looked so serious. 'I think that would be good, Mama. They were all so stupid in my class yesterday.' He nodded his head. 'I mean, really, you just wouldn't believe how stupid they are.'

I ruffled his hair, which he hated and immediately stepped away. 'How does it feel to be the brightest little boy in the world?' I joked.

But he replied without smiling. 'I'm brighter than a five-year-old.'

'Of course you are, darling.'

He tilted his head back and strode off back to his room, reminding me of a character called Johnny Head-in-the-Air from one of my favourite childhood books, *Struwwelpeter*.

Then I shuddered. They were all cautionary tales in that book.

Most of the children died horribly. Johnny Head-in-the-Air walked over the edge of a riverbank.

My phone rang. It was Julia Schmitt. Dr Borg could see Bruno at 9 a.m. I looked at my watch. It was just gone 7.30.

74

Half an hour later, Bruno sat next to me at the Refectory table, messily shovelling Coco Pops into his mouth, from a bowl of them drenched in milk.

As I prodded my spoon at a bowl of granola, berries and yoghurt, with no appetite, thoughts about Nicos were swimming in my mind.

Or about Nicos not swimming at all.

I just could not stop thinking, wondering, what had happened out there in that dark ocean.

I was feeling terrible. Had he made his rendezvous with the Saul Brignell boat and been killed and dumped overboard when they'd found out how little cash he had with him? I knew it wouldn't be good when they found out but I wasn't thinking he'd be drowned. I was expecting either he would get a beating or the boat would be intercepted by Customs. It made me sick to think that what I'd done may have been the cause of his apparent death.

I went over and over it in my head, my anxiety going through the roof again. Yes, he deserved to suffer for all the shit he had done to me and Bruno over these past few years. But no one deserves to be sent to their death. Maybe it was that damned Lutheran background instilled in me in early childhood: *Do the right thing.* And putting Nicos in that situation wasn't doing the right thing.

Or had Nicos cut a deal of some kind with the Brignell mob? He was persuasive enough to cut a deal with anyone.

Or had he simply, cunningly, faked his disappearance to escape from them?

And come after me?

I needed to re-read the newspaper article to see if it said anything about the *Bolt-Hole*'s lifeboat. Because if the lifeboat was missing, it could mean Nicos had used it. I knew from my times on *Bolt-Hole* that the lifeboat, a RIB, had a powerful outboard motor. It could reach any of the other Channel Islands, or even the French coast, in an hour or so in most weather conditions, and Nicos had told me he had on a number of occasions launched it off *Bolt-Hole* out at sea, at night, to collect or deliver drug consignments on remote parts of the French coast as well as Guernsey and Alderney, without fear of being picked up on a coastguard's radar.

Had fisherman Adam le Seelleur, who had ferried me to Saint-Malo, done the dirty and snitched to Nicos? Or would he, when he saw that the police wanted to speak to me, go to them?

But that would be insane. What could le Seelleur have to gain from confessing he'd illegally smuggled us into France, other than risking his licence?

'Hey, good morning!' said a man with a gravelly American accent. I smelled the reek of tobacco – forbidden here of course like pretty much everything else that was remotely naughty – and looked up, to see Shambolic Hair looking down with a broad smile. 'This your kid?'

I can't explain what it was, but he instantly fired me out of my dark thoughts and put a smile on my face. 'No, I don't know who he is – I just found him under a rock.' I winked at Bruno and he smiled.

Shambolic Hair grinned and held out a hand and in an American accent said, 'I'm Stoker.'

'Stoker? As in Bram?'

He looked puzzled, not getting it. 'Bram? No, I don't think so.'

I shook his hand back, and put him out of his misery. 'Bram Stoker wrote *Dracula*.'

He beamed and nodded. Then he tapped the side of his head. 'Yeah, well, you're too sharp for me, at this hour. I just spent the night in a coffin, cut me some slack, lady!'

I laughed, I couldn't help it. He had this face that was part impish, part handsome, part . . . rebellious. There was something wild about him. Something dangerous. 'You need to grind those teeth,' I replied. 'They look too blunt – for a vampire.'

He nodded, as if he wasn't sure I was joking, then stood awkwardly for a moment. 'Actually, I've come to say goodbye, which is kind of a bummer, as I've not yet even met you.'

'Was it something I said?' I fired back. I don't know what it was exactly, but I felt such an instant chemistry between us.

He shook his head. 'I guess it was something you didn't say. But, hey, who knows, if we're meant to meet again, we'll meet again. Until then, *tschüss*!'

'*Hasta la vista*!' I replied.

He made a gun out of his fist and pointed the barrel at me. '*Hasta la vista, baby*!'

Then he was gone.

There were more Coco Pops spilt on the table around Bruno's bowl than remained inside it, along with ocean-sized puddles of milk, but he continued eating, oblivious to the mess. I turned and looked towards the door. Shambolic Hair was standing there, on the far side of the room, seemingly looking back at me. Our eyes met briefly – unless I imagined that – and then he really was gone.

Leaving my insides all shaken up. At least it stopped me racing through thoughts about Nicos.

I certainly wasn't looking for a relationship at the moment. But to feel a flutter at a brief flirtation with this Stoker guy, along with the cold distance Hans-Jürgen had put between us, made me realize just how much I was missing the warmth I had always felt with Roy.

God, how stupid had I been to leave him?

Or was I just in a bad dip right now?

Stoker. Cool name. The American stranger. And now he was gone, out of my life. Ships in the night.

Although maybe that wasn't such a great analogy at the moment.

I looked at my watch. 8.45. Time to take Bruno to Dr Borg and see what he would make of my son.

And afterwards, to see what the doctor would prescribe me. I had done a calculation and worked out I had just one more day's supply of the tablets they gave me – dihydrocodeine – and I don't think the schloss will give me any more tablets. They do keep my cravings for heroin at bay.

Perhaps I could go to a chemist to get my prescription. Maybe pick up a bottle of nice wine. How I missed those pleasures.

As I stood up, and was about to tell Bruno it was time for us to go, I saw Julia Schmitt striding anxiously across the room towards us, followed by another, young, friendly-looking woman, in the same schloss tunic. I wondered why she was in such a hurry. Had I misheard the time of the doctor's appointment and we were late?

Then when she spoke, giving me a strange look as she did, I was seized with complete and utter panic.

'Sandra, there are two police officers who would like to speak to you.'

75

I stared at Julia numbly. My mind hung, my brain spinning like one of those infuriating little pinwheels on a computer screen. 'Police?' I said lamely.

I was frantically trying to think of all the reasons the police would want to speak to me. Had Roy finally tracked me down? Was I here illegally? But that could not be the case, this was the EU, I could travel freely anywhere within it if I wanted. It had to be something to do with Nicos, I concluded, but what?

Was he going to accuse me of stealing from him?

No way.

Julia Schmitt turned to the woman behind her. 'This is my colleague, Ellen Reinbach-Brenner. She will take Bruno to see Dr Borg, if you come with me.'

Her colleague gave me a reassuring smile.

'But – I – I want to be there for the consultation.'

Very firmly Julia replied, 'It is Dr Borg's preference to see him alone and then to speak to you afterwards. And these police officers must speak to you urgently.'

I leaned down to Bruno and explained quickly to him that this lady, Ellen, would take him to meet the man I'd talked about yesterday. He looked at her very closely, as if appraising her head to toe and then back up to the head, like a tailor or dressmaker. 'What computer games do you like?' he asked her.

I took the opportunity to slip away and followed Julia back

across the Refectory, then along the labyrinth of corridors, the stone walls lined with sconces holding unlit candles, and framed motivational quotes that were on just about every wall in this vast building.

Man cannot seek new horizons until he has the courage to lose sight of the shore.

A mind once stretched can never return to its original dimensions.

Failure isn't making the mistake. It's allowing the mistake to win.

Then we came into the entrance foyer. Standing by the reception desk, which Bruno and I had arrived at just two days ago, were two men in smart green uniforms that had a military cut. One, tall and wiry, in his forties, with wavy grey hair, had two pips on his epaulettes, and the other, some years his junior, with sleek black hair, and a good-looking but a don't-mess-with-me face, had just one.

Julia introduced me.

The tall one said, with no handshake offered, 'Good morning, *sprechen Sie Deutsch*?'

'I'm sorry, I don't.'

He smiled, pleasantly, but not that warmly. 'We are detectives from the Munich Headquarters. I am Kriminalhauptkommissar Ludwig Bollenbacher, and my colleague is Kriminalkommissar Jörg Steinmetz. We would like please to ask you some questions.'

'Sure,' I said, shaking with nerves. 'What about, exactly?'

They both looked at Julia, and I had the uncomfortable feeling she knew something I didn't. She led us through a doorway behind the reception desk into a small, cluttered office, with a table and four chairs surrounded by shelves loaded with a printer and a mass of files, and general office clutter. '*Kann ich Ihnen ein Getränk holen? Kaffee?*' she said to the police officers.

Both shook their heads and she left the room, closing the door behind her.

I felt very alone and very scared. I looked at Bollenbacher, who seemed the friendlier of the two. Was I about to be interrogated by the hard man–soft man technique I'd read about in books and seen in movies?

Bollenbacher spoke first. 'Frau Jones, we have been requested to speak with you by the States of Jersey Police, in regard to Herr Nicos Christoforou, who we understand is your partner?'

I stared at him for some moments, in silence. Wondering just how much he knew. Perhaps that I'd changed my name. But how far back had he drilled? Did he know who I really was?

I chose my words carefully before replying, not at all sure where this might be going. 'He is my ex-partner, I have left him.'

The two officers exchanged a glance, which unnerved me. *Just what the hell did they know?*

'How long have you been his *ex*-partner, Ms Jones?' Steinmetz said. From his cultured voice I could tell he was more comfortable speaking English than his colleague.

'I left him just under a week ago.'

'On Monday, September the twenty-sixth?' Steinmetz said. 'The last time anyone has seen him?'

I felt like I had just stepped onto the edge of an elephant trap. Gathering my thoughts quickly, I said, 'What do you mean, "the last time anyone has seen him"? Has something happened to him?'

The two officers exchanged another glance. Steinmetz responded. 'You are not aware that Nicos Christoforou has not been seen since the night of September the twenty-sixth?'

I had no idea what my rights were, here in Germany. Should I ask for a lawyer? I decided, for the moment, to play dumb and innocent. Both of them were looking at me, no doubt reading my body language and wondering why I was pale and trembling. I shook my head. 'No, I had no idea. He has not been seen since then? I did not know that. I just wanted to get away from him – and get my son away from him.'

'He is not your son's father?' Jörg Steinmetz asked.

'No. I did not move in with him until some while after my son was born.'

'Could you tell us your movements on Monday, September the twenty-sixth?' Steinmetz said, in perfect English, and only a slight German accent.

Again I was careful before replying. 'Well, yes. I returned from England on the Condor ferry at around 5 p.m.'

'And the purpose of your trip there, exactly, was?' Bollenbacher asked.

'I had not been back for three years. I wanted to see some old friends.' Then, in what I thought was a flash of inspiration, I said, 'I wanted to take my son to his grandparents. And I thought it would be good for Bruno to see where I lived before Jersey.'

I felt very uncomfortable about the penetrating way the two German detectives were looking at me. The scepticism on their faces.

I felt myself squirming. I was starting to blush. They could see I was lying. 'Tell me something,' I asked. 'How did you find me here?'

Bollenbacher replied first. 'We are informed by the States of Jersey Police that during the past months you have made phone calls to Hans-Jürgen Waldinger on the apartment phone. It was not hard. We contacted the schloss on their behalf and they told us you are here.'

I thought carefully before responding again. 'OK, what you need to know is that I was in an abusive relationship with Nicos Christoforou, which is why I left him. Years of hell, in which I felt that my life and also my son Bruno's were in danger.'

'Can you tell us, Ms Jones,' asked Jörg Steinmetz, 'when was the last time you saw Nicos Christoforou? The exact time, to the hour?'

'Yes, it was about 8 p.m. on the evening of last Monday. He told me the sea was quite calm and it would be a good night to go out fishing for bluefin tuna.'

'This is something he did regularly?'

I nodded. 'Fishing was his hobby.'

'Is it not coincidental, do you think,' Steinmetz continued, 'that the night you disappeared is the same night your partner, who you say was abusive to you, was last seen? Because it seems a little more than coincidence to the police in Jersey who have requested us to detain you.'

'What do you mean?' I blurted, panic rising inside me.

The Kriminalkommissar dug his hand inside his tunic and produced a document, which he unfolded. 'Frau Jones, I have a request here from the States of Jersey Police to arrange for you to be taken to our police headquarters in order that Jersey detectives can question you about the suspicious disappearance of Mr Nicos Christoforou.'

I jumped up in blind panic, yelling, 'That is ridiculous!'

My one thought at this moment was to get to Bruno. No one was taking me and making me leave Bruno behind.

But Steinmetz had read me, and was blocking the door seconds before I reached it. 'Please, Frau Jones, be calm.'

'Be calm?' I shouted, looking at him incredulously. 'You're accusing me of murdering my monster of a former boyfriend and you're telling me to keep calm?'

His colleague intervened in his clumsy English. 'Frau Jones, it is not we accusing, we are on the instructions of the police in Jersey. If you wish us to restrain you with handcuffs, we will do this, but I don't think it is needed?'

I took a very deep breath and tried my hardest to calm down. Then I sank back into my chair and began sobbing. 'This is not possible, it's not possible. There's been a big mistake, a terrible mistake.'

'There are two detectives on their way here from Jersey to speak to you, Frau Jones,' Steinmetz said. 'They will be here in Munich in around –' he checked his watch – 'two hours. We will take you to the police headquarters for processing and there they will interview you.'

'Processing?' I asked, the word freaking me out. 'Is my son coming too?'

'This has all been arranged,' Steinmetz said. 'Your son, Bruno, will remain here in the care of Frau Reinbach-Brenner.'

I felt close to throwing up from nerves, and from the anger inside me, as the realization hit me. Julia Schmitt already knew about this when she came to the Refectory to collect me. She had already been making arrangements. Presumably Hans-Jürgen knew also.

'You don't need to handcuff me,' I said lamely, through my tears.

76

Half an hour later, on the second floor of the Munich Police HQ, I was in a function room that felt like a laboratory. With its pale blue walls and ancient office furniture, on which perched a battery of modern high-tech equipment and a plump, smiling man with a crew cut and a badly fitting uniform.

I volunteered to provide my fingerprints and photograph as I didn't want to appear obstructive. The plump man indicated a chair that immediately brought to mind images I had once seen of Old Sparky, America's most infamous electric chair.

This was a contraption consisting of a wooden chair on a swivel, at the end of what I can best describe as a wooden plank, facing, by contrast, a modern camera.

'Frau Jones, please, a seat!' He positively beamed encouragement at me, as if to sit in this chair was the greatest privilege he could bestow on any human being in his charge.

So I dutifully sat in it. It was hard. He partially disappeared behind the camera and called out, 'At me, please, look here, *ja*!'

There was a brief flash.

Then he pulled a lever beside him that I hadn't noticed, and my chair swivelled 90 degrees to the left. There was another flash. He pulled the lever again and I swivelled 180 degrees.

Flash!

'All done!' he announced.

Then Kriminalkommissar Steinmetz, who was waiting in an adjoining room, escorted me, along with a female officer, to a side office. The officer offered me coffee, which I accepted, and asked if I needed anything to eat. But I wasn't hungry. It was 11 a.m. Steinmetz informed me that the two detectives from Jersey would be here in one hour.

Then the door slammed shut. And I realized for the first, and I hoped only time in my life, what a truly horrible sound that was. It shook every fibre in my body, and the sound echoed in my ears like the peal of a bell.

It was a tiny, windowless room, with the only place to sit an indented ledge at the far end.

The Jersey police couldn't seriously think I had murdered Nicos, could they?

But they had clearly gone to a lot of trouble to find me.

What had happened since I'd left in the fishing boat that night? Had they found something they hadn't told the press yet?

Nicos? His body?

Shit, was this going to backfire horribly on me? Oh God, I couldn't bear it. I could feel my anxiety rising.

Just over an hour later I was in another room with the officers from Jersey. They introduced themselves. 'Detective Constable Rosie Barclay and Detective Sergeant Jason Cowleard.' She was pleasant, in her mid-thirties, I guessed. Wavy brown hair and conservatively dressed. The female soft-man to her hard-man colleague.

Cowleard was tall, bald and looked like he wanted to be anywhere but here, in a Munich Police Headquarters interview room, right now. And I couldn't blame him.

It was small and horrible. Slime-green walls, a metal table, metal chairs, the sour, ingrained reek of a million cigarettes that had been smoked in here. Somewhere beyond these walls a glorious autumn day was happening – without us.

I had to hand it to these two, they had sure done their home-work, in rapid time.

They knew the gym I had joined in Jersey, the Carrefour, and they'd already spoken to one of my buddies there, Beth Pettit, who had told them she had recently seen the bruises below my neck and had quizzed me on them. They'd spoken to our cleaning lady, Vesma Jermaka, who had told them how one morning a month ago she had arrived to find me crying, with a cut lip. DC Barclay said that Vesma had also told them that Nicos terrorized Bruno and had come close to striking him on several occasions. She had told them it was only a matter of time before he did hit Bruno, in her opinion.

I'd told Vesma just how vile and abusive Nicos had been to me, but that I'd been more worried about how he treated Bruno, and that I was really scared he would hurt him one day. I'd also said I was seriously thinking of leaving Nicos and that I was beginning to plan how.

When I asked them if they had any news of Nicos they exchanged a strange glance and replied, a little too bluntly, that they hadn't.

'Ms Jones,' Jason Cowleard said. 'At 9 p.m. on the night of September the twenty-sixth, a taxi driver, Toby McMichael, dropped you and your son outside a small apartment block just above Bouley Bay. None of the occupants know you there. So what was your actual destination on that night?'

I looked at them both. And I could see in their eyes that they knew.

'Saint-Malo.'

'Where you had a hire car booked with Sixt, which you were due to pick up in the morning,' Cowleard said.

I looked at him, wondering how on earth he knew that.

'Your cleaning lady, Ms Jermaka, gave us your phone number. We obtained the records from that and the numbers you had called in the days immediately prior to September the twenty-sixth.'

'How did you get to Saint-Malo?' DC Barclay asked.

'On a boat,' I replied.

'So you were on a boat,' DS Cowleard said, 'heading out of Bouley Bay, shortly after the last time anyone saw Mr Christoforou?'

'I think you are putting two and two together and making five,' I said testily.

'Is that what you really think?' he asked, staring at me even more intently.

'It is, yes.'

'Ms Jones,' Detective Barclay asked. 'How much do you know about your partner – apologies – *ex*-partner's business activities?'

I should have anticipated the question, but I stupidly hadn't, thanks to my discombobulated brain, and it hit me like a cold slap. I suddenly felt very queasy, on the verge of throwing up. I took several deep breaths to calm myself before answering. They were both looking at me intently, scrutinizing my face as if it was an object of wonder in a museum display case.

My reply, popping out of nowhere, was little short of inspirational, I thought. 'Nicos regarded all women as just *her indoors*. Someone who should be at home, the little housewife, there for cooking, cleaning, laundry and sex – he never shared—'

Cowleard instantly interrupted. 'You said *regarded*, Ms Jones – why did you say *Nicos regarded*? Why did you use the past tense?'

That flummoxed me. I blushed – it was more of a hot flush. 'A slip of the tongue,' I mumbled. 'Once I'd left him, he became a *was* to me. Nothing makes any sense.'

They were still staring at me intently. 'You lived with him for more than three years?' Detective Barclay asked.

'About that, yes.'

'During this time were you aware of him being involved in any criminal activity?' She seemed to be turning increasingly cold and hard.

'Criminal activity?' I feigned astonishment. 'What do you mean, what kind?'

'Are you a drug user?' Detective Cowleard asked.

'Me?'

They looked at me in silence. I kept wondering, *what do you know that you are not telling me?*

'An empty prescription package, labelled methadone, with your name on it, was found in the apartment you shared with Mr Christoforou,' Detective Barclay continued.

I'd thrown that in the bin before leaving, just the outer envelope. They'd been going through the rubbish? Clearly, they'd been going through absolutely everything.

Shit.

'I believe methadone is prescribed for opiate addiction. That it is particularly effective for someone trying to get off a heroin dependency. Is that the case with you?' Barclay asked.

Something in the way she said it and the way she was looking at me told me she knew, she absolutely knew.

I didn't need to answer. The two detectives could see my red face.

'Ms Jones, were you addicted to heroin before you met Mr Christoforou, or after?' Detective Cowleard asked.

I was wary of saying anything that might incriminate me. I felt I should maybe have a lawyer present. 'I'm not prepared to answer that,' I said, more confidently than I felt.

'You should know that a substantial quantity of drugs has been found in the apartment. A commercial volume of heroin, cocaine and other substances. Are these yours?' he asked.

I felt the floor was sinking beneath me, as if I was in an elevator.

'A commercial volume? You're – you're joking. No, no, they are not mine and I had no knowledge of them.'

'Are you aware,' Barclay asked, 'that Nicos Christoforou spent five years of a twenty-five-year sentence in prison in Zanzibar on drug smuggling charges? That he would still be there today if he hadn't escaped, and there is an international warrant out for his arrest?'

I looked at her, dumbfounded. 'No – I – he never told me.'

Then, totally unexpected and out of the blue, Detective Sergeant Cowleard asked, 'Ms Jones, did you kill Nicos Christoforou?'

I was so stunned by the direct accusation it took me a moment to think clearly. 'Do you seriously think that?'

For the second time, I wondered if I should get a lawyer. But then I thought, why the hell should I? I'd done nothing apart from fleeing from an abusive monster.

Well, perhaps not *nothing*.

'You say you went on a boat to Saint-Malo on the night of September the twenty-sixth. What time was that?' DC Barclay asked.

'It was soon after the taxi dropped myself and my son in Bouley Bay.'

She glanced at her notebook. 'According to the driver, Mr Toby McMichael, he dropped you and your son at Bouley Bay at approximately 11.10 p.m. That is three hours after the last time your former partner was seen. Can you tell us what you were doing in that time?'

From three years of regularly going out with Nicos on his boat, I had learned something of the local winds and tides. 'What I was doing in that time was feeding my son and myself, packing and organizing the taxi pick-up. But as you clearly think I murdered Nicos during that window, let me explain some nautical facts to you. On the night of Monday, September the twenty-sixth, there was a south-westerly wind of 12 knots, gusting sixteen. The south-westerly is the prevailing wind of the Channel Islands, as I'm sure you know?'

The two detectives looked at me, frowning.

'The missing boat was, as has been reported on and detailed in the *Jersey Evening Post* extensively, clocked by the Corbière coastguard radar station heading on a north-westerly course at 8.30 p.m. that night. Some while later, the boat was found abandoned, drifting ten nautical miles off Guernsey, according to what I've read.' I looked at them for acknowledgement.

Cowleard nodded. 'Yes. Your point being?'

'Hear me out.' I suddenly felt my confidence surging. 'Someone was steering the boat, so, unless it was stolen, it was Nicos – he's never let me steer the *Bolt-Hole*. He was heading against the prevailing wind and tides. Many hours later, the boat was found drifting somewhere off Guernsey, which means that before it was abandoned it must have been several miles west of Guernsey for it to have drifted that way. Are you seriously suggesting that between the hours of 8 p.m. and 11 p.m. on Monday, September the twenty-sixth, I was on board the boat, murdered Nicos, and then miraculously got back? Because I sure as hell didn't swim thirty miles back to shore with a young boy strapped to my back in that time.'

Cowleard, unsmiling, asked, 'Could the skipper of the boat that took you to Saint-Malo vouch for you – as an alibi?'

I hesitated, thinking hard again. I didn't want to dump Adam le Seelleur in it, but then he hadn't actually done anything wrong, had he? He'd simply ferried me to France, a country I could legally enter as a European citizen. All the same, I felt a loyalty to him. 'I'm sure he could,' I replied.

'Can you give us his name?' he asked.

I looked at him levelly. 'Are you arresting me for anything?'

Cowleard and Barclay shot a glance at each other. 'No, Ms Jones, we are not arresting you – this is not our jurisdiction. All we are concerned with at this stage is establishing what has happened to Nicos Christoforou.'

'In which case, have a nice day in Munich, and enjoy your trip home to beautiful Jersey.'

77

Autumn 2011 – Roel Albazi

They called it 'doing time', and Prisoner Number FF276493 still had plenty more of the stuff to do. A minimum of six long years. Or to put it the way it was marked out on his wall chart, 2,163 days.

His last girlfriend had a grumpy teenage daughter, Izzy. Whenever he'd asked Izzy how her day had been she would yawn a reply, invariably, 'Same old, same old.'

If she wanted to know what same old, same old, really felt like, she should do a spell in prison, Roel Albazi thought. Every single one of the days inside would really be the same. Get up, shower, eat breakfast, keep out of trouble. Go to woodwork class, keep out of trouble. Eat lunch. Go to the gym. Keep out of trouble. Then visiting time, except he rarely had visitors. Followed by association half-hour with his fellow prisoners. Then he would be locked in his cell until 7 a.m. the next morning.

The only regular visitor he'd had was Skender Sharka but now that had stopped. The idiot, only recently released from prison, had been busted at Manchester Airport with enough Class A drugs in his carry-on to ensure he wouldn't be free again until pretty much around the time he himself was out. Occasionally he'd get a visit from one of his friends in the local Albanian community – mostly one of his team members from the regular Sunday football knockabout they had in St Anne's Well Gardens.

He went straight to his cell at the start of association. He had no interest in associating with any of his fellow prisoners. He didn't want to have to listen to their tales of woe, of how they were fitted up by the police, or just generally had screwed up.

He only wanted to do his time, the very minimum time – 2,163 more days before he would be freed on licence, provided he 'kept out of trouble'.

And he was utterly determined to keep out of trouble.

This morning, a new day, one day fewer to go, he picked up the black Sharpie marker pen and put another cross on the chart. Now it was only 2,162 days.

He was proud of his beautifully framed chart. He had made that frame in his daily woodwork class. His instructor there told him he had real promise, that when he got out he would be able to get a decent job in the joinery department of a building company.

Albazi went along with the guy, playing the game. 'Keeping out of trouble'. There were plenty of assholes in here, and not just the prisoners who were spoiling for a fight, it was some of the screws, too. No way was he going to risk adding one single day to his sentence.

No way was he going to let Sandy Grace, or whatever the bitch's name was now, live for one extra day longer than was absolutely necessary.

He put the marker pen down on the small table, then stripped off and pulled on his shorts, singlet, socks and trainers, all set for his daily session in the gym. Strength work and aerobic, keeping up both his ripped muscles and stamina. Crunches, pull-ups, planks, the rowing machine, the treadmill – concentrating, sweating, stopping prison from breaking him the way it broke so many people.

But the part of his daily sixty-minute workout he most looked forward to was pulling on the boxing gloves and attacking the punchball.

And imagining it was a certain person's face.

Turning round, about to head out of his cell, he saw a letter lying on the floor that he could have sworn wasn't there two minutes ago. One of the screws must have put it there. *Thanks, pal, you could have said something pleasant, something like, 'Hi, Roel, you've got mail!'*

Instead of just tossing it on the floor.

But not smart to get angry. Anger led to fights and fights led to your time in here getting longer and longer. Which meant letting Sandy Grace live longer.

He picked it up. A white, letter-sized envelope that felt bulky, with his name and address on a printed label, opened by one of the screws as all mail, except letters from his solicitor, was.

Inside was the folded page of a newspaper. Puzzled, he removed it and spread it on his bed, flattening it out. It was the front page of a paper called the *Jersey Evening Post.*

The headline, above a photograph of a smart-looking boat, read: MISSING SAILOR'S PARTNER QUESTIONED IN MUNICH.

Below this photograph were two more. One was of a swarthy-looking man, with short hair and hooded, brooding eyes. The other a woman with short, wavy hair. Despite the grainy photo, different hairstyle and the fact that it had been four years since he'd last seen her, he recognized her instantly, even before reading on.

The newspaper reported her as Sandra Jones from Jersey.

Albazi didn't care what name she went under.

He cared only about one thing. She was the face he punched every day, without fail – except on rare occasions when the prison was short of screws and he wasn't allowed to leave his cell.

Oh yes!

He punched that ball so damned hard every day.

And in 2,162 days, when he was out of here, her face wouldn't be on a punchball, in his imagination. It would be on top of her neck.

'Hi, Sandy,' he said quietly, not that anyone was listening. 'Just so you know, it doesn't matter what you call yourself. The day I get out of here, I'm coming to find you. So you'd better hide really well. Because I promise you one thing. If and when I do find you, I'm going to kill you. With my bare hands.'

78

'Ms Jones, there's a question I put to the parents of all children who have been referred to me. What three words immediately spring to mind when I ask you to think about Bruno?'

I stared back at the psychologist, Dr Ramsden, who looked so serious, and pondered a few seconds. 'Let me think. Thoughtful. Inquisitive. And I guess intense. In a nice way – if you know what I mean.'

He gave me a quizzical look. Difficult to read whether he was faintly amused, or in agreement, or concerned. His voice gave nothing away, either. 'That's what springs to mind?'

I nodded my head. 'Yes, though it's hard to put him into just three words. My mind is a bit blank after a rubbish week. I'm sorry, we're not here to talk about that!'

Actually, more than a rubbish week. It had been two weeks. Two weeks of feeling constantly strung out, thanks to charmless Dr Borg, at the Schloss Leichtigkeit. He had decided in his wisdom that the dihydrocodeine I was on was not the best drug for helping to wean me from my heroin addiction. Instead, he had prescribed something different, called Espranor, which was a wafer that dissolved on my tongue.

The taste reminded me of the communion wafers placed in my hand by the pastor of Seaford every Sunday of my childhood. It had the dry flavour of an ice cream wafer, but without the joyous taste explosion of the ice cream that went with it. A bit like my childhood God, really. I did all the worship, but the ice cream always seemed to be missing.

But it wasn't ice cream that the Espranor wafer delivered, it was diarrhoea, for several days, followed by the night sweats and shakes in the day. And the constant sensation of being in a very dark, scary place that I would never get out of.

Now, as I sat in front of the eminent British child psychologist, I had the shakes and I was struggling to think clearly.

My nerves had been shot to hell and back ever since the appearance of the German police officers and my subsequent interview with the two States of Jersey Police detectives. I knew from what Roy had told me in the past how difficult it was for police officers to get permission to travel abroad – because of the cost and resourcing. Permission was usually only granted when it was a suspect in a major crime, or a key witness. Maybe I was just regarded as a key witness, but the vibe I got from detectives Cowleard and Barclay was not that. They clearly viewed me as a suspect with a smart alibi.

Sure, I could drop Adam le Seelleur in it, but there still remained the issue of the three hours or so between when Nicos was last seen and my taxi ride to Bouley Bay.

Every few hours I looked up the *Bailiwick Express* online on my phone, and every morning I scoured the *Jersey Evening Post* app for updates. The story of the drifting boat and its missing owner had dropped from the front page to just a couple of column inches on page five. The rescue operation had been stood down, and a police spokesman said it had now become a recovery operation.

Subtext: *We're looking for a body.*

79

The Allied bombers had done a fairly thorough job of flattening most of the industrial city of Frankfurt am Main during the Second World War. But the chic district of Sachsenhausen, with its cobbled streets and elegant terraced houses, had miraculously escaped largely unscathed.

I'd read about this on Wikipedia before boarding my flight here, a fortnight after my friendly little chat with the two detectives from States of Jersey Police. I've always liked to know the history of anywhere I visit. Roy's the same. We always used to bone up on places in England or abroad we were going to for the first time, noting down any sights we absolutely should not miss. Other than cathedrals and churches. Neither of us had ever been big licks on those – maybe the Gaudí cathedral in Barcelona being one exception.

To be culturally honest, it was always bars and restaurants at the top of our lists. Museums and art galleries came second. Interesting architecture a long way third. The Department of Developmental Psychology was located in a handsome period building, adjoining a publishing house I had entered first by mistake. The exteriors of both buildings were designed by a famous German architect whose name I had forgotten. The interior of the building looked like it had been designed by a couple of drunk carpenters who'd bought a lot more partition walls than they actually needed, and decided to create a maze out of them rather than send any back.

First the reception area and now Dr Ramsden's office itself had had all traces of any former elegance removed, replaced by bland white chipboard. On his walls were hung several framed certificates attesting to his multiple qualifications in child psychology, and on his small, bland desk were two framed photographs of two normal-looking children sandwiched, smiling happily, between their two normal-looking parents. The message was clear. *We are a normal happy family! I know how to make that happen, trust me!*

It seemed slightly odd, here in Frankfurt, to be seeing a doctor who looked so reassuringly establishment British. Dr Borg – *Iceborg*, I'd privately nicknamed him – told me that Bruno was not on any autism spectrum, but, in his opinion, he presented early signs of sociopathy. I challenged him on that, but he felt sure this was the case. He said the person best placed to assess him was a visiting professor of developmental psychology, attached to the University of Frankfurt am Main, called Graham Ramsden – one of the world's top child psychologists.

Over the phone, Dr Ramsden's very stiff assistant informed me that before he would take on any child as a patient, first he needed to see the parents. Which was why I was now here, with Bruno back at the schloss.

It usually took a long time to get an appointment; the professor had only been able to see me this soon thanks to a cancellation.

Middle-aged, dressed in a grey, chalk-striped suit, shirt and tie, if you saw him in the street you might think he held some kind of clerical position in a law practice or a firm of accountants. But the moment he spoke, you'd have realized you were wrong.

His voice had a quiet, commanding authority. His whole demeanour was friendly, and seemingly genuinely caring, but he was clearly fiercely intelligent.

As I was ushered in, he stepped away from behind his desk and shook my hand, greeting me with a warm, 'Good afternoon, Ms Jones, thank you for coming in to see me.'

He'd grabbed a notebook off his desk, and led me over to two comfortable-looking chairs angled close together, with a coffee table beside them.

'Thank you for seeing me,' I'd replied.

It was then he'd asked me for the three words that immediately sprang to mind when I thought about Bruno.

He looked up at me. 'I know you have been talking to Dr Borg, who has asked me to look into some of the more difficult aspects he has observed of your son's behaviour. Is this OK?'

'That's why I'm here. I understood you needed to see me first, in order to decide whether you would take Bruno on as a patient.'

'That's correct, Ms Jones. Can I call you Sandra?'

'Sure.'

'OK, Sandra, can I start by asking how concerned you are about Bruno right now, on a scale of one to ten, with one being not concerned at all and ten being very concerned?

'I'd say two, but others might think more like an eight or nine,' I said, spontaneously. And saw his eyes widen.

'Nine is pretty high. How long have they had this concern? When did you start to notice things were not going quite right with how he was developing?'

'It's difficult to say. I think he's just an individual, someone in control of his own mind. I feel he gets misunderstood. But various people in the past few months have told me he steals things or isn't very nice to other children. I just don't want him heading in the wrong direction as he gets older. And Dr Borg said he showed early signs of sociopathy, which just seems ridiculous, to be quite honest.'

Ramsden looked down at a sheaf of printouts. 'I notice from the completed questionnaire you sent in last week that he talked very early. Indeed, he seems to have met all his developmental milestones early, which is great, but I've not got a real sense of how he got on with other children. How would you say his social-izing skills are?'

'To be honest, pretty crap,' I replied. 'He's rarely shown any interest in other children.' I hesitated, thinking about the recent incident when Bruno had taken another boy's wristwatch. 'Except when they have something he wants. He doesn't seem to have a grasp of what is right and wrong, however much I try to teach him. He's always seemed most happy with his own company, playing his computer games or keeping himself busy with his little projects and interests.'

'Projects and interests?' Dr Ramsden asked. 'What kind?'

'He's always been curious to see how things work. If I buy him a new toy, instead of playing with it, like I'd expect a child to do, he dismantles it to see how it works. Only once he's got it in pieces he loses interest in it. He also asks strange questions but that's just kids, right?'

'About what?'

I hesitated for a moment, embarrassed. But then I thought, *what the hell?* 'One time, when I was cutting up a raw chicken, I saw him just staring in curiosity, like it was the best thing he'd ever seen. He asked me if it was possible to stroke it like you might a dog.'

He made some notes, then looked back at me. 'You sound like you have a unique and fascinating little boy. If I were to take him on, what would your expectations be of me, Sandra?'

'If you could figure out what makes him tick, that would be a start.'

Dr Ramsden looked at me solemnly for some moments. 'That's a pretty big ask,' he said. 'Can you describe yourself in three words?'

I looked back at him. 'You like your "three words", don't you?'

'They reveal a great amount. Less can sometimes be very much more. So can you describe yourself in just three words?'

That damned pinwheel in my brain was spinning again. I stared at him blankly. Three words. To describe myself?

Then they came to me.

'On. The. Mend.'

80

Dr Ramsden stared back at me and had the good grace to smile. Then he shook his head vigorously. 'Sandy, I see people all day long. Not many people come to see me because they are happy or in a good place. The mere fact that you want to bring your son to me shows me just how on-the-mend you are.'

I didn't reply for a while. He was totally missing the point. But was that deliberate, because he was only interested in Bruno, or was he playing some kind of psychological game with me?

I shrugged. 'I have been in a very bad place,' I said. 'I don't know how much Dr Borg told you about me?'

'Very little beyond his opinion that your son might be on the sociopathy spectrum.'

'Yes, I'm not sure I agree with that, but let's see what you think. Am I right that there's not a lot of difference between a sociopath and a psychopath?'

'Some people think there is, others say it's semantics.'

'And what do you think?'

'Both are people who have little empathy and little conscience about their actions. In my opinion, the key difference is that sociopaths are impulsive, psychopaths are manipulative.'

'That's what worries me about Bruno. I can't see it in him myself, but I don't like what others say about him and I feel he's getting tarred with this brush that he could be on a sociopathic or psycho-pathic spectrum for just being a bit of an individual. He's not like all the other children, but he's had a very different start to his life.'

He raised his eyebrows. 'Let's hope you are worrying unnecessarily. But first, tell me about you. What did Dr Borg omit to tell me that I need to know?'

'We could start with my being a heroin addict for the past three years. I'm currently cold turkey, taking Espranor.'

He made some notes, solemnly, without reacting, and the fact that he seemed so non-judgemental – on the surface at least – made me really warm to him.

'Is Espranor working for you?'

'I'm not sure. I was on dihydrocodeine before and I felt better with that.'

'I'm sure Dr Borg has a good reason for changing your meds.'

'He explained it to me, but I didn't really understand – how Espranor would help me get off my heroin dependency quicker. It's making me feel lousy, and I'm always anxious.'

'Give it time,' he said. 'If you don't start to feel better, ask him to change the dosage, perhaps.'

I nodded. 'Another thing he probably didn't tell you is that I have anger management issues. One of the courses I've put my name down for at the schloss is for that.'

'OK. Do you want to tell me more about that?'

I shook my head. 'I want to focus on Bruno. I feel I have it under control. I've been a lot better ever since I became pregnant. Maybe my hormones changed, or something.'

He smiled. 'Maybe. So, Bruno.' He said nothing for a few moments, then he said, 'If you want me to treat him, I will need to see him three times a week for at least the next six months and quite possibly a lot longer.'

It took me a moment to absorb this. 'Three times a *week*?'

'I'm afraid there are no quick fixes with children or adults. Psychotherapy is most effective with regular, intense sessions.'

'How much – what – what would the cost be?'

'In English money, one hundred and twenty pounds a consultation.'

I tried not to look too shocked. At the same time I was doing the maths. Three hundred and sixty pounds a week. On top of that the train or airfare here. I'd be looking at a grand a week, and probably a fair bit more.

Unless we moved here, and . . . I had no idea what property rental prices were here – but perhaps a lot cheaper than a 250-mile commute three times a week?

I did a quick mental calculation, although arithmetic had never been my strong point. I had around £30,000 in cash still hidden at the bottom of my handbag. If I had to pay Dr Ramsden, plus rent on top of that and all other living expenses, I'd be burning through my reserves at an uncomfortable rate, unless I could get a job. But then I'd need to pay for Bruno to be in kindergarten as well as someone to look after him.

Hans-Jürgen Waldinger had been really sweet to me in these past two weeks. He'd not permitted Bruno to attend any more classes because he was so disruptive, but he had arranged a rota of tutors to keep him occupied. All of them had reported how astonished they were at his intellect – at least two to three years advanced for his age.

I'd tried to keep myself occupied by attending the daily courses assigned to me as a first-year student. But this whole mind-spirit stuff just wasn't my thing. Trying to get my head around some of the concepts the airy-fairy tutors spouted at us felt, at times, like trying to grab smoke.

I had dinner with Hans-Jürgen most evenings. Our bond of friendship had definitely deepened, but so had the divide between us. The more time I spent with him, the more I realized what different journeys we were on. He genuinely believed it was possible – and passionately wanted – to make the world a better place.

All I wanted was to stop feeling so utterly shit. To sleep through an entire night without being woken by nightmares. To wake one morning without a feeling of dread in every cell of my body and pore of my skin, and the sense that a cement mixer was churning in the pit of my stomach.

For a short while, I'd thought the *Jersey Evening Post* had lost interest in the story and it had gone away. Then I'd read a front-page splash from a few days ago.

MISSING SAILOR'S PARTNER QUESTIONED IN MUNICH

To make it worse, they'd used my name. *Sandra Jones.*

Perhaps I was being paranoid. Roel Albazi was in prison in England and going to be there for a long time. He was hardly likely to be getting the Jersey newspaper delivered to his cell every day.

But all the same, I needed a Plan B. Hans-Jürgen made it clear that while he was always here for me as a friend I could rely on, Bruno was a problem, and until he was capable of socializing with other children, he was not welcome here.

I had a good look around for child psychologists in Munich, but I couldn't find any who were a match for Dr Ramsden in Frankfurt – and nor, crucially, any who were sufficiently fluent in English. Bruno and I both needed to learn German if we were to stay in this country, but that would take time. Moving to Frankfurt seemed the only real option, to try to get Bruno sorted. Maybe Dr Ramsden could work enough magic on him in six months for us to be able to return to the sanctuary – of a kind – of the schloss.

If I was sensible, I could stretch my funds for some while by staying in a cheap hotel or rental flat. Tutor myself and Bruno in German and perhaps in six months, if Dr Ramsden had improved him, get him into a nursery school and maybe I could then get a job.

Another option I considered was to track down some of my relatives. How would that play out?

Hi, I'm Sandy, I'm a recovering drug addict and my son,

Bruno, is a borderline psychopath. Thought you might be pleased to see us!

The tutor in the last class I had attended at the schloss had banged on and on about karma. All of us, he said, by virtue of us just being here in the schloss, had good karma. Out there, beyond the schloss walls, there was more good karma awaiting us. Every act of good karma earned a karmic reward.

I thought he was talking bollocks.

What had I ever done to deserve karma?

The answer was provided by a conspicuous absence of karma in the months that followed.

81

The worst hotel I've ever stayed in and times by ten. That's the Gasthaus & Hotel Seehaus, on Elbestrasse in Frankfurt. The best thing anyone had said about it on TripAdvisor – and the only person to give it a review as high as three stars – was that their room was clean. The rest of the reviews were two- or one-star. Someone gave it two stars for its central location. Another person gave it two stars for it having laundry facilities. Someone leaving a one-star review said they'd seen the largest rat ever in their bedroom one night.

But it did have an amiable day-time receptionist, called Maria, fifty-five going on twenty, who had a black fringe like the 1950s American model Bettie Page and told me she had written a novel, which she was trying to get published. And if I ever needed anyone to babysit Bruno, she would always be up for earning extra cash when she was off duty.

At 6 p.m. every evening, except Sundays when there weren't any staff at all, Maria was relieved by a surly, heavily bearded goblin, who chain-smoked until midnight, then locked the front door and buggered off. The only other staff member was a cleaner as shy as a nervous sparrow. I tried to engage with her a few times but she made it clear she spoke no English and I don't think she spoke any German, either.

The bedroom, with one solitary bare lightbulb, had a single bed for me that felt as if I was at an angle all the time like a boat keeled over in the mud at low tide, and a bunk bed for Bruno that he said was fine. The view from the window was down onto a street populated by hookers, drug addicts and a fair percentage of Frankfurt's down-and-out population. But, hey, it was just forty-nine euros a night, breakfast not included. I saw the breakfast on our first morning, a sad display of nothing I would ever want to put in my or Bruno's mouth, and was glad it wasn't included, in case of the temptation to eat it.

Something that was included was an unusual line in gift toiletries. A bar of partially used soap on which nestled a small, curly hair. It lurked on a shelf behind the plastic curtain – with four rings missing – in the shower cubicle, where there was black mould in each of the four corners of the tray that looked like lurking spiders. There was a part-used mini tube of toothpaste with the top off, left over from a previous guest, that made me think of Roy.

He was pretty fastidious about tidiness in the bathroom, whereas honestly I was less fussed. Few things pissed him off more than when I squeezed the toothpaste from the middle of the tube and left the top off. Now in these years since I'd left Roy, I could do it to my heart's content, a small symbol of my new freedom!

Roy had a thing about an orderly bathroom. He was forever tidying it, but then, ironically, leaving clutter, including his vinyl collection, all over the rest of the house. Whereas I obsessed about keeping our minimalist home clutter-free, and didn't really care about the bathroom so long as the towels were clean and soft.

What I didn't know as I checked us in, on the first day of our new life, was just what a handy location this was going to prove to be. All I thought, gloomily, on that warm October morning as I stripped all the bedding to take it down to the row of washing machines in the basement, so that we would know it was clean at least, was that this was going to be a longer road to recovery than I'd first imagined.

And I was remembering a gloomy quote from *King Lear*: *The worst is not, so long as we can say, 'This is the worst.'*

I countered it with John Lennon's words. He said so many smart things. I had always particularly loved, *Everything will be OK in the end. If it's not OK, it's not the end.*

Except it was the end for him and it wasn't OK.

Shit.

I felt so badly in need of a hit that first night, after getting takeaway burgers and fries for Bruno and myself. I needed something stronger than the Espranor. I knew I couldn't go back to that life, so I worked hard to resist the temptation. But it was hard. A constant battle and an easy one to give in to if I let myself.

I also desperately needed some adult company or I would go crazy. But I couldn't risk leaving Bruno, especially if there were rats around, so that wasn't going to happen, not tonight anyway.

He had his first appointment with Dr Ramsden tomorrow at midday. It was now 7 p.m. There was an ancient television in the room that only seemed able to get German channels. The Wi-Fi did at least work – most of the time – three euros extra per day. And the electricity in the room, I discovered, when it plunged into darkness at 9.30 p.m., was on a meter. Luckily, Old Smokestack downstairs, as I nicknamed him, had a stash of coins he was able to give me in exchange for notes.

I went back up to my room, popped a euro in the meter, then stared down at the street below. It wasn't wide but the traffic was solid, lit by the glare of neon lights from the strip clubs and sex shops. The blare of music, some from a nearby bar, some from the stereos of the passing cars with deaf drivers. A large sign, directly across the road, flashed orange, blue and yellow, *CABARET. PIK-DAME.*

I realized I'd only viewed this room in daytime. I hadn't reck-oned on a ringside view of the seediest aspect of Frankfurt's night-time economy.

I stared down at a row of small, beat-up cars parked one-wheel on the pavement. A couple of down-and-outs were leaning against one, seemingly sharing a joint.

I drew the curtain, a flimsy piece of cheap fabric that was about as useful at keeping out the flashing neon light as the proverbial chocolate teapot, and turned to Bruno. He was on the top bunk, his head in a book, oblivious to all around him.

And at that moment, I envied him that so much.

Oh God.

I looked at the flashing lights against the curtain. Heard the sound of rap music booming out from a passing car in the street below. A siren somewhere in the distance. My bag with all the money I had in the world sat on the floor beside me. There wasn't even a safe in this room. I would have to hide it somewhere, but I had no idea where, and under the mattress seemed the only place at the moment. But not great.

Then when I stacked my coins into neat piles beside the meter, I realized that Smokestack downstairs had short-changed me by one euro. Deliberately or a mistake? I decided to swallow it for now rather than go down and confront him, but I would be wary of him in the future. Not great to feel ripped off, even by a tiny amount.

It really wasn't great being here at all.

What actually had been great since leaving Roy, I was thinking with a tinge of nostalgia?

Leaving the home I loved and had put so much love into.

Leaving the man who had never judged me. The man who if I'd given him the chance would have supported me in embarking in a career of my choice.

The man who had rarely raised his voice in anger at me, and never, ever, in a million years would have hit me.

A decent, honest human being who would have made a great and caring dad for Bruno, whether he was actually his biological father or not. Hell, he'd never have known.

I'd exchanged him for Nicos, a violent bully and a criminal.

Then for Hans-Jürgen Waldinger, utterly charming but now celibate and on another planet to mine.

I was here trying my best in an awful part of a strange city. Strung out, with my son, in a country where I didn't speak the language. With a past that was a train crash and a future that looked like an even bigger one. Leaving my home was my only option at the time; it wouldn't have taken Albazi long to find me and kill me, I had to escape from that. But was leaving Roy the biggest mistake I'd ever made?

82

Guten Morgen, meine geschätzte Damen und Herren!

I never imagined six months ago that I'd be saying a very polite *good morning* in German.

Bruno speaks it pretty well now, too – he picked it up quicker than me – and it's thanks to an online course on the internet and practising out and about. Learning it was a good way to fill many very long and lonely days for both of us – not that we mind each other's company, we are a good team. But the older Bruno gets, the more introspective I notice he is becoming.

Today, like most days now, I have company. I'm watching a man shooting-up in a corner of the room below me. Baseball cap, shoddy clothes and filthy trainers planted on the red-tiled floor. Like pretty much everyone who comes in here off the street, he looks a lot older than he probably is. And he has the typical bad posture. He's seated on one of a row of hard plastic chairs, hunched over the stainless-steel shelf that runs most of the way around the room, oblivious to the mirror in which he can watch himself steadily killing himself, jab by jab, day by day.

It's ironic that the word heroin comes from the German *heroisch,* which actually means *heroic.* And doubly ironic, it was originally used to treat a drug addiction – to morphine.

The man is cooking. He holds the flame from a plastic lighter beneath a spoon that contains white heroin powder and a saline solution. In approximately one minute the mixture will turn

335

brown. He will draw it into the hypodermic syringe and then inject – once he's found a vein that's not shot to pieces. I don't know this guy's name although I see him a couple of times a day, because he doesn't do conversation, but just watching him makes me so grateful for getting off all this. A year ago this would have been me. Nine months ago, even. Unable to function without my fixes, with the time gap between them growing steadily shorter and the doses stronger.

Now I'm on the other side of the fence – literally. It's a glass fence – well, a shatterproof screen – between those of us who work here and those who come to shoot-up. I'm working in one of Frankfurt's four drug consumption rooms. I discovered this place was just a few minutes' walk along the road from our hotel – I noticed people coming and going every time I walked past. Pretty sad-looking people, but I recognized something about them, something that had not long back been me.

Then by chance I got chatting to a guy in a bar, whose name was Wolfgang Barth. He told me he was in charge of this establishment. He explained they had a doctor on the premises 24/7, a rota of nurses and social workers and twenty beds.

The drug consumption rooms don't sell drugs, but users can bring their own drugs to these premises, be given a sterile spoon and needle, and take their drugs in the presence of someone able to administer instant medical help if required. Wolfgang joked that these places are known as shooting galleries. But the statistics are no joke. Since the first one opened, here on Elbestrasse in 1992, the annual rate of drug overdose deaths in Frankfurt dropped from 192 to thirty, year-on-year.

Wolfgang had no budget to pay me, but he was immensely grateful for my offer to volunteer, and that worked well for me, as I could fit it around taking Bruno to Dr Ramsden, and spending more time with him on his days off. It works well around my part-time paid job, which is flexible, cleaning and ironing for some clients. And it was giving me back my feeling of self-worth. The volunteering meant I was doing something positive. I was helping people. And I could understand something of the dark place they were in. I also felt that the desperation I saw through my work there shocked me enough to stay on the straight and narrow. A constant reminder that I did not want to be on the other side of the glass wall.

Where I'm sitting is known as the nurses' station. There is a constant, pervading smell of disinfectant that reminds me so much of the Brighton and Hove Mortuary, where Roy took me once, in those early happy days, to show me where he had to go to view post-mortems of murder victims. We are elevated, like having balcony seats in a theatre, looking down at the room itself. When people come in the door, which is always unlocked, they have to look up at us – which is for our protection. The occasional one is violent, especially when badly strung out, and we are out of reach, just.

A man is coming in the door now, and this one does like to talk. His name is Tomas Arlberg. He could be anywhere between forty and sixty – that's what years of shooting-up heroin do to someone. It's not so much the drug itself but the crap it's cut – mixed – with. Street dealers never sell 100 per cent pure heroin – or, for that matter, pure crack cocaine, methamphetamine or any other opiate – mostly it ranges between 5 and 15 per cent pure, with the rest of what you are buying normally being chalk or cement dust. And that's what Tomas Arlberg has been injecting into his veins every few hours for the past twenty-five years, if I understand him correctly.

And it's not too easy to understand him, because he mumbles. He has only a few teeth and lank, dark hair turning grey that covers his eyes until he remembers to shake it away. His face is gaunt and many weeks unshaven; his body looks painfully thin, enveloped in a charcoal herringbone greatcoat with holes in the sleeves and is at least three sizes too big. He smells pretty rank, like, I'm afraid, so many of our visitors. And yet he has beautiful blue eyes. Every time I see him I wonder about his past – that long distant past – and just how good-looking he might have been. I wonder what was his journey to here? He's clutching the large plastic carrier bag, white with red and black markings, stuffed full, which he always has with him.

Full of everything he owns in the world?

He looks up and smiles, seems genuinely pleased to see me, and asks, '*Wie geht es dir?*'

At least I think that's what he says. 'I'm fine,' I reply in German and thank him for asking.

He nods, seeming pretty happy about this. With my rubber-gloved hands, I lean over and hand him his kit of a sterile spoon, saline solution and needle, and he shuffles off towards an empty place in the far right-hand corner, which he always favours, settles, pulls his wrap of heroin from his coat pocket and finds his lighter in another. I stop watching, the memory of my three years of doing just this – albeit in nicer surroundings – too painful.

Everything has gone quiet in Jersey. I've heard nothing more from the police there. I had one scare soon after relocating to Frankfurt, when I read in the *JEP* that a male body had washed up in Guernsey. There was speculation for a few days that it might be Nicos, and I didn't know how I felt about that. I was relieved when it turned out not to be him, but a man from Guernsey who had mental health issues and had been missing for some weeks.

Although I didn't really understand why I felt that way, why I was happy to think that Nicos might still be alive and not murdered by Saul Brignell and his henchmen because of what I had done. Because there were moments – the way he treated Bruno – when I could have throttled Nicos myself.

Equally, I worried that all the time there was no body, it meant Nicos *might* still be alive. Out there somewhere – and coming for me?

I check my *Jersey Evening Post* app religiously every day; Nicos and the *Bolt-Hole* really do seem now totally to have fallen off their radar.

I guess that's pretty much it for the good news. The bad is that Dr Ramsden is not happy with the progress he has been making with Bruno. Actually, that's an understatement.

On the positive side, the psychologist does feel he can make progress with him. On the negative, he's taking a two-year view. Two years of therapy, three times a week. From now, on top of the almost £8,000 I've already handed over – thank you, Nicos – Dr Ramsden thinks Bruno will need two more years, at least. Which works out at a tidy £35,000 or so.

Which I do not have.

So far, while I've been as frugal as possible, our classy hotel lodgings and our living expenses over the past five months have still burned through nearly £10K. Which means, according to my calculations, that I've burned through a total of almost £18,000.

I have around £12K left.

And at the moment, although I am doing some paid work, it's not earning me much and I can only do this thanks to Maria – AKA Bettie Page – who has turned out to be a bigger angel than I could ever have imagined. She adores Bruno – they seem to be, in their eccentricity, kindred spirits. While I'm volunteering at the drug consumption room, ten doors along the road Bruno helps Maria on reception.

Bless her, she has convinced Bruno that she couldn't do her job without him, and he is being polite to people and they seem to like him. OK, so they are the hotel's weird ragbag of guests that he sees, but at least it's a start of his developing some normal social skills.

And they are a weird lot in the Gasthaus & Hotel Seehaus.

There's Erika, who's older than God, an Auschwitz survivor, who has lived in room 103 for, she told me proudly, forty-one years. She showed me her arm where she had the faded tattoo with her number from Auschwitz, telling me, 'I was the lucky one, I lost all my family.' She wears dark glasses and walks with a stick, but is still fiercely independent. And, most importantly to me, she spends time with Bruno and he seems to react to her in a good way.

He said, poignantly, one night, 'Mama, Erika says the Nazis stole all her family's money. Can't we go and find it and get it back for her?'

Another morning, Bruno met a Moroccan chef, from room 206, who worked in a restaurant somewhere nearby, and showed him a bunch of knives he carried in a belt around his waist. And another afternoon, he met Stefan Pfeiffer, a dopehead who came down unsteadily from his room – never rising before midday – and offered him a toke on his spliff.

Dr Ramsden didn't feel Bruno was ready enough yet, with his lack of association skills, to be enrolled in a normal kindergarten – or even a special-needs one. But I had the feeling that hanging out with Maria was giving him enough of an education. Approaching his fourth birthday, he was truly a willing – if un-witting – undergraduate in the University of Life.

Dr Ramsden's office was a forty-minute walk each way from the hotel, and to save money, and because it was good exercise – and helped make the day pass – I walked Bruno there and back three times a week, except when the weather was truly vile. And it had been horrible, cold and wet for the past month. Frankfurt had hot summers, but its winters were bitterly cold – at least judging by the one we had just emerged from.

It was late February, and there was a hint of spring in the air. I had been to see Dr Ramsden alone for a review session about

Bruno – who I'd left in the care of Maria back at the hotel. As before, the psychologist felt he was definitely making progress, but not as fast as he would have liked.

Crucially, Bruno had bonded with Dr Ramsden. And I could see small but significant changes in him, week on week. I had to keep the therapy going, but there was no way I could afford it. I was faced with a stark choice. Blow the rest of my funds – and then what? Or pull him out of his treatment and take my chances with him?

And then – maybe it was the months of working free at the drug consumption room or perhaps because I had a karmic credit carried over from some former life – the gamechanger occurred.

Totally out of the blue.

83

March 2012

I don't take taxis that often, but I can guarantee I'll get a what's-your-game look from the driver whenever I give my address. Elbestrasse. So what. Hey, one of the perks of living in my dodgy 'hood' is that the bars are cheap.

But today it's my birthday, it's Saturday night and we're not doing cheap, we're celebrating! It is girls' night out on me, and we are doing posh! I'm in a taxi heading towards the Frankfurter Hof, and the city's hotels don't come posher than this venerable grande dame, with its top-hatted doorman outside.

I know I should be conserving every penny, but what the hell, I'll blow a few quid – or rather euros – tonight and that will just bring the time I run out of cash a few weeks nearer. Unless, with my improving grasp of German, I can get a decent paying job. But I'm not worrying about that now. Tonight I'm going to have fun!

Ingrid and Cordelia are already at a table in a dark corner of the smart and very lively bar, both pretty much near the end of their first Cosmopolitans – it looks like – and they jump up to greet me with squeals of excitement. They are both nurses at the consumption room and we've become friends over the past few months. Like me, Ingrid is a single mum, with a nine-year-old son, and Cordelia's tales of her online dating disasters have had us in fits.

I order a bottle of wine for us to share and get to hear about her latest hook-up – if a man in a beanie, showing her pictures of his dick on his phone within five minutes of their drinks arriving, can properly be called a hook-up. It's not because of her stories that I haven't tried online dating myself, it's that since Nicos I haven't the energy or inclination to meet anyone. I don't want another relationship. Not another new relationship. I'm feeling more and more that I want what I had and threw away.

Roy.

Ulrike, a social worker at the consumption room, has texted to say she is five minutes away. She seems far too pretty to be working in such a grim environment, but she genuinely loves it, like we all do, it's a great team. When she first told me she was gay and single, almost a little suggestively, those desires I'd had for women pre-Roy flashed before me and I felt a momentary wave of arousal. But right now I'm not getting tangled into any kind of a relationship. I've got myself straightened out from my addiction – well, within reason – and my focus and priority, one hundred per cent, is getting Bruno sorted. I owe him that.

And in truth, I'm feeling a lot of guilt about being such a rubbish mother to him for the first three – almost four – years of his life. Pretty much a drugged-up zombie who found it easier to stick a games console in his hands, rather than actually do any activities with him. But that's different now, we do everything together and he's honestly my best friend.

No surprise Dr Ramsden talks to me about Bruno's lack of socializing skills with that upbringing.

But now I'm two glasses of wine down, with another bottle on its way. The bar is alive with chatter and laughter and feel-good music, and we four girls are totally lit up. Cordelia is telling us about yet another hilarious online dating disaster with a mistimed kiss, when suddenly, I hear Billy Joel's 'Piano Man' playing, and amid the haze of fun and oblivion, I have a fleeting reality check. *Someone walking over your grave*, my mother used to say.

Roy loves Billy Joel as much as I do, and this was one of the songs on our wedding playlist.

Sing us a song, you're the piano man . . .
And you've got us feelin' alright.

'Feeling all right?' Ulrike asks me and gives me a flirty smile. A come-on smile?

I ball my hands and dance my fists in the air. 'Never better!'

We all clink glasses so hard that Ingrid's breaks, spilling her drink down onto the table and the nuts and olives. A fresh one appears. And then at some point, we all stagger through into the dining room, to our table, where we don't care that our raucous giggles and loud laughter are totally out of place in this grand, elegant and discreetly calm room, and I don't give a toss about the frowns from several elderly diners near us.

THIS IS MY BIRTHDAY! I feel so elated – thanks to the booze – better than I've felt in – oh God – so long.

I try to focus on the wine list, which is the size of a telephone directory, and turn to the sparkling ones. I nearly select a Prosecco, which is a fairly eye-watering price, then think *what the hell* and plump for a Champagne at a price that, luckily, I can barely read. Well, how many times in your life do you have a birthday?

And later, after blowing out the candle on the tiny cake and blowing another bottle of champers, the waiter brings the bill. When I sign my credit card slip, my eyes even more blurry, I grandly add an extravagant fifteen per cent tip without even looking at the total.

Then we stagger back to the bar. Ingrid and Ulrike go outside for a smoke, and Cordelia heads off to the loo. When I reach the crowded bar, a hand grips my arm and a vaguely familiar face is grinning up at me from a stool.

My addled brain takes a moment to process who it is.

'They let me out of my coffin, for one night,' he says with a big grin.

I don't believe it!

It's the guy I met briefly all those months ago at the schloss. Shambolic Hair. Stoker. AKA *Bram*.

'I kind of figured we'd meet again,' he says with another grin. 'Get you a drink?'

And suddenly, at this moment, I wished all the three other girls I was with would disappear.

84

March 2012

Well, the three girls did disappear, but only after a showy magnum of Champagne bought by Stoker. Ingrid had to get back to relieve her babysitter. Cordelia, unbelievably, had swiped an app on her phone and was off to meet someone in a bar. Ulrike was the last to go, giving me a look that said: *Let me drag you away from this disaster-in-waiting.*

I had no idea what time it was, and I didn't care.

'You like gambling?' Shambolic Hair – Stoker – Bram asked. His voice was American with a German accent. Or was it German with an American accent?

I gave him a slightly unfocused look and raised my glass to take a sip, only to discover it was empty. 'Gambling?'

'Uh-huh.'

Then I sort of remembered, he'd told us – all four of us – he was from California but, in his words, had kind of gone to Europe to kind of find himself and had kind of fetched up in the Schloss Leichtigkeit because some dude he'd met told him he would find enlightenment there.

But they'd kicked him out for doing drugs.

'Gambling?'

'Wanna come to a casino?'

I looked at him, at his impish grin and his mesmerizing eyes. And I realized, although I barely knew him, just how glad I was to see him again. The sense of a kindred spirit. Naughtiness. I sort of fancied him, and liked him too.

'To gamble?' I asked.

He nodded. 'That's kind of what you do in a casino.'

'I haven't – sort of – gambled – in a while – like I don't sort of really do it. Not any more.'

'It's your birthday.' He looked at me quizzically. 'Birthday luck?'

'I can't really afford it.'

I might be drunk, but I wasn't so drunk that I was about to fritter away all I had left in the world – already significantly reduced after having paid the bill.

'We'll just go play for pennies. Bit of fun, right? I'll give you some and you can watch me. Yeah? I want you to enjoy yourself with no pressure. I will bankroll you for one thousand euros. If you lose it, *c'est la vie*; if you win, keep the winnings and let me have my thousand euros back. Do we have a deal?'

'You're joking, really?'

'The truth, let's go have some fun.'

I shot a glance at my watch. It was 12.15 a.m. I felt a flash of panic about Bruno. But then I remembered, lovely Maria had said she would put him to bed and stay in my room until I came back – and she had said not to worry. She would stay there all night if I needed. And she'd given me a broad wink.

No way was I going to need her to stay all night. But the mention of a casino fired something inside me I'd not felt since my fateful days at the Casino d'Azur. This could be a way of testing my resilience. I knew I could go to the casino now and not be sucked in. In and out, just playing around for fun. Then walk away. No problem. No loss. And if I won, well, that was a bonus.

Birthday luck?

'Do they really have casinos in Frankfurt?' I asked.

'Do bears shit in the woods?' he replied.

85

March 2012

The silver Mercedes glided to a halt the instant we stepped through the hotel's revolving doors, and a courteous, suited chauffeur jumped out to greet Herr Stoker by name, and then opened the rear door for me. It was then that I realized that the magnum of Champagne might not have just been an act of bravado to impress me. Stoker might actually be a man of substance.

As we crossed Frankfurt, cossetted in soft leather, to the quiet sound of Mozart's *The Marriage of Figaro* through the speakers, he produced an immaculately rolled cigarette from a silver case inside his leather jacket, lit it with a fancy lighter, then passed it to me.

I shook my head. *No way, José.* I might be drunk but wasn't drunk enough to smoke. My resolve lasted all of two seconds then I had a tentative inhale.

Followed by a longer one.

Nice!

It wasn't like the euphoria from all those heroin hits, this was different, mellow, just – well – just OK. I watched the lights of the city stretch past the window like they were elastic. Elastic lights. I giggled.

Then saw Stoker looking at me quizzically. 'Did I miss the joke?'

I shook my head. 'I think the Champagne and the cigarette have gone to my head!'

'You OK?'

'Weird how life works, isn't it?' I said. 'I met you in the schloss and now we're in a limo in another city. Maybe we're in a parallel universe?'

He asked me what had brought me to the Schloss Leichtigkeit. I told him, fully and frankly – omitting, of course, the little detail about relieving Nicos of some of his stash of cash and what might have happened to him subsequently.

When we finally stopped, the security guard outside the casino opened the rear door and greeted Stoker deferentially, by name. I noticed the banknote Stoker pressed into his palm. And the reverence with which my escort was greeted by the two glamorous ladies in the palatial reception inside, who signed us in.

We walked up a grand curved staircase and entered a vast room that would have taken my breath away, if I wasn't already puffed out by the climb, and squiffy from the booze. The phrase 'fin-de-siècle grandeur' was all I could think of to describe what I was looking at.

Gaming tables that stretched into the horizon down below, each of them beneath a gilded chandelier. Baccarat, craps, poker, blackjack, roulette, all populated by smartly dressed men and women, quite a few in tuxedos and ballgowns. Glamorous young women in skimpy skirts and black bow ties weaved around, delivering drinks on silver trays. It was, honestly, like something out of a Hollywood movie.

If I hadn't been so merry, I'd probably have turned and fled. But as it was, I just stood still, taking it all in. Inhaling the atmosphere. And it was a great atmosphere to inhale – amazingly, people were smoking, cigars and cigarettes! It took me right back to how delicious pubs smelled in those times before the smoking ban. A smell I loved. Even more intense now I was in my current state.

Stoker led me over to a cashier, put down a credit card and, after a few words in German, received a stack of chips. He handed me some.

I hesitated for a moment, then drunken bravado took over. I scooped them up and felt a buzz of adrenaline.

Ten chips.

Hell, I was feeling reckless. I couldn't lose.

'What do you want to play?' Stoker asked.

Trying to remember what Jay Strong had taught me, all those years ago, I looked around. Three of the four tables were busy, but the fourth, on the far side of the room, looked deserted. It was manned by a female croupier with razored blonde hair. And she was looking very bored.

Perfect!

Trailed by Stoker, I strode through the melee towards it. She was, in true casino tradition, spinning the wheel and flicking the ball, despite having no punters. I stopped short and watched the little white ball rattling around, bumping off the frets, before finally settling in black 22. On the outer edge of what they call, in casino parlance, *voisins du zéro* – zero's neighbours – or, in other words, the zero zone!

Beside the table was a column with a digital display, showing the most recent numbers the ball had landed on. Amongst them, zero had come up twice. Interesting. Was Jay right about all bored croupiers? Would she aim again for zero? I often thought that seventeen had been the age of my life where I'd had the best time and that number seemed to follow me like a talisman.

Good things always seemed to happen to me on the seventeenth of a month. It seemed always to have been my lucky number. Well, until it had become unlucky. But, hey, like the true gambler inside me, I ignored that bit. Black 22 was nine o'clock to zero. Number 17 was just before three o'clock and one number nearer. And suddenly I had a feeling. A really good feeling. She was going to adjust her aim and maybe she would go the other way, in her bored shot at zero.

Number 17 was the other way.

Reckless, for sure. But what the hell. I'd blown the best part of a grand already tonight on my bill. Why not enjoy this free gaming now? If I won big, it could change my life and Bruno's.

I bet the lot on 17. All ten chips. One thousand euros.

The *ranch*.

As I did so, I felt the presence of a few other people coming over. Like Stoker and I were a magnet? Stoker placed chips on several other combinations.

The wheel began spinning.

Shit.

I was tempted to grab my chips back. But I was too late.

I was in a bubble of silence.

The croupier announced, first in German then English, *No more bets!*

The ball bounced, danced, ricocheted. Into 22, then out. Into 8 then out. Dancing.

Shit, shit, shit.

I watched the wheel turning, slower and slower, in total disbelief. I was hallucinating. A tiny round ball, smaller than a quail's egg, nested in a tight little black box, sandwiched between red 25 and red 34.

Was it going to pop out again, just like it had popped out of 22 and then 8?

But the wheel was slowing too much. The ball snug between the frets, slowly passing in front of my eyes. Before it even came to a halt, the croupier announced, sounding totally bored, '*Siebzehn, schwarz.*'

And suddenly I felt giddy.

This could not be real!

I heard someone say an excited '*ja!*'

And '*super!*' from someone else.

I watched the croupier rake in all of Stoker's chips, then she turned to the various stacks of chips in front of her, took three off one pile and one off another, and placed them next to my original one-thousand-euro stake.

'Wow!' Stoker said. I think he'd already said it several times, but I'd barely heard him. 'Wow, fucking awesome, wow!'

I did a rough calculation – I had just won thirty-five thousand euros. Yikes!

A couple of other people were now laying down bets, along the side and on groups of numbers. More people had materialized and were crowding around the table. I just stared at my winnings, still sitting on 17. At thirty-five thousand euros. Enough money to maybe get me through another year in Frankfurt at the crappy Gasthaus & Hotel Seehaus. And even more importantly to pay for another year of Professor Ramsden's fees for Bruno.

Was this real, or was I imagining it all?

The stone-faced croupier had finished clearing away all the dud bets. And the little white ball still lay between the frets: 17.

My lucky 17!

A male voice called out: '*Nochmal!*'

Again!

Then a female voice: '*Nochmal!*'

Then it seemed I was engulfed in a wild crowd of people and the reek of perfume and cigar smoke, and all around me voices were calling, '*Nochmal! Nochmal! Nochmal!*'

Stone-face was preparing to spin the wheel again. Hands were appearing in front of me, laying down chips of different colours around the green baize.

I ignored them. I was going to take my winnings and bank them.

Through all the excited shouting I heard Stoker's calm voice urging, 'Take your winnings, Sandy, eh?'

I reached, then stopped. I could not explain it then and I can't explain it now, but at that moment I had a feeling. That was all.

'*NOCHMAL!*' bellowed a tall guy in a tuxedo, with wild hair and a bow tie hanging loose. '*NOCHMAL, NOCHMAL, NOCHMAL!*'

A feeling. Not a voice in my head and not an epiphany. Just like in that moment in time I could see the future – as if I was peeking through a curtain at it. At the immediate future. Just maybe a minute or two ahead of now. I could see the ball rolling around the rim of the wheel and I knew where it was going to land.

I knew, I absolutely *knew.*

More voices joined in the chant. '*NOCHMAL! NOCHMAL! NOCHMAL!*'

I had to leave those chips where they were.

The charmless croupier set the wheel spinning again, a little faster than before, and that made me anxious. Stoker was nudging me, then, almost shouting, 'Get those chips off the table! Grab 'em!'

'*NOCHMAL! NOCHMAL! NOCHMAL!*'

When he realized I wasn't going to remove those chips, he reached towards them himself.

But it was too late.

'*Keine Wetten mehr,*' the croupier said sharply.

No more bets.

The ball was rolling around the rim and slowing down.

I realized I might have just made a monumental error.

86

Shit, I thought, watching that ball. I'd just made a fortune and now I was going to lose it. Lose it all, the lot, on one spin of the wheel.

Because of those stupid, drunken onlookers urging me on. Idiots who were probably all so rich that the amount I had riding on the wheel now was just petty cash to them.

Stop, stop, stop.

I made a lunge towards my chips, then stopped in mid-air as the croupier gave me a withering look.

The ball fell off the rim and rat-a-tat-tatted over the frets.

Idiot, I thought. *Idiot, idiot, idiot. Oh God, you idiot.*

You stupid sodding idiot.

It popped into green zero. Then out.

Rat-a-tat-tat-tat.

It fell into black 6, but the wheel was still spinning fast and it was spat out. Into 18 red.

Please don't stay there.

It popped out. Rattled some more.

I couldn't bear it.

Just one minute ago I had thirty-five thousand euros. A fortune! Enough to solve all my immediate problems – and then some. And I'd blown it. Stupid, stupid, stupid loser me.

I closed my eyes. Turned away. Trying to remember Dr Ramsden's words of advice about controlling the rage that was building inside me.

Deep breaths. I listened to the sound of the ball.

Rat-a-tat-tat-tat.

The wheel slowing.

Thirty-five thousand euros.

A sudden moment of silence. Followed by a hushed gasp – or maybe I'd imagined that.

Then the deadpan voice of the croupier again.

'*Siebzehn.*'

Stoker's voice, 'Oh sweet Jesus!'

I heard cheering. Applause. Then even more frenzied shouts than before. '*NOCHMAL! NOCHMAL! NOCHMAL! NOCH-MAL!*'

'Leave it! Let it roll again!'

I was mesmerized. Was this real? Was I fucking dreaming? I heard Stoker's voice again, through all the hubbub.

'You've won! You've only goddam won!'

I felt his arms around me. He kissed me on both cheeks. I opened my eyes. It took me some moments to process what I was looking at. The roulette wheel, motionless. The little white ball nestled in the frets of 17.

In confirmation, I saw 17, followed by 17, on the column with the LED of the most recent numbers.

'*NOCHMAL! NOCHMAL! NOCHMAL!*' More and more people gathered around the table, crowding us, shouting. '*NOCHMAL!*'

I shook my head. I didn't care how disappointed they might be. I really didn't.

The razored-hair croupier scooped away all the losing chips, then added ten grey chips to my stack, as nonchalantly as if each of them represented just one euro.

'*NOCHMAL! NOCHMAL! NOCHMAL!*'

GO AGAIN! AGAIN! AGAIN!

I was momentarily numb with disbelief.

'*NOCHMAL! NOCHMAL! NOCHMAL! NOCHMAL!*'

The crowd was in a feeding frenzy. They wanted to see me go on. And some part of my brain was goading me on, too. It was telling me I was on a roll, I couldn't lose, I could only go on winning bigger and bigger tonight.

I was their hero!

God, it was tempting to go on. One more roll. I was intoxicated. My Warhol moment, my fifteen minutes of fame. Had I ever before in my life felt so much the centre of attention, so admired?

There must have been fifty people gathered around the table and they were chanting again.

'*NOCHMAL! NOCHMAL! NOCHMAL! NOCHMAL!*'

But they were baying for blood. I was their Icarus. They all wanted to see just how high I could fly before my wings melted and I crashed to the ground.

The croupier hadn't yet spun the wheel, as if she too was waiting on my decision.

How much money would I make on just one more roll? Untold millions. Thirty? Forty?

Oh my God, the temptation.

I would be rich. Seriously rich.

I looked at Stoker. I saw the almost imperceptible shake of his head. *No. No. Quit!*

But I didn't need that shake. I'd already made my decision. Somehow, somewhere in another part of my brain, I reached for the shutters and slammed them down on the part that was goading me on.

'Enough!' I announced loudly. '*Basta! Fini! Genug!*'

And saying those words felt so good. So damned good. As if I'd wrenched a crazed monkey that had been clawing at me for years off my back and thrown it into a ravine.

Then I reached out and scooped the whole lot towards us.

Towards me.

'You did it! You held your nerve!' Stoker said, as we walked away from the table.

'You swear it's mine to keep?'

'I am a man of my word, it's yours, have fun with it!'

I stared at the top grey chip on the tall stack. It had one hundred thousand euros embossed on the top. Then counted. There were twelve of them. Then I stared at the two pale blue chips with twenty-five thousand embossed on them and a single yellow ten-thousand-euro chip next to them.

If I was right, I was staring at one million, two hundred and sixty thousand euros.

One and a quarter million pounds, give or take.

'Here,' I said, taking a pale blue chip and pressing it into Stoker's palm. 'Call this my debt paid, with interest.'

And I knew, at that moment, I would never set foot in another casino again. I was done.

87

March 2012

When I woke, I felt quite groggy. I was in an incredibly comfortable bed. In a large, beautiful room, all black lacquered wood and cream soft furnishings. Minimalistic.

I was more on the bed than in it. Thankfully, I had my clothes on, and after an initial panic, I remembered speaking to Maria to ask her to stay over with Bruno. Jeez, I shouldn't have drunk so much. My brain started presenting me with a mosaic of events of the previous night, all in bite-sized chunks, as well as presenting me with the sensation that a road-drill was working its way through one ear and out the other.

The casino.

Had I dreamed it?

What the hell time was it? The curtains were closed but light was flooding into the room. I heard a knock on the door. Moments later it opened and I smelled the aroma of coffee. Stoker, barefoot, in jeans and a T-shirt, carried in a tray on which were a mug and a croissant. He put it down on a table by the window. Then, holding something between his forefinger and thumb that fluttered, came over towards me with a wry smile.

It was a piece of paper.

'Good morning, sleepyhead!' he said. 'Nice lie-in?'

'Yeah, I think I needed the sleep! I can't take the booze, it seems.'

'It's cool,' he said. 'Everything's cool!'

He held up the piece of paper, delicately, in front of my eyes, holding it at each end with his forefingers and thumbs.

It was blurry. I couldn't read it.

Sensing this, he held it closer. 'You did pretty good last night, crazy lady!'

'Uh?'

'Can you read what it says?'

Then, for an instant, time stopped.

Everything stopped. I could read it now.

It was a Deutsche Bank cheque from the casino made out to Sandra Lohmann.

I had to read it several times to be sure. In between each reading I looked up at Stoker's face and saw his reassuring nod.

It was real.

Unbelievable.

I was a millionaire!

Just one problem. Sandra Lohmann was a family name I had reclaimed for myself. And I didn't have a bank account.

88

So, to all those armchair sages who say that money doesn't bring you happiness, let me tell them something. They are right. I can say this five years after my win – it doesn't bring happiness, but it makes a miserable life a lot more tolerable.

One example of which is we've moved from Frankfurt to Munich. I've traded up from our dump of a room at the Gasthaus & Hotel Seehaus to a very beautiful fourth-floor apartment on Munich's Widenmayerstrasse. We have a gorgeous view across the road to the park and the Isar, the pretty river that flows at some speed through the city. And the location is unbelievably handy – it is half a kilometre's walk from the psychiatrist to whom Dr Ramsden referred me, who I now see twice weekly. His name is Dr Eberstark.

He's a strange guy, short, in his mid-fifties, I guess, who has the knack of almost making himself seem smaller still. Maybe it's the suits he wears, which all seem to be one size too big, as if he's waiting to grow into them, or maybe it's the way he sits in his leather chair, all hunched up, or maybe his large, black-rimmed glasses that give him the appearance of a hawk.

But I think he gets me, and we are currently working through – old ground, I know – the reasons I left Roy in the first place, and my old anger issues that I'd thought I had under control ever since my drug addiction days, but which were now periodically resurfacing. I've twice lost it with Bruno, once when he threw a tantrum because he didn't want to go to bed, and another time when he was just plain damned rude to me when he didn't like the sausages I'd cooked for his evening meal. It took a lot of effort for me to calm down and I hate myself for making him scared. We make up quickly, but the guilt doesn't leave me.

From what Dr Eberstark seems to be saying, I've never properly come to terms with having left Roy, and my anger is all part of this, which is why I can't properly move on. He's explained the treatment he's giving me, it's called DBT – dialectical behaviour therapy. Of course I've googled it dozens of times. It's a therapy developed to help people cope with extreme or unstable emotions and harmful behaviours. It's meant to be able to help me to regulate my emotions, like it's some kind of mental thermostat. And there's something that Dr Eberstark omitted to tell me about DBT. It's also a treatment for borderline personality disorder, particularly people at risk of self-harming.

Me?

I guess self-harm comes in different guises. It's not just cutting yourself. It's making choices that are ultimately harmful. Like leaving the person who loves you and will always take care of you, because . . .

Because . . .

Because, that old cliché, you think the grass is greener.

Stoker had been crazy for me. I don't know what influence he had, but it was pretty impressive. He managed to get me German citizenship in the name of Alessandra Lohmann, and a bank account, where I had finally been able to turn that cheque from the casino into real money. As well as an investment manager who was looking after my windfall, giving me an income more than sufficient for my needs, as well as growing my capital.

Stoker was fun, but I just couldn't give him the relationship he wanted. He even told me he wanted to marry me. But much though I liked him, I didn't want to sleep with him, or anyone.

I just had this constant, burning feeling that I ought to be back with Roy – however much I tried to forget about him. To put him behind me. Like he was someone I knew in another life but not this one now.

Except Bruno is a constant reminder of him. Although I still can't be sure Roy is his biological father, I have a strong feeling, which I can't explain, that he is. When I look at him I see Roy's eyes. Roy's nose. When he smiles I can sometimes swear it is Roy smiling.

I keep thinking I should do one of those DNA paternity tests. But there's a big problem with that – I don't have anything from Roy to get DNA from, for comparison. However, that is about to change.

I really like Munich, and I see a bit of Hans-Jürgen – we have lunch and sometimes dinner together. We're good friends now, although at times he drives me crazy with his weird views. Actually, he is always driving me crazy with his weird views. But I do like him. Every time I go to see him at the schloss, with its scented candles and all its intense weirdies in their white tunics, I'm just so pleased I can leave and go back to my gorgeous apartment.

He constantly tries to encourage me to return there per-manently, but it's not for me. I'm happy – well, content for now, anyway – in Munich. Frankfurt is a nice enough city, but Munich has a soul that I never felt in Frankfurt. It is beautiful and so walkable. And I guess the real reason we moved here was that Dr Ramsden was returning to England and put me in touch with a child psychologist in Munich whom he felt could really help Bruno.

He'd been right. Bruno, now nearly nine and a half years old, did seem to be improving and had made friends with a boy at school. His name was Erik. Erik Lippert. They hang out together almost to the point of being as inseparable as twins.

Their friendship cemented by their love of the Bayern Munich football team, they are often dressed in identical replica club shirts and their bedroom walls are plastered with posters of their heroes. Bruno's favourite player, Pascal Gross, is German but doesn't play for Bayern Munich. He and Erik follow his every move. I'm happy Bruno has developed such a passion for the sport and after treating them to go and see a couple of games live I found myself enjoying it too. Erik's parents, Anette and Ingo, are lovely, smart people. They are part of a small group of friends I have made here. I've not had any serious relationship in some years. But the Lipperts made a couple of efforts at matchmaking, resulting in a couple of embarrassing dinners with divorced single guys they knew, before I managed to dissuade them from any more.

Roy would have liked them.

Roy.

No matter what happened, no matter what I did, everything came back to Roy.

I set up a Google alert on his name so every time there was a mention of him, usually in the *Argus* newspaper, sometimes other Sussex newspapers, I got to read about his work and to see Roy's name. It does make me proud; he gets his fair share of mentions as the SIO on various murder cases. I wonder why I never felt so proud before, or did I? Did I just resent his work because it impacted our life so much? Hard to tell now after so many years. I'm not able to find out about anything to do with his personal life, though. And that's what I'm really curious about.

It's now almost ten years since I left him. But there hasn't been a day when I don't think about him. When I don't wonder what his life is like now. Does he have a girlfriend? Has he remarried?

Shit, that thought twists my heart.

Ten crazy years.

God, how I miss him.

Would he be impressed that I am rich now?

No. Money wasn't his motivation. He cared about people, about making the world a better place, in whatever small way he could.

He's a better person than I will ever be.

There's a line in Shakespeare's *Othello* that sometimes finds me in the middle of the night, as if it has tracked me down and wants to haunt me.

Like the base Indian, threw a pearl away, richer than all his tribe.

Maybe I should go to England. Tell Roy I'm sorry. Tell him he has a son. Our son. Tell him I made a big mistake and that I so much want him back.

Do I have the courage?

No, I don't. But I've just found a way to get his DNA.

I think it is bloody brilliant.

My psychiatrist does not.

Dr Eberstark tells me it's crazy and to put that idea right out of my head.

I don't think it's crazy at all. I think it's very smart.

89

Through my lawyers, I hired a private detective – he's called Jack Roberts. I like him, he's a smart guy, based in Kingston. He's found out a lot about Roy for me and pretty quickly. Every Thursday the *Argus* has a property page, something I've never really bothered to look at since I've been away. Jack sent me a screenshot of a page from this week's. I scan it quickly – amazing how values have shot up since Roy and I bought our house. Then I see it.

Our house. Our *home*.

For sale.

WTF?

Why was he selling?

After a burst of unexpected resentment and questions in my head, I started to think more calmly. I realized there may be a silver lining here that I could take advantage of. I'd contact the estate agents and arrange a viewing. I was sure I could find something to nab – a comb or a toothbrush, something like that.

Then I had an even better idea, which was the one that Dr Eberstark really, really did not like. But I've discussed it with my German lawyer, in Frankfurt, to whom Stoker introduced me. It's perfectly possible, and I have the cash.

My plan was that, under one of my false names, I buy the house. My longer-term plan was maybe a bit far-fetched, but you have to have dreams, right? This dream was helping me get my focus on. Maybe Roy and I will live there again one day.

90

It didn't take me long to find my favourite place in Munich, or München, as the Bavarians – well, all Germans, I guess – call it. Nor did it take Bruno long, either – his is the awesome multi-storey BMW museum, which we have to visit at least once a fortnight and ogle the automobilia there.

He also loves the huge olde-worlde beer cellar, the Hofbräuhaus, where we have become Saturday lunchtime regulars. We order our weisswurst – white sausage – with sweet mustard and pretzels, accompanied by a weissbier for me and a non-alcoholic one for Bruno, which he holds up proudly and always finishes. Often Erik Lippert joins us and sometimes his parents too.

Afterwards we stroll to the huge Viktualienmarkt, with its green and white covered stalls set in an enchanting square, and select some of the produce we'll cook over the weekend and the following week. Bruno takes food very seriously, often, intensely solemn, interrogating a butcher on the exact content of the wurst, or vegetable seller on where the produce was grown. Sometimes when I look at him doing this, he seems more like a little man than a nine-year-old boy.

But my favourite place of all is where I am now, on a wooden bench at a table in the beer garden overlooking the boating lake in the Englischer Garten. I've read this is one of the biggest city parks in the world. I like it even more than the amazing New York Central Park, which I visited a long time ago with

Roy, and we cycled on rented bikes around its six-mile circumference road.

There is so much beauty here in the Englischer Garten, with its two lakeside restaurant bars, a Japanese tea house and vast open spaces for walkers, picnickers and horse riding. At the entrance to the garden, we never tire of watching the local surfers riding the endless waves on that part of the river. The park stretches from the city centre out to the north-eastern extremity, and I can reach the lake within thirty minutes' walk of our apartment. Or much faster if, like today, I've run here, and then gone on to clock up 10k. I've never enjoyed running so much in my life. It's given me my mojo back, time to release some of my stresses, and I use that time jogging to plan and process. I'm now gulping a much-needed water, and then I'm looking forward to a cold weissbier.

It's a warm day and there's a wonderful scent of freshly mown grass and lake water and wood varnish – and pure, clean air. Every now and then I catch the waft of cigarette smoke and it sets something off inside me, again and again. The memory of the man I had once loved so much.

And, *oh shit,* still did.

My heart heaves.

A mother duck, followed by about ten of the cutest ducklings, appears from behind the tiny island in the centre of the lake. I watch them weaving between some of the rowing boats and pedalos; they look like they're all connected to their mother by invisible string, and they make me smile, as I remember something Roy once said – that ducks add a little extra joy to the sum total of human existence.

I go over to the self-service counter and buy a stein – around two pints – of weissbier and carry it to the far end of a wooden table, right by the lake, and settle on the bench. There's an elderly couple, with empty glasses, sitting at the far end, and after a couple of minutes they get up and walk off, leaving a newspaper, the *Münchner Merkur*, behind. It flaps in the breeze. The sound irritates and despite my good mood I feel a flash of anger at them for not taking the damned thing. Then my anger increases. There's a very determined-looking Nordic walker, in her sixties, wearing bright red Lycra, teeth clenched, ski poles clacking on the hard ground, heading straight towards me. She smiles at me.

And I glare at her.

It works. She veers away, her poles clack-clack-clacking.

I try to remember Hans-Jürgen's words, from his anger-management course at the schloss, about deep breaths and positive thoughts. Deep breath in for four, out for four. In for four. Out for four. It starts to work. I calm down, look around, try to just enjoy being here. I know another jog would help the stress disappear, but I'm done for the day.

This is my *me* time. When I have the solitude I crave. And this is pretty much the shape of my weekdays during the time Bruno is at school.

I love just sitting here, enjoying the breeze off the water. I'll drink my beer, get a sandwich, and think about my plan – until it's time to head off to collect Bruno from school.

I love my boy to bits. I just wish I understood him. And didn't worry about his future so much. It's like there's something he can't tell me; I can't explain it. Part of this is his fascination with death. Often at weekends, when he is not seeing Erik and I ask what he would like to do, he tells me he would like to visit a cemetery. He particularly loves the largest tombs and just stands and stares at them, in silence. And if there is any opening in the sides, he scrambles down onto his knees and peers through, looking for bones.

The damned newspaper is distracting me with its constant fluttering. I need a clear head to focus on my plan. I slide across the bench, grab it, intending to dump it in a bin, but the photograph on the front page catches my eye.

THEY THOUGHT I WAS DEAD

It's a large, silver motor coach that has rolled onto one side, straddling and buckling an autobahn crash barrier. Emergency service crews in orange suits are standing around it and there is a bleeding victim, partially visible – but not their face – on a stretcher.

The headline shouts – I'm translating from the German – SEVEN DIE IN AUTOBAHN COACH CRASH.

I read on. Disasters of all kinds have always fascinated me. Boats, planes, trains, cars, earthquakes, floods. I guess I'm a bit of a disaster junkie. Call me weird, but I love all this stuff. I read that all the passengers on board were members of a Christian fellowship group in Cologne. Seven dead and twenty-three seriously injured. I wondered, mischievously, what they all thought of God now.

I turned the page, feeling a twinge of guilt at that bad thought. There was a photograph of a cyclist who appeared to be fleeing from two police officers on foot, and another road accident – this time a VW Passat that had rolled over. I flicked on through the pages. There was a story about a factory closure that didn't interest me. Nor did a photograph of a school football team.

Then, as I turned the page again, I froze.

It was a small advertisement. Just one column's width and a couple of inches deep.

I read it.

Re-read it.

Re-read it again.

And again.

Then again.

369

91

June 2017

SANDRA (SANDY) CHRISTINA GRACE

Wife of Roy Jack Grace of the City of Brighton and Hove, East Sussex, England. Missing, presumed dead, for ten years. Last seen in Hove, East Sussex. She is five feet, seven inches tall (1.70 metres), slim build and had shoulder-length fair hair when last seen.

Unless anyone can provide evidence that she is still alive to Messrs Edwards and Edwards LLP, at the address beneath, a declaration will be sought that she is legally dead.

Wow. A bombshell. I can't even focus on the words of the ad any longer, I am so furious.

I'm not actually that dead at all. I'm not even slightly dead. *Presumed dead*?

Or should that read *assumed dead*?

That's a bit rich coming from you, Roy. Have you forgotten what you told me about *assumptions*? That you always tell your team that the word *assume* makes an ass out of you and me? And that you tell them that *assumptions* are the mother and father of all mess-ups?

You know what I'm going to do? I've no idea what your plans are, but I'm going to find out, and then I'm going to come to England. Maybe we'll reconcile. This has made me so sad, I can't understand why you are doing this. Surely you don't want me out of your life like this. It's going to be a big surprise when I tell you my side of the story.

92

Things have moved fast, a lot faster than this damned travelator – walkway – thing I'm on at Munich airport, heading to Gate E17 for my Lufthansa flight to London. It's half-term and Bruno has his little arm linked in mine. I so treasure these moments as I look at him proudly, my little human.

I see all the people coming the other way, so many of them stooped by backpacks that make them look like tortoises. And years of looking at their phones. But that's not my problem right now. I've something far more important on my mind.

Jack Roberts has discovered Roy has a new lady in his life. This was a heart-sinking but inevitable find. She's called Cleo Morey and she's a mortician, who runs the Brighton and Hove City Mortuary. Only they don't call them morticians any more. No, she has a much grander title. *Senior Anatomical Pathology Technician.*

She spends her days with people who are even more dead than I am.

But Jack Roberts has found out more still. Cleo Morey is very pregnant, in fact she may have already given birth, which makes me feel really sad.

But there's even more to come from Jack – and this plays to my advantage. Roy is now living with Cleo Morey – at her place, and I have the address. Given our old house in Hove is on the market, I have arranged an appointment to view it at 10 a.m. tomorrow.

My plan is coming together.

Then my phone rings. It is Hans-Jürgen.

'*Meine Liebe!*' he says. 'I—'

Then the call disconnects, as if he has gone into a tunnel. This happens all the time with him. Why does the stupid guy always pick the places with the worst reception to call me from?

My phone rings again. But as soon as I answer the connection has gone again.

Then I do a double take.

I see someone coming towards me, some way off, on the opposite moving walkway.

Albazi? It can't be? Oh God no, please. I am frozen in panic. The figure gets closer, and I try to hide myself. Not Albazi. Definitely not Albazi, but so very alike.

Why does he sit in my subconscious like this? It keeps me on edge, my adrenaline pumping.

Curiously, my mind darts back to a time last December. I was again on a travelator, and I was so sure I'd seen Roy. He had Roy's posture, Roy's height, and facially, from what I could see, so similar.

But I was so flustered I dropped my phone, and ducked down to retrieve it. When I stood up, he had passed. I turned to look at him and he turned to look at me.

But we were both too far away to be sure. It gave me goose-bumps. Like this Albazi double has just now. Like a fiendish Albazi shadow I can never shake off.

I'm half tempted to turn and run back. But the path behind me is totally blocked with people and their stupid luggage. And I know it wasn't him.

We reach the end and, cautioning Bruno, we step off.

Get a grip, Sandy, get a grip.

93

'And this is the master bedroom,' the estate agent said. 'It's a good size, that's what you get with these older houses, much more generous spaces than today's new-build homes. And there's an en suite, of course.'

He appeared to be barely out of his teens, with mussed-up hair, dressed in a cheap charcoal suit, white socks and snazzy grey loafers. There was a thin line of fur above his upper lip that looked like it might want to be a moustache when it was older.

I held the particulars in my hand, nodded and gave the pretence of looking at the document. But in reality I was looking around the master bedroom. *Our* room. *Our* king-size brass bed, *my* vintage mahogany dressing table, on which still sat, as if in a time warp, all my bottles of perfume and make-up items.

I stared at the Art Deco chaise longue we'd bought at the weekly antiques market in Lewes. At a silver-framed photograph on the dressing table. It was Roy's mother and father's wedding day. It used to be downstairs, I thought to myself. But instead, it was here replacing one of my favourite photos of Roy and me smiling on a beach in France, which must now be long gone. Tucked away in a drawer or thrown in the trash. Smiles of a couple in love.

That was the thing with photography. Those captured moments. Like the lovers in that Keats poem, frozen in time on the Grecian urn.

I stared at the dressing table a while, then felt tears welling at the thought he may have just thrown that photo away or ripped it up or burned it. I turned away and walked over to the window, which had a view of the rear garden, as well as the back of a house in the next street along, which was partially masked by three tall leylandii. One had turned brown – clearly dying or dead. When that came down, you'd see that house even more clearly. Smart of Roy to try to sell while it was still standing.

I looked down at the wide lawn, which was dominated by the water feature I'd created as the focal point. A cluster of smooth stones, with a dried-up channel around them and a fountain that was not switched on. And slime that had gone black.

The agent indicated the door to the en-suite bathroom and I went in. It was bare, denuded of toiletries. There were just two scented candles, that had long ago lost their scent, at either end of the shelf above the twin sinks. I had put them there. That's how long they had been de-scenting. There was also an unopened Molton Brown handwash. Presumably put there for the brochure shoot, to look classy.

'I'm afraid we need to keep moving,' he said. 'We have another viewing in twenty minutes – this kind of house, at this price level, is in high demand in this current market.'

He was an arrogant tosser, I decided, and I'd already forgotten his name. I decided to think of him as White Socks.

I walked across the bedroom to the doorway, then stopped and looked back, thinking hard about my plan. I glanced around the room. It looked too tidy, there was nothing lying around, no slippers, dressing gowns, nothing to indicate anyone had slept in this room for some while. It felt unaired, unlived-in. It didn't smell of Roy, it smelled of polish, sterile and slightly musty, like a room in a museum.

The bed looked like it had been made by a professional – Roy could never have got it to look this neat, he would never have thought of stacking cushions in front of the pillows, hotel-style.

A woman's touch? Roy's new lady? But there was nothing to indicate a woman had been sleeping in here. No lingering scent, nothing. No photos of them. I was thankful for that.

I had a couple in my bag that my PI had obtained for me. She was nice-looking, I guess. I had to admit she was attractive in a kind of classic English rose way. Which is how I always saw myself. Perhaps that's why Roy likes her. Because she reminds him of me.

But she will never be *me*.

And she doesn't know I'm still around.

I followed White Socks out, steering Bruno, his hand gripping mine, across the landing into the large spare room.

'This would make a great space for your son,' he said, looking at Bruno for approval, but Bruno stayed quiet.

But I reacted with interest. Because someone was clearly living in this room. Who? There was a row of polished, expensive-looking men's shoes by the skirting board. Several flashy suits – not Roy's taste – in dry-cleaner cellophane hanging from the dado rail. An untidily made bed. As I entered the bathroom I saw a whole stack of men's toiletries, an electric toothbrush, and a couple of towels, one lying on the floor. There were droplets of water inside the glass shower cabinet. And a strong smell of cologne – not one that Roy had ever worn. Not his type.

So who was living here? It wouldn't be Roy, not in his spare room, surely? And the intel I had from the PI was that he had moved in with this Cleo Morey.

Must not get distracted from my mission. From my plan.

'What's the owner's reason for selling?' I asked White Socks.

'He's a detective, I understand, with Sussex Police.'

'OK.'

'This was his marital home. I understand he's separated from his wife. I don't know any more really. I can find out if you're interested?'

'I'm not interested.'

'I've got a cousin in the police. He told me the divorce rate is very high among coppers,' White Socks said.

'Is that so?'

'Yeah, it's their lifestyle. Lot of shift work, late hours, stuff like that.'

Bruno and I followed him downstairs.

We went into the sitting room, and I took a deep breath. It was like entering a time warp. It was almost exactly as I had last seen it, almost a decade ago. The minimalistic style in which I'd decorated this room, with black futon sofas and a low, black Japanese table. I'd do it differently now. Darker cosy walls and a light sofa, a couple of chairs and a nice deep-pile rug is more how I'd see it, I think. In the far corner stood Roy's antique jukebox, but, to my surprise, on the floor in front of it were spread out, untidily, some of Roy's prized collection of vinyl records, many out of their sleeves.

Why had they bothered to tidy some rooms, but not others?

'Great room, this,' White Socks said. 'Lovely big windows and a working fireplace. Ideal family room. Converted with real taste!'

I stared around, smiling at his last comment, transported back a decade, thinking how funny it is that everything dates. Back then I thought this style would last for ever.

'Yeah, but I'd give it a makeover, looks like it hasn't been done for a decade!' I said, amusing myself.

'Well, we all have different tastes. It has huge potential, doesn't it?'

Still smiling, I followed through into the equally minimalistic open-plan kitchen-diner.

My emotions were all over the place. I wanted to tell him that this was my house too. My home! That he had no right to be selling this without my permission, and that I wasn't dead at all.

But somehow I managed to keep schtum and just listen.

'I understand this used to be two rooms, which the present owner knocked into one. It could of course be kept like this, or changed back to a separate kitchen and dining room,' he said.

Of course it could! I thought. And then I saw the goldfish. It was in a round bowl on the work surface, close to the microwave, with a plastic hopper for dispensing food clipped to the side.

Marlon? Could it possibly be Marlon, still alive after all this time? No way!

I walked over and peered closely. The fish looked old and bloated, opening and closing its mouth in a slow, steady, gormless rhythm. Whatever golden orange colour it had once had was now faded to a rusty grey.

I crushed away a tear. Could this really be him? The goldfish Roy had won at a funfair? He'd be fifteen years old now, at least.

Bruno suddenly joined me, peering into the bowl, too. '*Schöner Goldfisch!*' he said.

Stupid, I know, but I really was close to tears. 'Marlon?' I said, quietly, willing this so much to be him.

The fish opened and shut its mouth.

I was aware of White Socks watching us.

'Marlon?' I said again, louder, tears running down my cheeks now.

'*Warum nennst du ihn Marlon, Mama?*'

'Because that's his name, *mein Liebling!*'

'You know its name?' White Socks asked.

Could a goldfish really live this long?

At that moment, the front doorbell rang.

White Socks hurried out of the room to answer it.

And I took the opportunity. I told Bruno to stay where he was and I dashed back upstairs, into our bedroom and straight through to our en-suite bathroom. There must be something. For God's sake! I stared, frantically, at the bare shelf, and then at the equally bare shower cubicle.

Roy's washbasin was on the right. I opened the drawer beneath.

Bingo!

It was crammed with all kinds of bathroom stuff that had been removed from sight.

Toothbrush. Hairbrush. Oh yes! Brilliant. Perfect!

I'd learned all about DNA testing from Roy. How just one hair follicle could be enough to nail a suspect. I had a whole jungle here! I dropped the hairbrush and toothbrush into my ever-trusty handbag – a new genuine Louis Vuitton I'd treated myself to.

Then one more thing. Was it still here?

I walked furtively into the bedroom and was relieved to hear the crass voice of White Socks downstairs, no doubt starting the next viewing.

Then I had to look. Had to.

I opened my wardrobe door. And saw all my clothes hanging there, exactly as I had left them. I tugged open the drawers and my underwear, pullovers, T-shirts and everything else still lay there.

Have you moved on, Roy? Or do you keep all this because you hope I may come back into your life?

I hurried over to my bedside table and opened the middle drawer.

It was still there. The silver bracelet Roy had given me for my birthday. It was antique Tiffany and he'd bought it at one of the jewellery shops in Brighton's Lanes – one of the few shops he trusted. It had meant a lot to me, and I'd planned to take it when I left, but I forgot – guess I had a lot of other things on my mind.

It was tarnished, but I could still see the engraving on the inside:

RG ♥ SG

More tears rolled down my cheeks. Shit. Get a grip, girl.

I popped the bracelet inside my bag, then went back downstairs.

White Socks was standing in the hall with two almost indescribably dull-looking people, busily pointing out how wide the staircase was, and that you did not get staircases this wide in new-builds today.

'Will you send me a report on all the damp spots we found?' I asked him gaily. 'And that dry rot you mentioned in the kitchen floor?'

As he gave me a completely baffled look, I ushered my son towards the front door. Then I stopped at the threshold, as the couple stared at me, and added, 'I do hope you tell this couple about the subsidence in this area – that the houses on either side have needed underpinning. Such a shame, such a nice street otherwise!'

Then we were gone.

94

I have the cash to buy this house. OK, a bit mad, really, to buy my own house, but I can sort all the financials out with Roy in the fullness of time.

The car reeks of our cheeseburgers – although Bruno has eaten most of mine because I don't have much appetite – and greasy fries. I've got a clear view through the windscreen of the entrance to the gated townhouse development where Cleo lives. With my husband.

Of course at some point Roy was going to move on with his life – what the hell had I expected? But all the same it hurt so much. If I could just tell him the reasons I had to leave, maybe he could forgive me. He knew how dangerous Albazi was. There's no way I could've stayed. He'd understand, if I could just explain. But now it worried me he was trying to dismiss his past with a single wave of his hand. Among the many reasons for having me declared dead was so he could be free to marry that woman.

I looked again at the particulars of our house. Our *forever home*. It was on the market now, and it might never come back on again for the rest of our lives, because it was the kind of house people might live in for years. The kind of family home where people could grow old together.

Where Roy and I could grow old together.

That had been the plan when we'd bought it. What kind of an old couple would we have made?

'Mama, how much longer do we have to stay here?' Bruno asked suddenly.

I looked at him. Roy had always said he would be happy whatever the sex of our children. Was Bruno his son? I was about to reply to him, to tell him not much longer, when I saw a man striding down the street towards us. He was dressed in a dark suit and carrying a bulky case.

Oh my God.

It was nearly ten years since I'd last seen him – for certain anyway – but in this fading light it could have been just twenty-four hours. His trim figure was just the same and his face had barely aged. Only his hair was different, cropped short and gelled. It suited him. And he looked happy.

Shit. So happy.

I knew there was no chance of him recognizing me – I was wearing a baseball cap pulled low, large dark glasses and my hair was completely different. But even so, I lowered my face, a thousand thoughts going through my mind.

How happy was he with Cleo? How long had they been seeing each other? Did they bicker like we used to?

What do I do next?

I raised my head and had a cautious peep. He was tapping on the entry panel keypad. Then he pushed the wrought-iron gate open and entered. Moments later it swung shut behind him with a clang I heard.

It swung shut on me.

Locking me out of his new life.

I watched until he had walked out of sight.

Then I twisted the key in the ignition so hard I thought for a moment I had snapped it in half. The engine fired. Then I accelerated away so furiously it sent Coke spurting over Bruno, who protested loudly.

I can't remember ever feeling so low in all my life.

382

95

I realized what it was about Dr Eberstark that made him look like a hawk, albeit a wise hawk. It was his nose, a big hooked proboscis that could almost be a beak, partly concealed by the enormous black-rimmed glasses he wore. He had kind, sympathetic eyes through those lenses, smiling eyes, but an almost permanently bemused expression.

In all the times I had seen him, I'd not figured out whether he reserved that expression for me, or it was simply how he viewed the world – or at least, the world as seen through the eyes of his patients. Not a very happy world, I would think.

So am I now officially dead? It seems ages since I picked up that copy of the *Münchner Merkur* in the Englischer Garten and read the advertisement my husband had placed, to have me declared dead.

So was he my husband still, even if I was legally dead? Was he my ex-husband, my was-husband? My lawyers weren't sure. No one was sure.

This Monday afternoon we were having one of our long, habitual and expensive silences, punctuated only by the sound of the traffic three floors below on Widenmayerstrasse. I say expensive because it was costing me the same whether we talked or not. I had started to speak but then hesitated, feeling embarrassed, although Dr Eberstark was the one person I should be able to talk to about anything, because he wasn't there to judge me. Just to help me.

But there were times when I felt he was like a judge at the Bench, looking at me, the villain on trial in the dock. Even though I was on the couch facing him, I could feel his eyes on my back.

'I do horrible things sometimes,' I said, finally getting it out. Then fell silent again.

After a while he asked, 'What kind of horrible things, Sandy?' His voice was always calm.

'I put an advertisement in their local paper's Deaths column that their baby had died.' As I say the words out loud I am so embarrassed it feels as though I am hearing someone else speak them. *Come on, judge me, be shocked!* He stays as calm as ever as if what I am telling him is just so routine. I bet inside he thinks I'm nuts. Who wouldn't?

The problem was I was upset and fuming. I drank far too much and made two very bad decisions that I now regret. Not only did I put the advert in their local paper, but I had also scratched into the bonnet of Cleo's car: 'COPPER'S TART. UR BABY IS NEXT.'

What on earth was I thinking? I am deeply ashamed, but alcohol had made me feel confident and heightened my emotions. The day I left Roy I was so wrapped up in the threat and my own danger I didn't give him or his future enough thought. I didn't consider that he would have a new girlfriend or children. But now I wanted him back, everything was different.

I tell Dr Eberstark about vandalizing Cleo's car. I'm on a roll now, may as well get it all out in front of the expert.

Did I detect a hint of admonishment in his tone?

'What did you think you would achieve by doing that?'

There was a framed photograph on the doctor's desk of him with an attractive, rather academic-looking woman and two very serious-looking girls in their late teens. They stood in a posed group, all looking so prim, so perfect, so anodyne. As if none of them, ever in their lives, had farted.

'Sometimes I feel I'm like the scorpion in that fable,' I told him.

'Which fable?'

'The one where the scorpion asks the turtle to give him a ride across the river to the other side. The turtle replies, "I can't do that. You might sting me to death." The scorpion says, "Look, I'm not dumb. If you carry me across the river and I sting you, we will both die – you from my sting and I will drown."

'So the turtle says, "Okay, that makes sense!"

'They get halfway across the river and the scorpion stings the turtle. The turtle, in agony and starting to sink, turns and looks at the scorpion and says, "Why did you do that? Now we're both going to die."

'The scorpion replies, "I know. I'm sorry, I couldn't help it. It's in my nature."'

Dr Eberstark asks if I think I'm the scorpion, if that's how I justify my anger and what that tells him. I don't know what it all represents but I know it makes me sad that Roy's moved on without me.

Then, totally changing the subject, he asks, 'In our last session you were going to tell me something about the baby. Do you want to tell me now?'

The baby? Cleo's baby?

No, I realize. He means Bruno. 'The thing is, I'm not sure it was Roy's.'

He barely reacted at all. Maybe he'd been expecting something like this. 'Oh?'

'I was having an affair. With one of his colleagues.'

He looked at me, silent and a little expectant, which made me feel I ought to continue.

'A short while before I left Roy, I had an affair with a man called Cassian Pewe. Well, more a fling than an affair. More like a few one-night stands. I saw him a handful of times right up until the time I left Roy before I realized that actually I really didn't like him. I'm in the process of having a DNA test done now, to see if I can establish whether it's Roy or him who is the father.'

I watched him nodding, absorbing this.

'Interesting,' is all he replied.

Then, infuriatingly, as he so often did just when things were getting going, he looked at the clock on the wall.

'OK, time's up. I'll see you on Wednesday.'

96

September 2017

After leaving Dr Eberstark's consulting room, and running the gauntlet of the receptionist in the adjoining room who acted as his sentinel, I crossed busy Widenmayerstrasse and strolled over the grass towards the path that ran along this side of the Isar river.

It was my ritual after every session, to stroll or jog along the bank. A time for collecting my thoughts and reflecting on what we had discussed. An hour to myself, before I had to head off and collect Bruno from school.

The sky was a wintry grey, with faint drizzle falling, and my thoughts were grey.

Although I'd rented a really beautiful apartment on Widenmayerstrasse, in general my lifestyle during our recent years in Munich had been pretty modest. I'd bought a second-hand VW Golf, similar to the one I'd had in England. Bruno was in a private school but the fees were reasonable. And all our holidays had been relatively local. In summer we'd gone to Lake Constance, Bodensee, and to a ski resort near Salzburg in the winter months, where I'd enjoyed watching Bruno learn to ski – and really take to it.

As a result of being reasonably frugal, and the prudent invest-ments of my gambling win in Frankfurt, made by the finance management company my lawyer had introduced me to, my portfolio had increased to over £2 million.

The asking price for our house in Welbeck Street, Hove, was £880,000. I'd contacted the estate agent first thing this morning and put in an offer of £850,000. He'd told me he already had an offer for £875,000 and it was a cash buyer.

Without hesitation, I told him I was a cash buyer too and upped my offer to £900,000.

He told me he would speak to the vendor and get back to me.

Actually I AM THE VENDOR! I wanted to joke with him. *Or at least 50 per cent the vendor.*

Except I wasn't. Not any more. I was dead. Legally dead, anyway.

I'd called my lawyer in Frankfurt to try to understand where I stood. He didn't know the procedure and promised to get back to me. By the time of my next session with my psychiatrist, two days later, he had still not come back.

And in this strange status, I realized I was the very embodiment of Schrödinger's cat, which was both alive and dead at the same time.

I decided I would begin my next session with Dr Eberstark, on Wednesday, by telling him this.

Then I pulled my phone out and saw there was a text from the estate agent, saying he'd just tried to call me.

Damn, stupid me, I'd put my phone on silent for my session with Dr Eberstark and hadn't put the sound back on. I called him back immediately. When he answered he sounded, as he always did, like he was chewing gum. He told me the news that the other party had raised their offer to £910,000.

'Are you playing silly buggers?' I asked him, straight out.

'I'm afraid it's a bidding war, Mrs Lohmann. This is happening a lot these days.'

I could imagine him lording it at some desk in an open-plan ground-floor office in full view of the street and, with each increased bid, going *kerchinggg!*

'All right,' I said. 'I'll go to nine hundred and fifty thousand.'

'Nine hundred and fifty thousand?' he said, double-checking, still chewing.

'Correct.'

'Final offer?'

'Final offer.'

97

The soundtrack to the start of our Wednesday session was the *beep-parp . . . beep-parp* of the sirens of a succession of emergency vehicles, six floors below, racing along Widenmayerstrasse. Although it was chilly outside, it was stuffily warm in Dr Eberstark's consulting room, and the window was open a few inches, to let some air in – but it came with the traffic noise.

'Are you intending to tell him you are actually alive?' he asked.

I was feeling very distracted today. He keeps coming with the questions. I answer them as best I can. To this one, a *no*.

'So you are a dead person?'

Er, no. '*Sandy Grace* is a dead person. That doesn't make me a dead person.'

'Legally you are.'

No again! 'Legally I am Frau Lohmann.'

'You told me that you got your German citizenship by paying someone. Was that lawful?'

'No one died in the process.' My tone was sharp, I was annoyed by his sudden prurience. And I was annoyed that the estate agent had not yet come back to me on my raised offer on Monday. I mean, surely that was a knock-out offer, a slam-dunk?

We talk about right and wrong, about what my disappearance might have done to Roy, but really what choice did I have? Yes, I did think about Roy and what it would do to him, but I was being chased down by madman Albazi, who no doubt still wants to kill me, and it really was better for Roy and me that I left.

'It was the best of a bad set of options. In my view,' I say.

'And that is still your view, isn't it?'

'I've made a mess of my life. I guess that's why I'm here. People don't come to a shrink because they're happy, do they? Do you have patients who are happy?'

'Let's just focus on you.'

'I'm a train wreck, aren't I?'

'I would not say that, not just yet. But you are heading towards becoming one, in my opinion, if you go ahead and buy that house.'

I looked at him. And had the sense of staring into Nietzsche's abyss. That thing about the abyss staring back at you.

98

I waited, after leaving Dr Eberstark's office, until I had crossed Widenmayerstrasse and found an empty bench along the river-bank. It was cold and the sky was an angry grey. A few drops of rain were falling. Then, watching the beautiful crystal-clear water flowing past from the waterfall, I called the estate agent.

'Ah, Mrs Lohmann, congratulations, you've seen my message?'

'I have.'

'You must be delighted, and frankly even at nine hundred and fifty thousand, you are getting this beautiful home at a good price, it will be worth over a million by the end of this year, no question.' He was gushing. This was him but rebooted. He didn't even sound like he had gum in his mouth.

'Right,' I said, aware I probably sounded like the least enthu-siastic person he'd ever delivered good news to.

'Are you back in Germany at the moment?'

'I am.'

'OK, what I'll do is email you a draft sale agreement memo-randum for you to fill in. If you can put in the name of the solicitors you will be using for the conveyance, I can start the ball rolling this end. I imagine this will be subject to survey?'

Subject to survey. I liked that. The house was over eighty years old and there had been plenty of minor things wrong with it, including damp patches and a roof that wasn't in the best shape. It was a get-out if I needed it.

'Yes, subject to survey.'

There was a brief pause then he asked, more tenderly than I would have given him credit for, 'Is everything all right, Mrs Lohmann?'

'It's fine, why?'

'Just checking you are happy to have secured the property. You sound a little – flat?'

'I've just offered nearly a hundred grand over the asking price. Do you think I'm not happy maybe because of that?' Then I ended the call.

Shit.

I stood up and walked along the towpath, barely noticing just how cold it was. All around people were wrapped up well; even some of the dogs being walked had coats on. It seemed it was already growing dark, or perhaps that was just the darkness of the abyss in my heart.

Had I just blown it with the house deal?

Maybe it would be a good thing if I had.

But half an hour later, just as I was about to drive out of the car park at the rear of my apartment building, to go and collect Bruno from school, an email pinged on my phone. It was from the estate agent.

My heart sank.

It was full of platitudes. *Delighted for you, Mrs Lohmann! Such a good decision! I'm sure you and your son will be so happy in your fabulous new home. You've made a great choice.*

The sale memorandum was attached.

I had to open it and read it, right now. It all seemed so surreal. Was I really buying a house I already owned?

99

My little man sat in the Golf beside me, looking very self-important, as ever. He was neatly dressed, in his herringbone tweed overcoat, with not a hair out of place, giving the impression more of someone who had just stepped out of an important board meeting than a nine-year-old boy who'd just finished school for the day.

He gave me a very serious look as I drove then said, '*England, warum England?*'

I tried to speak to him in English as much as possible, in the hope I would bring him up to be bilingual. It was working, if it got a little confusing for both of us, switching between the languages at times.

'You were born in England, darling, and I'm English. Wouldn't you like to go and live there? To give it a try?'

'*Warum?*'

'Because . . .' I was struggling. 'Because it's beautiful. It's my homeland.'

'Germany is now our home, Mama. Germany is beautiful. And anyhow, Erik would not be in England, would he?'

'You could make other friends – new friends.'

'Erik is my friend, I don't need other friends. I don't need new friends. I'm happy with the friend I have.'

That was one of my worries about Bruno. His lack of interest in making friends. At least he had one in Erik – but they were very different personalities. Erik always seemed to be smiling and looking relaxed, whereas Bruno carried a sense of responsibility and sadness.

I drove on in silence as he looked out the window. I was thinking about the results of the DNA paternity test that I'd had through from a firm in Berlin.

So now I know Roy is the father.

What now?

The danger from Albazi felt like it was subsiding a little after all these years but I couldn't stop myself being wary, on my guard, jumping at my shadow, seeing his double haunting me. I wonder if that will ever stop. Could I find a way to pay him back to clear my debt and we could all move on? That might help. Go ahead and buy the house, lure Roy back and tell him he is Bruno's father?

Then what?

At another of my appointments with Dr Eberstark he'd asked me two things and I'd misled him about them both. Firstly, did I know who the father of my child was? It had annoyed me, to be honest, all these questions I really didn't want to answer, so I just said stuff to delay it. I know it's his job to try to understand, but I am just getting so tired of it all. I told him I thought I was paying him to help me, not interrogate me, and asked that we change the subject!

That's when he asked me if I had bought the house in Hove. To which I didn't answer, I couldn't tell him, he'd think I was truly crazy. I wanted these questions to stop. I just sat and stared, almost through him, in another world. A bit like I feel now.

Suddenly, Bruno asked, 'Mama, are we having bratwurst for supper?'

I smiled. Sometimes the sheer simplicity of my child's life brought me back to earth with a pleasantly soft landing. OK, bratwurst really wasn't the healthiest food to give a growing lad, but it was his once-a-week treat. I subjected him to my on-and-off vegetarian and vegan diet on most of the other days.

'*Ja!*'

'*Hast du daran gedacht, Senf zu kaufen?*' He said it as if it was the most important thing in the world. And, casting my mind back to my own childhood, I remembered that such seemingly trivial things as this really were important.

'I have, darling,' I replied in English. 'I bought more mustard when I went shopping this morning.'

As soon as we got home, Bruno headed off to the privacy of his room, and I reminded him to do his homework before playing any more online games with Erik, knowing Erik's parents, Ingo and Anette, who were much stricter than I was, would have told him the same.

I sat down at my rather grand desk, with a great view of the park and the Isar, and checked my emails, wondering yet again what I should do about responding to the sales memorandum I had been sent.

There was a Google alert and I clicked on it.

And immediately wished I hadn't.

100

October 2017

Having me declared dead had shocked me to the core, but the Google alert I was reading now rocked me in a way that nothing before ever had. It was a piece in the *Argus* online, under NOTICES.

TOP COPPER TO WED ON SATURDAY

The wedding of Detective Superintendent Roy Grace, of Surrey and Sussex Major Crime Team, and Cleo Morey, Senior Anatomical Pathology Technician at Brighton and Hove City Mortuary, will take place at St Margaret's Church in Rottingdean at 2.30 p.m. on Saturday, 2 November. Many senior police officers, including Chief Constable Tom Martinson, are expected to attend. The marriage will bring to a close the detective's years of sadness following the unexplained disappearance of his former wife, Sandra (Sandy) Christina Grace, over ten years ago, who was formally declared dead in August of this year.

God knows how long I sat there, staring ahead. It was Bruno's voice that finally snapped me out of the kind of trance I was in.

'Mama?'

'*Ja, mein Liebe*?'

He was hungry.

'I'll cook your bratwurst in a few minutes, OK? I just need to finish something I'm doing.'

He padded off, disgruntled, to carry on with his homework, or, more likely, to try to kill more futuristic warriors than Erik on an intergalactic battlefield, or whatever.

I logged on to the Lufthansa website, then British Airways. After that I went on to expedia.com. It was good timing, a holiday for German schools next week, so it would be no problem to take Bruno with me. I booked flights to London and a well-reviewed bed-and-breakfast hotel in Brighton called Strawberry Fields for the two of us.

How very convenient to have me declared dead. Getting married, are you, Roy Grace?

I don't think so.

101

I wore a veil and felt every inch the black widow. Which just shows how messed up the inside of my head is. The only person here who's dead is me, and this isn't a funeral; it's a wedding.

But it was sure going to feel like a funeral to me.

It's quite a pretty church, I'll give Roy credit for that, the kind of olde England Norman and Saxon mishmash that looks great in photos in *Hello!* And on the mantelpiece. Not as pretty as ours – the one we got married in – but a good second best, for a second marriage.

There's a long queue of people waiting to go in, a few of them in smart police tunics, the rest in suits and dresses, many of them wrapped up against the biting wind.

'Bride or groom?' says a male voice and my heart stops. For a moment, all I want to do is turn and flee. *Shit, shit, shit.*

It's Roy's best friend, Dick Pope. We were due to go out to dinner with Dick and his wife, Leslie, to celebrate Roy's birthday that night. That day I disappeared.

Why the hell hadn't I thought that he'd be here? An usher, of course.

But he was pretty distracted and clearly had not recognized me through my very dark veil and with my short hair. And why would he? Sandy is dead.

'Bride,' I said, to obfuscate. He handed us each an order-of-service sheet and indicated the left side of the church.

Every pew was full, but that suited me fine. We made our way to the back of the church and stood. Bruno had a clear view down the aisle and I could see over the tops of the sea of heads in front of me.

I'd been rehearsing my lines rigorously. Well, I say *lines*, but, to be honest, it's not much more than one line, really.

Then, suddenly, I was stricken with panic. This was crazy, I had to get out. I grabbed Bruno's arm and half pulled the confused boy out of a side door at the rear. No one noticed. I stood, gulping down air, while Bruno asked me what was wrong, why I was so upset. I shook my head. I had to go back inside. We hadn't come this far to just walk away.

I just had to calm down enough to be able to say that line, that one line. I said it silently now.

'Mama, why are you whispering?'

We slipped back inside. I said that line to myself again. Then again. Finally, I sort of felt ready. Sort of.

When the vicar, quite a jolly figure with a white beard, queries if anyone knows of any legal impediment to the marriage, I will listen like everyone else. To the same words most of the congregation will have heard so many times.

And I guarantee that not one of these people in this packed church will ever before in their lives have heard someone speak up who is actually not prepared to forever hold their peace.

Boy, were they in for a treat today.

I was shaking, feeling as if I was on some alien planet, in someone else's world where I totally did not belong. It wasn't a massive church and I could see Roy, his hair short, cutting an elegant figure in his grey tails standing by the front right-hand pew chatting nervously to a tall black man, also in tails, who was smiling. He put a reassuring arm around Roy's shoulder. His best man, presumably, but who was he? He looked like a cop. Of course he would be a cop.

Suddenly the organ struck up loudly. Pachelbel's Canon.

No, really? How cheesy.

Roy and his best man sat down. Roy, on the end of the pew, turned and stared up the aisle. Smiling, all soppy.

The bride appeared, on the arm of a silver-haired man who looked a total toff. Here was Barbie. About to wed Ken.

Moments later, Ken and Barbie were standing, facing the vicar.

This was just nuts. Too nuts. Like one of those panic dreams where you try desperately to stop something and you can't.

'Are those people getting married, Mama?' whispered Bruno.

I barely heard him. All I could think was: *My husband is getting married to another woman, right in front of me! My husband with a best man I've never met. My husband getting married in a church full of many people I have never met.*

I felt the anger swirling through me, like the first gust of a brewing storm.

'Mama, are they?' he whispered again. 'Are they getting married?'

'Maybe,' I whispered back.

But maybe not. I can stop it.

'Only *maybe*?' whispering still, but a little louder. 'Why are they standing there if they are not going to get married, Mama?'

The vicar, blocked from my view now by Ken and Barbie, boomed through the speakers, 'The Grace of our Lord Jesus Christ, the love of God and the fellowship of the Holy Spirit be with you.'

His name, according to the service sheet, was Father Martin.

There was a typically murmured, self-conscious response from the congregation. 'And also with you.'

Everything became a blur. I felt in total turmoil. Roy looked so confident, so handsome, so mature now. Such a different person from a decade ago.

He had had his faults, I was thinking, but in the eight years we were together I was certain of one thing, from the deep love he had always shown me, that he had never been unfaithful. Thinking back, I'd never, in all that time, even seen him eye another woman. He had told me, many times, that he loved me to bits, that I was his soulmate, that something incredibly powerful had drawn us together. And I had agreed with him each time then. In those early days, I had truly believed we would be together for ever.

Until.

I shuddered.

'God is love, and those who live in love live in God and God lives in them,' Father Martin intoned.

In just a few minutes, Roy would be gone for ever. Married to another woman.

I felt a tear trickle down my cheek.

'Why are you sad, Mama?'

Almost the entire congregation read aloud the words printed on their order of service sheets. I clutched Bruno's left hand tightly and held my sheet, which I'd not yet looked at, with my free hand. On the front was printed *Roy, Cleo*, with the date and a dinky drawing of church bells between them.

I was starting to hyperventilate. Tears were flooding down my face now, stinging my eyes and blurring my vision. I only had moments left. I had to stop this. *Had to*. Stop this lie. This sham. Bigamy was about to happen. I had to stop it. I was duty-bound, surely, to stop it?

Wouldn't I be breaking the law if I forever held my peace?

And I wanted him back so desperately at this moment. So damned desperately. I didn't care what anyone would think when I blurted out – shouted out – those words, I was damned well going to do it.

I had to do it.

Yes, me! I can show just cause. He's already married – to me!

THEY THOUGHT I WAS DEAD

'God of wonder and joy: grace comes from you, and you alone
are the source of life and love. Without you, we cannot please
you; without your love, our deeds are worth nothing. Send your
Holy Spirit and pour into our hearts that most excellent gift of
love, that we may worship you now with thankful hearts and
serve you always with willing minds; through Jesus Christ our
Lord. Amen.'

Grace. The word kept coming up in the service. *Grace.* The
word – name – seared my heart. The sight of the man I had once
loved so much, and still loved, standing with his bride-to-be.

I have the power to stop it.

I have come here to stop it.

I am going to stop it.

102

I will be an accomplice to a criminal act if I do nothing – despite the fact that I have been declared legally dead. No one has actually told me I've been declared dead. Shouldn't someone have to notify you if you were dead?

I held that thought for a moment. Then realized how absurd it was.

I still wasn't thinking completely straight.

The organ struck up again, the strains of 'Jerusalem'. The congregation began to sing, loudly, lustily; everyone knew and loved this hymn. Their voices rose to the vaulted roof of the building and echoed off its walls.

'And did those feet, in ancient time, walk upon England's mountains green? And was the Holy Lamb of God on England's pleasant pastures seen?'

And my anger, which had been simmering close to boiling point, turned to near blind fury.

This was the same damned hymn everyone had sung at our wedding.

For God's sake.

It was Roy's favourite, because it was the English rugby anthem. I remembered so very clearly, all those years ago, standing at the altar at All Saints Church, Patcham, with Roy on my right, on the happiest day of my life. About to be married to

404

the man I loved, and with whom I wanted, without any question, to spend the rest of my life.

Was Barbie, standing beside him now, as happy as I had felt?

I blinked away tears but more replaced them. Bruno squeezed my hand for a moment. He didn't understand what was going on but he knew I was upset. I fumbled in my handbag for a tissue, lifted my veil a little and dabbed my eyes.

'Mama?'

I silenced him with a raised finger, then stood still, shaking, listening.

'I will not cease, from mental fight, nor shall my sword sleep in my hand, 'til we have built Jerusalem in England's green and pleasant land.'

Hans-Jürgen was always spouting quotations at me. There was one, his favourite, that was resonating now. It went something like, *For all of us, life is a series of journeys, and at the end of each journey, we arrive back at the place we started from, and know it for the first time.*

That was me, now. Here in the church. Listening to the fading sound of the organ and the echo of our wedding hymn. Realizing just how much I loved this man standing at the altar, and had always loved him.

And knowing it so deep inside.

Time was running out.

I had to stop this.

I took a deep breath.

Roy looked so calm, standing so upright, so confident. Was this how the congregation had seen him on our own wedding day?

Father Martin began speaking. 'In the presence of God, Father, Son and Holy Spirit, we have come together to witness the marriage of Roy and Cleo, to pray for God's blessing on them, to share their joy and to celebrate their love.'

'Mama, who are they?'

He said it so loudly an elderly woman in front of us turned round, glaring.

I raised a silencing finger again. 'Sssshhh!' I said.

'Marriage is a gift of God in creation through which husband and wife may know the grace of God. It is given that as man and woman grow together in love and trust, they shall be united with one another in heart, body and mind, as Christ is united with his bride, the Church.'

I had to stop this. Somehow, I had to find the strength to do it. This was what I had come to do.

'The gift of marriage brings husband and wife together in the delight and tenderness of sexual union.'

I couldn't help it. I let out a stifled cry.

'Mama?' Bruno looked at me, alarmed, squeezing my hand again tightly with his own tiny one.

'And joyful commitment to the end of their lives. It is given as a foundation of family life in which children are born and nurtured.'

More words went over my head as I thought more and more how I had never before considered Roy making love to another woman. About him doing the same things to her that he had done to me. He'd been an incredible lover. Always considerate, always determined to satiate me fully before himself. None of the other sexual relationships I'd ever had came close. And now, tonight, he would be going to a bedroom somewhere, and would make love as a new husband to his new bride, and no doubt do all the things to her we had done. And he'd be telling her they were soulmates. And not think for one damned second about me. About all we had once been and once had.

If I didn't intervene.

The moment was getting closer. Less than a minute or so away, now. Father Martin continued towards the point of no return.

'Roy and Cleo are now to enter this way of life. They will each give their consent to the other and make solemn vows, and in token of this they will each give and receive a ring.'

I realized I was twisting the ring Roy had put on my finger nearly two decades ago.

'We pray with Roy and Cleo that the Holy Spirit will guide and strengthen them, that they may fulfil God's purposes for the whole of their earthly life together.'

I took a deep breath. Another. Then another.

NOW!

This was my moment. The chance to change my life. To go back to how it all had once been. I took yet another long, deep breath. Ran through the words again in my head.

YES, I KNOW A REASON! HE'S ALREADY MARRIED. TO ME!

Father Martin said, loudly, but with a smile, 'First, I am required to ask anyone present who knows a reason these persons may not lawfully marry to declare it now.'

And suddenly, without warning, Roy turned and looked half comically back down the aisle, staring straight at me, it seemed. Staring straight through the veil into my eyes.

I froze.

He turned back to face the altar.

My legs had become unsteady and I had to hold on to the back of the pew in front of me for some moments. I thought I was going to throw up.

Had he seen me? Could he somehow know I was here? How? It wasn't possible.

But, I realized, what I wanted to do now wasn't possible.

I had made this long journey to stop the wedding, but I couldn't do it. I didn't have the strength. I didn't have . . .

A tornado of confusion was raging in my mind.

I have to do it.

Have to.

Have to.
NOW!
But I just stood, frozen. Terrified suddenly.

'The vows you are about to take are made in the presence of God, who is judge of all and knows all the secrets of our hearts.'

I gripped Bruno's hand so hard. Then, ignoring the sea of faces, I dragged him, half running, out of the church and out into the sunlit afternoon.

'Mama!' he protested.

Behind us I heard Father Martin's voice. 'Therefore if either of you knows a reason you may not lawfully marry, you must declare it now.'

I stood still, listening hard. Hoping. Half hoping.

'Mama?'

'Ssshhhh!'

'Roy, will you take Cleo to be your wife? Will you love her, comfort her, honour and protect her, and, forsaking all others, be faithful to her as long as you both shall live?'

The silence seemed eternal. Then I heard the words I dreaded. Faint, but distinct enough. Like the whisper of a ghost.

'I will.'

Dragging Bruno by his hand again, I ran, stumbling, blinded by my tears, down the church path to the road, and back up the hill towards where I had parked the rental car.

103

Two men, one very tall, one very short, stood in protective over-suits and face masks, inside the lock-up garage in Munich. They looked a bit like a pair of rather shabby CSIs. This garage was shabby too, the kind you could rent cheaply pretty much the world over. Plasterboard inside a corrugated iron shell and a roller-shutter door. Big enough to fit a large car and to be able to work on it without bashing your elbows on the beat-up walls.

'Wouldn't it have been easier just to have bought a used one?' the short guy asked. 'There must be ones for sale all the time.'

'The boss said no,' the tall guy responded. He was adjusting the nozzle on the gas cylinder with which he would, in a few moments, begin spray-painting the stolen five-year-old Mercedes E-Class estate a specific shade of cream. The car was sitting up on jacks, minus its wheels, with its bumpers, mirror and chrome grille covered in protective tape.

'You know your problem?' the short one said. 'You're halfway up the boss's backside.'

'And you know yours?' the tall one replied. 'When you were born they threw the best part away.'

Both of them pulled their masks down over their faces as the tall one fired up the spray gun and set to work.

When he had finished, the short one set to work on the electrics, checking everything was in working order. And, most important of all, the yellow and black roof light.

104

'Tell me, how did you feel in the church, Sandy?' Dr Eberstark asks.

Bruno and I had flown back yesterday, just managing to get the last two seats on the only afternoon flight to Munich. With my head all over the place, I hadn't thought to book any return tickets to Munich. Why? What had I thought was going to happen if I stood up and halted the ceremony?

I was still trying to process it all. What I had done – or rather oh so nearly done – scared me, because I realized I still wasn't right in the head.

'I felt like an alien. I realized I didn't know his world any more. And I kept thinking what a mistake I'd made.'

Dr Eberstark said nothing, as if giving me space to continue. After some moments, I did, but my voice was faltering, and I was close to tears again.

Eventually I had to stop and sobbed, feeling so sad. I just couldn't help thinking, why did I let it all get so far? Why didn't I tell him I was alive much sooner? I might have had a chance of getting him back. It was going around my head in a loop.

Then, sniffing, trying to keep it together, I said to Eberstark, 'Such a big bloody mistake. When I realized that, I wanted him back so much, I wanted to be there, I wanted to be that woman.'

'Yet you left him,' he said unhelpfully.

'Yes. I left him. I guess I didn't know then what I know now.

I wanted him back so badly. Really, at that moment when the priest guy – the vicar – asked if anyone knew any reason they should not be joined together in holy matrimony, I nearly shouted out that I did. Really, I so nearly did. That's what I had gone there intending to do.'

The psychiatrist waited silently.

I was gathering my thoughts. I know I've made a total mess of everything. I wouldn't do it the same way again. I have learned and matured. But I wouldn't be sitting here if I didn't care. I told him I feel I've screwed up my life. How every day I wake up in the morning and I lie to my son. He asks me about his father and I don't tell him the truth. I'm scared I'm going to screw him up. That some days I think I should kill myself. He replies by asking me if I've thought about the consequences of that on Bruno. Like I haven't thought about that! Of course I have. But these things are all in my thoughts. Some days are more positive, some not so much. Some days I just feel desperate and want someone to come along, give me a hug, take over and tell me everything is OK again.

I talk for a few minutes before Dr Eberstark glances at the clock on the wall.

'We'll have to leave it there,' he says. 'I'll see you on Thursday. Is that OK with you?'

Always.

After I closed the front door of Dr Eberstark's building, wrapped up in my coat, scarf and gloves, I walked out onto the pavement alongside the four lanes of heavy traffic on Widenmayerstrasse, and stopped, staring at the wide grass bank of the Isar river across the street.

How many sessions with strange – and expensive – Dr Eberstark had I now had? Were they getting me anywhere? Sometimes I left his consulting room feeling strong, but other times, like now, I left feeling more confused than ever.

As the traffic thundered past, I wondered if now was the time, finally, to tell Roy – newly married Roy – about Bruno. Surely he needed to know, in case anything happened to me?

That would sure as hell throw a spanner into his newly wed bliss.

How would Cleo take the news?

How would Roy?

Roy was a kind man at heart. He would take responsibility, because he would have no option. But how much did he care for Cleo, really? He'd kept telling me, during our life together, that he could not live without me. Well, he seemed to be doing pretty well, so far. But maybe she was just a poor substitute. Maybe he was still burning a candle for me?

It was cold, bitterly cold. I felt cold through to my bones and thought for a moment about abandoning my usual constitutional along the riverbank, after my sessions with Eberstark, and just heading for the warmth of home. But I decided the air would do me some good, clear my head.

My sodding confused head.

I looked right then left. For an instant I was back in Brighton, in England. Where the traffic drove on the opposite side. I looked to the right, and the road was clear. Then some kind of clarity returned. I was in Germany, they drive on the right here. Then I stepped out. *Look left, then right then—*

The roar of an engine.

I fleetingly saw the front of the cream Mercedes, with the yellow and black roof light. It said TAXI.

Then it felt like a brick wall had hit me broadside.

105

Murmured voices intermittently intruded into the constant loop of weird movies playing inside my head.

I repeatedly heard the kind-sounding voice of a man who told me he was Dr Stockerl. I was under his care.

I wasn't able to open my eyes or move anything, but I could hear them, and piece together, bit by bit, what had happened. I was in a coma, I heard them say. Apparently no one had told them that people in comas could hear everything that was going on. Well, I could.

The narrative went that I had stepped out in front of a taxi. It had hurled me 10 metres along the road. As I lay there, some bastard on a motorbike had stopped, grabbed my handbag and ridden off.

Another time, I heard them talking about a small boy.

I wanted to open my eyes and tell them. This was my boy, my son. But they wouldn't open. My mouth wouldn't work. Nothing worked. I was like a corpse but still alive inside my dead body. I had the sensation of being underwater, in a swimming pool, and there were people on the surface totally disconnected to me. But I could hear them. Every word.

They were saying a small boy, upset that his mother had not turned up to collect him from football, had gone to stay the night with a friend.

That would be Erik.

413

Erik's mother had come to the hospital the next day and identified me as her friend. Frau Lohmann.

Then I heard them talking about the police. That Frau Lohmann was not my real name. That I seemed to have several names and was connected to a missing Greek drug dealer who had lived in Jersey. Gossip was I might have been involved in his disappearance.

I so much wanted to wake – and see Bruno – and tell them the truth.

One nice lady, who told me she was a nurse, talked to me every time she was on shift. I had the sense she knew I could hear her. She told me I was in the Intensive Care Unit of the Klinikum München Schwabing.

At some point when she was talking I did open my eyes, blinking against the light, and saw a woman in hospital scrubs looking down at me. The badge on her chest read, *Stationsschwester Frau Koti Fekete.*

But my eyes closed again almost immediately.

'Come back to us,' she said, quietly. 'Wake up! Your son needs you!'

My son. Bruno. Roy's son.

I needed her to tell Roy. Desperately needed her to do that. To tell him so much. But it took all my strength to say just one thing.

'Tell him I forgive him,' I murmured.

'Tell who?' she replied.

106

March 2018

It was four months since my accident, Stationsschwester Frau Fekete told me – as I had no sense of time at all – when I re-entered Planet Earth in some small capacity as a sentient human being. Almost every part of my body hurt and I had only limited mobility without excruciating pain – despite being attached by a cannula to a morphine drip, among other drip lines plumbed into me.

There's a word in German that I particularly like. I like the way it sounds and I like what it means. *Gemütlich.*

It translates as 'pleasant', but actually it means so much more than that. I don't think there's a word in the English language that adequately conveys the feelgood factor of the word.

That's what it felt as I stared up at a man in scrubs, with warm brown eyes that seemed almost to be dancing. The badge on his lapel read *Dr Stockerl.*

'I think you are back with us now, Sandy,' he said in English with a strong accent. 'Would you prefer I speak in English or German?'

'Either. Maybe English, bitte?'

I was on a bit of a morphine high at the moment and I smiled at him and wanted so much to tell him just how *gemütlich* he was. But then he talked me through all the injuries I had sustained in the accident, and suddenly he seemed so serious. He delivered a litany of bad news about my condition.

And suddenly he wasn't at all *gemütlich* any more.

When he had finished dispensing all the gloom and doom I thought it was possible to hear, he added further to it. 'Munich Police are very anxious to speak to you about your accident. Do you feel up to talking to them?'

I didn't feel at all up to speaking to anyone after the information dump I'd just had. But I was curious. My memory had returned – at least some of it – and I was thinking back to the last time I'd spoken to Munich Police – soon after I had arrived at the schloss. How many years ago? Six, seven?

With a stab of alarm I wondered: was there news of Nicos after all this time?

I didn't have to wait long. Soon after, Stationsschwester Frau Fekete came into my room with a tall, rather fine-looking and confident man in a green tunic. It took a moment before I placed him. He looked a little older and his black hair was now shot through with silver flecks. He also looked a little stiff.

'*Guten Morgen, Frau Lohmann, ich bin Kriminalhauptkommissar Steinmetz. Erinnern Sie sich, dass wir uns vor einigen Jahren kennengelernt haben?*'

I replied to him in English, because the German translation software in my head wasn't working that great. 'I remember, we met some years ago. You were just a humble Kriminalkommissar then.'

He softened a fraction. 'You remember.'

I looked directly back at him. 'I think most people would probably remember when they were detained. Particularly if it was the only time in their life.'

He looked as if he wasn't sure whether to frown or smile. Instead he did neither, he just looked serious. 'Frau Lohmann, I am in charge of the investigation into your accident, and I would like to ask you some questions, if you are feeling strong enough?'

'I'll try. But I don't really remember anything – only what I've been told.'

'According to eyewitnesses, you were struck by a Mercedes taxi as you attempted to cross Widermayerstrasse. But what the four witnesses we have interviewed have each said is that this vehicle appeared to deliberately drive at you. There were not any tyre marks on the road to indicate it had braked, and three of these witnesses have said they heard the roar of its engine, as if it was accelerating.'

I thought about this for some moments. 'I was standing near to the traffic lights, and I was confused, I remember, about how the English drive on one side of the road and Germans on the other.'

Steinmetz nodded. 'Yes, and this may be the simple answer. But there are two things that are concerning to us. The first is that the taxi did not stop – of course the driver could have been drinking and was scared he would lose his licence. Unfortunately no one got his registration number. But the second is that a motorcyclist, seconds after, stopped, grabbed your handbag and rode off. One of the witnesses did manage to write down his licence plate – and it turned out to be false.'

He looked down at me as if waiting for me to provide an answer. But I didn't have one.

'What are you actually saying?' I asked him.

'What I need to ask you, Frau Lohmann, is do you think you might have any enemy?' He gave me a long, penetrating and knowing look.

'Are you referring to Nicos – my former partner?'

He continued looking at me, as if he was convinced I was hiding something. 'It is possible, Frau Lohmann, that this was just an unfortunate accident, and this motorcyclist was a criminal opportunist. We do not have enough evidence to suggest for sure you were targeted, but, bearing in mind your past association with a former criminal who went missing, this is something we cannot rule out. Perhaps you could think hard if there is anyone who might have – what do you call it in English? – a *grudge* against you, and let me know. I will leave you my card.'

I thanked him. But the way I was feeling after all the bad news Dr Stockerl had delivered, I didn't care if anyone did have a grudge. If they wanted to kill me, I would embrace them with open arms for taking me away from the life I was left with.

107

March 2018

It was two weeks later when I was alerted by Stationsschwester Fekete that a man and a woman were here to see me. They had flown from England, apparently. She understood it was my former husband and his new wife and asked if I would be up to seeing them. If I did not wish to see them, she would tell them I was not well enough to receive visitors.

She clearly had no idea of the backstory here.

Roy and Cleo, here? In Munich? In this hospital?

So they both now know about me? They thought I was dead. What the hell do they think? What on earth can I say to them?

Why were they here?

How . . . How did they know? Was Roy angry . . . Happy?

'Why do they want to see me?' I asked.

I knew it was a stupid question.

'Perhaps because they care and want to help you?' she suggested.

I couldn't cope with this, not how I was feeling. Nor how I imagined I must be looking. And yet I had a burning curiosity as to why they were here. How had Roy found me?

'Please tell them I'm not great but if they want to come in, that's OK.'

A few minutes later I heard the sound of the door opening. I kept my eyes closed, opening them just a fraction, very briefly, to check them out. Roy looked anxious – dare I say it, distraught?

She looked nervous as hell. Less like a new bride now, more just – just plain girl-next-door.

Roy wore a leather jacket over a T-shirt. She had on a navy coat, black sweater, blue jeans and knee-high suede boots. And a large blue Mulberry handbag. They weren't cheap.

She looked so damned, sodding, bloody perfect.

Then I heard his voice. 'Sandy?'

I didn't react.

'It's Roy. I'm so sorry – about your accident.' God, his voice sounded so emotional, so choked. I stayed silent, feigning sleep when I heard him say the words that hurt so much. That he's moved on. I heard the shuffle of feet and it sounded like he'd moved away a little. I risked opening my eyes just the tiniest fraction, and could make them out. He had his arm around his new wife. Then, as he turned back towards me, I closed my eyes tightly again.

I heard his footsteps, then I felt something touch my forehead. Stroking it. Then his voice again.

'I – I can't believe it's you. It's really you. After all this time.'

I still did not react. How did he sound? Pleased? Relieved? Hurt?

But not like he was exactly ecstatic to see me.

I maintained steady breathing, like I was asleep.

I knew I'd have to open my eyes and deal with this at some point, but keeping tucked away gave me some protection for a few moments.

Then I thought, *OK, what the hell*, and opened my eyes. That clearly startled them!

'So you're Cleo?' I asked. 'You're the woman he married?'

She looked really uncomfortable, as if she wanted to be anywhere but here. Her voice was posher than I had expected but very nervous. 'Yes, yes I am.'

'Good luck,' I said in the most acid tone I could muster, and closed my eyes again.

She'd be dwelling on that for a long time to come.

There was then the sound of the door opening again and I heard a nurse saying she needed to change some of my dressings, so could they step outside for a few minutes? She told them they could get themselves water or coffee just down the corridor.

As I heard them leave the room, I felt a flash of anger. Why the hell had he brought her with him? If he'd managed to track me down after all this time, didn't he have the balls to come alone? Did he seriously think I'd be interested to meet the woman who had usurped me?

Maybe that was an indication of just how little he had changed and that I'd made the right decision in leaving him.

But as I lay there, while the nurse faffed around, I desperately hoped he would come back.

Finally she left and the door closed. It seemed an eternity before it opened again. To my relief, through my flickering lids, as I pretended to still be asleep, I could see it was Roy. Alone this time.

108

I heard his footsteps, then felt his weight on the end of my bed, by my feet. His voice was different now, gentle, intimate.

'Hi, Sandy, I – I can't believe it's really you. After all this time. Nearly eleven years.'

I didn't answer.

'What happened? Tell me. Why didn't you contact me?'

I felt him hold my left hand. Had he noticed I was wearing my wedding ring? Of course he had, he was a sharp detective.

I wondered, at this moment, what would have happened if I'd thrown my arms around him and showered his face and neck with kisses.

'I've got a son,' he said. 'Noah. He's eight months old. Maybe one day, when you're better, we can meet and be friends. I'd like to think that's possible.'

God, I felt so many good emotions welling up. *Yes*, I so wanted to say. *Yes, please!*

Then he threw a dampener.

'But before any of that can happen I need some answers. I need a lot of answers. Why did you leave? Why didn't you make contact? Do you have any idea of the hell you put me through?'

He stopped for a while. I wanted to reply, to break this silence, but it felt easier just to keep my eyes shut.

'Do you not care at all? I think I deserve to know.'

He was still holding my hand. It was a hand I had once known so well but now did not feel belonged to him.

'You were always so ambitious for me, Sandy, wanting me to get to a higher rank than my dad. Well, I've been lucky, I've reached Detective Superintendent. Did you ever think I'd do that?'

I didn't want to tell him I already knew that, because I had tracked him online since I had left, looking for mentions of him. That might come across as odd. He spoke some more, and I just listened until I felt him let go of my hand and the weight rise from the end of the bed.

I opened my eyes and looked directly at him. He was looking at me. 'Going already, Roy?'

He gave an awkward smile and sat back down.

It was hard, speaking, my throat was raw from the breathing tube that had been down it for a long while, but I managed, my voice sounding a little raspy. 'I'm pleased you've done well at work, that you've got to where you always wanted to be. Head of Major Crime. *Detective Superintendent.* I like that, it sounds good, sort of suits you.'

'Thanks.'

He shot a glance at his watch and I realized, disappointedly, he probably had a plane to catch. With his bride.

'And you've got the son you always wanted. Noah. That's a nice name. Very biblical.'

I've no idea why I added that. Roy wasn't remotely religious.

'Yes, I suppose it is. We both just liked it.' He smiled awkwardly. 'OK, so you've heard my download; now tell me what's been happening in your life. I've heard bits and pieces.'

He was looking at me intently and I wondered just what he did know about these past years. 'I expect you've heard the bad bits, the drugs and the depression and failed relationships. I've got some good bits too – I'm independently wealthy and I've got a son who's ten.'

'OK, so what I have to know is why you left me? What happened, where did you go? Did I do something wrong?'

'It's a long story, Roy, but not for today. I will explain, I promise.' I really do want to explain it all to him, to show him how sorry I am. To start again. I just don't feel he wants to. And that breaks my heart.

'OK, tell me about your son. Bruno, is that his name?'

I nodded, completely dispirited.

'Who's the father?'

I hesitated. 'That's also for another day, Roy.'

'OK, let's focus on the future then. How's your recovery going? What are your plans when you get out?'

'I haven't been doing that well. They told me a while ago that I was lucky to be alive – that when they brought me in they didn't expect me to survive. I've had a serious head injury, I've got a spinal injury and I don't know yet if I'll ever be able to walk properly – without a limp or a stick. They've removed my spleen. My face is a mess, I'll be permanently scarred – who's going to want me? And I worry about Bruno.'

'Where is he now?'

'Friends are looking after him for the moment. It's not been easy bringing up a child as a single mum, even with the money.'

He nodded. I could see sympathy in his face, but I could also see anger.

'Have you spoken to your parents?'

'No,' I lied.

'Do you want me to call them?'

'No, I'll speak to them when I'm – when I'm ready.'

'Are there any other people you'd like me to contact?'

I suddenly felt his questioning was intrusive. This was not the reunion I'd planned. This was not our eyes locking, then us embracing, telling each other how much we had missed each other. And Roy forgiving me.

'No, certainly not. How did you find me anyway? I didn't want you here, I really don't want to be doing this. I don't need this right now, it's too much, Roy.'

'You know there are all kinds of legal ramifications. I'm going to have to report this to both the German and Sussex Police.'

'You had me declared dead,' I said, almost raging.

He raised his voice, just a little, but enough for me to feel his pent-up anger. 'What the hell did you expect me to do?'

I closed my eyes. It was too painful to look at his face. 'I'm due to see the consultant this week, he's going to talk about my treatment in the future and my prognosis. Now I'm starting to get stronger, slowly, they'll be wanting to move me out of this hospital. But I'm quite worried about that, I don't know how I'm going to cope on my own. I feel so alone, Roy. So alone in the world. Now you're bringing me all this, I can't face it.'

I couldn't help it. I started crying.

He took my hand again and held it tightly.

'You'll be fine. I'll do what I can to help. It wasn't my intention to upset you, but I have to know the truth – you turned my life upside down, and now you're doing it again.'

He fell silent for a moment, then his expression changed and he told me all about dear Marlon the goldfish. How he loves him because he's the one connection he still has to me.

I stayed silent. I didn't want to tell him I'd seen Marlon only a few months ago.

It felt like he was messing with my head. I was in shock that he had come and even more shocked that he had brought Cleo with him. But most of all, I guess, I was angry that both of them had seen me like this. I wasn't a pretty sight. Most times when I used the bathroom, I couldn't even bear to look at my face in the mirror.

'I think you should leave now, Roy, I didn't ask you to come. I'm getting tired,' I replied.

He let go of my hand. 'I still need answers. I'll come back and see you again soon.'

I said nothing as he stood up. I could barely see him through the blur of tears streaming down my face. He reached the door, turned to look back at me, fleetingly, then was gone.

I lay there for a long time, hoping no damned nurse or doctor would come in. So much to think about. Roy's anger, for one.

What were he and Cleo talking about now, probably in a taxi back to the airport? What was she thinking? Was she wondering what he had ever seen in me?

Was he wondering the same?

Cleo must be a decade younger than me. She was everything that I wasn't, and now would never be. I would be permanently disfigured as well as a semi-invalid. If he was ever going to take me back, it would have been here, when he had come alone into this room. He would have thrown his arms around me and held me tightly, told me it did not matter how I looked, nor how badly injured I was, he still loved me to bits and we'd repair everything and start our life together all over.

Instead he'd been angry.

Almost bitter.

Demanding answers.

Brought his new wife in as if to gloat.

Oh shit. I am never going to be happy. I have no purpose in this life.

There was a large light fitting directly above me. It looked like it had been way over-engineered for its purpose of shining a light down onto the bed, it was more like one of those gantries you see on motorways. It was fixed to the ceiling and looked like it could support an elephant hanging from it.

It would take my weight, no question.

109

March 2018

I pressed the bell for the nurse and was pleased when, a few minutes later, my favourite, Stationsschwester Koti Fekete, came in.

I asked her if she could bring me a notepad, three envelopes and a pen. A *lined* notepad if possible, because it might help my writing be more legible.

When she returned a short while later with the items, she suggested if I was going to write, I might like to sit up a little, and she pressed the button to raise the back of the bed. Then she left me alone.

The first letter was to my lawyer in Frankfurt. I kept it brief, and I found it surprisingly easy to write. The next was gut-wrenching. It was to Bruno. My poor young man. He's been more of a parent to me than I have to him at times in his short, complicated life. I choose my words carefully and throw my heart into it. I know he will be better off without me in his life. I tell him how loved he is, and the words flow. But Roy's was the most challenging one.

It was a lengthy process and I went through several drafts. Each time that I made a mistake I tore the sheet off, balled it and stuffed it into the drawer beside my bed. A couple, in frustration, I threw on the floor. Finally I had a draft I was happy with. I omitted a fair amount, including any mention of Albazi, and bent the truth in places so that it is easier for Roy to hear. I am probably a bit self-indulgent in my recollection given my state of mind but I think it says all I need it to.

> Dearest Roy, If you are reading this, then you will know I am gone.

I think there's comfort in getting straight to the point and I am happy with the next bit I read through about how I want to give him some answers, but that I just can't carry on now that it is known I'm alive. I'm not sure it reads perfectly but it will have to do. I scan down further.

> Now I've got a whole shitload of stuff dumped on me. All the people I'd have to tell – my parents, friends, authorities – I just can't cope with this – the shame and the embarrassment. I don't know how to start or where to go.

I stop and consider striking through some words. It's hard to think of the ways this may all be interpreted and the impact that it could have. I need Roy to know things, but it would be helpful to have someone to read it to see if it's coming across how I intend it to. The person who would be best to do this is, absurdly, Roy.

> I discovered I was pregnant and I had some fast decisions to make. Either I stayed, in which case I would have been trapped by this child into remaining with you – for a while, at least. Or I had an abortion.

It goes on. About his work, whether I have the courage to leave. And the part I find truly embarrassing. But I have to tell him.

THEY THOUGHT I WAS DEAD

You need to know I wasn't a saint, I wasn't the good person you always believed I was. This may hurt to read, but you need to know that I wasn't always faithful to you – I had some one-night stands. I'm not making any excuses – nor am I going to name names.

More about what I kept hidden from him. The mess I am in and my depression. The drugs. It's all just so shameful. I feel those same feelings of self-hatred I always felt when my parents came down on me for being such a disappointment to them.

There's so much I wanted to tell you – and ask you – when you came here last. I don't know why I didn't. I was so shocked to see you, my head was all over the place. I guess I knew then I couldn't see any future. My face is going to be permanently scarred. I've got motor-control problems – the consultant neurosurgeon just told me that my head hit the road at a bad angle – the worst bloody angle it could have hit – all my grey matter is jumbled up inside the box that's meant to protect it.

No hope, no future, a long dark tunnel. And then to the final part.

When I am gone, take care of our son, Bruno. He worries me; you'll see what I mean. Don't give him to my parents, they'd never cope and it would be hell for him.

I'm leaving you plenty of money for him, to pay for his education and set him up in life. I've also left you DNA proof that you are his father. You won't know this but I took some samples from our house when I visited Brighton last year.

I do still love you, even though it might not have seemed that way to you for all these years. Sorry, but this is really the end for me. I know I'm a coward, but then maybe I always have been.

Sandy

110

March 2018

I smiled, in sorrow, as my supper tray arrived. One of the games Roy and I used to play during a date-night dinner in one of our favourite restaurants was choosing our last meal if we were to be executed in the morning. Both of us agreed we would be gluttons. And we would totally large it on the desserts.

It's strange the things we remember from our past. I can clearly recall the last time we played it. Roy said he would have the biggest banoffee pie on the planet. I had chosen chocolate fondant with hot chocolate sauce. Grilled lobster as a starter for Roy, then a rib-eye steak with chips and broccoli – health-conscious to the last – well, the broccoli bit. I'd have gone for an aubergine parmigiana, then a Dover sole – off the bone, I don't like to see dead fish faces – and mushy peas. And chips, too. It has to be chips.

I was thinking about this as my meal tray arrived tonight. It had some horrible, tasteless lake fish, pike or perch, with a green vegetable that was so overcooked it fell apart when I prodded it with my fork. It might have been spinach in a former life. Dessert was trifle, which – well, let's be polite, because it tasted better than it looked – looked like the remains of a roadkill reimagined by Tracey Emin.

Not exactly my fantasy last meal. But I guess so much in life doesn't live up to our hopes, and that part of growing up is learning to manage our expectations. Oh well, let's hope this is the final disappointment.

431

The clock on the wall read 7.45. I knew the ritual. In ten minutes a quiet male nurse would come in to take my tray and give me the two small pills, in a plastic container, to take half an hour before I wanted to sleep. I wouldn't be swallowing them tonight and I wouldn't be needing them ever again, but I didn't say that to him when he came. I watched him leave with the tray and close the door. A few moments later, scrupulously punctual, a female nurse came in to insert my night-time catheter.

When she had left, I felt completely at peace with myself. I'd made my decision, my affairs were all in order. The three letters, all in envelopes and addressed, were on my bedside table. I felt crashing waves of sadness about things I would never see – most of all, Bruno growing up, becoming a teenager. But at least I wouldn't be an embarrassment to him. An invalid mother with a scarred face. I'm sparing him that, my dear, sweet boy.

They normally left me alone at night, now that I was out of danger. No nurse had come in after my catheter had been inserted for several nights now. I would just have to take that risk. If anyone did, I would plead my screwed-up mind, that I had no idea what I was doing and divert to Plan B. Which I didn't yet have. And hopefully would not need.

Now I needed to focus on the task in hand.

I'm really not feeling great.

The whole room seems to be wobbling.

111

But I can't do it. I just can't do it.

I lie there, crying. Scared. And I'm realizing that I just can't do this to Bruno. He's been through such shit with me, during all my years as a drug addict and then as a recovering addict. None of it is his fault. Don't I owe it to him to care for him? I was the one, even more than Roy, who so desperately wanted a child. And now I have one, can I really just abandon him, because it suits me to bail out?

Shit. Shit. Shit.

I'm feeling even more light-headed now. Even weaker. I sink back down into the bed, then look at the three envelopes I've addressed and pick up the one to Roy. And realize in my addled state I hadn't sealed it. I try to pull the letter out because I want to rip it up. I'm going to rip all three letters up.

My hands are shaking so much that the moment I get the letter out of the envelope it falls. The paper is so flimsy that I see it, floating down from side to side like a crappy paper aeroplane, and it lands on the floor several feet from my bed.

My brain is all over the place. I need to get up and fetch it. I need to replace the catheter I have pulled out. I need—

The door opens suddenly, and I'm frozen with panic.

The clock says 11.55.

I don't know why I'm looking at it.

A medic comes in, wearing the scrubs and gauze mask that all the doctors and nurses here wear. A male.

433

Part of a crash team?

Had I triggered an alarm at the nursing station when I pulled out the catheter?

He shuts the door and walks over towards me. As he reaches me he raises his mask and, with a faint foreign accent that is very definitely not German, he says, 'Hello, Sandy, remember me?'

I do. It is not a happy memory.

112

March 2018

Roel Albazi looks pretty much as I had last seen him a decade ago. Apart from a large scar down one side of his face.

He's smiling. But not with a lot of warmth.

'It's been a long journey to find you, Sandy,' Albazi says.

'If it's about the money I owe you? I can pay it back – with interest. I always planned to pay you back. I have the cash – I could pay you tomorrow when the banks open.' My voice comes out as a croak. I'm shivering.

Albazi shakes his head and gives me another smile, this one almost sympathetic. 'It's not about the money, now, Sandy. And just to show my bona fides on that, I've brought your handbag back for you. I believe you lost it when you had a little altercation – shall we say – with a taxi.'

I see my beige Louis Vuitton bag dangling from his arm. I'm shaking with terror. I think I'm about to throw up.

'This is about my mother, my father, my grandfather, my sister and her girl,' Albazi says. His voice sounds horrible. 'All of them were murdered because you defaulted and disappeared. Any ideas how you can pay me back for destroying my family? No? Final answer?'

I lie there, utterly petrified.

He suddenly bends down, and then stands up holding a sheet of lined paper with handwriting on it.

My letter to Roy, I realize.

435

'Give me that, please,' I blurt. 'It's personal.'

He stands and reads it carefully, taking his time, taking several minutes. When he has clearly finished, he looks at me, then at the equipment around me. Then he smiles. 'Trying to take your own life, Sandy?'

'No, please listen to me. We can sort this out.'

He shakes his head. 'No, Sandy, we could have sorted this out ten years ago, when I was waiting for you in my office in Shoreham and you never turned up with the money you had promised.'

'I have the money now. I can pay you any amount of interest.'

'Did you not hear me very well, Sandy? This is not about money any more. There is no amount of money you could pay me. No amount in the world.'

'So – what – what – how – how can we sort this out? Listen – there were so many issues I had.'

'Did your mother get tortured to death, Sandy?'

I look him in the eye. It was like staring into the crevasse of a glacier. 'No.'

'Did your family get tortured to death?'

I shake my head.

'Did you ever spend ten years in prison dreaming of this moment, Sandy?'

'What moment do you mean?' I was whimpering.

He holds the letter in front of my eyes. 'I dreamed of this moment every single day when I woke up, and I dreamed of it every long night while I slept on my shitty, hard bunk. I dreamed of meeting you again one day, somewhere. And I dreamed that the day I met you, I would kill you. But I never dreamed you would have made it so easy for me.'

113

Kriminalhauptkommissar Marcel Kullen sat in his third-floor office at the Munich Landeskriminalamt headquarters, sipping his scalding first coffee of the day, while staring at his screen, viewing the video footage he had just been sent.

It was a woman in a hospital gown, in a room at the Klinikum München Schwabing. She had hanged herself from the arm of a ceiling light.

According to early estimates from the attending police officers, she had been dead for some hours. Her last visit from any of the nursing staff at the hospital had been at 8.15 p.m. yesterday.

Her death had all the hallmarks of a carefully planned suicide. There was a lengthy note to her former husband, Roy Grace, which Kullen had just read, as well as notes to her son, Bruno, and to her lawyer.

He liked Roy, from the brief times they had spent together, and was sure he would be very upset at this news. The English detective had been so convinced his long-vanished wife might still be alive and living in Germany – in Munich. As had turned out to be the case. Her letters – all three at her bedside, in sealed envelopes – were even greater evidence of this.

With a heavy heart, he picked up his phone and dialled Roy Grace's number.

ACKNOWLEDGEMENTS

I never knew when I started the Roy Grace series just how much Sandy would passionately interest so many of my readers. She didn't just captivate Roy Grace fans, but she has captivated me, too, and I've been with her through her highs and lows and many personas. She has, over the years, become an icon of the entire Roy Grace series. I've always felt I owe you, my readers, this book – and I owe Sandy, too, the chance to be judged fairly.

I have so many people to thank for all the time and help they have given me in my research for this novel. I would love to detail the input of each person listed below, but that would take a whole other book! Instead, my heartfelt thanks. Please know each of you is far more than just a name in an alphabetical list: Martin Allen; Sue Ansell (RIP); Graham Bartlett; Jon Bennion-Jones; Inspector James Biggs; Clare Butcher; DI Louise Clayson; CI Callum O'Connor; Emily Denyer; Jane Diplock; Martin Diplock; Dr Matt Doyle; Dr Deryn Doyle; Linzi Duckworth; Kelly Frost; Jonathan Gready; Chris Hamsey; Anna-Lisa Hancock; Kevin Lemasney; Jonathan Jones; Anette Lippert; Dr James Mair; Tom Ogg; Richard Pedley; DI Aiden Quenault; Dr Graham Ramsden; Chris Robinson; Guy Rolliston; Alan Setterington; Andy Sibcy; Anita Simmonds; Helen Shenston; Julian Short; Chief Officer Robin Smith; Hans Jurgen Stockerl; PC Richard Trundle; Dr Orlando Trujillo; Darren Twort; Ludwig Waldinger; Sven Müller, Polizeihauptkommissar.

Thank you to my wonderful publishing house, starting with a sad and fond farewell to Wayne Brookes, my friend and wonderful publisher for fourteen years, and a big, excited welcome to my new publisher, Francesca Pathak. Pan Macmillan have been publishing my books since 2003 and I owe them so many thanks.

To single out a few: Jonathan Atkins, Melissa Bond, Charlotte Cross, Stuart Dwyer, Brid Enright, Claire Evans, Jamie Forrest, Lucy Hale, Daniel Jenkins, Andy Joannou, Becky Lloyd, Sara Lloyd, Poppy North, Joanna Prior, Jeremy Trevathan, Charlotte Williams, and my brilliant structural consultant Susan Opie.

Huge thanks, too, to my tireless agent, Isobel Dixon, and the fabulous team at Blake Friedmann, including Julian Friedmann, Conrad Williams, Sian Ellis-Martin, James Pusey, Nicole Etherington, Susie Bloor, Daisy Way and all the other people there!

I'm also blessed with three wonderful publicists – Caitlin Allen, Emily Souders and Niamh Houston at Riot Communications.

I have a dream team at Team James: Dani Brown, Chris Diplock, Emma Gallichan, Lyn Gaylor, Sarah Middle, Mark Tuckwell, Chris Webb. And two extra-special mentions to my front-line edit team.

First, to David Gaylor, who, as befits the real-life model for my fictional Roy Grace, used all of his detective skills in quite brilliantly rising to the enormous challenge of aligning all the events in this novel to the countless appearances and mentions of Sandy in the preceding nineteen Roy Grace novels.

The second extra-special mention is to my wife, Lara, who really got inside Sandy's head and provided so many invaluable insights and ideas that really helped to shape both her erratic but very human character and the novel itself. Without her input, it would have been a lesser book.

And, of course, I owe thanks as ever to all our furry and feathered friends in our ever-growing menagerie, who help make me smile no matter what, and none more so than our gorgeous dogs, Spooky and Wally, and our mischievous cats, Willy and Woo.

I always love to hear from you, my readers. Message me through any of the channels below. Thank you for being such wonderful and loyal readers – and now, finally, you know the truth about Sandy . . . how she filled in that little dash, which all of us will one day have, between the dates of her birth and death.

Peter James

contact@peterjames.com
www.peterjames.com
www.peterjames.com/youtube
www.facebook.com/peterjames.roygrace
www.twitter.com/peterjamesuk
www.instagram.com/peterjamesuk
www.instagram.com/peterjamesukpets
www.instagram.com/mickeymagicandfriends

NOW A MAJOR ITV SERIES

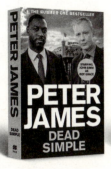

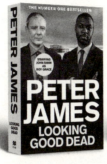

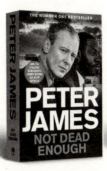

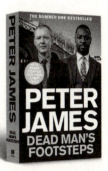

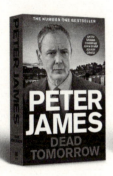

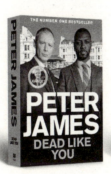

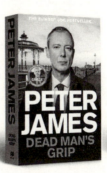

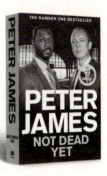

Peter James's first eight books in the Detective Superintendent Roy Grace series have been adapted for television and star John Simm as Roy Grace.

Discover Peter James's books at peterjames.com

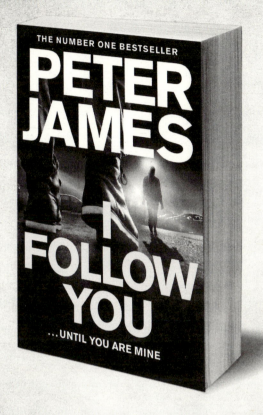

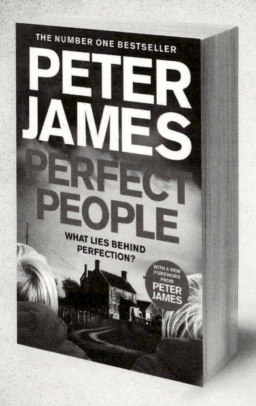

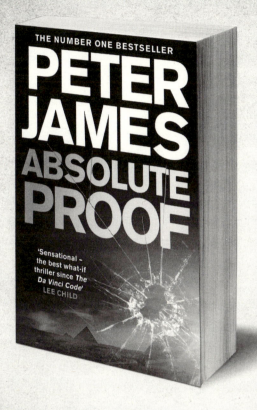

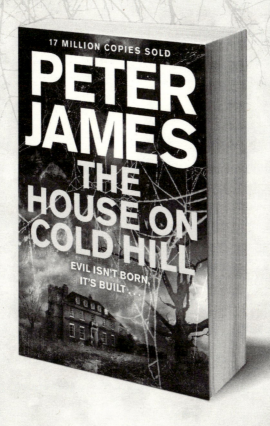

ABOUT THE AUTHOR

Peter James is a UK number one bestselling author, best known for his Detective Superintendent Roy Grace series, now a hit ITV drama starring John Simm as the troubled Brighton copper.

Much loved by crime and thriller fans for his fast-paced page-turners full of unexpected plot twists, sinister characters and accurate portrayals of modern-day policing, Peter has won over forty awards for his work, including the WHSmith Best Crime Author of All Time Award and the Crime Writers' Association Diamond Dagger.

To date, Peter has written an impressive total of nineteen *Sunday Times* number ones, has sold over 21 million copies worldwide and has been translated into thirty-eight languages. His books are also often adapted for the stage, with his six stage shows up to now grossing over £17 million at the box office.

www.peterjames.com

@peterjamesuk

@peterjames.roygrace

@peterjamesuk

@thejerseyhomestead

@mickeymagicandfriends

You Tube Peter James TV